A Searchlight and a Silence

Chris
~ Enjoy &
share!

~ Susan K. Hach

ISBN: 978-1-060920-105-0
Printed in the United States of America
©2015 Susan Flach
All rights reserved

API
Ajoyin Publishing, Inc.
P.O. 342
Three Rivers, MI 49093
www.ajoyin.com

Please direct your inquiries to admin@ajoyin.com

For Mom
whose encouragement never wavers

A Searchlight and a Silence

SUSAN K. FLACH

Book III of *A Song and a Seashell* series

Prologue
Winter 2017

Icy gray water hangs, hovering like a giant blanket, stirred only by the occasional fluid movement of a fish or other marine life seemingly unbothered by the cold. Somewhere above, a bitter waft of air sends a series of tiny ripples across the steely liquid surface. Curling wisps of morning fog reach out to obscure the corridor from sea to land, blurring both worlds into one. For a period of time all sound is subdued, ostensibly frozen as if in cahoots with the surrounding elements of nature.

Nearby the muffled sound of a groan breaks through the quiet, followed by a shrill, bloodcurdling shriek. Many minutes later a small, shadowy figure can be spotted rising like a specter out of the mist. As if just waking from a deep slumber, the female configuration commences to rub her eyes with her fists after sliding slender fingers repeatedly through the brown tendrils of her ratted hair. Cold air slaps her face, jolting her into a kind of renewed awareness. Like an untamed animal, her head darts in all directions as she takes in her surroundings.

With unsteady feet she begins traversing through the hovering clouds that are hugging her body like a silky robe. A purposeful determination arrives to cover her spritelike features, and resolutely, almost frantically, she begins rifling through a forest of wild brush, carving out an instantaneous pathway with each step. A disoriented rabbit crosses her path, and she kicks it ruthlessly out of her way in order to continue on at the current pace. A blue jay swoops through the air, flying from tree to tree, coming inches away from her head. Lifting an arm high into the air, she smacks her hand all around trying to make contact with the bird, but it darts easily away landing on a nearby branch, seemingly watching as she continues on.

Finally she stops. Eyes wild, nostrils flared, she breathes through short, panting gasps. Hands on hips, she stands on an elevated parcel of land overlooking the tranquil community nestled among the winding coves of the coastline: pricey, boarded up cottages; rows of shops locked and closed for the season; wooden docks devoid of swaying watercrafts; Barren boardwalks. Indeed! Dormant for now, but soon enough the village will transform into a charming population of vacationers. A regular summertime wonderland.

She's seen enough.

Snapping her head away, she turns to the left, allowing her gaze to take in the sea—miles and miles of open sea. Almost instantaneously, a flash that can only be interpreted as hatred is revealed through the bitter contemplation of her eyes. Then slowly the look disappears, and in its place forms the unmistaken semblance of an eerily wicked smile.

Chapter One
Spring 2017

Bright, cheery daylight pours through the east facing windows of the cabin, lighting a trail for me to follow into the kitchen. That and the stream of mouthwatering smells coming at me are assaulting my senses—bacon and eggs cooking on the stove; fresh, ground coffee percolating; the citrusy flavor of oranges being peeled and squeezed. Without a second thought I begin padding in that direction, passing through the rays of sunshine that are lighting up my bare feet with each step. The wooden floorboards creak and groan below the transferring weight of my body. When I reach the galley, I pause in place, and once more that familiar, but still uncontrollable feeling instantly spreads through my body, causing a hitch in my breathing. Standing with his back to me, facing the countertop that serves as a connection between the sink and stove, is Tristan. The strong muscles in his back shift with each movement as he goes about making breakfast for me—for us. An old, tattered tee shirt hugs his shoulder blades, and a pair of sweatpants rest low on his narrow hips. I have only a split second to swallow before he detects my presence and turns around. For two seconds there is a pause between us, and our eyes connect.

"Hey, sleepy. Good morning."

"Morning." My voice sounds slightly breathless, and a knowing smile spreads across his lips. I shake my head to focus my thoughts. "Breakfast smells so good. I'm starved."

"I'll bet." He laughs lightly before turning back to the eggs in the pan.

Unable to resist, I walk across the room and wrap my arms around his strong body from behind, resting my head on his back. "I wish we didn't have to go to work," I whisper into fabric that is skimming the surface of my lips. I don't have to see his face to guess his reaction to my words. By now I just know.

"Well, we *could* just—"

My pulse accelerates and I pull away, seating myself at the breakfast nook instead. "If only we wouldn't lose our jobs if we did."

He sets a steaming plate of food in front of me, and suddenly my stomach is rumbling. He is such a good breakfast chef. I will never get tired of the mornings when he decides to use his culinary skills in the kitchen. I glance up at the chiseled cheekbones so close to mine as he leans in to slide a glass of orange juice my way. I catch a trace of his soapy-clean smell and drink it down. No, I will definitely never tire of this—of him!

He takes a step back from me, and a teasing grin spreads across his face. "*Maybe* . . . maybe they wouldn't mind just one more time. I could call in just for today. I'm pretty confident they like me enough. It would be okay. And Marine Studies likes you too—what do you say . . . are you in?"

Am I in? *Of course I'm in!* I shake my head and laugh nervously. "You better get over here and eat, or else we're both going to be late."

He grabs his plate and sits opposite of me. After taking a large bite of bacon and a swig of juice, he looks back up at me. "If you are sure—"

No, I'm not sure at all! I bite my lip and throw my napkin at him. "We better get going."

After showering and arranging my hair into a low ponytail, I meet Tristan once again in the kitchen, this time with both of us dressed in business apparel, getting ready to exit the cabin for the day and spend the next several hours at our jobs: he at NEC Systems Group, and me at Center for Marine Studies, Rhode Island.

Grabbing my keys, I look up, and he's there in front of me, getting ready to tell me good-bye. He looks down into my eyes and involuntarily my pulse begins to beat at a faster rate.

"Have a good day, okay?"

I nod. "You too."

He leans closer. "I'll see you later?" His voice is soft.

"Okay." I barely have time to answer before I feel the gentle pressure of his lips on mine. A dizzying sensation immediately begins to swirl through my body, and I feel myself getting pulled into him. I fight the built-in response to collapse against him, instead allowing myself only long seconds to kiss him back. Finally I pull away, slightly disoriented and breathless. "Yeah . . . tonight. I ah . . . I'll see you tonight," I tell him. Then touching my fingers to my lips, I watch as he turns and walks out the door. A short time later I follow suit.

Sliding into my black, four-door jeep, I shake my head to clear my thoughts of Tristan, preparing myself to enter work mode for the day. It has been several months since we said our wedding vows on Tristan's remote island, and still I had not tired of him—can't wait to be with him every chance I get. The sight of his strong, well-formed body still sends my pulse tripping with just a glance. His sea green eyes still make me lose my train of thought so easily. And he still looks at me like he just can't get enough. Will that ever change for us? I grip the steering wheel in front of me and squeeze. *Geez, I hope not!*

The winter had been trying at times with Tristan in hibernation for days at a time. But as he had promised, he came back to be with me as often as he could. And we made every minute of our time count. Now spring has arrived, and we can be together for many more hours of each day. My spirit is beginning to blossom just like the surrounding greenery that is trying to come awake, renewed with fresh hope for the coming season.

Since the very beginning, right after the wedding nuptials were complete, our transition into marriage was as natural as breathing. Sharing dinners, dish duty, and the general upkeep of the grounds around the cabin felt like it was made just for the two of us together. Like one of the two of us could never possibly be responsible for all the daily tasks that came to us, but together—together it was no work at all. We had eased into our roles as husband and wife with very little effort.

I still enjoy my job: spending my days at the Center for Marine Studies in downtown Westerly, setting up workshops and classes that encourage the general public to have a better understanding and respect for the marine environment. And Tristan still works as a consultant engineer for NEC Systems Group, traveling to nearby coastal villages and cities, advising companies on how to best set up structures that will protect the ocean ecosystem.

It is a beautiful spring day, and the world outside the Center for Marine Studies is coming alive, making it very difficult for me to sit in a cubicle all day. I am antsy to get outdoors and experience everything that is becoming new again: the warming air temperatures, the transition of the local vegetation from lackluster brown to vibrant green, the smell of raindrops sinking into the softening earth, the promise of flowering plants waiting to bloom. And the call of the ocean preparing to host another summer by mesmerizing the locals and the visiting tourists with its transfixing beauty.

Finally the hours pass, and I am heading back toward our cabin with the windows of my jeep wide open, fresh air pelting my face. When I arrive, Tristan's already there with a ladder perched against the north side of the house, putting a loosened piece of siding back into place—leftover damage from a recent vicious storm. He hears my car tires as they crunch against the gravel drive and edges himself back down the rungs. His hair is slightly damp, clueing me that he's been out for a swim. He greets me with a grin.

"The weather's great, isn't it? Before long it's going to be time to get *Blue* back out again." I nod my head, laughing on the inside. *Blue*, the boat that he worked so hard to fix up—that he gave to me as an unexpected gift. *Blue*, the boat that *he* drives whenever we go out together, that he spends his free time polishing and tinkering with that feels more like *his* baby than mine.

"I know. I love this weather. It means summer is almost here. How's the water?"

"It's warming up. Are you ready for a swim?" Tristan watches my face as he asks the question, and immediately I feel my cheeks heat up as I think back to our last *swim* together. Back to last fall before winter came roaring in like a lion—keeping me from immersing any part of my body into the waves of the ocean.

But this doesn't stop Tristan, of course. His need for daily sustenance from the water keeps him in the ocean any time of the year regardless of temperature—regardless of winter, spring, summer, or fall. I still have such a hard time wrapping my mind around this concept—that the guy that is snuggled up with me in bed at night keeping me so warm will be headed out into the frigid breakers of the ocean minutes later—leaving the comfort of my body heat for hours spent in near-freezing liquid. But this is Tristan—this is how he exists—so even though I can't fathom it, I just inwardly shake my head, give him one more kiss good-bye each time he leaves, and look forward to his return, thankful that I don't have to join him on his Antarcticlike swim.

"I'm sure my next swim is still months away. But I *would* love to go for a walk on the beach." The tone of my voice is light and teasing. My eyes twinkle with playfulness. Nodding slowly, Tristan watches the expression on my face, trying to read into my words.

"Let's go."

Tristan's hand is wrapped securely around mine as we traverse the winding shoreline that is taking us farther and farther away from the cabin. A soft breeze is ruffling the air, stirring up the fresh scents of spring—sending Tristan's intoxicatingly salty, clean smell my way periodically. I inhale deeply, enjoying the euphoric feeling that comes with each lungful. Beside us whitecaps romp spiritedly toward the shore. The sun shines down liberally, heating the skin on our forearms, creating the sensation that the air temperature is actually warmer than it is. I let go of Tristan's hand to take off the hoodie that I had worn, tying it around the waist of my jeans instead.

When I break our physical contact, he takes the opportunity to slip off his Docksiders and wade a few inches into the surf, getting the bottom of his jeans all wet in the process. Bending down, he picks up a handful of rocks and begins tossing them onto the surface of the water. I observe as each one skips toward the horizon and then disappears into the waves. When the supply in his hand is depleted, he turns back around and catches me watching him. His green eyes narrow marginally, and he goes very still.

I suck in a breath.

He looks so good! His long-sleeved shirt is fitted snuggly across his chest, hinting at the strong muscles that I know are hidden just beneath. His faded jeans are resting slightly low on his hips, accentuating his perfect form. I bite my lip and wait for him to move—wait for myself to breathe again. Slowly he takes a hand and runs it through his wind-tousled, blond hair, and suddenly I am taken back to age seventeen when we first met at beach volleyball. And even though we are still in our low twenties—not that much older really—so much has happened since that first evening at the lakeshore. A lifetime of ups and downs, of joys and disappointments, of happiness and devastation. In some ways it feels like we have already lived through decades together, and yet right now in this moment we are still just two kids.

Self-consciously I begin playing with the escaped strands of hair from my ponytail as I wait for him to cross the sand toward me. It seems as though his steps are slow and deliberate, and my heart beats loudly and impatiently in response. He is almost to my side when a loud splash interrupts the tension in the air. Simultaneously we both turn in the direction of the ocean.

Yards away from where we are standing, our favorite pet dolphin is shooting into the air showing off to the nth degree with each acrobatic flip, clearly enjoying the warm spring weather as much as anyone. In and out of the waves he gyrates and dives, obviously ecstatic that the long winter is finally over, and his owners are now out for a shoreline walk with the unspoken promise of many more to come.

Immediately I am grinning. "Drake . . . hi, Drake."

Tristan presses his lips together and shakes his head. "Hello, Drake . . . the *moment spoiler!*" His voice is loaded with sarcasm, and now I am laughing.

"Aw, he misses me. I hardly ever got to see him this winter." I continue watching Drake's playful antics feeling slightly frustrated that I can't go to him and pet him—the water is still too cold for me to wade through. Tristan rolls his eyes and I playfully grab his waist, throwing myself into his arms for a hug. While my face is pressed against his chest, he runs his fingers through my ponytail before giving it a spirited tug. At that I push away from him, using my hands and hip to free myself. Tristan shakes his head, and I chuckle outright.

"You just wait!" his voice calls to me.

I wink before backing away, all the while holding his gaze. "I *can't* wait!"

He moves his head slowly back and forth two times feigning complete seriousness, but the light in his sea green eyes betrays the resoluteness of his tone. "You are in *so* much trouble."

I crinkle my nose while continuing to back away faster and faster, almost stumbling over a piece of driftwood in the process. Finally I turn around so I can see where I am going. From there I take off in an all-out sprint. My breath comes in quick gasps as I run through the uneven piles of sand that line the shoreline, adrenaline shooting through my veins initiated by the thrill of the chase. Somewhere behind me a repetitive thudding sound spurs me into lightning-quick speed. But I'm not naive. I know that even though I am swift as the wind, it won't be fast enough. Soon the rhythmic pounding behind me gets louder, and I know that Tristan is effortlessly closing the gap. *Oh crap!* An anxious thrill skyrockets through my blood.

In a flash I am taken back to Tristan's island late last summer on our honeymoon. There had been similar chases—all amidst the surroundings of a tropical paradise. And as expected, Tristan had always won. But I never minded. Because somehow the punishment of getting caught always ended up seeming more like a reward. Even now I get a chill as I recall the two best weeks of my life—two weeks in luxuriant heaven with Tristan and I finally getting the chance to know each other intimately, appreciating that after all we'd been through we'd never have to be separated again.

During the winter on lazy evenings at the cabin, lying together by the flickering light of the fireplace, we'd sometimes fantasize about future vacations the two of us could take together—the most imminent one being a Caribbean cruise. It was easy to imagine careening around the open seas in luxury—eating fancy meals and dancing the evening away under flashing disco lights, then allowing Tristan to slip discreetly away during the midnight hours for his necessary swim. It seemed like the perfect idea—like a vacation destination created with just the two of us in mind.

The image of our dream getaway fades quickly into the background of my mind, however, as I feel strong arms reach out to grab me from behind. *Game over!* Helplessly I shriek as I get pulled to the ground, pinned easily by Tristan's grasp. Hovering just above me, slightly winded, his green eyes are dancing, and a *ha-I-got-you* grin covers his perfect lips. Completely breathless, for a second or two I try to uselessly wiggle away from him.

"I'm pretty sure you're not going anywhere," his deep voice teasingly admonishes me.

I give a couple more squirming bursts of effort before eventually succumbing to the sand under my back, wholly captured.

"When are you going to learn?"

"Learn what?" I giggle as my respirations finally start to slow.

"That you can't outrun me. That you will never get away from me . . . ever."

"Someday . . . *maybe?* Not sure." My flippant answer is laced with flirtation—the game *is* still going.

He finally lets go of my arms and tickles the skin just below my neck. "You enjoy playing with fire, don't you?"

I silently lift my eyebrows and bite my lip in answer. At that Tristan goes very still, and the look in his eyes has now changed, the playfulness from seconds earlier completely gone. My heart begins beating rapidly in my chest, my breathing increasing its tempo once more—this time for different reasons. Taking a strand of my hair, he gently tucks it behind my ear, all the while watching my face. I swallow hard. For a second or two all is quiet around us except the sound of waves somewhere in the background.

Then slowly he begins inching himself closer to me—his mouth now only centimeters from mine. As an involuntary reaction I sigh and my body lifts itself ever so slightly from the sandy ground reaching for him—needing him to be closer—as I wait for his soft lips to finally touch my own.

Finally I am not disappointed. Immediately every thought fades far away into the distance. And then it's just me and Tristan and a blanket of sand tucked away in a perfectly hidden alcove next to the shimmering sea.

Two days later I am in the bedroom changing out of my work

clothes when I hear the front door open and shut, clueing me that Tristan has just arrived home from work as well. "I'm in here," I call out to him while pulling a knit, long-sleeved tee over my head. There is no answer and I pause in place, furrowing my eyebrows in question. *Maybe he didn't hear me.* After sliding dark gray yoga pants up over my hips, I pad into the kitchen and find him peering into the refrigerator, rummaging for something to eat. "Hey." I send my greeting to him once more.

Finally he turns around and smiles. But there is something about the way it doesn't quite reach his eyes that causes my heart to pick up in tempo. "Hey . . . how was your day?" He shoves a handful of grapes into his mouth as he talks and turns back to resume his search.

"It was okay." I lean against the countertop and wait for him to finish scrounging around for an after-work snack. But the longer I remain, the more he keeps looking—now having moved on to the cupboards, examining their contents for something suitable. *Well, dang! I guess he is hungry then!* I maneuver myself into an upright position and reach my arms high into the air for a stretch. "I'm going to go for a run, so I'll see you in a bit."

Finally he stops what he is doing and looks back over his shoulder. "Okay . . . yeah, I'll see ya."

I locate my running shoes and head outside into the crisp air that now feels more like winter than spring. How quickly things can change in two days' time. I shiver and pull a knit hat over my head, leaving my ponytail exposed beneath. After long minutes of stretching, I take off on a shoreline run, allowing the chilly wind to bite my cheeks with each step. After several miles of high-speed feet-pounding-against-the-wet-sand sprinting, I arrive back at the cabin with sweat pouring from my skin in spite of the cold, outdoor temperatures. After a hot shower, I head to the kitchen to think about fixing dinner. Everything is quiet in the interior of the house, so I assume Tristan is somewhere outside working on a project or possibly even out in the water for a swim. Unexplainably a feeling of sadness washes over me—usually he lets me know what he's up to, where he's headed, what outdoor project he'll be working on around the property. *Doesn't he?*

After pulling out the ingredients to make spaghetti and mixing them into a saucepan, I sit back and wait for the dish to simmer on the stove while I thumb through a magazine. Tristan doesn't pop his head in the house even once during this time. Eventually I set the table and decide to go in search for him—dinner is ready. After looking around the premises, I spot his well-built frame carrying a box into the shed. The wind is blowing his blond, rumpled hair. His cheekbones are highlighted pink from the nippy air. Something inside of me pulls tightly in my chest at the sight of him. I hold back on my approach, waiting for him to set his load down. "Dinner is ready," I finally call to him.

Wiping his hands on his jeans, he looks up at me. "Okay . . . I'll be right there." He attempts a grin, but it quickly disappears and I head back into the house feeling oddly unsettled.

Dinner is pleasant enough. The atmosphere at kitchen table is quiet but not ill-natured. Tristan stabs at a meatball with his fork and takes a bite. "This is really good."

"Thanks." I try to meet his gaze, but he is looking at his plate, continuing to eat. The longer dinner goes on, the more the spaghetti seems to curdle in my stomach. But the reason for my discomfiture isn't blatantly obvious, because in all actuality Tristan is treating me cordially. I can't exactly say that something is amiss. But deep down in my gut, it just feels wrong between us somehow.

Finally I cannot take another second of whatever it is that is hanging in the air. I am carrying my plate to the sink, warring with myself over these feelings of unease that are running through my mind, when I stop walking midstride. "Tristan?"

He is taking the pot of leftovers off of the stove. "Yeah?" The word is spoken as an after-thought, like his mind is a million miles away from the room we are in.

I sigh and turn to look at him. "What is going on?"

He is halfway to the refrigerator, and now he too has stopped midstride. "What? How do you mean?"

Now I know I am 100 percent right in my assumption. I turn to face him and quickly detect the muscle in his jaw twitching. He doesn't look me in the eye—hasn't looked me in the eye all evening really. "I *mean* why are you acting like this . . . all cold and stuff?"

His head snaps in my direction. "I'm not trying to be cold. I just—"

"Just what?"

For two long seconds Tristan doesn't say anything. "I know you might not like—"

"Like what?"

He lets out a slow breath. "That I have to go away for a while . . . for work." Again he faces away from me. My heart is beating a little more rapidly in my chest, but I try not to panic. This may not be a big deal. After all, he had gone away all winter long for a couple days or so at a time, and it was okay.

"For how long?"

"I'm not sure. A few weeks, maybe longer. *Hopefully* not longer."

I let out a soft breath and close my eyes. *I don't like it.* If he thought it was only going to be a few weeks, why the attitude? "Where will you be going?"

"The Pacific Ocean." *The Pacific Ocean? That's so far away.* "There's been some stuff going on out there, and they really need a good consultant. Apparently . . . ah . . . they tell me I'm one of the best."

I nod resolutely. "I believe that." *But I don't like it.* For a few long seconds the room is quiet. "What happened to 'I'll never leave you again, Bethany.'?"

Tristan closes his eyes as if in pain. Then finally he opens them again and looks right at me. "I know . . . I know I said that but—" He pauses midsentence and runs a hand through his blond, tousled hair. And I wish he would stop it, because he looks so sexy and I don't want him to look sexy, because now he's going to be gone for who knows how long, and I'm going to miss him so much. I hug my arms around my chest and look at the kitchen floor. He begins speaking again. "But they really need me . . . so I have to go. I'm . . . I'm sorry."

I nod my head and look back up. "Okay." My one word is a choked whisper as I try hard to fight back the tears that want to come. What else can I say? I know how strongly Tristan feels about his work and what he is doing for the ocean—for his people. Without a second's hesitation he sets the pot of spaghetti on the countertop and crosses the room to me. Taking me gently in his arms, he holds me to his chest while I fight back the tears that are trying to come. And he feels so good pressed against me. But it is a double-edged feeling, because I know that very soon I won't be feeling his strong body next to mine anymore—possibly for a long time. And the idea of that hurts so bad!

Chapter Two

"Hey, baby . . . it won't be forever." Tristan wipes an escaped tear from my eye with his thumb. I had resolved to hold it together, but here it is the day of Tristan's departure, and I can feel myself teetering on the edge of falling apart. *But I won't!* I take a step back from him and swallow down the giant lump in my throat, attempting a smile instead. Tristan's lips form into a grin in return as he winks at me. "Besides, we can use this as an excuse for a vacation together. In a week or two you can come out for a visit, and I'll spend all of my free time exploring the area with you. I hear there is a lot to do."

I nod my head, still not trusting myself to speak. I've never been to the West Coast and it *does* sound like a great idea—a sightseeing venture with my gorgeous, young husband. Although by then we'll miss each other so much, I have to wonder how much time would actually be spent *outside* of our hotel room on tours and the like. Then again, by the time I arrive in California Tristan will already have discovered all the secluded beaches and coves. So maybe a lot of time would be spent outdoors after all. At this thought my cheeks blush bright red, and I look away.

Tristan's soft laughter pulls my eyes back to his. It seems I'm not very talented at hiding my thoughts from him. It's one of the many things he claims to love about me—or so he says. For a second or two his gaze holds mine. "I'll be counting the days until your visit, okay?"

I nod in return. But deep down inside I want to scream out, "Don't go! Stay right here with me in Rhode Island, and don't ever go away." Instead I fall into his arms for a bear hug.

"I love you, baby." The tone of his deep, sexy voice whispering into my hair sounds so sincere, it's almost my undoing. Somewhere inside of myself I know that it will be those words I'll be hanging tightly onto for the weeks to come.

I squeeze back. "I love you too."

The loneliness of Tristan being gone is softened somewhat by technology. By now he had acquiesced to the practice of texting—a little marital compromise. That, along with nightly webcam sessions, soon becomes the thread that holds me together while he is gone. Each evening we set a time to meet up on the computer and visit with each other, talking and laughing for at least an hour or more. It is the highlight of each day. Every time we connect via the Internet, he is such a sight for my sore eyes. I love being able to see him and talk with him live. But there are moments while we are conversing when I want to just crawl through the computer so I can touch him, feel his warm, strong body pressed up against mine. It's in these instants that I wonder why they haven't invented teleporting yet. If I could just be with him, lay my fingers on him even for a few minutes!

The day following one late-night Skype, I am at work trying to organize statistics and ideas from various groups that have been successful at implementing ocean cleanup projects—flourishing ventures that are being carried out to beautify shoreline communities. Pulling together ideas from these alliances, I am compiling data and vignettes into a pamphlet designed to inspire others into duplicating similar actions.

While I'm trying to concentrate on the task at hand, two cubicles over I can hear Calista, Center for Marine Studies' self-designated brownnoser, kissing up, as usual, to our manager, Jada. Along with spewing empty words of praise over the way Jada looks, runs the facility, and in general is such a terrific person, Calista is currently singing her own acclaims as well. "Have you seen how well my dolphin project is coming together? Check it out; accolades are heading our way, I'm sure. Jada, you are going to be well-renowned when this goes live in the community."

Blah! I resist the urge to vomit. Can one person be so blind to such obvious flattery? *Apparently yes.* I'd been noticing in the past several weeks that Calista's fawning words *had* at times made their mark, enabling her to get certain jobs that seemed above her level of expertise. Holding my breath, I shake my head, waiting to hear Jada's reply. In my head I imagine the approving tone of her voice. *Oh, Calista, this is fabulous! You are so committed to our company!* I narrow my eyes—*the company*? But what about the ocean itself? Isn't that what we are all really here for?

Instead, surprisingly, that's not how it goes at all. A long pause filled only with the diffused shuffling sound of papers hovers in the air before I finally hear Jada's response. "This material looks so similar to SeaWorld's website, it almost seems like plagiarism. You don't want to mess with that. *I* don't want to mess with that. I hope you take me very seriously when I say I expect a complete revision."

My eyes go wide while I listen to the obvious disapproval in Jada's voice. Breath held, I cover my mouth with one hand, trying hard not to make a peep. Seconds later I detect the sound of Jada's retreat from Calista's cubicle. Startling into motion, very quickly my fingers find the keyboard at my computer and I begin earnestly typing, not wanting to get caught eavesdropping while Jada passes by. *Holy cow! That was unexpected!* But completely spot-on in assessment, I'm sure.

The next few hours I suffer through the annoying sound of sniffles and repeated nose blowing coming from two cubicles over. Over and over I have to resist the urge to shake my head and smile. And pretty much for the *most* part I do—resist. Because that wouldn't be very nice. *Would it?*

I'm still thinking about the whole SeaWorld-dolphin episode when I arrive home from work later that day, and how I want to share this little piece of work news with Tristan, knowing he will *get it*—because he's heard the *Calista* stories before. But when I am finally all settled in, hair freshly combed after a shower, sitting on my bed firing up the modem, getting ready to talk on the webcam, Tristan doesn't show up on the other end of the computer.

Automatically I glance at my watch to make sure I got the time right, 7:03 p.m. By 7:20 p.m. I'm still under the safe assumption that he's just checking in a little late tonight. But after an hour goes by, still his face hasn't lit up the screen. My heart does a slow dive in my chest as I begin sending him a series of texts that he never answers. Chiding myself for being so on edge, I eventually give up on my venture and prepare for bed. I've been so spoiled by his consistency and timeliness—so what if something came up tonight and he couldn't Skype just this once or answer my texts? I'll catch up with him tomorrow. No big deal.

Tomorrow finds me very distracted at work. The figures that I'd been compiling only the day before now repeatedly become a blurred mess on the page in front of me—it's so hard to make any sense of them at all when my thoughts keep taking me back to the empty computer screen in my bedroom from the night before. *How many days in a row would a second-grade classroom need to pick up one piece of trash in order to make an impact on the environment in one month's time?* Time after time I have to shake my head in order to clear it and attempt to refocus on the project at hand. Over and over again I have to remind myself that one episode of Tristan not contacting me is not an earth-shattering event. But in spite all of the self-talk, the hours drag and I can hardly wait for seven o'clock to arrive so I can reconnect with him again—so I can be reassured that everything is just fine, that Tristan is still breathing and smiling and is still his same beautiful self like always.

By eight o'clock I am pacing the floor of my cabin, and it feels like a lead ball is resting uncomfortably in my stomach.

Tristan has not shown up on the webcam once again.

By now my nerves are shot. I've barely touched my dinner, and I have to pee but I don't want to leave the computer, so I carry it with me into the bathroom. I can't risk the chance of missing him. But it doesn't really matter whether I leave the computer on the bed or set it on the sink top in the bathroom, because he doesn't show up while I'm sitting on the toilet either. Two, three, four times I text him—uselessly. I unplug and replug the computer, check and recheck the Internet connection, and pace the length of our bedroom floor at least a thousand times. But none of the tinkering and fidgeting behavior makes any difference.

Because Tristan never does text, or appear on the webcam, or in any way try to contact me at all that whole evening.

It's well past midnight before I finally talk myself into going to bed, determining in my mind that I will go to NEC Systems Group early the next morning to find out what they know—see if he's reported in to them lately. But at best I toss and turn restlessly. *Everything is okay. Everything is perfectly okay,* I keep telling myself before eventually popping out of bed to grab a drink of water, then crawling back under the covers and turning onto my right side. He was probably sent on some type of excursion to a remote nautical setting where communication just isn't possible. *That's got to be it. It makes sense.* Positioning one arm over my eyes, I settle onto my back and take a long, slow breath, finally at peace with my reasoning. Now I can sleep. For a minute or two I feel my body begin to relax into the mattress, my respirations coming in regular patterns. Then out of nowhere my heart begins palpitating, and I am wide awake once more. *Everything was okay between us before he left, right? I mean, right?* I squeeze my eyes tightly together and turn onto my left side. *Of course it was!* I just need to chill and go to sleep. By six o'clock a.m. my head is beginning to throb, and I feel a little lightheaded as I step into the shower.

My hair is still damp, but I am dressed and have already left a message at work telling them I will be a little late when I hear a knock at my front door. Nerves frazzled, I startle with the unexpected sound, and it causes me to jump and bump my elbow on the kitchen countertop in the process. My heart is pulsating through my veins as I walk in slow motion toward the door. Reaching for the blind louvers on the window adjacent to the entryway, I get ready to check who might be visiting at such an early hour. Tristan had cautioned me to be careful in this secluded setting while he is gone. In other words—*word to the wise*—don't open the door to strangers. But a sickening feeling is working its way up from my stomach into my throat, because I have a bad feeling that I will not find a burglar or any other type of criminal when I peer through the window.

My heart has quickened its pace, now practically exploding in my chest as the blinds fall back into place while I run at a lightning-quick speed to undo the locks. Hands shaking, I throw open the door. "Can I help you?" a voice that doesn't sound at all like my own says to the police officer and the gentleman dressed in a gray business suit that are standing on my front porch. *That man looks so familiar. Why does he look so familiar?*

"Bethany Alexander?" The police officer's tone is firm but compassionate. And his brown eyes look so sad. *Why does he look so sad?*

I nod my head just once. "Ye—yes?"

"Bethany, I am Officer Jackson, and this is Neil Barry from NEC Systems Group. May we come in?"

Once again I nod my head and take a few steps backwards, leading them into the interior of my cabin. All the while, recognition is setting in: *the divisional head of NEC Systems Group.* But why—? Immediately I begin shaking my head. *No! No! It's nothing bad!* Suddenly it is difficult to breathe. I stare both men directly in the eyes. *Just say it! Just say what you came to say and get it over with!*

Again Officer Jackson speaks. "Bethany, would you like to sit down?" *No! No, don't say it! Don't say a word. Nothing is wrong!* I shake my head. *No, I don't want to sit down!*

The police officer and Neil Barry exchange glances, and finally Neil clears his throat. Suddenly I am back in first grade, and I have to resist the urge to cover my ears with both hands and hum loudly to drown out his voice. Because that is what a six year old might do, but I am not six years old, so I narrow my eyes and tighten my jaw instead. "Bethany, I am sorry to tell you there has been an accident where Tristan was working out on the West Coast. Offshore in the Pacific Ocean, Tristan's vessel was found floating empty near some rocks. There was blood that matches his DNA . . . but we haven't been able to locate his body. We are still searching—" The head of NEC Systems Group, Neil Barry, pauses briefly to hang his head before looking back up into my face while I pinch my lips together tightly because I don't believe a word he is saying. *Because it just can't be true!* Once again he clears his throat, looking more and more uncomfortable by the moment. "But at this point we aren't very hopeful that we will find him alive."

All at once I feel numb all over. Suddenly I have an overwhelming sensation that I am going to collapse onto the floor in a lifeless heap. Immediately Officer Jackson is at my side, guiding me to the tweed couch in my living room. "Bethany, who can we call to come be with you right now?" *Who? Who can be with me right now? Who can he get?* I swallow down the pasty feeling that is trying to devour my throat—that is trying to choke me. I look into Officer Jackson's compassionate face. *Tristan! I need you to get Tristan to come be with me right now!* Sucking in a big, dry breath I weigh out my chances of being able to speak out loud. Unable to find my voice, I plead with my eyes instead. *Tristan. I just need Tristan. Can you please just go get Tristan to be with me right now?*

Neil Barry fidgets nervously as he sits with me on the coach while Officer Jackson uses his trained resourcefulness to search my cabin, looking for a number to call. The next thing you know, my best friend Lucy is sitting there beside me on the couch, taking Neil Barry's place. It is only after the two men exit the cabin that I am finally able to speak. Grabbing Lucy's wrist, I begin pleading with her to stop them from leaving. "I need to talk to them. I need them to come back and give me more information." *There has got to be more information.* "I really just need more details."

Lucy pulls me into her arms. For a long time she holds me there comforting me, willing me to cry. But I can't do it. I can't just sit back and cry when there is so much more to the story that I need to find out. I glance around the cabin that Tristan had worked so hard to remodel over the past few months, adding another bedroom in the back and refinishing the wooden floors so that they now gleam like new. The kitchen cabinets were going to be the next project on the list. Soon I will have to make a trip into Westerly to help pick out the material he'll be needing. For just a moment I try to imagine the style that will work best in the space allotted. Because I know Tristan will like it if I have everything ordered and arranged for when he gets back in town. *And that should be soon!*

One day passes, then another. Lucy brings a suitcase full of clothes to stay with me at the cabin. It occurs to me at some point through the barrage of miserable thoughts that are swimming through my brain that I am thankful she ended up moving to Watch Hill, even if it was mostly to be with Ethan Vaughn. At my request, she eventually takes me to the police station and then to NEC Systems Group so that I can gather and re-sort all the available information about the accident. Because I must have missed something. Because I just can't believe that Tristan is really not locatable.

And because he certainly can't be dead like they are trying to tell me.

But the only answers I get at either place are that they will keep me posted with any breaking news regarding the search. At this point there *is* no new information. So I go back to the cabin once more and nervously wait for any break in the case while Lucy stays right at my side keeping me company: making sure I eat plenty of food and taking me on daily walks so that I get the fresh air and exercise she insists I need to keep my body and mind healthy. A week has gone by with constant supervision and pampering from my best friend when I eventually tell her I'm okay, that she can leave if she wants, that I'll be just fine on my own now. *Really!* After much convincing she finally, reluctantly, leaves.

And I begin making my plans.

The next day I am on a 747, flying to California. With a seatbelt pulled snuggly across my lap, I begin squeezing my hands tightly together anxiously as the landing gear hums and the wheels of the plane prepare to touch down on the runway of San Diego International Airport. Where will I go? Where will I begin looking? Back home I had mentally explored all the Skyping sessions that Tristan and I had shared. After repeatedly sorting through our nightly conversations, I had jotted down any information I could extract from my memory about the detailed landmarks he had described of the all the coastal places he had been frequenting. Then I had contacted Neil Barry at NEC Systems Group personally and asked him to fill me in on the exact location and intricate details of the accident so that I could finally have the closure that I needed. Little did he know that the only closure that was happening concerning the whole West Coast incident was the closure of my eyelids while I prayed to God repetitively for Tristan's safe return.

Because I just *had* to find him!

Palm trees sway in the breeze as I walk past the Thirty-Second Street Naval Base. Normally the sheer size of the black ships lined up at the docking station dwarfing my small frame as I traverse beside them would have held my attention. But right now they are just a starting point for my geographical navigation which has only one end in sight: *finding Tristan.* After grabbing a sub sandwich at a gas station, I find a small seaside motel and check in. Sitting on a springy mattress that shifts squeakily beneath my weight, I spread out the pile of maps and list of markers that I'll be using to plan my route. Over and over I rehash the strategy for the search until eventually the scratchy, floral bedspread that is now burning into my bare thighs becomes a blur in front of me.

Standing abruptly to clear my mind from the overwhelming details, I quickly run my fingers through the long strands of my blond hair before pulling them into a ponytail and heading for the door. With a quick flick of my wrist I glance at my watch. First on the agenda—flag a cab and get over to South Bay Marina by One o'clock. There a hired captain will be waiting to take me on a personal tour of the Pacific to the location ten miles offshore where Tristan's accident reportedly took place.

Water sprays up all around the retired Special Forces RIB boat as Captain Jim and I speed through the open seas, closing in on the area where wreckage of Tristan's vessel had been found. Just up ahead, protruding like a miniature version of the iceberg that destroyed the *Titanic,* I spy the infamous rocky island formation that supposedly took Tristan from me, and my stomach suddenly becomes gnarled and painful. With bated breath, I hug my arms to my chest as our boat eases in closer and closer to the scene. Rock after jagged rock. Boulder after jutting boulder. Pile after pile of hostile, sharp-edged stones. An unyielding shoreline void of swaying trees and powdery sand. I swallow hard and am immediately chilled to the bone as I realize that I'm searching for blood splattered on the pointed rock formations when I should be keeping an eye out for a very alive Tristan sitting tucked away, waving down at me, telling me he's okay—that he's just had an inconvenient injury and could use a little help.

"Can we get any closer?" I call to Captain Jim.

"Not *much* closer without ripping out the bottom of the boat. But I'll do the best I can." Now that we have reached our destination, he seems to sense my growing angst and begins to shift uncomfortably in his seat, not quite knowing how to handle a girl in distress. In an effort to soothe my outward show of anguish, he circles our watercraft in and around the formidable island repeatedly, trying his very best to angle it into the rocky shoreline so that I can get a closer look.

Over and over again he listens to me when I say, "What about over there?" or "I think I just saw something over here—can we pull up for a closer look?" But every time he maneuvers our boat to the place where I direct him, we only find yet another pile of jagged rocks.

The sun is starting to lower in the sky when Captain Jim finally looks at me with sympathetic eyes and tells me we'll have to call it a night in order to get the vessel safely back to the marina by nightfall. He looks worried as he hands me the news, like he's afraid I might break down crying in the Special Forces RIB boat right out in the middle of the ocean. But I don't cry. I *won't* cry. Because I am not giving up. My hand reaches for the side pocket of my khaki shorts to feel if all my lists and maps are still tucked away safely where I'd put them. The sound of crinkling paper rubbing against fabric tells me they are. I won't give up hope. There are still many more places, shorelines, and landmarks to check out.

And light or dark, sun or moon, I won't sleep a wink until I've searched them all.

The sun is just slipping beneath the horizon when I thank Captain Jim, hail a cab, and head to my next destination—La Jolla, a development twelve miles up the coast from San Diego. During our Skyping sessions, Tristan had told me what a beautiful area La Jolla is and that he is just sure I would like it. And he is right. Resting my head on the seat in the rear of my cab, I watch as our vehicle becomes immersed in the wealthy, hilly, oceanside neighborhood. Our tires hug the curving roads as we wind through the upscale community. In the background, the sky is an artist's color palette full of lilac, rose, and tangerine, diffuse and shifting every few minutes. I let out a soft breath. West Coast sunsets are truly an awe-inspiring sight. But right now no amount of picturesque scenery or breathtaking ocean views matter, because until I find Tristan this is all just a superfluous painting inserted into the background of my venture.

After paying the driver, I pull out my maps and begin finagling my way through the cliffs in an attempt to locate a pathway that will take me down the steep incline to the sandy shoreline below. Eventually I find what looks like a traversable passage and begin to carefully edge myself downward. When I finally reach the bottom, I am greeted by the gentle push of the waves as they spill onto shore. High above me million dollar-mansions are everywhere, facing the wide-open sea. For a moment I imagine high-profile executives, arms resting across their wives' shoulders, watching through floor-to-ceiling windows as some crazy girl, all alone, begins a shoreline excursion on the cusp of the fading daylight hours.

But I don't care how I look or who might be observing me, because right now I just need to find Tristan.

I do, however, realize it is a race against time as I begin searching the winding coastline full of inlets and protective coves—all the areas Tristan had described to me in detail. The remaining glow of daylight is quickly waning, and soon I won't be able to see a thing—including my way back out of this twisting, nautical landscape. It occurs to me then that I'll be needing some type of light source, because I'm not willing to quit my search anytime soon. Recalling

Lost his memory? The blood in my veins turns to ice. I am frozen in place, listening, waiting for Britton to explain.

"At first he couldn't remember anything at all. But recently he's gotten bits and pieces back. Now he is finally able to recall the place he calls home. The Atlantic. The Pacifics have contacted us, and they are bringing him back to us. He'll be home in a few days." Britton pauses as if he is waiting for me to say something, but I am so overwhelmed trying to process this curve ball that he has thrown me that it takes a minute to think of what questions I want to ask. Finally I open my mouth to speak, but by now Britton doesn't notice. He resumes speaking, this time staring through me instead of at me.

"But—" He looks away and I get chills. *But what?* "I just wanted to prepare you. From what I've been told, there is a good chance he may not recognize certain things . . . certain people at first. It may take some time for his brain to heal, but hopefully he will recover more of his memory. And hopefully soon."

After Britton leaves I am a complete mess. I can hardly think straight. With tears rolling down my cheeks and the sound of laughter coming from my throat, I pick up Nate from his crib. Eyes blue and wide, Nate studies my face as if trying to decipher where all these new emotions are coming from. *Mommy seems happy, and yet maybe sad too. And squirrely—definitely squirrely!* Ignoring his perplexed looks, I hug him to my chest before taking him to the kitchen for breakfast. I tuck him into his highchair and then seconds later pull him right back out again. I have forgotten to change his diaper. But it is so hard to focus on anything when all I can hear is Britton Alexander's voice ringing in my ears. *Tristan is coming home.* My beautiful Tristan is coming home! *Yes,* this last piece of news about the memory loss is disheartening, but still, *Tristan is alive!* Tristan is alive and on his way back to me at this very moment!

The day Tristan is due to return I am a nervous wreck, continually pacing around the cabin. Repeatedly I pull my hair into a ponytail, then let it fall in soft waves around my face once again. Stopping midstride, I stare into the hallway mirror, running my hands over the simple white skirt and floral blouse I have chosen to wear for the reunion. My cheeks are pink with excitement, my blue eyes sparkling with energy. I have to pinch myself because I can't believe it! I can't believe that very shortly I am going to get to see Tristan again. Lucy has taken Nate for a few hours giving Tristan time to get used to our initial meeting. I will introduce his son to him a little later. I don't want to blow his healing mind all at once. Trying to remember people from his past and meeting Nate might be too much for him to process in one short time period. My escalating enthusiasm over reuniting with Tristan is dampened just a little when Zepher and Seth show up at my door alone. I knew they or Tristan's parents were supposed to be bringing him to the cabin. "Where is Tristan? Did he come with you?" The words spew from my mouth without any greeting for the twins.

"Actually," Seth says, "there has been a slight change of plans. We are here to take you to his beach. He is already there. We came to take you there too."

For a second my pulse rate increases in tempo. "I . . . I don't understand. Why isn't he just coming out to the house?"

Zepher and Seth glance at each other uneasily, and a weird, weightless sensation begins to climb up my limbs. Finally Zepher is the one to answer my question. "Because he . . . ah . . . doesn't remember it." *It?*

It the house or *it* meaning me? I nod my head slowly just one time. *Does he remember me?* I want to ask the question that is now burning in my mind, but I can't bring myself to verbalize the words. Because in all actuality, I don't want to know the answer. Panic begins eating away at me, and I have a sudden, desperate urge to get to Tristan's beach. I just need to get to him, lay eyes on him, let him lay eyes on me, and then once that happens everything will be okay. It will all come back to him, he will remember me, remember our strong love and everything that we've ever shared together, and everything will be okay again.

I take a deep breath and pull my hair into a ponytail once again. "Okay, I'm ready. Let's go."

Seth chats animatedly as we travel along the shoreline route that will take us to Tristan's beach, but Zepher is quieter than usual, sending an occasional nervous glance in my direction. I tune both of them out. I can't read into either one's take on the situation of what is about to go down. This is my situation and my situation alone. It doesn't matter what anyone else thinks about how it is all going to play out. Well, mine and Tristan's situation, that is. No one else matters but him and me. We keep walking.

Each bend that we round, each cove that we wind through is one step closer to finally getting to see Tristan after all of this time. My stomach is in ropes, and it is getting more and more difficult to breathe as my sandal-clad feet march through the sand. Step after step through the sandy shoreline. Puff after puff of salty ocean air coming in and out of my lungs. It is a breezy day, and the waves are trimmed with whitecaps as they advance toward the shore just to our left. The blue, cloudless sky allows the sun to shine brilliantly on the water, filling me with hope for what is about to come.

At last the terrain begins to look intimately familiar, and a waft of past memories begins to flood through my mind as we near his beach: Tristan and I talking on the beach; Tristan and I kissing and touching, lying in the sand; Tristan singing to me while I'm lost somewhere in a trance. My heart pounds in my chest as we round the final corner. Seth and Zepher are now both silent at my side. The sound of hushed voices conversing comes in contact with my brain, and I realize that Tristan must not be alone. *Of course they wouldn't leave him here alone!* I hold my breath as the dune grass clears and everyone comes into view.

Britton and Charlize Alexander and a small group of others that I recognize from the sea, close friends of the Alexander family, are all congregated in the protective alcove celebrating their love one's return. The crowd blurs, and now there is only one person crossing my line of vision, capturing my full attention. Now the rest are only nonentities smudged somewhere in the background of Tristan's private beach. All I can see is him.

I freeze in place, an ache clutching at my chest as I lay eyes on Tristan's stunning form for the first time in so long—in way too long. It is instantly obvious to me that he's lost weight. His shorts hang a little more loosely on his hips, and his cheeks are slightly more hollowed than before. But he is still the most beautiful specimen that I have ever seen. He is completely perfect.

A slight sigh escapes my lips, and unadulterated love seeps through every pore in my skin. It is hardly containable. I feel as though I am going to burst. The muscles in my legs are twitching and flexing as I prepare to run at full speed into his arms. But something stops them, because as of yet he has not once looked in my direction. I watch from where I am standing flanked by Seth and Zepher as Tristan is engaged in a conversation with his mom, not seeming to notice our arrival. I am suspended in limbo, every cell in my body wanting to close the distance and throw myself into his arms. And yet a piece of my brain is flashing me warning signals—telling me to hold up, because something is not quite right.

I have never been so unsure of what to do. A tumult of emotions are assaulting my mind, and I don't know what to do with them. My heart is singing with joy over seeing Tristan again. And yet disappointment is flooding through my veins over him not immediately tuning in to me the way I am so instantaneously tuned to him. Does he really not see me standing here? Can he not sense my presence—like he always had so easily before? Confusion and awkwardness surround me, because now I don't know how to act around him. I had been so excited to see him, I never gave this type of dilemma a second thought. Not knowing what else to do, I take a deep breath and wait—wait for him to turn and see me. Shifting restlessly in the sand, I contemplate calling out to him from where I am standing. Or should I start advancing toward him, hoping that eventually he will notice my approach?

Finally Charlize detects my presence out of the corner of her eye. From my distance I watch as she taps Tristan's arm and leans toward him, her lips moving as she speaks quietly into his ear. My heart hammers in my chest. Slowly he turns to look my way. As his green eyes pass over my form, I am immediately undone, and I have to press my fingers together to stop them from trembling. But the visual contact between us is very brief, and before I can register any real thoughts on the matter, he is turning back to his mom once more. My heart dives in my chest. *Oh God, no—does he really not recognize me?* Tristan says something to his mom and she nods in return. Suddenly I feel desperate to know what was just said.

"Bethany!" Britton's booming voice so close by causes me to jump. I had been so absorbed with Tristan I hadn't even noticed his approach. "Let's go say hi to the long-lost boy, shall we?" *The long-lost boy?*

I swallow, trying to get rid of the pasty feeling that is devouring my throat. "Okay." Together we begin advancing in Tristan's direction. Now he is looking at me again as I walk with his father through the sand, but his face remains completely stoic. Not an ounce of emotion crosses over his perfect features as his eyes scan over mine. I forget to breathe, hoping, waiting. Long seconds pass as I watch for his countenance to change, for something, anything to happen between us. For a flicker of recognition to pass through his green eyes.

But it never does. Instead, for a fleeting moment he looks away. I feel the tears that are threatening to pool behind my eyelids and force them away. "It's me, Tristan. *It's me!*" I want to desperately whisper aloud. Instead I curl my fingers into tight fists at my side and wait for Britton to take the lead.

"Tristan . . . ," Britton speaks cautiously as if he doesn't want to overwhelm his son with anything—doesn't want to overwhelm him with *me*. "This is Bethany. Bethany, the girl who we talked to you about." He pauses. "Your wife."

My pulse flutters nervously as I wait for Tristan to respond. As I wait for it to dawn on him. As I wait for him to say, *Bethany . . . Bethany, it's you. It's really you.* Instead his eyes connect with mine only briefly before they sweep over the rest of my form as if he is scrutinizing me. Trying to figure out what it is that he saw in me to begin with—what is it is about me that made him want to marry me in the first place. Suddenly I feel exposed, and for some unknown reason completely inadequate. I hug my arms to my chest. *Tristan is so hot!* As he stands in front of me, shoulders back, legs slightly spread, every inch of his being radiates self-assuredness even after having had his accident. In comparison, I am so small and plain. And the funny thing is, a year and a half ago I didn't feel that way at all. I felt beautiful and desirable and alive.

But now in the matter of a few minutes all of that has changed. Now I am an awkward, insecure teenager who is faced with having to interact with a drop-dead-gorgeous guy. Tristan nods his head in polite acknowledgement of the situation. "Hi," he says as he shoves his hand into the front pockets of his shorts. No "Hi, Bethany," or "Hi, how are you?" Just "hi." But his deep voice reaching my ears causes goose bumps to surface across my skin.

"Hi," I say back. Tristan presses his lips together and after a moment of silence looks uncomfortably away. I know I should say something else, but suddenly everything feels so awkward. I want to run a million miles away. And yet I don't want to leave him at all. I clear my throat. "I . . . I'm glad to see that you are okay. That you are . . . back." Polite conversation between two old acquaintances or near strangers. I can't believe this is happening. But there is nothing I can do to stop it.

Tristan looks back over at me and smiles for the first time, but the action seems almost forced. "Thanks. It's . . . ah, good to be back." Once again strained silence fills the air. This time Britton and Charlize step in to fill the void, chitchatting about Tristan's trip back from Pacific and his faithful dolphin friend who traveled with him the entire way. *Drake!* My gaze shifts toward the ocean, and after a few seconds of searching, I detect his smiling, black head bobbing against the horizon, waiting for Tristan to resume his place in the water beside him once again. I can't help it—now I am smiling too. Tristan's head shoots over to watch my face. But when I look back at him, he diverts his gaze. The conversation led by his parents continues without any acknowledgement of the miniscule, silent interaction between Tristan and me. At times when asked, although self-conscious, I attempt to say a few words in contribution to the discussion. Tristan too is drawn into the four-way, though mostly two-way, interchange by his parents as they ask him to describe various aspects of the trip. Then eventually the topics dwindle, and they finally step away and leave us alone.

Now the air surrounding us seems thick and uncomfortable. The waves keep a steady rhythm in the background, and I notice that Tristan keeps shifting his attention toward them—away from me. Somehow I get the sinking feeling that he'd rather be out there with them instead of standing here on land. I wait for him to say something but he doesn't, so I am forced to think of something to say, myself, because if I don't, he looks as though he's going to bolt at any moment. And I'm not ready to let him leave! *Oh my word, Tristan, it's me, the girl you love so much, remember? You told me so yourself so many times. Showed me so yourself so many times. Couldn't ever get enough of me, remember? Said you would never*

want to live without me. For a moment I close my eyes tightly together and then reopen them. I have to hold it together. He didn't
try to lose his memory. He's going to remember again. He is going
to remember how he used to feel about me. *Used to!* A chill shoots
up my spine as a new thought occurs to me. What if he doesn't get
those same feelings back?

"So the people . . . or the, um ones that helped you out in the
Pacific . . . were they pretty nice then?"

Tristan's green eyes look up at me, startled, as if he is surprised
to hear me talk. "Oh . . . yeah. Yeah, they were fine. Very good to
me actually." He pauses for a second to crack his knuckles. *Funny,
I never remember him doing that before.* "They say if they wouldn't
have found me and decided to take me in . . . I probably wouldn't
have . . . you know . . ."

I nod my head and swallow, trying hard not to imagine the alternative: *Tristan alone and dying in the Pacific.* "Well, good thing
they did then . . . right?"

Tristan chuckles lightly though almost awkwardly. "Right."

The dialogue between us continues with many long pauses filling
the air. By the time Seth and another sea person step in to rescue
the situation, my lungs are aching in my chest, and it is becoming
increasingly difficult to breathe. Eventually Tristan drifts off to join
another group of sea friends while I do my best to put on a show of
remaining upbeat as I mingle and talk with this person and that.
The topic always being the same—*isn't it great that Tristan returned.*
And when Britton and Charlize Alexander pull me aside to tell me
that it will be best due to the circumstances if Tristan goes home
with them for the night, but they will bring him by tomorrow for
another visit, I am not at all surprised. At this point, the way our
reunion has gone down, any other option would be hard to imagine.
I nod my head in silent acknowledgement to their suggestion, trying hard to fight back the drops of liquid that are trying to surface

behind my eyelids. As I am preparing to leave, I look for Tristan so that I can tell him good-bye, but he is busy talking with some of the others, so I begin making my retreat away from his beach quietly and all alone.

When I reach the comfort of my cabin, the tears that I had been holding back for the past couple of hours now come at full strength. And I cry unrestrainedly for the rest of the afternoon.

The following day I have conflicted emotions when I know Tristan is due to arrive at the cabin for his parents' proclaimed visit. I am still desperate to see him, but although I had been warned of the memory loss, I was completely unprepared for his blasé reaction to me. It hurts so bad! And even though I still have hope, I am so scared! I am so scared that he won't ever remember, and we won't ever get back what we once had.

I dress in a tan shorts and a gray tee shirt. After pulling my hair into a loose ponytail, I splash water on my cheeks to wake up the color on my skin and soothe away the puffy circles under my eyes. The past twenty-four hours have been long—too many tears, not enough sleep. The cabin seems quiet. Too quiet. I have made arrangements for Nate to be gone during the visit today. And now there is no one left inside the empty walls but me. According to Britton and Charlize, it is still too soon for the father and son to meet. And I couldn't agree more. Right now Tristan can barely stand to look at me, let alone be introduced to a son he doesn't know he has. Over and over in my mind I had pictured Tristan and Nate's first encounter as a joyous occasion. But as things stand—now is not that time.

The hesitant knock at my door comes around 5 o'clock in the afternoon. I take a deep breath, adjust my ponytail, and pad across the floor toward the sound. By the time I turn the knob, my heart is pounding in my chest. For a long moment nothing is said as I stare at Tristan's perfect features while he stands, looking slightly uncomfortable, on my back porch. I squeeze my fingers into tight balls. *He is still so unnervingly hot!* Taking my gaze off of his face and lean, muscular build, I peer behind him, expecting to find his parents or the twins. But he is all alone. My heart picks up in tempo. Considering how our initial meeting went down the day before, this is a bit of a surprise.

"Um . . . hi." He is the first to speak.

"Hey," I say back. As a nervous gesture, I begin playing with my ponytail. Silently I reprimand myself, knowing that my voice sounds self-conscious and breathless. I need to get control of the situation, or I'm going to appear like a swooning fool. As I open the door and step out onto the porch, Tristan takes a step back—at least six inches. My heart takes a momentary dive, but I choose to ignore it for the time being. Maybe he is just allowing me a comfortable space, after all, the porch is rather small. I motion to the ocean. "I thought we could go down by the dock. I thought you might like—"

He doesn't wait for me to finish. Instantly relief spreads over his face. "Yeah . . . sure."

As we walk the path from the cabin to the beach in quiet, I experience an overwhelming wave of discouragement, wondering if it will ever really work out between us again. After long stretches of silence, we finally reach the shoreline, and immediately Tristan's gaze is drawn to *Blue*. Now his eyes light up, and I am given a small surge of optimism. *Maybe his antique wooden boat will be what it takes for him to remember!* "Hey . . . this is cool." He begins walking the length of the dock. "Is this . . . is it yours?" His voice sounds so much like the schoolboy voice that I used to hear coming from him that I can hardly stand it. The sound is so endearing.

"Yeah . . . it's mine." *Ours. Yours, really.* The optimism from Tristan's enthrallment over *Blue* soon begins to wane, however, as he becomes so absorbed with the boat that I am left hanging out on the dock alone for most of his stay. After a while I have to wonder if his excitement over the boat has now become an opportune escape from our visit, the perfect solution for him. He can be here with me, look like he's putting an effort into our relationship, and yet conveniently avoid me at the same time. After an hour of him mostly tinkering with the boat, he prepares to leave, and our time together—though mostly not together—is over. After telling me good-bye, he glances uneasily over his shoulder several times as though he isn't quite sure whether or not he should dive in the water right in front of me. Then after one final, fleeting look, he chooses to walk down the shoreline instead. After he is gone, I want to sink to the sand in frustration, because I don't feel any closer to him than I had felt the day before. He barely even looked at me when he said good-bye. I squeeze my eyes together tightly, trying to push back the tears. I don't want to spend another night crying. I am already exhausted from the previous night's episode.

Once Nate gets dropped back off at home I hug him tightly to my chest, trying to draw some comfort from his affectionate, loving nature. After acquiescing to a few minutes of snuggling, he wiggles free, and I set him back down so he can run around the living room gathering up his favorite toys. As I head into the kitchen getting ready to fix dinner, I hear a noise on the back porch. Pushing a chair away from the table, I round the corner to see what it is. When I get to the door, the view through the screen causes me to freeze in place.

It's Tristan. He freezes in place too. My heart begins to pound. In his hand he is holding a windbreaker. He lifts it up for me to see. "I . . . ah, forgot this earlier. I left it on your porch." He bites his lip as he watches me through the screen, and my insides clench.

"Oh . . . okay." I had been so absorbed with how poorly our visit had gone that I hadn't even noticed his jacket lying there as I walked by on my way back into the cabin. "Okay . . . well, I'll see you—" Even though I don't want to, I feel my hand reaching for the doorknob to close the inside door. I know that this action will seem rude, but I don't know what else to do. I would love to try to initiate a conversation with Tristan and see if he would be up to staying for a while, but now is not the right time. As I'm running through this dilemma in my mind, I pause one second too long.

"Mom . . . ma . . . ma." A sweet little voice reaches out to me as Nate comes running headlong down the hallway. Instinctively I reach for the door but then freeze in place. It's too late. Finally Nate reaches my legs and stops short, his round, blue eyes making contact with the man standing out on the porch. For two long seconds Nate stares through the screen before burying his face into the back of my knee. Moments later, he lifts two arms toward me. Reaching down, I pick him up. Straddling his small frame against my hip, I finally allow myself to look back toward the porch, scared of what I'm going to find.

Tristan looks dumbfounded. As many times as he has avoided my gaze since he's been back in Watch Hill, now he is staring openly in my direction. And now I don't know what to say. How do you tell someone something this big? I didn't want him to find out like this. My pulse is throbbing in my veins, and I hug Nate a little more tightly to my side. Inside I am like a mother bear wanting to fiercely protect my son. My eyes, wide and unwavering, stare right into Tristan's. *Please like him. Please don't let this be an ugly thing. Nate is so wonderful! I love him so much! Please love him too!* Finally Tristan's deep voice breaks through the moment.

"Who is . . . who is this?"

I swallow hard. "This is Nate." *And he is beautiful and wonderful and perfect!* I motion toward the door. "Would you . . . would you like to come inside?"

Tristan hesitates before answering, still watching my face. "Okay?" The word is drawn out slowly, sounding more like a question.

Butterflies flutter around in my stomach as I feel Tristan's strong form following behind me into the living room, into the house where we've created so many memories. Now in some ways it feels like they never happened at all. I motion to a chair in the corner and he sits. I take a seat adjacent to him on the couch with baby Nate settled onto my lap. Nate is now staring with unbridled interest at Tristan. At his dad. *Can Nate sense it? Does he know? Is the inherent connection obvious?* I glance over at Tristan too, albeit nervously, trying to think of a good way to tell him what I am about to tell him. But there doesn't seem to be any perfect way. Any long introductions or stories will just prolong the information that he has the right to know, that I *want* him to know. Just not quite like this. I didn't want for it to all go down like this. I breathe a quick prayer, clear my throat, and look right at him. *Here goes.*

"Nate is your son, Tristan."

Chapter Seven

"Nate is *our* son." The words as they leave my mouth are just a whisper. Now I sit back and anxiously wait for the ramifications to fly across the room. Even from this distance I can detect the tiny muscle in Tristan's jaw as it begins to twitch. Uncomfortable moments pass and I am getting more and more nervous by the second, but on the defensive too. *Don't!* I dare him with my eyes. *Don't say anything bad about him!* Finally he shakes his head one time as if to clear it.

"Oh . . . okay . . . wow! I didn't know. No one told me so . . . so I just didn't—"

"Well, we wanted to wait until you were a little more adjusted to . . . um, everything, so that you wouldn't be *as* overwhelmed. But trust me. I wasn't trying to keep him a secret. I wanted to introduce you to him. Just not like—"

Tristan shakes his head, interrupting me. "No . . . no, yeah, I get it. Just not like this." His gaze shifts to Nate's small frame as he sits spellbound on my lap, repeatedly squeezing my arm with his small fingers. The skin on Tristan's face becomes pale, and his Adam's apple bobs up and down several times in his neck. "So . . . ah—" He clears his throat, but even his voice still sounds like it's cracked and unsure. "How old is he . . . ah . . . Nate?"

I soothe Nate's wispy, blond hair gently in a repetitive motion, almost protectively. "He'll be one year old soon."

"All right . . . okay . . . one year."

In all the years of knowing Tristan, I've never seen him look so overwhelmed. I can tell he's trying hard to pretend like he's in control of the situation—like I have not completely freaked him out by what I've just told him, by what he's just discovered. But I know him too well. Once again I get the now all-too-familiar urge to cry—the same urge that I've been experiencing on a regular basis for the past thirty hours. I inhale a large, shaky breath and fight off the feeling once again. But the lump in the back of my throat is still there, lurking. Tristan's green, piercing eyes alternate between carefully avoiding my gaze and shooting Nate tiny little glances from across the room.

All at once I have the sinking feeling in my chest that he is about to bolt.

And I know I need to let him. Pulling Nate a little more tightly to my chest, I get ready to say what I really don't want to say at all. But I know I need to. It hurts, though. It hurts so bad to just let him go. There is a part of me that wants to demand he stay and be the husband and the father that he really is. And knowing Tristan's strong character, he probably would acquiesce to my ultimatums, but what then? We'd have his presence in the house, but would we have his heart? I shake my head and ignore the answer to that question as it shouts back loud and clear in my mind. "Well, it's getting late . . . and you probably want . . . I mean you probably need to go."

Tristan's troubled countenance immediately relaxes, telling me that I just did the right thing. Just said the right thing. But if it *is* the right thing, then why does it feel like a knife stabbing me in the chest? Bracing his legs with both hands, Tristan raises to a standing position. His well-built frame devours the room, causing an ache to replace the spot where the knife has just been. I don't look at him, because I'm afraid that if I do he will see into my thoughts—all of the thoughts that I didn't used to have to hide from him. But now I do.

As he begins to exit the room and then stops moving, I avert my gaze. I get the feeling that he is waiting for me to send him a look of approval on his departure even though he hasn't once interacted with his newfound son. But what is it that he wants to hear from me—that he wants me to convey with my eyes? *Sure, it's fine. Just go ahead and leave and don't talk to your beautiful son. Don't pick him up or touch his perfect little cheeks or let him grasp your finger with his own tiny ones? Oh, and while you're at it just go right ahead. Go ahead and leave me too!* I sigh and look back up, pressing my lips together.

His green eyes are uncertain as they watch my face. After an uncomfortable pause, he begins to crack his knuckles. I flinch at his newly acquired habit. Finally he speaks. "So does Nate . . . should I—?"

"Nate isn't going anywhere." *Just go.* My tone holds no expression.

"Okay . . . well, good-bye then. Good-bye . . . um, Nate." As he talks, he continues walking out of the room, this time backing away for several feet before finally turning around and heading the rest of the way to the door. I rise to my feet with Nate straddled on my hip and follow his trail. Tristan is still a good distance ahead of us by the time the screen door closes behind him. Pausing, he turns and shoots us one last look though the woven mesh. I give a halfhearted wave in acknowledgement to his glance and then wait until he is out of sight before closing the interior door behind him.

With a heavy heart I continue into the kitchen and finish preparing Nate's supper. Sitting across from his highchair, I watch while he alternates between babbling and shoving food into his mouth. Periodically I offer him an absentminded, feeble grin. But I eat nothing. I have no appetite. After tucking him into bed for the night, I walk past my bedroom and notice a flickering light coming from the closet. In a panic I rush toward the wavering glow. *The searchlight!* I throw open the doors. For a moment or two the light dims until it is almost nonexistent, and then as if getting a second wind, it returns to full strength again. *The batteries!* The batteries must be getting low. Pivoting away from the light source, I hurry to the kitchen and rummage through the all-purpose drawer until I find what I'm looking for. Fresh batteries in hand, in no time I am back on my bedroom floor huddled in a crouched position while I insert them into the correct compartment on the side of the cumbersome device. After I am finished, I lean my head against the wall behind me, relieved. *Such a close call!* I will have to do a better job in the future of keeping the batteries replaced—because I not ready to let the light burn out. I close my eyes and allow my breaths to come in a heavy but steady rhythm. *I just can't let it burn out!*

Nate is holding onto my hand, tugging, trying to persuade me to go farther out into the water. It is a calm day and the ocean is placid, stretching on for miles without a ripple in sight. The familiar sound of the rhythmic waves is absent from the air, causing the shuffle of our feet against the liquid to seem that much more pronounced. The playful splish-splash of Nate's persistence is soothing in its own way, filling my mind with something other than thoughts of the blatant absence in our family. But I'm not ready to cave to his demands.

"No, no, Nate. We're not going farther out today."

Nate's green eyes look thoughtfully up into my face for a moment before he resumes his previous tugging, not at all deterred by my unwanted retort. But in spite of the resilience, his one-year-old strength is still no match for mine. Trying to distract his attention, I reach down to the water and send a spray of liquid his way. He squeals in delight. I am about to repeat the motion when I spy movement out of the corner of my eye. My hand stills in the water. To my right, standing silently on the shoreline, are Britton and Charlize Alexander. I gather Nate into my arms and head their way, nonchalantly peering over their shoulders to see if anyone else happens to be with them. Involuntarily my heart sinks when it becomes obvious that they came alone.

Upon my approach, they greet me with a brief smile before turning their full attention to Nate. Nate hesitates for a fleeting interval before finally deciding it's safe to wiggle out of my arms and run to his grandma and grandpa. They spend a few minutes doting on him before turning their attention back to me. Charlize's green eyes fill with compassion as they reach out to mine, and I feel my heart sink a little further in my chest. *Compassion usually means nothing positive.*

"So how are you doing with all of this, Bethany?" Even her voice is warm—laced with concern. My pulse picks up in tempo, and I shrug my shoulders.

"Oh, you know, things could be going better. But I'm hopeful." *Should I be? Hopeful? What has he said? What has he told you?*

Charlize presses her lips together and nods. And Britton, who had been the one that was so supportive at our wedding, encouraging me to go back to the altar and finish what we had started *because Tristan and I definitely belonged together—because Tristan is a good man and he knows Tristan loves me completely and unconditionally,* now glances uncomfortably away, unable to look me in the eye.

I can't breathe.

For a moment no one says anything. Everything is completely still. Today even the waves are silent, contributing nothing to the conversation. Suddenly I long for their dull roar in the background to interrupt the unwanted thoughts that are screaming in my mind. *Say something! Will someone please just say something?* Charlize sighs and offers me a small smile. "Yeah . . . some things just take time. This may be one of those things."

I nod my head resignedly and bite my lip.

"You know Tristan wants to do the right thing. He doesn't want to shirk his responsibilities now that he knows he has a son . . . and of course with you too. He wants to be there for both of you but"— *But what? But he doesn't love me? He doesn't love Nate? Because you never mentioned love*—"but he just needs a little time to collect himself and heal. This whole loss-of-memory thing has really thrown him for a loop. There is so much he doesn't remember, and it is really hard on him. He doesn't know which way to turn. But thankfully he is recovering some of his memory. Thankfully he does remember a lot from his childhood. So for now—"

So for now what? I bite my lip and brace myself. Nate, who is busy playing with the chain around his grandpa's neck, glances back at me with imploring green eyes. Almost like—*are you okay, Mommy?* But he can't possibly know. He can't possibly understand the unsettling undercurrents that are flowing through the conversation attacking my self-assuredness. Charlize sighs.

"For now Tristan is going to stay with us." Then she adds hastily, "Not for good, of course. Just until he remembers more."

I swallow down the bile that is rising into my throat. "What if he never does . . . remember?" *Will he never come back?* The implied question hangs heavy in the ocean air, choking me.

Charlize offers a sympathetic smile. *More compassion.* My fingernails dig into the skin on the palms of my hands. "We have to believe he will . . . *you* have to believe he will—"

"He *will* remember!" Britton's booming voice interrupts his wife's reassurances. It's as if suddenly he can't take it anymore—can't tolerate any more of this nonsense. He is bound and determined to state the final outcome and fix the problem. End of story. Nate startles in his arms.

I nod my head in acknowledgement to his resolute statement, but I am not fooled. Britton can rant and rave. He can pound his fists and send the waves into a tailspin with the thunderous sound of his voice. But he can't force Tristan to change his mind. After all, Tristan married me, didn't he? And that was not in Britton's original plan for his son. He wasn't able to stop that. And he won't be able to change the outcome of this either. In the end, Tristan will make up his own mind.

Charlize interrupts my thoughts, jumping back into the conversation where she left off before Britton offered his adamant opinion. "Because he does seem to remember many things from his growing up years, by him coming back to his childhood home, he may be able to build his memory on that secure foundation. It is a good place to foster the healing he needs, so that he can get back to you . . . and Nate."

I sigh and tell them okay. After all, what else can I do or say really? In many ways, what they are telling me makes sense. But deep down it still hurts so bad. Why can't he just resume his place with me and make it work? After visiting with Nate for a while longer, Britton and Charlize leave, and I am left alone with my son to stew over the newest plan concerning my long-lost husband's return.

And I don't like it at all.

It is so hard to retrain my thinking. I'd spent the last year and a half thinking that if Tristan was found on the Pacific Coast, if he was indeed discovered alive and was able to return, he would return to me and resume his place as my husband. And all would be just as it was before he had left. It's so hard to let go of that assumption. It doesn't feel right to let it go. But for sanity's sake I have to. I have to think of our situation in a whole new way. I have to let the intimate relationship that we shared disappear into the past.

But even though I know I need to let go of that relationship, I'm not ready to let go of him altogether.

So every chance I get, I begin hanging out by the water: choosing a shoreline route for my runs, taking Nate wading often, and going for long walks through town out to Napatree Point. Every splash in the water instantly draws my attention. Every disruption in the pattern of the waves has my head spinning in that direction. Every marine animal bobbing through the surf appears to be a dolphin at first glance.

But every time I do a double take in the direction of the ocean,

I'm never quite sure of what it is that I see out of the corner of my eye, of what I have just heard. Mostly my encounters are just empty splashes or protruding boulders or large fish cavorting close to the surface of the water. Deep inside though, when no concrete object materializes to explain the disturbance, I sometimes fantasize that it really is Tristan swimming somewhere just offshore watching me while I'm out for a walk. *Secretly he wants to be with me, but is unsure how to initiate the approach.*

But then after a few minutes of allowing that daydream to play out in my mind, I remind myself that it probably isn't true—that it is just a silly and whimsical thought, and that I need to get a grip on reality. The reality of it is that Tristan is not here with me, and until he figures out if he wants to be again, I am all alone.

It is early afternoon. Isabella is with Nate back at the cabin, and I am out for another all-too-familiar shoreline run. It is a cool summer day, and the sun is hidden by an overcast sky. It is the perfect temperature for stepping up the tempo, pushing myself into an all-out sprint. I am stretching my limbs, pressing them harder and faster. Sand flies beneath my feet. The wind is whipping across my face, and sweat is pouring off of my skin. Loose pieces of my hair intermittently flutter over my eyes while the rest of it sticks to the nape of my neck where it is held in place by a ponytail holder. One time as I am tucking a flyaway strand behind my ear, from out of my peripheral vision I think I detect movement in the water. Instinctively my head snaps in that direction.

I stop running. *Something* is out there. This time I'm sure. For a few moments I stare at a blur of shifting liquid several yards offshore. My heart slams against my chest in a state of perplexity while it decides whether to slow down from the abrupt end to my run or to speed up in anticipation of what I'm going to find stirring in the waves. More rhythmic splashes in the water, and I become increasingly confident of what I am seeing. I can't look away. I don't want to miss one flicker of movement. The first flash of skin sends a shiver down my spine. *It's him!* It's *got to be!* For a long minute all movement disappears, and I begin to lose hope. The cadence of the waves resumes a regular pattern, and disappointment sets in. *Whatever it was, now it's gone.*

I am just about to walk away and begin a light jog back to the cabin when a streak of blond hair captures my attention. *It is him!* I stand frozen in place watching as liquid from the rising tide seeps up around my feet, loosening the sand between my toes. Now Tristan is above the water, diving in and out of the waves with the sleek grace of a dolphin, unaware that he is being observed. A small ache in my chest begins to grow. I am suspended in the spot where my feet are planted. The surf continues to whittle away at the sandy foundation around me, and I am sinking farther and farther into the watery paste. But I don't move an inch.

One large spray of liquid, and Tristan's repetitive motion stills. Now his head is above the surface, water dripping off his head onto the skin of his face. He appears to be taking a break. Taking one hand, he runs it through the saturated strands of his hair while he glances behind him. I hold my breath. The sound of my heart rate is deafening in my ears. *Will he look my way?*

Do I want him to? For a moment I feel a flush of panic spread through my body. If he looks my way, he will see me staring at him. I shift my feet, but by now they are buried deep. The sand is like cement. My legs are like two pillars of mortar. I can't move. Suddenly I feel exposed. I can't get away if I want to. There is nowhere to hide on this open shoreline. Before I can give another thought to my predicament, Tristan's green eyes shift in my direction, and his gaze freezes on my face.

Now I can't breathe.

But I can't look away either. And neither does he. With eyes slightly narrowed for several moments, he stares hard into my face.

My throat feels as pasty as the sand that is swallowing up my feet. What is he thinking? Surely he recognizes me. Is he considering coming toward the shore? Hope and anticipation surge through my veins.

I blink and the eye contact is broken. Abruptly Tristan turns his head away, and before I can swallow twice, he is diving under the waves once again. Never once does he resurface. My lip trembles slightly as I press my eyelids tightly together. Using all of my strength, I pull my feet from the sand and walk away.

I'm still fighting away the disappointment of being within sight of Tristan and having him swim away instead of coming to shore when Lucy shows up at the cabin later that day. We had made plans to spend the evening together in town shopping at sidewalk sales, followed by dinner and a fireworks display. I eye her pretty face and her contagious grin as she taps her painted fingernails against my kitchen countertop while waiting for me to finish getting ready. It's hard to shift gears and accelerate into an evening of fun when I can't quit thinking about my earlier encounter with Tristan. Did he not recognize me? I narrow my eyes in contemplative thought. He *must* have recognized me. *Why then?* Why then did he just swim away? Is it that he wasn't ready? Or that he just didn't want to come talk to me—plain and simple. A shudder racks my body and I push it away, grabbing the keys that are hanging on a hook next to the hallway light switch.

"Okay . . . ready."

After kissing Nate good-bye, we make our way down to the cabin beachfront, a warm breeze ruffling the material on our sundresses. As we walk, Lucy's high heels keep getting stuck in the sand. As I watch her repeatedly struggle to keep her balance while her stilettos dig into the ground, my lips form a smirk. "Are you sure you want to wear those things? You realize it's just going to keep happening over and over again all night long."

Lucy presses her lips together, determined. "Yes, I'm sure. Gotta have my heels."

"All right. It's your feet getting stuck, not mine." I eye the sandals on my own feet, stylish but comfortable, and wonder how long before they'll be coming off for the evening. Since meeting Tristan I tend to go barefoot most of the time, especially while walking anywhere close to a shoreline. Once we reach my beachfront, I pause and observe *Blue* swaying back and forth in the water next to the dock. Lucy shoots me a look. She knows I'm still a little apprehensive about driving a boat. I have been ever since the near-drowning accident my first summer in Watch Hill. But lately I've pushed myself beyond that fear and have begun to take it out on occasion. With Tristan being gone for the past year I had to. I had to learn how to be okay on my own—had to learn how to depend on myself and no one else. And besides, today seems like a good day to take the boat instead of a car.

Still, it's with slight trepidation that I step into the crème-colored interior. My eyes connect with Lucy's, and I send her a shaky grin. *I can do this!*

In return her brown eyes sparkle with warmth and encouragement. *Yes, you can do this!*

I take a deep breath. "The water is relatively calm tonight, don't you think?"

"Very calm. No storms or bad weather on the radar for miles. It is going to be a perfect night." *A perfect night for driving a boat.*, she tells me with her eyes.

For a moment I watch her face. Finally I bite my lip and nod. "Okay . . . all right, let's go."

The ride over to Watch Hill municipal docks takes forever because I refuse to push *Blue's* accelerator past a slow troll, but Lucy doesn't say a word. After skimming the surface of the open water for close to thirty minutes, finally the familiar curve of the landscape and an inlet filled with parked, swaying watercrafts comes into view. Even from our distance I can see the crowds of tourists that are filling the sidewalks and the sectioned-off streets in the town. The energy of the event reaches out to grab me. Lucy turns to look at me and smiles. She can feel it too. I relax my shoulders. It is going to be a fun night in spite of the disappointment from earlier in the day.

After two unsuccessful attempts at parking, I finally pull *Blue* into a slip and tie her to a post. Once on the docks, Lucy loops her arm through mine and tugs me toward the sales. Eye-catching displays of merchandise are everywhere. Dodging shoppers, we weave in and out of the booths and food vendors. Smart arrangements of summer clothing and entertaining trinkets repeatedly draw our attention, luring us from exhibition to exhibition and store to store. At a booth overflowing with outerwear accessories, Lucy grabs a wide-brimmed, straw hat and places it on my head. She winks and tips the outer rim so that she can see my eyes. "Smile, Bethany. This is fun." After pulling on a similar hat, she leads us to a mirror and takes out her phone. We stick our heads close together and giggle like two schoolgirls as she snaps a picture.

The sun is dipping low in the sky before we finally settle into a table at an outdoor café and grab a bite to eat. By now I am famished, and the seafood chowder that I've ordered slides down my throat like water. Lucy takes a bite of her crab legs and points at my bowl with her fork. "I'm glad you've decided to eat seafood again. It seemed odd to me when you went on a stint when you wouldn't eat it. I know you always loved seafood . . . especially shrimp cocktail. I don't know, it was just kind of weird how you all of a sudden quit eating it. It's not like it is bad for your health or something."

I suck another spoonful of soup into my mouth and work hard to act nonchalant. My mind is racing as I search for an answer that will be acceptable to my perceptive friend Lucy. "Yeah . . . I don't know . . . I think I was just eating it too much for a while and finally got sick of it. I guess I just needed a break." I can't let her see into my thoughts—can't let her know the real reason for my abstinence—that I did it out of respect for Tristan's heritage. I ease into a smile and meet her gaze across the table. "I guess it is true what they say—there really is such a thing as having too much of a good thing."

Lucy watches my face thoughtfully for a second longer than I like, and my heart rate begins to accelerate. Finally she breaks eye contact. "Yeah, I guess."

We are just finishing the last bites of our dinner when the vibration of loud, echoing music fills the air. In unison Lucy and I turn toward the noise. Across the street adjacent to the municipal docks a patio is lit in colored, twinkling lights. In the corner a disc jockey is geared up with a conglomeration of electronic paraphernalia all set to fill the evening air with musical dance sounds. The flicker of the lights and the beat of the song stir something inside of me. I glance into the air directly above me and notice the darkening sky. It is later than I thought—soon it will be full-fledged night.

Lucy shoots me a look. "Are you thinking what I'm thinking?"

I nod my head. "I think *so*."

She throws her napkin on the table, her brown eyes shining bright. "Well, what are we waiting for? Let's go."

"But . . . shouldn't we wait for our food to digest?"

Throwing money on the table for our bill, Lucy reaches for my hand and pulls me out of my chair. "We'll be fine. Come on, I love this song."

I stumble to my feet and quickly shove the boat keys into my pocket as she begins guiding me across the street, in and out of pedestrians, closer and closer to the music. As we near the dance floor, the rhythm of the drums begins to pull my heartbeat into sync with the souped-up tempo. The twinkling lights that once seemed demure from our table are now everywhere, taking over—flashing and flickering, casting shadows—momentarily illuminating eyes, satiny fabric, and glistening skin. I lick my lips and take a look around. It seems we are not the only ones with this idea. A large conglomeration of people has begun to gather around us, getting ready to partake in the nighttime entertainment. Lucy and I take our place in line, impatient to get onto the dance floor before the song is over.

We are next to be admitted onto the patio when my heart unexpectedly slams against my chest. Everything around me becomes muted and distant. Immediately all lights and movement flash-freeze into an icy stillness. Even the oxygen in the air around me seems to freeze because now I can't breathe. My eyes focus through the crowd, staring beyond the blurred refractions of the twinkling bulbs, past the deafening silence of the immobilized stereo speakers. *It can't be!*

It just can't be!

I blink in an effort to clear my vision as I try to make the music and the lights and my breathing start back up again. Maybe I am mistaken. Maybe I'm dead wrong. Maybe the person that I am seeing on the other side of the dance floor is not who I think it is. But the blood in my veins tells me otherwise as it turns to frost, a slow chill creeping up my spine as I try to unsuccessfully convince myself—as I try to convince myself that the person that I am seeing through the mass of tangled bodies in this outdoor nightclub is not really Rye Markane.

Chapter Eight

In desperation I glance to my left to catch Lucy's reaction over what I've just seen, but the look on her face holds no recognition of anything amiss. Once again my eyes shoot back to the spot where I've just spotted Rye. But now all that passes through my line of vision are hordes of people crowding into a small space as they begin to shake it up on the dance floor, moving to the rhythm of the music. None of them remotely resemble Rye. Standing on my tiptoes, I hastily shift my head from side, to side trying to discover where she might have gone, but she is nowhere to be found. A second time I scan my surroundings. Still nothing. Narrowing my eyes, I stand frozen in in contemplative thought. *Was I mistaken after all?*

Lucy's tug at my elbow interrupts my thoughts. "Come on . . . we're on," her bubbly voice speaks spiritedly into my ear. I force a smile to cover up my distraction and allow myself to be led onto the dance floor. Soon the flickering lights and the pulsating sounds take over, and I am right there with Lucy, cutting loose in the moment. But there is a tiny part of me that can't quite free itself from the disturbing vision of what I may have just seen.

Two days later while I am perusing the lakeshore, flicking pebbles against the waves, still trying to make sense of Rye's apparition from the other night, Britton Alexander shows up on my beach again. This time he tells me that Tristan has decided that he would like to stop by for visits. *Visits?* Why does that word sound so formal? We are many minutes into the conversation before it hits me why—it reminds of me of girls in the break room at work talking about the inconveniences of having to arrange times for the fathers of their children to *visit*.

Tristan is going to be coming by to *visit* Nate. His visits are going to have nothing to do with me.

My heart sinks in my chest as I begin to sort through the multitude of disappointing feelings that are swirling around in my mind. Britton's words begin to blur into background noise as he proceeds to go over the details of the arrangement. Finally his green eyes look pointedly at me, and I realize that he is waiting for a response. Only I don't know to what. "I'm sorry, can you say that one more time?" My voice sounds small in my own ears, barely heard above the rumble of the ocean waves that are pushing onto shore behind me.

A concerned look crosses over Britton's features as he studies my face. "I said . . . ," he pauses for emphasis, "is tomorrow afternoon okay?"

I shake my head to clear it. "Yeah . . . tomorrow will be fine."

Only tomorrow is not fine at all. By the time tomorrow afternoon arrives I am a nervous, self-conscious wreck as I wait for Tristan to arrive. Over and over again I remind myself that he is just coming over to see Nate, not me. But I can't stop checking my appearance in the mirror as I pace up and down the hallway of my cabin. I can't stop smoothing the strands of hair, making sure my ponytail is neatly in place. When the knock at my door finally comes, I practically jump a mile. My hand is trembling slightly as I turn the knob and push open the screen entry. For a second my heart palpitates in my chest as I take in Tristan's familiar but now not-so-familiar form on my side porch. With hands shoved into his front jean pockets, he looks back at me with the same uncertainty that is currently twisting the insides of my stomach. His tousled blond hair and green eyes reach out to grab me, and I have to stifle a groan. *He is still so freakin' hot!* For a moment I avert my eyes and let out a slow breath. *Why does he have to look like that?* It just makes things that much more difficult.

"Hi, Tristan . . . come in."

Is it just my imagination, or does he seem to flinch as I say his name? Now I am even more guarded and my pulse accelerates, tripping apprehensively through my veins. It occurs to me then that Tristan's uncertainty is not a mirror of my own at all, but is caused instead by his trepidation of not wanting to be here—around me. At this thought a lump begins to form in the back of my throat, and I have to work hard to push it away. *This is about Nate,* I keep whispering repeatedly in my mind, trying to steel myself against the rejection I am feeling. Tristan follows me into the living room. I pause and gesture toward Nate's bedroom. "He is just finishing up a nap, but I'll go check on him."

Tristan's green eyes stare back at me incredulously like *What? I'm here to see Nate and you'll just go check on him? I thought I was going to be laying eyes on him and interacting with him, not sitting in the next room while he enjoys a nap!*

I clear my throat. "Yeah . . . I'll just go get him."

"All right."

Tristan's deep voice is still echoing through my ears as I slowly push open Nate's door. Light spills into the room illuminating his small shape. He is already awake, standing and hanging on to the crib railing while he stares back at me expectantly. His blond curls are tousled, and his eyes look sleepy. "Hey, baby," I murmur as I pad over to him. Immediately Nate's lips form into a smile. He starts to lift his arms toward me and then pauses midmotion, peering around my shoulder instead. *What is it, baby?* As I turn to see what has captured his attention, unexpectedly my heart picks up in tempo. Tristan has followed me into the nursery. Suddenly the space surrounding the three of us seems small and intimate. And the fact that this scene could have easily played out a million times already had Tristan never had his accident is screaming inside of me, making me feel completely flustered. Ignoring my hammering pulse, I lift Nate into my arms. "Someone is here to see you." I cringe inwardly at the shakiness that is evident in my voice.

In the shadows of the dimly lit room, I can barely detect the unease that is written across Tristan's face—the unease of the situation. But it's there. I can feel it. Hugging Nate a little more tightly to my chest, I turn toward Tristan. "This is your daddy, Nate." I pause, trying to ignore the apprehension in Tristan's eyes. "Your daddy has come to see you today."

"Hi, Nate." The confidence in Tristan's tone catches me off guard, but it helps me to snap out of the awkwardness of the moment. I point at the entryway to Nate's room.

"Should we . . . I mean, let's go out there."

"Oh . . . yeah, okay."

Less than a minute later we are situated on opposite ends of the couch with Nate nestled onto my lap when the discomfiture in the air finds its way back to encircle us once again. I bite my lip and soothe Nate's hair with the palm of my hand. Tristan cracks his knuckles and watches Nate with growing curiosity, careful to avoid my eyes. Finally he sucks in a barely detectable breath. "So does he take a nap often?"

Often? What constitutes often? My hand pauses midstroke, resting on the top of Nate's head. "Usually once a day. Sometimes twice."

"Oh. Oh . . . okay."

Silence.

Tristan shifts uncomfortably on his cushion. I resume soothing Nate's wispy, blond curls.

"So would he want . . . do you think he would come to me? Like I could hold him or something?"

I hesitate, trying to search for the right answer. *Why is this so difficult?* If it were anyone else over at the house visiting Nate I would know exactly what to do to make things go smoothly—to make both Nate and the other visitor feel completely comfortable with their interaction. *Why is this time so different?* Why is Nate huddled against my chest, seemingly frightened? Why am I so tongue-tied that I can't even talk playfully with my own son, encouraging the exchange between him and his visitor? *Why does his visitor look like he would rather be eating seafood?*

For a brief moment I close my eyes, searching for clarity, and suddenly I know what I need to do. I have to pretend. I have to ignore that it is Tristan sitting only feet away from me ripping my heart out with each breath that he takes, and act like it's no one special over at the house trying to get to know Nate better.

"I think so. Yeah . . . he'll come to you eventually. Just . . . just talk to him a little first." Gently I pry Nate away from me so that he is sitting on the edge of my lap. "That's your daddy over there, Nate. See your daddy?" Surprisingly my voice sounds playful and confident, and I can feel the tension immediately begin to ease away from Nate. Glancing up, I catch Tristan's green eyes watching our interaction. *Don't think about it. Don't think about him. He's just a person. Just any old person.* I force a smile and tickle Nate's tummy. Tristan's shoulders begin to relax. Nate eyes Tristan curiously.

"Hey . . . Nate. Hey, little guy." Tristan's voice is deep and steady.

A half hour later Tristan is on the floor, handing Nate toys, and Nate is toddling around his legs beginning to playfully engage with his dad. I leave the room for a few minutes to throw some clothes in the drier, and when I return Nate is situated on Tristan's lap while Tristan is lightheartedly tweaking his nose. Nate crinkles his nose and giggles. My heart catches in my chest. For a moment Tristan goes still as he watches Nate's face. Finally sensing my presence, he turns to me. "I could have sworn a few minutes ago Nate's eyes were blue . . . similar to ah . . . yours. Now they are completely green . . ."

Walking slowly across the room I take a seat on the couch. "Green like yours." I finish his thought.

Tristan nods as he continues looking into Nate's face. "Yeah . . . like mine. How is that? I mean I'm right, aren't I? Weren't they just blue?"

I sigh. "Yeah, you're right. They *were* just blue. I was confused the first time I figured out that it was happening, thinking that I had to be mistaken. But now that it happens on a regular basis, I'm used to it."

"But why—" Tristan studies Nate's face some more. "I mean, I wonder why that is—"

"I'm not completely sure, except that I've come to the conclusion that it is because he has half of me and half of you in him. Maybe it is just another way his combined genes are manifesting themselves."

Tristan's head snaps in my direction. "How is he . . . I mean in what other ways is he like you . . . and like me?"

I know what he's getting at, and suddenly I'm bursting with pride, eager to tell him the news. "Nate is like me because he can breathe air for an unlimited amount of time. And Nate is like you because he seems to be able to breathe water for an unlimited amount of time as well."

Tristan bites his lip in contemplation as he processes the information that I've just handed him. And although he doesn't verbalize his thoughts on the matter, I can tell that he is secretly pleased. My heart soars in my chest.

After that Tristan's visits with Nate begin to take place on a regular basis, and although he stays mostly focused on Nate during the hours he stops by, I can't help but look forward to each and every encounter, hoping that sooner or later his affection for me will be rekindled. Or that this will help his memory to return so that we can resume what we once had.

One visit as he is preparing to leave, instead of walking right out the door, he hesitates, standing awkwardly at the exit while fumbling with the knob. It seems as though there is something he wants to tell me before he leaves. Immediately my heart rate begins to accelerate in anticipation.

Finally he spits out the words—the words that tell me he wants to move back in—that he wants to live here with me and Nate. Instantly my joy-meter shoots up to overload. I can hardly believe my sudden good fortune! The next afternoon when he brings over his box of clothes and personal belongings, it's hard to pretend I'm not ecstatic over his return. But I keep my smile under wraps and instead shift awkwardly back and forth on my feet while he stands in the entryway hall, waiting for me to give him direction as to where they should go. Nate is asleep with his bedroom door closed most of the way, and I feel suddenly exposed without him on my hip as a shield. I glance uncertainly up into Tristan's green eyes. *Where does he want to put his things?* I don't want to assume too much by thinking that he is planning on moving back into the bedroom that we once shared for a brief but amazing time. As I recall some of the intimate memories from that short time frame, without warning my cheeks begin to burn. While I work to recover from the blush, a flicker of something that I can't quite put my finger on passes through Tristan's eyes. Now I look at the floor.

"You have a place you want me to put this stuff?" His deep voice causes me to startle but helps me to focus on the present too.

"Ah . . . sure. There are basically two good closets in this place. The hallway closet or our . . . I mean the main bedroom closet. You are welcome to either." I lead him an arm's reach from the hallway closet and point toward it while gesturing at my bedroom at the same time. "In here or there. Whatever you like." For a brief moment I detect the indecision that is written across his face before I look away, allowing him privacy to make the choice without my blatant stare as an influence.

Unwittingly my heart begins to pound in my chest as I hear him walk into the bedroom.

st of the afternoon and evening although he is polite,

s an indication that he holds any type of affection

this point he is just a roommate. A roommate who has decided to put his things in our shared closet. A roommate who is really the father of my beautiful son. A roommate who is really my husband, that I am completely in love with and attracted to. Only he hasn't come to recognize this last bit of truth yet. *Will he ever?*

In spite of the platonic lines laid out clearly between him and me, Tristan eases right in to his fatherly role, holding none of his affection back from Nate. And I get it. Nate's spirited eyes and charming smile are like a magnetic force pulling you in. How could he *not* be instantly drawn to him? Nate returns the affection openly, seemingly aware that this new guy in the house holds some meaningful connection to him. Each time I catch the two of them in some type of interaction together, I instantly feel a strong tug at my heart.

That night while I lay in bed with my mind racing a million miles a minute as I prepare for sleep, I can't stop thinking about Tristan's close proximity somewhere on just the other side of my bedroom wall. Earlier I had shown him blankets that he could use for the couch and then at the same time had nonchalantly pointed to my room and said, "Or there is room in there too or whatever. Wherever you want to crash will be okay." It had been so hard to keep the shakiness from my voice as I relayed his sleeping arrangement options for later that night. Now without wanting to, I keep finding myself straining my ears listening for the sound of him getting himself situated in the room adjacent from me. I am deep in concentration trying to catch the snap of the blankets unfolding or the creak of the couch from Tristan's shifting weight when the squeak of my bedroom door opening causes me to practically jump a mile.

My breath catches in my throat. *Oh my word, Tristan is heading my way right now! Does he just have a question? Does he need another blanket? Is he coming to bed?* My pulse is now tripping at lightning-quick speed through my veins, and my mind is becoming a jumbled mess. Should I keep my eyes shut and feign sleep, or should I go for eye contact and let him know that I know he is here? Maybe he has something he wants to ask. I should probably open them. Too timid to make a move, I opt for keeping them shut. Frozen in place, I hold my breath while I wait for him to quietly exit the room. Instead I feel the mattress move beside me as Tristan crawls in next to my side.

That night it is so hard to sleep. I can tell Tristan is being careful not to touch me. But once in awhile his arm or thigh accidently brush against mine, and each time they do my muscles clench deep in my stomach and my heart rate skyrockets. It's so hard not to look over at him and stare at the perfectly formed cheekbones and sexy tousled hair that I know is resting on the pillow only inches from mine. It is so hard not to take a deep breath of the salty, clean smell of him that I've missed for ages—that is reaching out to me like an addiction that I've kept subdued for way too long. Most of the sleeping hours that night are spent alternating between holding my breath, too afraid to move, or conversely trying hard to concentrate on relaxation breathing in order to calm the embarrassing sound of my heartbeat that I am convinced must be keeping Tristan awake.

The next morning Tristan carries on like nothing out of the ordinary has passed between us by him sleeping in the same bed as me. And so I take his lead and assume the same role. Day after day pass until at least two weeks have gone by with us living in the same house. We are polite strangers. Tristan resumes going to work, and each day that he comes home he begins to help with things around the cabin and of course spends much time playing with Nate. And for this I am grateful. But I can't help but be disappointed at the same time. His affection toward me does not seem to be rekindling in any shape or form. It almost seems worse that he is treating me with respectful courtesy instead of any other emotion. Love, hate, irritation—anything else. It is secretly my worst fear coming true—that he has no thoughts toward me one way or another.

Every moment of every day I have to work hard to ignore these depressing thoughts and remind myself to take it one step at a time, remind myself that I need to be thankful that Tristan is here now, taking on his fatherly responsibilities toward Nate. That is what is most important now anyway. *Right?*

It is these thoughts that are pummeling through my mind as I am walking up to the cabin from the beach with a small bag of garbage in hand after cleaning out *Blue*. I am almost to the porch when I get a sense of someone watching me. Glancing to my right, I detect Tristan standing next to the outbuilding in the corner of the yard. When I look over at him, for the first time since he's arrived back in Watch Hill, he doesn't look away. For several surprising seconds our eyes connect. My heart catches in my throat. This is so unexpected. I am immediately flustered. Finally he continues on into the shed, and I keep walking toward the cabin feeling completely shaken.

And completely alive.

At dinner that night I look up to find him watching me several times, and each time I blush bright red. Each time I feel his eyes weighing down on me as I scoop a fork full of pasta into my mouth, my heart slams uncontrollably against my chest. *What is going on?* A couple of times I lift my lowered lids to meet his gaze. *Has he—? Is he—?*

Has he changed his mind then?

Later when I am getting ready to put Nate to bed, Tristan approaches me from behind so he can tell Nate good night. Nate is situated in my arms as I prepare to carry him to his crib. I can feel the strength of Tristan's chest as he presses up against my back while he leans over to kiss Nate's cheek. This intentional physical contact between us is new. He had been so careful the past couple of weeks not to touch me—almost painfully so. Now he is close enough I can feel his warm breath on my neck as he pulls away from Nate after the kiss. It is suddenly difficult for me to breathe as I think about the closeness of Tristan's mouth to the bare skin of my shoulder. Tristan gives Nate one last show of affection by brushing his hair away from his face, his hand brushing against the goose bumps that are now forming on my arm in the same sweep. Finally he steps away from us, allowing Nate and me the freedom to continue on into the nursery. By now every nerve ending in my body is pulsating. I can hardly concentrate as I finish Nate's nighttime routine. What will I find when I come back out of his bedroom? Will Tristan carry on with his recently found attraction for me? Has he discovered that he loves me after all? I am soaring with the new prospect of it all.

When I leave the security of Nate's presence, I head to the kitchen instead of going to the living room where I know Tristan is currently lounged on the couch. Although it is difficult, I am determined to play it cool like it's no big deal—all of this sudden attention he is sending my way. Like *oh really, you've been giving me the eye all evening and putting on the moves like crazy? I hadn't even noticed!* I take a big drink of water and suck in a slow breath.

Yeah, right!

Finally I make my way into the living room and take a seat on a reclining chair next to the window. Tristan glances up from his sprawled position on the couch and shoots me a look like he is surprised that I am sitting so far away. But really, does he think that I am that easy? After all of this time of him essentially ignoring me—as a husband anyway. I swallow hard, trying to disregard the truth that is fighting to be heard in the back of my mind. *Yes, I am.* That easy. At least when it comes to Tristan. I press my lips together resolutely, determined to hide this fact from him. Maybe he won't remember. I can't let him figure it out!

"What are you looking at?"

At the sound of Tristan's deep voice I jerk my head around. I hadn't even realized that I'd been staring out of the window. *Avoiding him, obviously.* Quickly I peruse my mind for an acceptable answer. "Oh . . . I don't know, I guess I was just checking out the tree line, thinking that it is kind of too bad that there is no direct view of the water from the house."

"Yeah?"

A second too late I realize that my answer must have seemed like an invitation for Tristan to join me and scrutinize the view for himself. *Oh crap!* On cue Tristan jumps up and begins padding across the creaking planks of the wooden floor as he heads my way. Every fiber in my being is aware of his overt sexiness as he approaches. Instantly I know that I am in trouble. Kneeling beside my chair he leans in to take a look out the window in an attempt to duplicate my view. "You see what I mean?" The words seem breathless as they leave my lips. Tristan leans a little closer. Now his arm is brushing against mine. Fire rushes through my veins.

"For sure. I know exactly what you mean. There can never be enough views of the water." The playfulness in his tone catches me by surprise. I relax just a little and dare to look up into his eyes. *Mistake.* He holds my gaze for a long second. "Are you thirsty?"

"Sure . . . I—"

Tristan jumps up. "Let me get us something. I'll be right back." He heads to the kitchen. Minutes later he is back with two glasses filled with a concoction that looks similar to lemonade. Eyeing the shimmering liquid in the crystal cup, I take a small sip. It tastes like lemonade but a little different too. It has a sweetness to it as well and a little bit of a bite. Tristan watches me take a drink. "You like it?"

I nod my head. "Yeah, I do. What is in it?"

Tristan's green eyes sparkle with mischief. "It's a secret. I could tell you but . . ."

Laughter peals from my throat. "Yeah . . . I get it. I wouldn't want that." I look into his face as he crouches beside my chair. *What would I want though . . . instead?* I suck in a breath. *Oh my word, what am I doing?*

A knowing smile crosses over Tristan's perfect features like he realizes the effect he is having on me. And he is enjoying it. I take another drink of the liquid in my glass, and it slides down my throat, instantly transforming from cool to warm as the effects of the mixture reach my veins. I turn and find myself smiling over at Tristan, and it hits me then how pleasant this situation is—this blatant flirtation between us for the very first time since his return. But the coquettishness doesn't last long.

Seconds later Tristan's grin disappears, and all the air inside me exits my lungs. Watching my face, he reaches over and eases my glass out of my hand, setting it on the small table next to my chair instead. Grasping my wrist, he slides his fingers between mine and pulls me to my feet. I shiver with the contact. *I can't believe this is happening!*

"You cold?" Tristan's voice is just a murmur.

Yes. No. Maybe. I don't know. I shake my head.

With a gentle pressure he pulls me toward him, wrapping his arms around me. "Because you shouldn't be cold."

I nod my head and swallow. *Okay.*

He rubs his hands up and down my arms as he looks into my eyes, leaving a trail of fire on my skin. "Better?"

"Better." My voice is just a whisper. My vocal cords are nearing paralysis, rendering me virtually speechless. My lower lip begins to tremble, and I bite down on it gently in order to get it under control. Tristan groans and his green eyes go dark and serious. *So serious.* My heart slams against my chest. *I remember that look.* He stops rubbing my arms altogether. For two long seconds time seems to suspend, and I lose all ability to breathe.

Tristan is leaning closer.

And closer.

His lips and mouth are so close. I reach for his blond, tousled hair and impatiently pull his head the rest of the way down to mine. The connection between us is immediate and desperate. It had been so long. *Way too long!* His mouth moving against mine feels so good. His strong body pressed up against mine feels so good. I run my hands over the strong muscles of his back and draw him in closer yet. *I can't get close enough.* I can tell by the way he is kissing me that it is the same for him. He can't get enough of me. It had been so long and finally this is it. Our connection is back. *He loves me again!* My beautiful Tristan is finally back! The idea of it is so overwhelming I want to weep. Instead I show him all I am feeling with my kiss and my touch.

Reaching for his tee shirt, I attempt to pull it over his head. Suddenly everything that we are wearing only seems in the way from our complete unification. Tristan figures out what I'm doing and shudders. He stops for a second to help by yanking it the rest of the way off. Now he is bare chested. Taking a step back toward me, he reaches for my tank top as well and then pauses. He motions his head toward the bedroom. "Do you want to go in there?" His deep voice is raspy.

I nod. *Yes,* I tell him with my eyes. A thousand times yes! This is the Tristan that I know and love. That I am going to be with for the rest of my life until we are very old and gray. And he is finally back and ready to show me how much he loves me once again.

Silently he takes my hand in his and leads me down the hall and on into the bedroom. *Our bedroom.*

It's early morning when I awaken the next day. The first signs of dawn are beginning to pour through the window, casting a faint bluish glow across the floorboards and furniture in the room. I turn and reach for Tristan, but the space beside me on the bed is empty.

As all of last night's memories come flooding back to me, I instantly feel warm all over. On instinct I lay quietly, frozen in place as I listen for Nate. All is quiet. It is too early—not time for him to be up at this hour. So if Tristan isn't taking care of Nate's needs, then he must be somewhere else—the bathroom or maybe the kitchen. Immediately I want to go find him. A grin spreads across my lips as I roll off the mattress and slip into my pastel blue terry robe. My whole body is tingling and refreshingly achy. *Oh my word, I have missed him!* And I miss him in bed with me right now as well. Now that he has come back to me, I want him with me every second that I can get. Opening the bedroom door, I pad into the hallway past the living room and on into the kitchen in search of him.

The minute I see him, my breath catches in my throat. He is standing with his back toward me, fully dressed, staring out the kitchen window that is situated just above the sink. Even from this view I am immediately pulled toward his raw beauty. His jeans are hanging slightly low on his hips, causing a strip of his plaid boxers to show above the waistband. I blush faintly and swallow hard, chiding myself for letting something as mundane as a thin slice of underwear get to me after all we did last night.

"Hey," I whisper, not wanting to wake Nate.

Tristan turns to face me, seemingly surprised by my presence. "Oh, hey." His voice is nonchalant, and my heart takes a fast dive in my chest. *What is this?* The light and warmth that was so evident in his eyes last night is now gone, replaced by a certain type of apathy instead. Unwittingly my body begins to tremble all over, and I hug my arms tightly to my chest to stop the motion. I take a step toward him. Maybe I've misinterpreted his demeanor. Maybe it's just early and he's still tired. I mean it *is* early. I take another step.

As I am slowly crossing the kitchen floor, Tristan leaves where he is standing and heads toward the refrigerator. I stop walking. Am I only imagining that he moved away from my approach just to avoid me? A lump begins to form at the back of my throat. Tristan opens the refrigerator and pulls out some juice. Pouring a large glass, he drinks it down without saying a word. The icy chill in the room is causing me to shiver all over. *Oh, my God, what happened? Why is he being so cold?* Tristan sits down the empty glass and begins cracking his knuckles without looking at me. Suddenly I can't take another second of his aloofness.

"What is going on, Tristan?" My voice is shaky, betraying the tears that are lurking close by.

Finally Tristan looks at me, seemingly confused. "Going on?"

"I mean last night . . . you were . . . we—"

Tristan runs a hand through his tousled blond hair and sighs. "Yeah . . . about that." Once again he sighs and then looks away. "I think maybe—"

"Maybe what?" I can't hide the slight tremor that is etched into my voice.

For a moment Tristan presses his lips together. "That it was . . . it's . . . it's just too soon." *What?* Even though I don't want them to, tears begin streaming down my cheeks. *No! No, this can't be happening!* Tristan glances over at me and notices me crying. Now he looks uncomfortably away. "Shit!" He shifts positions, putting me back in his line of vision without quite making eye contact. Twice he runs his fingers through his hair. Then after cracking his knuckles several times, he finally speaks again. "I ah," he pauses, while peering over at me anxiously, "I think it would be best if I . . . moved back with my parents . . . for now."

I can't speak. The achiness from our night spent together that had possessed my body like a thrilling caress only minutes ago now feels like a vise of unadulterated pain. Cold, stabbing pain! By now wet liquid is plastering my cheeks, consequently obscuring my vision. But in spite of the blurriness, I can tell Tristan is heading toward the door, getting ready to exit and leave me once again.

I stifle a sob. *What about Nate? What about his things?* Will he just leave Nate high and dry? *Coldhearted bastard!* As if reading my mind, he goes still in his tracks.

"I'm gonna just go . . . I'll be in touch . . . you know, with Nate and to ah . . . get my stuff." The knob to the side entrance jiggles, and I know he is getting ready to step into the out-of-doors, back to the ocean—back out of my life. I am standing in the kitchen doorway, my shoulders shaking, staring at the ground, listening as he goes. For a brief pause the wiggling doorknob stops and he turns back around to face me, but he won't look me in the eye. "I'm . . . I'm sorry. I just . . . yeah . . . ," he pauses. "I'm sorry."

Moments after his final words, the door slams and he is gone.

A couple days later I am out for a shoreline walk, trying to sort through my depressive feelings over all that happened the night before Tristan exited my life once again, when a semblance of clarity settles over me. As of yet Tristan has not been back to visit Nate, and I can tell by the occasional bewildered look in Nate's eyes that he realizes something important in his life is missing: his daddy. His daddy that he was growing to adore more and more each day. I clench my fists at my side as my feet skip through the surf. This thought alone causes anger to shoot through my veins. But there is another thought that causes me to be infuriated as well.

My stupidity.

Involuntarily I keep replaying the scene from our bedroom that night. All the kissing and the touching and the intimate acts that we shared had completely convinced me that Tristan was in love with me once again. Only he really wasn't at all. And isn't. The only thing that *really* happened that night was that I was used! Completely used and discarded! I had filled a need for Tristan and that was it. As I saunter down the beach rubbing my arms with my hands while watching the plummeting whitecaps roll past me, I can't help feeling cheap and stupid. *How could I be that stupid?*

I am still sifting through the resentment and anger in my mind when I realize that I've walked farther downshore than originally intended. Now I am getting close to East Beach, and the landscape around me is beginning to fill with people. My usual energy depleted, I pause to rest against a large boulder for a minute before I begin my walk back to the cabin. I am staring mindlessly out to sea, trying to relax my mind from a swirl of negative thoughts, when a conversation shared by two lady beachgoers close by causes me to perk up my ears.

"—so it keeps happening. More and more frequently too."

"I know and it's strange. Now they are saying a large vessel was just capsized by a wave that was more like the size of a tidal wave, from out of nowhere. Meteorologists say they didn't even know it was coming."

"That is weird. And then the group of whales that the tourists saw swimming too close to shore, bumping into one another like they were confused or drugged."

"Is that the same incident that caused several small watercrafts to lose control, and then afterward the water in the same area turned black?"

"I believe so. The thought of black water just creeps me out. I haven't seen it, but they say the water is mostly back to blue again at least."

"Oh, well, that is good . . . it's so strange . . . makes me wonder—"

The dialogue fades away into the ocean air as the ladies continue walking down the beach, out of hearing range. A chill slowly creeps up my spine as I sort through all I have just learned in that one short conversation. Immediately I am taken back to the day on the beach where Nate and I witnessed an episode similar to what they have just described, when the fish around our feet all started swimming topsy-turvy. *Strange!* Making a mental note to look further into the issue, I decide to continue on into town to pick up some fresh fruit at the market for dinner before heading back to Nate and Isabella.

After perusing the fresh produce stands for many minutes, my arms are filled with a bag of peaches, plums and blueberries. As I near the boardwalk that leads to the hub of town, the air suddenly leaves my lungs. At the far end of the boardwalk standing on the edge of the ocean with his body turned slightly away from me is Tristan. Nausea climbs to the top of my esophagus as I notice that he is not alone. Tristan is with a girl. A cute, petite, brown-haired girl who I am now positive is the very same one that I witnessed the other night at the downtown dance patio.

Rye Markane.

She is back!

I swallow back the bile that is now filling my throat. Rye Markane really *is* back in town! And Tristan is with her, and they are talking and laughing and skipping rocks. And Tristan looks happier than I've seen him in a very long time!

Chapter Nine

I have just hugged my mom and dad good-bye.

Now I am in the kitchen sorting through bruised peaches and plums, deciding which ones are still salvageable and which ones are on a fast track to rotting. The minute I'd figured out Tristan was with his old childhood girlfriend, Rye Markane, my purchases from the market had fallen from my arms, causing a landslide of fruit to spread over the ground. Snapping out of my initial state of shock, I had stooped down and tried my best to unobtrusively pick up each piece, shoving them back into my paper sack through tear-blurred vision. Keeping my misty eyes focused on the ground, I desperately hoped that I wasn't drawing attention to myself, especially where Tristan and Rye were concerned. I definitely didn't want to give them the satisfaction of knowing that I had just seen them together.

That was two days ago. Since then I'd gotten the call from my mom—my brothers wanted to come for a visit. When first presented with the question, my instinct was to say no, thinking that having the boys around might be a hindrance to any chance of Tristan and I rekindling our relationship. But as I cleared my throat and pulled the phone a little more tightly to my mouth, preparing to give my answer, I eyed the bag of fruit that was sitting untouched on my countertop half-bruised and dying. It was right then that it hit me—our relationship wasn't going anywhere at the moment anyway. They might as well come. Besides, having their energy in the house would probably be a welcomed distraction from all the pain I was currently experiencing.

Now my parents have come and gone since dropping off the boys, and I am just getting around to salvaging the fruit. I am still reeling from the initial shock of first laying eyes on my twin brothers when they arrived at the cabin. Had it been that long since I'd last seen them? And do fifteen-year-old boys really look like that? Where had I been while they were growing into such strapping young men? Had I not visited home often enough? My jaw had gone slightly slack as they breezed into my cabin with an unmistakable air of confidence while Mom and Dad stood in the doorway eyeing all three of their children with a sense of pride.

"Bethany." Jake wrapped his arms around me in greeting. After pulling away, his blue-gray eyes scanned the interior of my cabin. "I always did love this place. This is so great." Running a hand through his dark brown hair, he shot a look at his twin. "Right? Am I right?" I shook my head and smiled. I couldn't get over how dark Jake's hair had become, rendering him a spitting image of my dad.

Josh nodded his light brown, sunstreaked head, smiling, while he pushed his brother out of the way so that he could give me a hug as well. After squeezing me hard he took a step back. "This place *is* total awesomeness. I can feel the good times coming on already." Inwardly I cringed a little at his statement, remembering the fiasco of their visit two summers ago. Hopefully this one would be a little more contained. Josh detected my look of worry and patted me affectionately on the back. "Don't worry, sis, Jake and I are all grown up now. This summer will be completely legitimate. Bury your concerns right now."

Laughing outright, I rolled my eyes. *Smooth, Josh. And by the way, fifteen isn't all grown up.* Although looking so much older and now that much more male, Josh still had the same features as Mom and I. "I have to admit, it's nice to have your word on the matter. Good times without any issues sounds like a good plan to me."

After their arrival into town, it doesn't take long for the boys to migrate away from the cabin and head toward the beach. They seem eager to check out the waterfront, the place where I imagine they'll be spending most of their time during the visit. As I watch their youthful muscles flex through their tank tops as they saunter away from the side porch, I can't help but think of Tristan. And his well-built frame.

The well-built frame that I saw hanging out with his ex-girl-friend/ex-fiancee on the beach just the other day. A sharp knife stabs deep into my chest as I picture them together having so much fun. He certainly hadn't acted that way with me since he'd been home. I close my eyes and groan over my stupidity once again, the stupid-ity of thinking that Tristan was magically in love with me suddenly and ready to get back what we once had. *Like that was why he was in such a hurry to take me to bed that night.* User! Why had I fallen for it? I should have forced his hand and made him take the time to at least have a real conversation with me—get to know me again a little. After all, he hadn't even said anything remotely personal to me during the entire time that he'd moved back in.

I should have known better!

I should have known that his actions—his sudden interest in me—didn't add up to love. And since when did he change so much? Because the old Tristan that I knew and loved wouldn't have tried to use me. Dump me—yes. But not use *and* dump me.

Gritting my teeth, I hug my arms to my chest. I should have at least called him out on what he actually is before letting him leave my house that morning. Why hadn't I told him he was a bastard and possibly slapped him across his face for effect? Instead, I stood there weeping softly like a wounded animal. And now he's off spending his free time with Rye, laughing and having a good time without giving me a second thought. Squeezing my hands into tight fists, I sigh loudly and shake my head.

He really is a creep!

The minute Josh and Jake burst back through the door of my cabin after checking out the beachfront, my thoughts about Tristan are pushed to the back of my mind. Their vibrant, youthful energy immediately takes over the room, pulling me in the second the screen door closes behind them. I smile back at the animated expression on their faces, suddenly thankful they are here. *Just what the doctor ordered!* Josh smiles back.

"Hey, I forgot how awesome your boat is. Will we be able to take it out while we are here?" he asks.

"Possibly. On occasion. But Dad has also arranged for a rental while you are here, so we'll have that here for your use too. We can pick it up first thing tomorrow morning after your boater safety lesson."

Jake narrows his eyes in question. "Boater safety?"

"Yes, boater safety. You'd want to take that class even if you were driving in a small lake. But in the ocean ten times more so. That water is no joke. It will swallow you up if you are not careful." Watching their captivated faces, I can tell I have their complete attention. "Promise me here and now that you'll take the whole water thing seriously and be careful this summer."

Jake nods his head. "Got it."

"Yeah . . . got it." Josh echoes. After a short period of silence, he proceeds to punch Jake in the arm. "But seriously, Dad got us our own boat to use this summer? It just keeps getting better."

In answer, Jake can't contain the smile that lights up his face, causing his blue-gray eyes to shimmer. And for a split second it hits me just how handsome my brothers have grown up to be. Another second later I am mouthing a prayer of bereavement for all the young girls of Watch Hill. They won't even know what hit them now that Josh and Jake have arrived on the scene.

Nate's cries interrupt my thoughts. Jake and Josh follow me to my bedroom, where I'd transported Nate's crib in order to give them his room during their stay. Tousled blond hair and sleepy blue eyes greet us as the door squeaks open. Immediately fascinated, Nate stops babbling the minute he sees his teenage uncles. And they are fascinated as well. All three boys have changed so much in such a short time—in the months that they'd been apart.

It doesn't take long before Nate is warmed up to my brothers' company, laughing delightfully at the over-the-top antics they use to keep him entertained. I smile to myself as I listen to their playful interactions while I prepare dinner in the next room over. There might be an added bonus to having my brothers here for a visit. I eye the meatball sandwiches in front of me that are now stacked high on a plate ready to be served. That was one of the quickest dinner preparations I'd had in quite some time. *Yep, this might work out well.*

"Dinner is ready," I call out into the living room.

Jake and Josh don't waste any time coming into the kitchen. Jake is carrying Nate awkwardly in his arms while Nate stares up into his face, mesmerized, not even caring that he is strapped uncomfortably around Jake's hip. I laugh outright as I take Nate from Jake and am soon joining in the exuberant conversations of two fifteen year olds as they rehash all the ways they've spent their summer so far.

It isn't long after the boat rental, a Boston Whaler, is picked up the following day and brought back to the cabin that the first group of girls shows up to hang out for the afternoon. That evening they are joined by a handful of boys. Jake and Josh talk me into allowing them to have a beach bonfire, and I make them double swear that they will keep things under control with no serious mishaps or injuries if I do. The twins agree wholeheartedly with my demands, and soon the sound of teenage laughter is echoing off of the water, filling the night sky as it circulates through the air up to the front porch of the cabin where I am sitting.

The following day two blond girls that I recognize from the

previous evening's group show up at the house ready to have some more fun with the boys. I shake my head in amazement as I wait for Josh and Jake to make their way to the door. It definitely didn't take them long to find summer friends. I guess I didn't need to worry about them being bored. Not that there'd ever been a concern really. Knowing the innovative personalities of my brothers, bored is not a word that is usually in their vocabulary.

I don't miss the slight jab that Josh offers his twin while they round the corner into the hallway just as the girls come into view. In acknowledgement to his brother's apparent form of communication, Jake nods his head ever so slightly without ever looking over at him. This whole interaction goes completely undetected by the girls. I shake my head, wondering if this means they like the girls, or is it just that they knew that girls had a thing for them from the night before and now, *bingo,* here they are just as they'd suspected. Inwardly I roll my eyes. Who would ever know?

"Hey." Jake is first to offer a greeting.

"Hey," the girls both reply in unison.

Josh runs a hand through his sunstreaked hair and bites his lip like he is trying to figure something out. Seconds later I know what it is. *Their names.* My brothers don't even remember the girls' names. "You are . . . I'm sorry, I'm really bad with—"

"Anna," the shorter blond offers graciously without appearing at all insulted. She points to the girl beside her. "And this is Elle."

"Right. I was going to say that." Josh is all smiles, and the girls simultaneously giggle. *You were going to say that? Really?*

"Well, in case you forgot, we are Jake and Josh." Jake's voice is playful, and once again the girls giggle. Stifling a cough, I turn away. I am willing to bet the girls hadn't forgotten their names for a second. And I am also willing to bet Jake is well aware of this fact. After they introduce Anna and Elle to me and Nate, the foursome is soon out the door getting ready to take the boat out on the water for the day.

The days that follow are more of the same, filled with nonstop social gatherings and impromptu get-togethers for the boys, mostly taking place at the cabin. It seems I am continually mixing up lemonade and refilling jugs of ice water. And my culinary skills get lots of practice while I try my hand at making a variety of dips, sandwiches, and fun snacks. Anything I set out for the visiting teens is immediately devoured. At times I feel like I am running a full-time catering business. Occasionally I jokingly wonder whether I might need to hire some part-time cooking help.

But after setting all teasing thoughts aside, I realize that it is a good thing for me to be keeping so busy. It leaves me very little time to deliberate over the pain that is gripping my mind from all the current heartbreak Tristan has sent my way. As long as I keep myself well occupied, I am okay. But the moment downtime presents itself, I am attacked by the reality of Tristan's amnesia that no longer includes me as his love interest. And now even more fresh in my mind are the memories of our recent episode together in bed. Over and over flashbacks of all the things we did together that night keep coming back to haunt me, stealing my breath with each thought before repeatedly sucker-punching me in the stomach. The way he seemed so into me—I was so sure that he had been feeling the same things I was feeling. How could I have been so dead wrong? And worst of all, did it really matter anymore anyway? Because now that he is hanging out with the first love of his life looking like he is having a really good time, there *is* going to be no me.

No Tristan and me.

I press my lips together and squeeze my fingers into tiny balls as I allow anger to replace the hurt. *Screw him!* If he wants Rye, then I don't want him anyway. It's this very thought that is playing in my mind as I hear the screen door slam, jarring me back into the present. Jake and an entourage of two other boys and a dark-haired girl are soon standing in the doorway to the kitchen. "Hey, sis, we are heading out to East Beach to play some volleyball. You got a time you want us to back for dinner or anything like that?"

Pulling my hair back into a ponytail, I think about the plans I'd made with Lucy that evening. "Tonight might be a good night for you and Josh to grill your own hot dogs. There is a pack in the fridge and some buns in the cupboard."

Jake's blue-gray eyes instantly light up. I can tell the wheels in his brain are spinning. "Or what about a beach bonfire tonight? And we can roast the hot dogs down there?" As his voice becomes more and more animated, I can feel the chain reaction of his enthusiasm filling up the room. Now his friends look energized with the idea, their eyes bright, smiles forming on their lips.

I pause for a moment to contemplate the idea.

Jake runs his fingers through his dark hair as he studies my face, taking my silence as possible dissention. "And," he hastily interjects, "I will tell everyone, if they want to attend the bonfire they need to bring their own hot dogs or any other food they might want to eat." Again a pause. "How does that sound?"

"That should be fine. You and Josh know the drill. Keep it under control. No injuries. And clean it up when you are all done. No littering on the beach or the water. Right?"

Jake is all smiles. "Right."

Nate is pressing the lid on a pop-up toy over and over with the palm of his chubby little hand. Isabella is sitting beside him on the living room floor keeping him entertained while I try to get some work done around the house. The twins' bonfire had gone on until well after I'd arrived home from my evening out with Lucy. The last time I had checked on them down on the beach, the group had finally dwindled down to a quiet handful of kids sitting huddled around the flames, talking in hushed tones. Satisfied that every-thing was under control, I had gone to bed.

Now it is midmorning, and I am waiting for Jake and Josh to

crawl out bed before putting all the breakfast food away. I am just about to go check on them when I hear male voices coming from the living room. Wiping my hands on a towel, I pad into the room where they are. Josh is kneeling on the area rug next to Nate, pressing the lid on the pop-up toy that Nate has been playing with while Nate watches with a happy look on his face. Jake is sitting next to Josh. He proceeds to tap Nate on his head with his index finger in an effort to capture his attention. It works. Nate's blond, wispy curls spin in Jake's direction.

"Hey, buddy," Jake says.

"Ba ba ja ja," Nate answers. Josh continues to play with the pop-up toy, seemingly in no hurry for breakfast. Expanding my gaze, I notice Isabella has removed herself from the group and is now staring out the front window, winding her wavy brown hair into a twist at the nape of her neck.

"Good morning, boys."

Jake and Josh snap their heads in my direction. "Good morning," they both say in unison.

"You guys going to eat before I put the food away?"

Josh pats his stomach. "Breakfast," he teasingly growls. "I'm ready." He pops up and stretches his arms over his head, causing the muscles on his bare chest and arms to flex. Seconds later Jake jumps up and prepares to follow his brother into the kitchen. I am so busy watching the expression on Nate's face as he stares up in awe at his teenage uncles towering above him that I just about miss the look in Isabella's chocolate-colored eyes from where she is positioned across the room. *What is this?* I blink and Isabella catches me observing her. Immediately a blush covers her cheeks, and she averts her eyes. I stifle the urge to smile and walk over to Nate. Crouching down, I place a kiss on the top of his head while looking in Isabella's direction.

"Isabella, would you like something to eat too? You are welcome to bring Nate and join us in the kitchen."

I can tell it takes a lot for Isabella to look back at me, but when she finally does, a faint glow of red is still evident on her olive complexion just above the indentation of her dimples. "No thanks . . . I think I'll just stay in here. Nate . . . he . . . he seems to really like this toy we were playing with."

"Okay then." I nod my head. "But you are welcome if you change your mind." Inside I know she probably won't though. Not with that much shirtless testosterone sitting at the kitchen table shoving food into their mouths while they make wisecracks and roguish gestures combined with overconfident grins.

The boys are still sitting at the table enjoying a leisurely, late-morning breakfast when I decide to go out for a run. A cool breeze from the ocean is twisting up the path, hitting me gently across the face as I make my way down to the beachfront. The freshness of it is invigorating. Today I feel like I can really tear up some sand below my feet. I am more than ready for a run, the run that will help me to shed some of the hurt and frustration that I have been carrying around with me for the past few weeks. A shot of adrenaline is shooting through my veins as I mentally prepare for the speed that I know I am capable of when suddenly I go still in my tracks. After rounding the last bend of the beach trail, I have now arrived to the shoreline. While my vision fine-tunes to *Blue* as it sways gently against the dock, unwittingly I suck in a breath.

Because Tristan is on the boat.

Hearing my approach, he turns to look at me.

Right away I feel my cheeks heat up in anger as I recall the way I had so recently been used by him, and discarded—for Rye. Tristan stares back at me, seemingly surprised to see me. Now my cheeks are on fire, but for other reasons than anger. *Blast it, why does he have to look like that?* I dig my fingernails into the palm of my hand, determined not to look away. Narrowing my eyes I bite my lip. "What are you doing here?" A look of disbelief flashes over Tristan's features, and even I am surprised by the sound of contempt in my voice.

For a moment he seems to contemplate my question. "Zepher told me *Blue* was stalling and he couldn't figure out the problem. He said I should come by and look at it myself. So here I am."

I press my lips together and shrug my shoulders. "Okay." *End of conversation.* Looking away I prepare to ignore him as I gear up for my run.

"Yeah . . . I should have told you I was coming, but I thought I could just come and fix it without disturbing anyone."

My eyes freeze on the ground in front of me. *I guess the conversation is still going. Oh, you mean not disturb anyone like your son who adores you and wonders why you never come to visit anymore?* I swallow hard, trying to fight away fresh feelings of resentment. *And me. Surely you wouldn't want to disturb me!* Uncomfortable silence causes me to finally look back toward the boat.

Seconds too late I realize my mistake.

Tristan is standing there wiping black grease from the engine on his ripped tee shirt. The expression on his face registers momentary confusion. It's then that I notice the wet stands of his hair as they drip onto his perfectly contoured cheekbones. The muscles in his arm flex as they pause midmotion. *I want to cry.* I want to run to him and slide my fingers through his sexy hair and kiss him and sob into his chest and tell him how much I love him. I want to remind him how much he still loves me too. Self-loathing takes hold of my thoughts. *Why can't I make up my mind?*

Instead I clear my throat. "No biggie . . . hope you can figure it out. You know . . . the problem with the boat. I . . . I'm just going to . . . I was just getting ready to go for a run."

Tristan nods and turns back to what he'd been working on before I had arrived to the beach. Facing away from him I begin to stretch. Focusing on the task at hand, I try to tune out what I know is behind me. But it is so hard with every part of my body on high alert. Leaning to the ground I reach toward my feet, extending the muscles in my calves and thighs until they burn with pain. As I bend and twist and reach I keep telling myself to ignore the person I am sharing the small space on the beach with and focus on the sting in my limbs instead. But just once I disregard the little voice inside my head and sneak a quick peek out of the corner of my eye toward the boat.

Red-hot blood rushes to my cheeks as I get a stolen glimpse of Tristan's blatant stare while he watches me stretch. Heart pounding, I focus my eyes back on my feet, feeling relatively certain that he is unaware that I'd caught him looking. *Oh my word!* Feeling unexplainably embarrassed, I suddenly can't get away fast enough. As I begin my run down the shoreline, it doesn't take long before I am pushing my warm-up jog into a breakneck sprint. And all the while I can't help but wonder if Tristan's green eyes are still on me, watching as I go farther and farther away.

Chapter Ten

Humidity hangs thick in the air. There are sure to be storms later—I can feel it in the atmosphere—can practically taste the salty, metallic flavor of it. It is relatively early in the morning, and I have Nate loaded up in the car, driving down Watch Hill Road as I head into town to grab some pastries and coffee and a couple of items that I need from the local drug store. I glance up at the sky through the windshield of my car in search of dark clouds, but there aren't any—just a dull, gray-white haze. For a moment my thoughts shift to Jake and Josh. They were up and gone from the cabin hours ago, off on a sailing excursion with a couple of other boys whose parents have a summer home in the area. According to the twins it is a ginormous home with a large collection of boats. Hopefully they checked the weather report thoroughly to make sure they were in the clear before they headed out onto the open water. Gripping the steering wheel a little tighter, I cringe at the thought of my brothers out in a helpless watercraft fighting the waves and wind from a storm.

After a brief struggle with Nate's stroller, I finally have it unloaded from the back hatch of my jeep, and we are perusing the aisles of Macost's Drug Store. When my basket is eventually filled with toiletries and other items of necessity, I begin to check out a variety of other fun trinkets that are reaching out to grab my attention: a book of local poetry, a pair of flip-flops artistically turned into a *welcome to my beach* sign, an array of brightly colored stationary.

"Ma ma ma." Nate begins to wiggle impatiently in his seat.

"Just a minute, baby, and we'll go."

I continue to skim though the collection of packets in my hands. Seconds later, Nate has figured a way out of his safety strap and is proceeding to climb out of the stroller. A box of postcards boasting breathtaking sunsets instantly falls from my fingers and lands on the floor. Bending down to pick it up, I quickly set it back in its place on the shelf before reaching for Nate's arm. By now he is toddling down the aisle at a speedy pace. I take off after him. "Oh no, you don't. Get back here, young man." Nate screeches and runs faster. Quickly his momentum becomes too much for his small legs, and he begins to trip and fall just as I scoop him into my arms. My heart beats fast as I eye the sharp edge of the shelf he was heading toward on his way down. *That was too close.* And I don't need any accidents or injuries today. *Shopping over.*

Hugging Nate tightly to my chest, I give him a reassuring squeeze which is really meant for me, before setting him back into his seat. Pulling up to the checkout counter, I hand Nate his favorite toy—a green, stuffed octopus—to keep him occupied while I pay for my purchases. Even this doesn't hold his interest for long today. Shoving my wallet back into my bag, I hurry to get the wheels of his stroller into motion in an attempt to pacify him once again. Knowing my son well, I realize that if I can just get him out of the tight quarters of the shop and back out into the unrestricted air of the outdoors, he will most likely settle down and I will have him under some semblance of control once again. But until that happens, every nerve in my body is skittish as I wait for him to break into loud, protesting cries. Hastily I head for the door.

I am pressing the push-lever handle open with my back, edging out onto the sidewalk as I keep Nate's wiggling form in secure view, when I feel myself collide with a moving form. Now my edginess is heightened. *Oh my word, really? This shopping excursion can't be over soon enough!* "I am *so* sorr—"

The words in my mouth go dry as I turn around to view the

person I've just collided with. Shock would be too inconsequential of a word to describe what I'm feeling the second I lay eyes on the small frame and pixielike features standing directly in front of me. *Rye!* Gray eyes large and round stare into my face, seemingly shocked as well. But there is a flash of something in them that tells me that this is not the same Rye that I dealt with years ago. In seconds an icy chill creeps up my spine, turning my initial shock into alarm and then transforming just as quickly to hurt as I take in the person standing next to her. *Tristan!*

Oh my word, no! Why did I have to run into Tristan and Rye out on one of their cozy little excursions together? My day of running errands in town was already heading downhill quickly. Now it is taking a spiraling, deepwater dive. I blink and glance up at Tristan. *But I don't want to.* I don't want to look at him at all. I want to kick Nate's stroller into high gear and push him down the sidewalk at a lightning-quick pace as I race toward the safety of our parked car. But what can I do? Tristan is standing there directly in front of me, and I have just run into him and Rye—literally. And for a few heartwrenching minutes I know I have to acknowledge them. Rye detects my and Tristan's eye contact and takes a step toward Tristan, almost possessively. I suck in a breath. *You are wrong, Rye. He's not yours. He's mine! He is my husband, after all.* Swallowing hard, I set my jaw. *What am I saying? If he doesn't want me, I don't want him either. Go ahead, just have him!*

"Bethany!" Rye's greeting startles me. It's the same mousey voice from summers ago, but now with an edge to it. An edge of something I can't quite put my finger on: insincerity, triumph, disdain? Again I get a chill. "It's been so long."

Not long enough! I nod my head, still speechless. I try hard not to look at Tristan's windswept hair as it as it flutters lightly above the contours of his cheekbones. But from the way I'm positioned on the sidewalk, he stays in my line of vision anyway. Holding my breath, I try not to remember the way I caught him checking me out yesterday as I prepared for my run. And now here he is a short time later back with Rye. Once again I had obviously read too much into his actions; I could just shoot myself. My heart palpitates strongly in my chest as I detect something akin to guilt spread across the perfect features of his lightly tanned face. *Guilt means nothing good.* Suddenly I feel nauseated. Reaching for my stomach, I rest my hand against it in an attempt to stop the churning motion inside. Detecting my movement, Tristan's gaze moves to where my fingers are resting, and his eyes widen faintly. Abruptly I get an urge to laugh—loud, gut-splitting, tears-come-to-your-eyes laughter—as it occurs to me what he is probably thinking. *No, Tristan. No, I'm not pregnant!*

I narrow my eyes. *But I could be, you stupid shit. Wouldn't that just be a lesson for you—what do you know, there are consequences for our actions after all!* Inwardly I shake my head. What am I thinking? That would only compound the nightmare I'm living on a day-to-day basis. Fleetingly I send up a prayer of thankfulness that I'd gotten my period last week.

Finally Tristan clears his throat. "Ah . . . hi, Bethany."

"Hi," I more or less mumble.

Tristan's eyes shift to take in Nate. I turn to look at Nate as well and realize that he's been sitting motionless in his stroller this whole time, stunned into good behavior by the collision. His wide, staring eyes transition from blue to green right in front of me. *What does this mean?* Does he recognize his dad? Can he sense their shared connection to the water? Tristan blinks and I wonder whether he has detected the transformation as well. Again Tristan clears his throat, but it still sounds like he has a frog in it.

"Hey . . . Nate."

Light immediately spreads across Nate's countenance, and the hint of a smile begins to form on his lips. Tristan's expression softens. Rye's jaw hardens ever so slightly. My shoulders stiffen. This entire chance meeting is so awkward I can hardly stand it. I can't get away from this storefront quick enough. Tristan takes a step toward Nate's stroller. Nate's green eyes twinkle in response.

"How have you been, little buddy?"

"Ba ba ba," Nate pauses and looks inquisitively into Tristan's face before he starts up again. "Da da da."

Tristan immediately shoots me a look like *did he just say that? And do you think he knows what he is saying?* Shrugging my shoulders, I begin soothing Nate's wispy waves away from the brow of his forehead. *What do you care? You never come to see him.* As if reading my mind, Tristan glances at Nate and then back at me again. "I'd like to come visit him. I mean . . . I miss him." An unsolicited tug pulls at my chest. Tristan continues, completely unaware of my feelings. "Can we set something up sometime?"

"Sure," I tell him, avoiding eye contact.

"Okay, well, I'll be in touch." I can feel Tristan's gaze on me while he waits for me to glance up and confirm our tentative future appointment. But somehow I just can't bring myself to look his way.

"Come on, Tris, let's go. I really need to get to the water right now. Are you ready?" Rye's syrupy voice interrupts my dilemma, and for a split second I make the mistake of looking her way just as she reaches for Tristan's arm. I flinch at the familiarity of their contact. Rye's eyes are gray ice as they stare back at me. Tristan shifts uneasily in the spot where he is standing. And suddenly I can't take one more second of this unsightly exchange.

"Ready, baby?" I question while peering into Nate's stroller and maneuvering the wheels around at the same time. Without any formal good-byes I begin walking away from Watch Hill's newest couple, all the while trying to fight the giant lump that is forming at the back of my throat. From out of my peripheral vision souvenir shops, clothing boutiques, and restaurants whizz past me as I walk, and I don't see one of them. Eyes focused on Nate's stroller and the blur of the cement under my feet, I can't get away from Tristan and Rye fast enough. I am almost back to my black jeep when I finally glance up to the sky. So far there are still no storms brewing on the horizon, but I can't help but think that somehow the color of the atmosphere above me is just a little darker shade of gray.

The sky continues to deepen throughout the rest of the day and into the afternoon. And my mood grows dim right along with it. After trying unsuccessfully to push thoughts of Tristan and Rye's budding intimacy away, I finally decide to go for a shoreline walk to clear my mind. Leaving Nate asleep in his crib under Isabella's care, I wander down the coastline taking large, cleansing breaths of sea air. Behind me *Blue* sits tied to the dock post, swaying against the waves as I walk away. For a minute my thoughts go to another boat, the one Josh and Jake had been riding earlier in the day. I was relieved when I had received the text telling of their successful return from the sailing excursion. And by the looks of the billowing and blackening clouds on the horizon, their homecoming had come none too soon. A quick glance at the stirred-up water to my right causes me to question my own trek and the risk I'm taking of exposing myself to the pending, agitated elements of nature. For a moment I consider turning back around.

But the way I'm feeling right now, even a looming storm can't make me care enough to change my course. I just want to walk far enough away from Watch Hill to take at least the edge off of all the unwanted thoughts that keep circulating around in my brain. So I keep taking one step after the other, all the while ignoring the threatening sky. When the first drop of rain hits my cheek, I once again reconsider my itinerary. *Maybe this walk isn't a good idea after all. Maybe I should just head back.* Up ahead in the distance I detect a rumble of thunder, and a momentary shudder rips through my body. I pause, listening for more of the same. Then shrugging my shoulders, I resume my pace, wondering if my self-preservation has all but vanished.

It's not long before the initial drops of rain have turned into a steady stream of liquid running off of my face and onto my body, soaking my clothes. Fighting to see beyond the downpouring precipitation that is now obscuring my vision, I am trudging through murky sand when I hear a voice calling to me out of the whipping motion of the wind. Instantly the blood in my veins turns to ice.

"Going somewhere?"

A startled gasp leaves my lips as I go still in my tracks.

"Funny, I didn't take you for the type of girl that would enjoy this type of weather. The wet look isn't exactly your thing."

Rye! "It is not my first choice, but I can deal with it." *Not that it's really any of your business!* "And anyway, talk about me . . . what about you? Apparently you don't seem to mind it either."

Chilling laughter leaves Rye's lips as she steps directly in front of me. In spite of her petite size, the overt hostility in her eyes as she stares directly at me causes my stomach to twist into knots. "Why would I . . . mind it?" She pauses. "I was born into water. It's part of me." She takes a barely detectable stride in my direction, but enough that I feel myself unwittingly taking a step backward to get away. To get away from her! For a moment the irony of this seeps into my brain. The first summer I had met and hung out with Rye in Watch Hill, she was nothing but a timid waif of a thing—albeit strange at times. My, how time had changed things. And circumstances? Had her circumstances changed her too? Had she really been that affected by Tristan's rejection that she had evolved into the person that is now flashing ice cold daggers at me? Or had she been this crazy all along and had only hid the extent of it relatively well? Once again, her biting voice pulls me into the present. "But you really don't get that, do you? You don't get that about Tris either. We *both* belong to the water. You can't ever change that."

Anger and unexpected fear course through me at the same time. "I wasn't try—"

"That's right . . . *don't* try." Her lips curl into a sneer. "Because you *won't* ever change that!" By now the sky has turned black as midnight in spite of the early evening hour. Rain is coming in torrents, soaking both Rye and me. I hug dripping arms to my chest, shivering, feeling so completely out of my element in this inclement weather. Unlike Rye, who, having the home court advantage, appears completely at ease in the storm. Liquid is streaming from her shagged, brown hair onto her lips, repeatedly saturating her already sopping wet tee shirt and cutoff jean shorts, but she doesn't blink an eye. The water is clearly on her side.

A flash of brilliant light fills the sky all around us, startling me into motion. A loud, earth-shaking crack of thunder follows. "I've had enough of this conversation," I say loudly enough to be heard through the inclement weather. Shifting my body sideways, I turn to leave, surprised that my voice holds none of the fear that is currently ripping out my insides. Funny, I had never considered Rye to be dangerous before. Why am I suddenly so apprehensive and afraid? Another burst of lightning fills the air beside me along with a long, jagged bolt of electricity as it reaches for the ground, zapping a piece of driftwood in the process. I practically jump a mile.

"He doesn't want you anymore, you know." The words as they reach my ears through the sound of pelting raindrops and the swirl of scourging wind cause me to freeze in place. Inside I know I need to run for safety—both from the imminent threat of the storm and from the venom being spewed in my direction. But instead I turn slowly back around to meet the poisonous gaze that holds me momentarily riveted in place. Rye takes a step closer, positioning herself directly in front of me. And although she is at least a couple of inches shorter than me, I figure she must be standing on some type of incline, because our faces are completely lined up, less than two inches apart. A chill runs down my spine.

Her voice is a controlled whisper as she speaks into my personal space. The warmth of her breath as it spills onto my cheeks is a stark contradiction to the iciness of her words as they leave her lips. "You little bitch . . . You stole him from me. And now paybacks suck, don't they?"

Goose bumps instantly cover the skin on my arms. I inhale quickly, my mind spinning as I try to think of a retort. A series of loud booms shakes the sand below my feet, drowning out any chance of speaking aloud. Afterward the sky glows ghostly white. For one, two, three, four seconds Rye's face illuminates, and the coldness in her gray eyes seems to pierce my own—reaching deep down as if into the very depths of my soul. Then the light disappears, and once again I am surrounded by darkness.

By the time another flash of lightning pervades the air, Rye is gone.

And I am alone on the beach.

Taking a sweeping gaze of the shoreline and finding it empty, I begin shivering from head to toe. Inhaling a calming breath, I spit out a mouthful of rainwater and start making my way back home through the now receding storm. Even though Rye did not technically lay a finger on me, I feel like I have been physically assaulted. Her unexpected approach, cold stare, and venomous words felt like a direct attack. And although she never actually gave any verbal threats, I am somehow coming away from the whole episode feeling forewarned, forewarned to stay away from Tristan.

He is hers!

But in all actuality, from the direct usage of her words I shouldn't feel threatened at all. She has just pretty much informed me that it's *game over*. Tristan no longer cares about me. So really—according to her, I *am* no longer a threat.

Even so, the tenor of the conversation leaves me feeling anything but reassured.

Pulling a wet strand of my hair away from my eyes, I keep a fast clip as I wind around the bends in the landscape, making my way back toward the cabin. For a few minutes I contemplate going to Tristan's parents with news of the confrontation. Surely they would want to know. They of course are aware of Rye's past frailty made evident by the whole wedding episode and all, followed by the years of rehab she had undergone down in the sea. And now everyone thinks she is completely well. But the unsettled way I felt during the altercation just now and the eerie look in her gray eyes as she spewed her words of venom at me cause me to feel like she is anything but well.

I am almost back to the cabin before I decide that telling Tristan's parents would not be a good idea after all. Although completely shaken to the bone, at this point I don't *really* feel physically unsafe. And I don't want to appear like a whiner. And since Tristan seems to be spending time with Rye lately, I'm afraid that is exactly how it would come across if I went to them—like a whining baby. Then my next thought is to talk to Zepher and Seth. They had told me that Rye seemed to have worked through her issues where Tristan is concerned and had been cleared to be on her own again. She seemed to acting appropriately in their world. But it might be wise to update them on the opposite so that they can keep their eyes peeled for any unusual behavior. I make a mental note to fill them in on this episode the next time I run into them.

The following morning I awaken feeling completely exhausted.

Like every ounce of my energy has been zapped. And it has been zapped—by Rye. In spite of the bright rays of sunshine that are pouring through my bedroom window, another light catches my attention. Sitting up in bed, I catch a glimpse of the searchlight's perpetual glow coming from underneath the closet's bifold doors.

For a second or two I imagine that the light flickers. But instead of running to it in an effort to protect the continual blaze, I close my eyes and will nature to finally take its course. *My fight is all but gone!* When I open my lids again, I half expect to find darkness creeping from underneath the crack in the closet door, but instead the little thin line along the wooden boards of the floor shines brightly as ever. Sighing, I turn away. Running my fingers through my sleep-tangled hair, I hop out of bed. *Whatever!*

Grabbing Nate from his crib on my way to the kitchen, I begin preparing something to eat for breakfast. After heating up some oatmeal on the stove, I am seated at the table alternating between taking bites out of a steaming hot bowl and offering Nate spoonfuls of smashed bananas. Nate smacks his lips, enjoying every mouthful. I am angling another morsel toward his opened lips when his head suddenly turns away from me and toward the window instead. Through the open screen a conglomeration of energetic teenage voices can be heard making their way up the path that leads from the beach to the cabin. It's early for visitors—especially teenagers. I glance at the clock on the microwave: ten thirty. It's not really that early after all. *My, I really overslept!* Apparently that whole confrontation with Rye had done me in.

Two confrontations actually! The run-in I'd had with Tristan and Rye earlier in the day before the more recent beach encounter now comes floating back into my mind. Involuntarily I shake my head to clear a day full of unwanted thoughts. *Well, no wonder!* No wonder I'd overslept and am now sitting lifelessly at the breakfast table feeling like I've been hit by a speeding locomotive.

An explosion of knocks and exuberant voices at the side door pulls me out of my overwhelmed state. The twins' friends have now finished making their way up from the beach and arrived at the house. Leaving Nate's wide stare and messy banana face at the table, I pad toward the commotion.

"Hi. Are Josh and Jake around?" the tallest boy with blond hair asks as I unlatch the screen. Another boy with sandy hair and two girls with brunette ponytails are huddled behind him, peering in. Right away I recognize the boys from other times they've been over at the cabin. And although I am not completely sure, the girls look relatively familiar too.

I pause, studying their faces. "Conner . . . and Matt, right?"

Conner, the spokesperson, smiles warmly and nods his head in the direction of the girls. "Good memory. And this is Justine and Sara."

"Hey, guys. Well, hang on . . . I'll go see what my brothers are up to."

Letting the screen shut behind me, I make my way down the hall toward the twins' summer sleeping quarters. Behind me I can hear the beginnings of Nate's protests over being left sitting alone at the table. After two sessions of knocking and no reply from inside, I push my brothers' door open slowly. The room is a dark cave. Light filters in from the hallway, and I eventually detect a burrowed form on each bunk.

"Hey, Jake. Hey, Josh," I call into the obscurity of the room. My voice is a loud whisper. No one stirs. "Hey guys." This time my tone is a little louder. Through the dimly lit shadows I detect minute movement coming from the top bunk, but still no answer. Heaving a sigh, I walk to the window and open the blinds. Bright sunshine pops in through the louvers. Instantly there is a ruffling of covers on both beds. Jake, who is on the top bunk, rolls over onto his stomach, still ignoring me. Youthful muscles ripple through the bare skin of his back as he attempts to find a comfortable position. Josh groans on the bottom bunk and proceeds to pull a blanket over his head.

I can see I am getting nowhere. Briefly considering going to get a pitcher of ice-cold water from the kitchen tap, I clear my throat and try one more time. "Josh! Jake! Wake up! Your friends are here.

It's almost noon." *Well, ten thirty actually, but still.* "And they are waiting for you out on the side porch."

This time Jake groans. Shifting his position in bed, he turns his head so that he is facing my direction. His blue-gray eyes peer out at me from the side of the pillow. The blanket that is ensconcing the bottom half of his body falls away from his hips, revealing American Apparel underwear. He makes no attempt to re-cover himself. "Just tell them we'll catch up with them later."

Really? "Are you sure? I think they are going to be a little disappointed. Don't you even want to know who it is?" At my questioning, Josh appears dead to the world, still offering no response. Jake maneuvers his body so he is once again facing away from me. I have to strain my ear to hear his muffled answer.

Something something, " . . . see 'em later."

"Okay, fine."

After shutting the door behind me, with slight exasperation I shrug my shoulders and return to the kitchen. Pulling Nate from the highchair where his voice has now escalated into a series of disgruntled yelps, I head back to the side porch to give the twins' friends the news that Jake and Josh won't be joining them. As expected, the group looks a little disappointed as they turn to leave, their voices now a little more subdued while they make their way down the steps and back onto the trail that will lead them to their boat. With Nate in my arms, I pad back to the kitchen so we can resume our breakfast, all the while wondering what time my brothers will decide to eventually show their faces to the world today.

Chapter Eleven

A dull knife is carving away at my chest. I sit up in bed holding one arm across my breastbone, gasping for breath. *Something is not right!* My thoracic cavity feels like it's been hollowed out, whittled away by an unsharpened blade, leaving a bereft ache in its place. Shaking my head to clear the disorientation from sleep, I try to focus on the early morning light that is pouring through the window of my room. *What day is it? What time is it?* Did I just have a bad dream? Within seconds my mind drifts back to yesterday, and I recall the subdued day at the cabin after my stormy encounter with Rye on the beach the evening before. Even the twins had seemed affected by the dim mood around the house, not dragging their butts out of bed until well after noon. And then it was still many hours after that until they were functioning at full speed once again. It was like we all couldn't shake it—that certain something that was holding us in a depressive funk.

But that was yesterday, and now this feeling that is gripping me, cutting right through me, is far worse than the gloomy haze that I experienced yesterday. It is real and sharp and urgent! And getting stronger by the second. All at once a sinking dread shoots right through me as it occurs to me what is wrong.

It is too quiet!

It's too quiet in the room!

There are no soft, rhythmic breathing sounds filling the air with their familiar, soothing pattern. Immediately my eyes dart over to the corner of my bedroom where Nate's crib sits tucked into the crowded space between my dressing table and closet door. Even in the faint glow of daybreak I can see his favorite blanky as it lies abandoned in a heap. *Oh God, no!* Immediately my mind becomes a jumbled mess as I leap out of bed. Heart pounding in my chest, I run to check on what I can clearly see is an empty crib. *Nate, Nate! Where are you baby?* I begin screaming in my mind while taking a sketchy breath in an attempt to calm myself down so I can think. *This may be nothing. There is probably a completely plausible explanation for this.* Maybe Nate was fussing and I was so soundly asleep I didn't hear him, and one of the boys came to get him to take care of his needs. Maybe they have him this very minute in the living room reading him a book to pacify him or in the kitchen giving him a drink. Maybe the twins are even more mature than I have given them credit for.

Maybe!

Holding on to that tiny thread of hope, I dash through the doors of my bedroom into the common areas of the cabin. The living room is just as I left it the night before with a couple of toys still scattered on the floor. Pivoting to my left, I rush into the kitchen, but the only sound filling in that quiet, darkened space is the steady hum of the refrigerator. The table sits empty and alone. Distraught, I stand staring at the blinking light on the stove. *Think! Think!* A rush of frantic tears begins to form at the back of my eyes. *Nate, where are you? Nate! Nate! Nate!* I can't think straight. I can't sort this all out. I can't do this at all. *God, please help me!* Pinching the skin on my arm in a desperate attempt to focus, I consider another option. Could he have climbed over the railing of his crib all by himself? Searching my mind, I try to recall his efforts to maneuver himself into various positions around the house. Had I sold him short? Was he more capable of mobility than I had thought? And if so, where would he have gone on his own? He can't open locked doors—this I know for certain.

Abandoning my thoughts, with lightning-quick speed I run to the twins' room. Bursting through their door, I take in their sleeping forms on the bunks. No Nate! "Josh, Jake, wake up." The urgency in my voice elicits an immediate response, and they practically jump to their feet. Hair rumpled from sleep, they stare back at me with drowsy but instantly alert expressions. *What is it? What is going on?* Their gray-blue eyes call out to me in unison. "It's Nate. He is missing. He isn't in his crib." Just saying the words aloud as if officially admitting the truth makes me feel instantly sick inside. Suddenly I get an overwhelming urge to double over and puke onto the floor. I press a trembling hand to my throat. Josh and Jake look confused.

"What do you mean? Nate's . . . how, I mean where—" Jake's voice is focused but still thick with sleep.

"He's not in the house? Have you looked everywhere?" Josh interrupts.

"Yes, everywhere . . . he's not . . . he's not in—"

"How about outside? Maybe he got outside."

Outside. Outside. He couldn't be outside; the door is locked. Outside. Outside. Yes, maybe he is outside! "Yes, let's look outside!"

Within seconds Josh and Jake jump into the shorts that lay discarded on the floor beside their bunks. Still dressed in cotton pajama pants and a tank top, I take the lead as we rush toward the side exterior door of the cabin. With each twist of a lock that my trembling fingers unfasten, I remind myself that this is really just a futile search; there is no way Nate could have gotten himself out of the house. But at this point what else is there—what other options do I have? Where could he have gone?

Switching my racing, tangled thoughts to search mode, I tell Jake to comb the yard and the surrounding woods while Josh searches the driveway heading up toward the road. And I take the path that leads to the beach.

The beach and the water.

The water! The most likely place that Nate, if capable to get out of the house on his own, would go. *But there is no way!* It just isn't possible. What else then? What could have happened to him? With no definitive answers to my own questions, I force myself to come face-to-face with a little nagging thought that had been creeping around at the back of my mind from the moment I had startled awake with a dull pain of emptiness in my chest.

Rye!

The instant my eyes had flown open that morning, my mind disoriented, I had somehow connected the ominous feeling I was experiencing to Rye. It was just a premonition I had, but a very strong one. The moment I had woken up, my first thoughts were, *Something is wrong—and it is because of Rye.* I didn't know why or how. But deep down, I just *knew*! And then in the seconds that followed, after I discovered that Nate was missing from his crib, the feeling only continued to grow stronger. And now with each passing moment, although with lack of any concrete proof, I am increasingly sure.

Deep down in my gut this is what I know to be true: A). My precious baby boy is missing, and B). Rye Markane is somehow responsible.

Now the question is: What should I do about it? What *can* I do about it? Call the police? While considering that option, I almost trip over a fallen tree branch that crosses the winding path I'm rushing down as it leads to the beach. Every second that I don't make the right decision about the best way to search for my baby is another second that his life is in danger. This overwhelming thought alone is enough to make me want to throw myself facedown in the sand and cry my eyes out while I beat my fists against the ground. Once I reach the lakeshore I begin pacing, running my fingers through my hair as I try to contemplate what move to make next. From all appearances, I am a crazed lunatic roaming the beach. If I do involve the police, I risk exposing the sea people in the process. Am I willing to do this in order to save my son?

Without a doubt!

But if Rye has taken Nate into the sea, how will I lead the authorities to him and her—to their world—when I don't even know how to get there myself? And besides, in all actuality Nate is a sea person himself. What will they do if they find him immersed deep in the sea, breathing without a problem? No; the police idea just isn't going to work.

I need to find Tristan.

"Tristan . . . Tristan," I begin calling into the sea air. "I need you right now. We need to find our baby. Nate is missing." Splashing though the early morning tide, I make my way out into the water, knowing full well that it's the first place I need to start looking. But little good two feet of ocean depth is going to do me if that is all the farther I am capable of going out. My eyes shift to *Blue*. I could definitely cover a lot of footage with her. Maybe she is my best option. But as that thought flutters through my mind, another one comes in to take its place: short of renting a submarine, any type of human intervention or man-made watercraft is not going to get me any closer to finding my baby. No; *Blue* will do me no good either. "Nate . . . Nate . . . where are you, baby? Come back to Mommy, Nate!"

In desperation I begin running through the water, soaking my pajama pants and tank top while I alternate between calling out to Nate, begging him to come back to me, and then calling to Tristan, begging him to help me. But neither ever emerges from the depths. Adrenaline kicked into overdrive, I finally tear myself away from the ocean waves and head back to the cabin to check on the boys' progress. But they have nothing to report either. With solemn faces they listen while I give them specific instructions to keep an eye out here, while I try to get ahold of Tristan. Never once do they suggest that we involve the police or Coast Guard, and somewhere in the back of my mind I briefly wonder why.

I barely remember driving to Tristan's beach. My first conscious thought after leaving the cabin's driveway is of rounding the final bend in the shoreline that leads to Tristan's protective alcove, hoping with desperation that when I do, I will find him there strumming on his guitar like I had in times past. But when the dune grass finally clears, offering me an unobstructed view of his beach, all I find is a familiar blanket of sand and empty waves pushing to shore.

"Tristan . . . Tristan."

The sound of the surf seems to swallow my words the minute they leave my mouth. But this doesn't stop me. Over and over I call Tristan's name while one thought alone keeps pulsating through my mind. *I need to get to Nate! My precious baby Nate! Time is wasting, and I have to get to Nate!* But I can't do it on my own. I need Tristan's help. I desperately need Tristan's help.

"Tristan . . . Tristan."

My voice escalates until it finally becomes high-pitched and frantic, begging and screeching. Tearing up the sand with my scattered, frenzied movements, I continue to circulate the circumference of Tristan's beach until I finally realize that he isn't going to materialize anytime soon. Without a thought of what my next plan might be, I take off running down the shoreline desperate and helpless as tears begin to stream down my face. Intermittently I swipe at them so I can see where I am going. *But where am I going?* All I want is to get to my sweet baby, and yet there doesn't seem to be any way. Frustration overcomes me. I just can't bring myself to give up, and yet what else is there? For a brief moment I consider throwing myself into the waves. If I don't have Nate, I don't want to go on. At least this way I can console myself by knowing I *tried* to go after him—it's just that the water wouldn't cooperate with my lungs. I take a deep breath of air. No, I haven't come to that point yet. *Yet!* With helpless desperation I continue on.

I am running headlong down a stretch of sandy coastline, vision blurred, getting ready to round a corner past jutting, rocky terrain when I collide with a solid, unmovable force. The intensity of the impact causes me to bounce backwards, toppling toward the ground. But as quickly as I lose my footing, strong hands reach out to grab me, securing me in an upright position.

"Whoa, Bethany . . . what is going on?"

Zepher!

Oh, thank God!

"Zepher, oh, Zepher, what can I do—I have to get to him and I can't and I don't know where he is but I think it's the water and I can't go in there and oh God please help me he can't be missing I need him I don't know what to do—"

Zepher tightens his grip on my arms and gives me a brief shake. "Hey . . . hey . . . hey, slow down, Bethany. What is going on?"

I inhale deeply, trying to catch my breath, and Zepher lets go of my arms so I can brush away the tears that are mixing in with my words. "Nate is missing. Someone took . . . he's not in his crib!"

A look of alarm immediately covers Zepher's face, concern filling his blue eyes. "You sure . . . have you looked—"

"Yes, everywhere. We've looked everywhere. He's got to be . . . he must be down in the ocean. Can you help me? I know Rye—" *Never mind.* "Zepher, *please* help me!" Even though I am trying very hard to speak calmly, I can feel desperation infusing itself back into my voice with each word spoken.

Zepher's eyes narrow. "Wait . . . what about Rye?"

"Nothing. It doesn't matter right now. Can you please, *please* help me?"

"Okay. Yes. Yes, I'll help you. I'll get Seth, and we'll dive in and start looking right now. You go back to the cabin and wait for us, okay?" He pauses to contemplate my tear-streaked face. "Will you be all right? Will someone be there to stay with you? Your brothers?"

"No!" My voice is unyielding and strong, surprising even me. I take a shaky breath. "I want to go too. I want to be there. I want to help find him."

Zepher shakes his head, looking somewhat confused. The beauty mark above his lip twitches momentarily. "But you can't. You *know* you can't." His voice softens minutely. "It will be okay, Bethany, we'll find him and bring him back to you."

"No! I want to go too. And I know I *can*! You know I can too . . . you saw me down there before. *Please* . . . take me with you! Let me help you find my baby. I've got to find my baby."

Zepher shoves his hands in his pockets, looking away from me as he stares toward the sea, considering.

"Please, Zepher—" The words as they leave my trembling lips are filled with desperation. "The only way I can go is with your help . . . can you help me?" It seems like forever that he has his tensed shoulder blades facing me as he ponders his decision. And I don't have forever. *Please, Zepher! Please help me!* Finally he turns back in my direction. His demeanor is hesitant as he takes in my trembling form. For a moment the dimple in his right cheek becomes evident as he sets his jaw and bites his lip, still trying to decide. Finally he lets out a long, slow breath.

"Okay."

What! Really? "Thank you," I whisper. "So what's next? What do we do?"

For a moment Zepher regards me uncertainly. "I'm not . . . I'm really not all that sure. I've never done this before, so—"

"But you *can*! You can do it. It will be okay. I'll relax . . . really relax . . . and let you. And it will work." *It's got to!* "Where do you want me to lie? Do you need . . . should we go somewhere else? Does it need to be somewhere more private?"

Zepher rakes a hand through his light brown hair and takes

a sweeping glance of the beachfront we are on. "No . . . no, this should be okay. I guess . . . just . . . you could probably lie down up there by that rock."

Quickly my eyes fine-tune to the spot where he is referring, and I waste no time situating myself in the sand. Closing my eyelids tightly together, I wait for Zepher to start singing. After what seems like long minutes, the absence of his voice causes me to reopen them. Propping myself up on one elbow, I find the place where he is sitting adjacent from me on a large, protruding rock. The waves are splashing up all around it, getting the pant legs of his jeans all wet. Hesitancy radiates from his demeanor. It looks as if he is not planning on starting to sing anytime soon. A bad feeling begins to settle in the pit of my stomach. *Is he changing his mind?*

"Zepher . . . what? What is it?"

He hesitates before he speaks. "This probably isn't a good idea. It might be too much for you . . . going under like this. You have already done this before and each time—"

Yeah, yeah, yeah . . . I know, each time it gets harder on me. Well, I don't care. I have to get to Nate! "I'm well aware of this, but my adrenaline is really intense right now. I don't think it will affect me that way. I feel really strong right now. I think I can handle it. I'll be okay," I pause. "Besides, the other times I've gone under I did just fine. I'm pretty sure I must be immune to the effects of the deep sea." *Lies! All lies!* I think back to the last time Tristan had taken me under to meet his parents. Afterwards, it was days before I could stand on my own two feet again. Back then Tristan had been very concerned for my health, telling me I should never attempt the dive again. *But so what?* The way I am feeling right now, my strong drive to find Nate could carry me on forever. This time will be different.

Zepher sighs deeply. Now both of his dimples appear. "All right . . . let's just do this. Let's go find Nate."

Thank you! Thank you, Zepher, I tell him with my eyes before settling back down on the sand once again. For a brief moment I lie there contemplating what his voice will sound like when he starts to sing. Or even what song it will be. I have never heard him or Seth sing before. But I know that music is a big part of them. It's a part of all those that live in the sea. Still, I can't help but wonder. It's hard for me to imagine his voice sounding anything like Tristan's. Tristan's voice when he sang to me was so sexy—I was immediately sucked in by the sound. I couldn't have resisted being pulled into a trance even if I tried. Will it be the same way with Zepher? Will I be able to relax enough to let myself get pulled into *his* trance? *I have too!* For Nate's sake. Shifting my legs and bottom in order to get more comfortable, I roll my neck and try to sink farther into the sand.

Hey, not too bad—! Those are my last conscious thoughts as the sound of Zepher singing fills the air, and I drift into a deep sleep. When I open my eyes again, I am momentarily disoriented. I can't remember where I am—where it is that I'm supposed to be. *What is going on?* A strange feeling of weightless settles over me, and my eyes begin darting in all directions as I fight down feelings of panic. *I can't breathe! I can't breathe!* Is this a dream? Am I dying? Who will take care of Nate if I do?

Nate!

I am down in the ocean searching for Nate! The second this realization hits me, I detect a form swimming at my side, slightly to my rear. My head swivels until I can see who it is. Blue eyes are smiling triumphant back at me. *We made it!* I offer a brief smile in return. *It's Zepher, of course.* "You doing okay?" he asks through the muffled sound of the water. I take a relaxing breath, and the panic I was experiencing only seconds before begins to ease away.

Nodding my head, I try to contemplate my current condition. "Yeah . . . yeah, I think I'm okay."

"Good . . . let's go find that boy."

Yes, let's go find Nate! My true purpose for being down here in the first place immediately takes precedence in my mind, and raw determination edged with adrenaline begins coursing through my veins. Allowing Zepher to take the lead, I swim with resolute speed and complete focus through a rippling haze of blue. On and on we soar deeper and deeper into the depths of the ocean until the scenery begins to fill with color and the promise of sea life. For what seems like many minutes we continue our route, heading toward what I assume will be the same city Tristan once took me to—his hometown.

The hollowed caverns and stone formations in the distance are just beginning to look vaguely familiar when Zepher and I encounter a rough patch of water. Suddenly the world around us begins to gyrate and swirl out of control. Schools of fish, seahorses, turtles, any creature that is within swimming distance from us begin to flail and scatter, unable to get a grip on their underwater reality. The instant I am sucked into the chaos, I begin to lose my ability to breathe. Zepher is getting pulled away from me, caught up in the swirl of the water. And he is my life force. Without him at my side sending me the energized sustenance I need to stay alive, it will only be minutes before I am dead—suspended lifeless under the sea. While continuing to gasp for air, the world around me becomes darker and darker as I descend into an unconscious state. But through my fight to stay alive, it suddenly occurs to me that the darkness is moving, shifting and repositioning itself as if fighting to sustain some type of equilibrium in the midst of the pandemonium. *How can this be?* Then it occurs to me: the darkness is not my fading conscious state at all, but a giant squid. A giant squid has been disturbed from the comfort of his elusive home and is now hovering like a storm cloud, feet from where I am flailing in the water.

A new fear shoots through me as I am covered by the immense shadow. I am in the midst of closing my eyes, preparing to give myself over to the magnitude of the formidable creature that I know will soon devour me, when I detect Zepher riding on one of its tentacles. All around us the ocean floor continues to rock tumultuously, stirring up the deep sea. Clinging for dear life, Zepher hugs the squid's limb like a jockey at a horse race while making his way closer to me just as the last few breaths of air are ebbing from my lungs.

When Zepher reaches the spot where I am thrashing through a blanket of unstable liquid, he throws himself into the space next to me. It takes a moment or two before I fully take advantage of his presence and realize that I can breathe once again.

At the very same time, the ocean all around me begins to calm, returning once again to its normal state. For a long minute all sea creatures are suspended motionless as they try to regain their balance. The giant squid is the first to make a move. Removing itself from the upheaval, it discreetly disappears into the deep recesses below as if it were never there to begin with. Instantly a sigh of relief escapes my lips.

I look hard into Zepher's eyes. *What was that all about?*

"I'm not sure." I am almost surprised to hear the sound of Zepher's voice as he answers my silent question. Tiny bubbles ripple through the water with each word spoken. Immediately my thoughts are taken back to the day at the lakeshore when Nate and I had witnessed a similar disturbance on a much smaller scale. Then my mind shifts again as I recall the other reported incidents on the edge of town. An uneasy feeling shoots down my spine. *What is going on with the water?*

Now my need to get to Nate is tenfold. Will he be all right after that oceanic disturbance? Taking a few minutes to recompose ourselves, we finally begin swimming once again. As we gain entrance to the outskirts of the city, I keep my eyes peeled for the presence of a small, blond boy swimming. *Nate! Nate!* I want to scream, but am unsure how to do this without making a complete spectacle of myself. As we begin drifting through the city streets, the desperation that is welling up inside of me starts to supersede any thoughts of normalcy. Suddenly I no longer care about creating a spectacle. *What if we don't find him? What if he is not here after all? What if Rye did something to him besides kidnap him—something horrible or worse!*

My pulse begins tripping hard in my veins, my eyes filled with frantic desperation as I search in and around every crevice of each underwater domain that we encounter, under and in between carefully constructed edifices and ornamented sculptures, through crowds of people swimming on their way to somewhere—carrying on like my baby boy has not just been stolen from his crib that very morning. Suddenly panic rises in my throat, and I want to scream. I want to cause a complete scene so everyone will just stop what they are doing and help me find my precious little son. Zepher notices my troubled demeanor and does his best to stay right by my side, offering me continual support through the energy of his force field.

"Ma ma ma."

What? My eyes begin darting wildly in all directions. Did I just imagine the sound? I glance to my left. Zepher's expression is on high alert, eyes scanning the water around us. No, I didn't just imagine it—clearly he's heard it too. "Nate! Nate!" I begin calling though the diffuse sound of the liquid.

"Ma ma ma." This time the voice is closer, so close I can almost feel the bubbling effect it makes as it travels through the water.

"Nate . . . Nate . . . Nate. Where are you, Nate?" My heart pounds, frenzied and hopeful, in my chest. Then I blink and he is there in front of me swimming and smiling, clearly happy to be in the presence of his mom once again. "Nate . . . oh, baby, it's really you," I cry out while gathering him into my arms. "I got you, baby . . . we found you." His little blond head burrows into my chest as I hold him in a tight grip. Zepher is grinning from ear to ear, genuinely relieved. I offer a small smile in return before glancing discreetly over his shoulder into the nooks and fissures of the cityscape around us— looking for Rye. Narrowing my eyes, I ball my fingers into a fist and take a sweeping glance through the immediate vicinity of the hollowed-out caverns, daring Rye to show herself. Because I know she is there. *Somewhere. Lurking.*

But she never does come into view.

Turning my gaze back to Nate's sweet little form as it rests against my body, for a split second out of the corner of my eye I detect a slender silhouette disappearing into a patch of waving sea grass. Clenching my jaw, I hug Nate a little tighter to my chest. Was the shadowy movement just my imagination? Suddenly I can't wait to get back home.

But the return swim is so tiring!

At first I attribute the fatigue to the fact that I am holding onto Nate, refusing to let go of him even for a second, and his added weight is draining my strength. But after Zepher finally talks me into giving Nate up and letting him swim tethered closely at his side instead, my exhaustion only continues to increase. Zepher keeps sending me worried glances, telling me to hold on—we are almost to the spot where he'll put me under a trance once again and take me to the surface. But the longer I swim, the weaker I get—too weak to go on any farther. "I can't do it," I hear myself whisper into the misty blue haze surrounding me.

"Yes, Bethany . . . you can—" is the last thing I remember before all thought and sensation ebbs away from me, spiraling my mind into a pool of darkness.

Chapter Twelve

Beep beep beep beep.

I am vaguely aware of a soft, pulsating tempo being played somewhere close by, but am unsure of where it is coming from. But I do know it's near—possibly only feet away from where I am. *Where am I?* For a long minute I listen to the sound of the signal which seems to be reverberating in complete sync with my own heartbeat. I have a strong notion that I should know the circumstances surrounding the noise, but I just can't seem to open my eyes and figure it all out. Exhausted from the effort, I finally give up and allow myself to drift back into a peaceful sleep.

The next time I wake, the beep seems louder, and this time through sheer determination I am able to force my eyes open. But it takes so much work. Fighting the sheen of a bright light, I blink several times. "She's awake!" A familiar female voice jars me into further alertness. "Kevin . . . Bethany is awake!" *Mom and Dad?* "Bethany . . . baby, you're okay? How are you? Never mind . . . shshh . . . just relax . . . you're okay . . . it's okay." I attempt moving my head to take in my surroundings, but it seems as though my hair and my brain are glued to the pillow. Shifting my eyes, I turn to the sound of my mom's voice. Tears are running down her cheeks as she stands next to my dad. Both are staring down at the place where I am lying in bed. *But why am I in bed?*

I lick my lips. My mouth feels like a desert. "Why . . . whe . . ."

"Shshshsh . . . don't try to talk . . . you are okay. You are going to be okay." My mom is now sitting on the edge of my bed holding my hand. Dad is kneeling beside her. For a quick moment he wipes a fist across his eyes before forcing a smile. *What is going on?*

Why am I so tired? Why do Mom and Dad look so overwhelmed— sad and yet delighted at the same time?

Nate!

Now the beeping noise beside me increases, ringing high and fast like a Salvation Army bell at Christmastime. The sound of it along with the intense lighting in the room only adds to the feeling of panic that is shooting through my veins. *Where is Nate?*

My baby, Nate!

The fuzzy image of a deep-ocean dive begins to emerge from the recesses of my memory. *I was searching for Nate. Nate was missing. But I found him! I found him!*

Where is Nate?

It takes all the strength I have to lift my head off the pillow and throw back the covers so I can look around the room. It seems as though someone has filled my mouth with hot glue. It is so hard to speak. "Whe . . . where—"

My mom looks anxious as she reaches for the sheet, trying to cover me back up. "Shhh . . . Bethany . . . you are okay . . . There was an accident in the water. You are in the hospital . . . try to—"

"No . . . Nate—" I finally manage to blurt over the shrill of the loud bells that seem to beating directly inside my chest, ripping me apart from the inside out.

"Shh . . . shh . . . Nate is okay." As my mother's reassuring words are spoken, instant relief begins to placate every nerve in my body.

"Where . . . ?"

"Lucy has him at this very moment, and he is his usual sweet little active self, doing just fine. He is perfectly fine."

That's what I needed to know. As I nod my head, the beeping noise begins to slow, and unwittingly my lids close once again.

The next time I lay eyes on the bright walls of what I now know is my hospital room, it seems like days, weeks, maybe even months have passed. Blinking three times, I try to clear my mind of the sluggishness that seems to be a new part of my daily routine. Sleep, sleep, and more sleep. That is all I seem to do these days. Pressing my lips together, I imagine how good the taste of water would be right now. *If only I could just get a drink.* Shifting my head on the pillow, I turn to see how I might go about getting some help. I still feel so exhausted, but if I could just get a drink, then I might be okay. I have just finagled myself sideways and am about to call for my mom and dad, thinking that they might still be around, when I freeze in place.

Instead of finding my parents sitting across the room, I find Tristan instead. *What?*

At my movement his green eyes widen in surprise for a brief moment before narrowing into a disapproving gaze. Involuntarily my heart begins to pound hard in my chest, and for the first time since awakening it occurs to me that there is no longer a telltale beeping noise to echo my inner-most emotions. All of a sudden I am very thankful that the bells have somehow been disconnected.

"Hey," he says while shifting awkwardly in his seat.

"Hey," I manage to mouth, though it comes out sounding like an undecipherable croak. Lifting a weak arm, I attempt to reach for a Styrofoam container with the word H20 scribbled across the side. It is sitting on a table next to my bed, so close, but just out of my reach. *Crap!* My arm falls back to the mattress. Rising to a standing position, Tristan pads across the floor toward me. Lifting the container filled with water from the nightstand, he hands it to me. And for some reason, this simple act causes me to feel awkward and embarrassed. *What is he doing here?* I feel like I hardly know him anymore. What is he doing in my hospital room, sitting there quietly while I sleep? Avoiding eye contact, I concentrate on the cup that is resting in my feeble grasp, realizing that my appearance must be a miserable sight. *And why do I still feel so weak?* Tristan waits by my bedside while I lift shaky hands to take a drink. Afterward he retreats back to his seat. Before returning he slides my table a little closer—close enough that I can now reach it should I want to. "Thanks," I whisper with a voice that is now somewhat intelligible.

Tristan nods, his brow furrowed. He is seated on the chair across from me again. Silence fills the room.

I clear my throat. "How long . . . do you know how long I have been . . . out?"

"Almost two weeks."

Wow! "Oh. I didn't know. I figured it was probably awhile. I just didn't—"

"You almost died, you know," Tristan interrupts. His voice is laced with anger.

"No, I—"

"What were you thinking?" he interrupts again. "You shouldn't have gone under the water like that. You are lucky to be alive." Running a hand through his hair, he rumples it more than it already is. For a few seconds the muscle in his jaw twitches as he pauses, apparently contemplating his next words. "Did you know that at first you couldn't even breathe on your own? You required intubation. For a while it was touch and go . . . you were playing with death."

I take a deep breath. I want to answer all his questions and accusations, but he seems to be on a roll, unwilling to hear anything that I could possibly say anyway. And I am *so* weak. Too weak to argue. Besides, what does he care? It seems like he is perfectly happy to be spending all his time with Rye. Why the big effort to pretend he cares about me? *But speaking of Rye!* Anger begins to swell inside of me, bolstering my strength. I take a long drink of water and look toward Tristan's chair. "Someone stole Nate! That's why."

Tristan's head snaps in my direction.

"Yeah, that's right," I continue. "Someone stole Nate. And I *had* to go after him. I woke up and Nate wasn't in his crib. I was in a panic . . . I *had* to get him back!"

Tristan seems to think about this for a while. "What do you mean, stole him? He seems very drawn to the water . . . couldn't he have just gotten there on his own?"

"No! That just isn't possible. I've considered that option, and there is no way he could have done that. Someone stole him . . . and I think it was Rye!" The minute I say the words, I detect an incredulous look forming in Tristan's eyes. He looks completely taken aback by what I've just said. Then seconds later, a grin forms on his lips, and he laughs out loud.

"Rye?" He laughs some more, and suddenly I feel very tired. And stupid. He shakes his head, and I sink farther into the mattress. "I really doubt that . . . yeah, I doubt *that* . . . What are some of your other theories?"

"Yeah . . . just like she didn't steal the seashell either," I mutter under my breath. As the mumbled words leave my lips, I am immediately taken back to our wedding day with Tristan and I standing at the altar, getting ready to seal our consecration with a kiss. It was during that exact moment Rye had shown up in her disheveled attire to stop our union, sporting the seashell she had stolen from my neck during the middle of the night only weeks before—the very same seashell necklace that Tristan had given to me as a gift—a representation of his devotion and love.

Tristan goes very still, cocking his head in confusion. "What did you say?"

I let out a long, slow breath, exhausted. "I said I have no other theories."

Deep in thought, Tristan continues to watch my face. For a split second his gaze travels to the exposed skin above the scoop-neck of my hospital gown, and my heart begins to pound in my chest. To the place where my seashell necklace would be—where it still is. *Did I say too much? Should I have just let it go?* I know I'm not supposed to influence his memory—he is supposed to gain it back in his own time. But somehow the anger got to me, and I let it slip. Finally he shakes his head as if to clear it. "Well, anyway, no matter how Nate got into the water, you shouldn't have gone down there to get him. You should have gotten me to help you. I could have gone after him safely, and you wouldn't have had to risk your life."

"I did look for you, but I couldn't find you," I pause before continuing. "Thankfully I did run into Zepher though, and he was able to help me out."

"Again, to state the obvious, Zepher could have gone down there on his own, and you wouldn't be lying here right now, lucky to be alive."

I turn away and face the opposite wall, suddenly too exhausted to continue the conversation any longer. *I'm not sure why you care anyway, Tristan: it seems as though you don't love me anymore anyway.* A lump begins to form at the back of my throat.

"What?"

I suck in a startled breath and freeze in place. *What do you mean—what? Oh no! Did I just say that out loud?* Suddenly I feel completely drained. I don't half know what I'm doing or saying at the moment. *Oh my word—maybe I did say it out loud!* Finally I turn my head slowly back in Tristan's direction. The look of perplexity that is covering his perfect features causes an ache to form in my chest. *Don't look at me like that! God help me—I still love you.* Stop it! *That look! It's making me still love you.* I bite my lip and swallow hard. "I said I'm really tired and think I'll go back to sleep now. But thank you for stopping by. I appreciate the gesture and all the concern." *But you are free to leave anytime because I can't stand to have you sitting there across the room any longer when I just want you to take me in your arms.*

It seems to take a few moments for my words to register. Finally

Tristan startles into motion. "Oh . . . okay, sure . . . yeah, I'll just go." Standing, he rubs his palms against his jeans before shoving them into his back pockets. Butterflies begin to flutter in my stomach in spite of my overwhelming exhaustion. Pressing my lips tightly together, I try to stop the involuntary way my body is reacting to the way he looks—so hot—standing there in the doorway to my hospital room as he prepares to leave. "Okay . . . well good-bye," he says.

In answer, I nod without saying a word.

"Feel better," he mouths as he begins edging outside of the room.

I swallow hard and nod once again. And then he is gone. And I fall effortlessly back into a drugged-like sleep.

When I am finally released from the hospital, my mom decides to stay in town awhile longer to help me get back on my feet. Between her and Lucy and Isabella—who continues to come over on weekdays—I have all the help I need to get nursed back to good health. But although I hate to admit it, Tristan is probably right. I probably shouldn't have gone back down into the ocean to look for Nate. I really could have sent Zepher by himself. But I was in such a frantic state at the time, I couldn't think straight. But now after everything is said and done I am paying for it, because even though I am getting stronger every day, I feel much weaker than I did the last time I went under. And there is a small part of me that wonders if I will ever be the same again. Just the thought of jogging causes me to want to take a nap. It's hard for me to imagine running barefoot on a shoreline ever again.

But one hug or *I adore you Mommy* smile from Nate, and I forget about the struggle I am having with my restoration to good health. So relieved and happy to have him back safe and sound, I want to shout with joy every time I lay my eyes on him. I ask for my brothers' help to push his crib next to my bed so that he will always be close to my side at night. I consider having an alarm system put on the windows, but figure that my parents and Lucy wouldn't understand the need.

As far as they know, Nate fell in the water, and I almost drowned trying to save him. At least that is the story Zepher has passed on to everyone. And the odd thing of it is—my brothers never try to negate the account or bring up the fact that Nate had been missing that morning, and that is why he'd been in the water to begin with. It is the unspoken part that we all silently agree to never talk about. Occasionally I wonder if Josh and Jake think I was in some way negligent and therefore responsible for Nate's disappearance, and by their silence they are covering my butt.

Sometimes it's so hard not to tell them the truth.

Sometimes it's so hard not to tell everyone the truth.

I am thankful to have my mom and Lucy around helping me to get stronger every day, but there are times when they look at me with genuine concern, and I know they are thinking back to the time when I had fallen into a deep depression my first summer in Watch Hill, seemingly too weak to get out of bed for a good chunk of the vacation. I want to reassure them this is not like that—this is real; this is actual physical damage to my body from a deep-sea dive—without scuba gear.

It's the carefully worded questions they ask about how am I doing—*you know with Tristan back and yet not back?* I try to reassure them that I'm okay in that department. Taking it day by day, moving forward, realizing that he may never remember *us*. But I can tell they don't quite believe me—*that I'm really okay*—and that his distancing himself from our marriage is not somehow contributing to my weakened state. There seems to be no way to convince them—at least verbally. So I make every effort to get stronger each day, eating right and adding additional minutes to my exercise routine during each workout session, determined to get stronger as quickly as I can—therefore proving them wrong.

As the days go by, at times it is a relief when my mom is off running errands in town or Lucy hasn't stopped by yet for one of her frequent check-ins, and it's just me and Isabella along with Nate at the cabin, and I can just be myself. Because Isabella doesn't know my long, complicated history with Tristan, I don't feel the need to put on a brave front when I'm with her.

Today is one of those days. My mom has just left for town, taking Jake with her to pick up some groceries, and Isabella is playing with Nate in the side yard. I am just thinking how proud I am of my progress—I haven't even felt the slightest urge to take a nap today—when I hear a male voice added to Isabella's and Nate's playful banter through the open window in the living room. I glance through the screen to check it out.

Isabella is on her haunches next to Nate, inches away from where he is standing, grinning, while she lightly tosses him the toddler version of a football. Josh has just arrived in the yard coming back from the beach and is heading in their direction. He is wearing blue swim shorts with neon green graffiti etched into the fabric and a tight fitted tee shirt that reads *sand surf or sail*. Upon Josh's entry to the yard, Isabella glances toward him and then immediately averts her eyes. Her cheeks now glow a soft shade of pink.

"Heeeey . . . Nate. The Natester," Josh calls as he crosses the yard to where they are. Nate's face immediately lights up. Isabella begins playing with her ponytail while inadvertently looking up at Josh through lowered lashes.

"Ja ja ja. Ba ba." Nate's blue eyes twinkle as he picks up the football that is resting at his feet. When Josh finally stops directly in front of him, Nate looks up questioningly into his eyes. *Want to play catch, super-cool uncle?* Nate glances down at the ball in his hands and then back up at Josh once more. *Can I throw you this football?*

Josh gets it. "Hey buddy . . . throw me that ball," he says.

Nate immediately smiles and tosses the ball in Josh's direction. It falls a few inches away from Josh's feet. Picking it up, Josh lightly lobs it or more or less hands it back to Nate. Once Nate has it tucked safely in his arms again, he beams from ear to ear. As far as he is concerned, he just made the catch. Now he looks up into Josh's face for approval.

"Good job, Natester." Josh reaches out to lightly tickle Nate's tummy. "Now throw it back to Uncle Josh."

Nate seems to contemplate the directive for a moment before tossing the ball once more. Isabella watches the interaction from where she is sitting, looking on. And I can't help but notice the way her eyes take in every move Josh makes when she thinks he isn't looking. After Josh has the ball in his hands once more, he surprises me by not making the handoff back to Nate. Instead he turns toward Isabella.

"Hey, Isabella . . . think fast!"

I can tell by the way Isabella's chocolate eyes widen, that she is surprised too. But with quick reflexes she startles into motion and manages to catch the ball that Josh sends flying in her direction.

Josh's blue-gray eyes widen as well. "Hey, not bad." Isabella's cheeks are now a brighter shade of pink than before, and my heart feels for her. It looks like she would rather disappear into thin air than to have to interact with my brother Josh, let alone take any type of compliment from him. For a moment Josh seems to study her. "By the way, do you talk?" he blurts unexpectedly.

At that Isabella's head snaps in Josh's direction. "Yes!" Her voice is an unusual combination of shyness and indignation. For a long moment Josh watches her face, and I wonder if he is noticing the way her dimples are now showing, made evident by the way she is setting her jaw almost defiantly. Or if he is seeing the raw beauty of her pink, naturally swollen lips and flawless, olive complexion. Or the way her deep brown eyes seem to go on for miles, matching the coloring of her wavy hair. Breaking eye contact, she furrows her brow. "Yes . . . I talk."

"Okay . . . so talk." Josh walks over to the patch of grass where she is sitting and takes a seat on the ground a couple of feet away.

Now they are lined up side by side. Isabella shifts uncomfortably in her spot. Close by, Nate busies himself playing with a toy truck and a plastic shovel.

"What about?"

"About? How about where do you go to school for starters?"

Isabella begins fingering her ponytail as it winds around to the front of her chest. Keeping her gaze on the wavy strands, she inspects the ends. Anything to avoid looking at Josh. "Westerly."

Josh picks up a blade of grass and rolls it casually between his fingertips. "Yeah? Your whole life?"

"Yep."

"That's cool." For an instant Josh gets a faraway look in his eye. Then just as quickly he shakes his head, seeming to snap back out of it again. "Yeah, that's cool you live around here." He pauses and shakes his head for a second time. "This town, this place . . . yeah, this place is something else." For another lingering moment it looks like there is something more he wants to ask Isabella on the topic. But after opening his mouth twice to speak, he hesitates and switches to another subject, telling about his school, about life in the big city, and about all the sports he's played over the years. Intermittently he asks Isabella about her life around here and about whether or not she plays sports. And although Josh is the one doing most of the talking and Isabella is giving only short answers, I can tell by the way she is making increasingly longer bouts of eye contact that she is beginning to feel slightly more comfortable in Josh's company as the conversation continues.

She is still smoothing her ponytail, periodically glancing over at Josh, when he looks over at her, and for a split second their eyes connect. "So what grade did you say you were going into this fall?"

Isabella quickly adverts her gaze to the ground. "Eighth." Her voice is soft. Too soft. With a furrowed brow Josh searches her downcast face.

"What?"

She lifts her head. "I said eighth grade." This time the words come out loud and clear.

Josh appears to choke, and Isabella sets her jaw, causing her dimples to show. "Eighth grade?" Josh pauses. "How old are you, anyway?"

"Thirteen."

"Thirteen?" Josh practically gasps. "Oh . . . hey, that's cool." He runs a hand through his sandy blond hair. "Yeah, that's cool." Abruptly he turns his gaze to the right and begins watching Nate's efforts at shoving a stick into his Tonka truck. "Hey, Natester . . . are you trying to destroy that truck? I doubt if that stick is going to fit, buddy." Nate stops what he is doing and looks at Josh with round eyes. Seconds later his attention is turned back to the truck, and Josh jumps up and walks over to where he is sitting while Isabella watches though lowered lids. Rumpling Nate's blond, wispy hair, Josh kind of half glances over his shoulder in Isabella's direction. "Well, I am *hungry* . . . I am going to get some *food*," he announces with exaggerated loudness. "Hear that, Nate, Uncle Josh is *hungry!*"

From there he begins heading toward the cabin while Isabella watches through eyes filled with a mixture of disappointment and yearning. My attention shifts from Isabella to Josh. As I survey his slow, steady gait and the slight stoop of his shoulders while he walks through the yard up to the side porch, I begin to question whether it's just my imagination, or does his step lack some of the zest that it possessed when he first arrived to the cabin?

I am almost completely back to good health when my mind clears and I become more certain of the observation. Not only of Josh, but Jake as well. They both definitely lack some of the vivaciousness that had been a big part of their youthful personalities when they originally came to town. Now as I observe their faces during the daytime hours while they lounge on the couch mindlessly playing their video games for hours, I begin to detect the hint of faint shadows beneath their eyes. Once as I carry a basket of clothes from the bedroom to the laundry room, I stop midroute and stare hard in their direction, contemplating the reason for the change. Is it possible that they have been overly worried about me after my deep-sea excursion? After all, I *did* have a near-death encounter—and if I think about it—all the people that are closest to me have been hovering at my side ever since. Maybe I really *had* scared everyone, Josh and Jake included. Maybe I was sicker than I thought. Maybe to appease all that are concerned, now I need to work that much harder at putting on a good front, proving that I am once again back to normal. *Besides, I really am feeling a lot better!* It wouldn't be *that* hard to pretend just a little more.

Chapter Thirteen

"Good-bye Mom . . . I'm going to be okay. Really!"

Mom shoots me a look like *promise?* I have finally convinced her to go back to Philadelphia, and she is pulling down my gravel driveway sending me one more fleeting look of concern before she curves around the bend that will take her out of my line of vision entirely. Besides, I still have Lucy to pop in now and then, and my brothers who I have talked my mom into leaving for added aid with outdoor chores around the house. And of course there is Isabella, who still comes on her regularly scheduled days to help with Nate, so I'm all set. Even Zepher and Seth continue to stop by on occasion, offering their assistance with the bigger projects on the grounds of the cabin.

And then there is Tristan.

Tristan has been coming over on a regular basis to take Nate for parental visits. And although I wish he had an ulterior motive for coming around—like me—I am happy that he is stepping up to the plate being a father to Nate. It warms my heart each time I witness their affectionate interactions with one another, causing me to secretly wish I could be included in their group—making it a trio. Making it a family of three. But instead I allow them space to be alone, thinking that this is what Tristan wants. To date he hasn't given me an indication that he wants it any other way. But furtively I can't help but look forward to each scheduled visit, hoping beyond hope that something inside his heart has changed since the last time he stopped by, and that this time he might say something or send me that one look that lets me know that he's interested again. But so far the only looks he has sent me are ones to confuse. Because on occasion when I think that maybe he is showing interest in some way, the next moment he is standoffish and distant.

A knock at the door lets me know he has arrived for today's visit. Scooping Nate into my arms, I head in the direction of the sound. Nate begins wiggling in my arms the minute his dad comes into view. Tristan's hair is dripping wet, making it seem like he just stepped out of the shower, but I know it's really from the ocean of course. For a split second he catches my eye as I step out onto the porch and my heart flutters in my chest. A soft gust of wind stirs around us, causing his wet hair to ruffle ever so slightly. At the same time his fresh soapy, salty scent reaches my senses, awakening every nerve ending in my body. For a moment I press my lips together and look away, trying to get ahold of myself. *But he makes it so hard.*

When I look back in his direction, I catch him studying my expression questioningly, but the moment our eyes connect, he quickly focuses his attention on Nate. Without hesitating I hand Nate over. The bare skin on our arms brushes as I do, causing goose bumps to form on my arms. Immediately I take a step back and begin rubbing them with my hands, hoping that Tristan hasn't noticed. *It is so embarrassing—my uncontrolled reactions to him!*

But if he notices he doesn't let on. By now he is captivated by Nate's smiles and babbling as Nate tries in earnest to tell his dad a story about the time they'd been apart. And I can't help but smile as I watch the way Nate's eyes light up, now so green, when only moments before they had been blue. After a few minutes Nate notices some of his favorite toys in the front yard and wiggles to get down. Tristan brings him over to the pile of trucks and outdoor plastic yard equipment, and I contemplate going back inside to allow them their father-son alone time. Situating my ponytail over my shoulder, I turn to leave.

"Hey . . . Bethany."

I pause and turn back around.

"I know I've been coming around four o'clock to see Nate, but for the next two visits I'd like to come later. I have something going, and I was hoping to come in the evening."

"What time were you thinking?"

"Around seven."

I nod. "Seven should be—" Out of my peripheral vision I detect Nate abandoning his dump truck in the yard as he makes a beeline for the path to the beach. "Nate," I call to him while he continues to run as fast as his little toddler legs will take him. On instinct I take after him, chasing his disappearing form before he gets too far. It doesn't take long until my loftier stride catches up with his baby steps. "Nathan Milton Alexander, you get back here," I playfully reprimand him just before scooping him up in my arms. Kissing his soft cheek, I tuck him against my hip and bring him back to where Tristan is standing. I shake my head. "This little guy . . . like I was saying, seven should be—"

But the perplexed look on Tristan's face stops me from finishing my sentence for the second time. I go still in my tracks. *What is it?* For a long moment, Tristan seems lost in thought like he is trying hard to remember something. Finally he speaks. "Mr. Horton . . . Milton." Narrowing his eyes, he runs his fingers through his hair before looking over at me. "Milton was Mr. Horton's name. Milton Horton." It sounds as though the idea is just dawning on him.

I nod my head slowly, not wanting to interrupt his moment of discovery.

"So you named Nate after Mr. Horton then?" Tristan's voice is soft, contemplative.

"Yes."

He bites his lip, looking like he is still trying to figure something out. "So . . . you liked . . . I mean you must have thought a lot of him

. . . Mr. Horton . . . to name Nate—"

"He was a great man. He will always have a place in my heart." I pause. *And he was always in our corner, Tristan—he knew we were meant for each other—he knew we were meant to be together.* "And I knew . . . I knew how much he meant to you," I finally spit out.

Tristan studies my face for a few seconds before acknowledging my statement with a barely perceptible nod. Afterward he looks away, and I am left feeling very unsure of his thoughts on the matter. Part of me is hopeful that his memory has been stirred up, but the other part of me is less encouraged by the way he seems so ready dismiss the whole thing as if it were insignificant. Out of nowhere I experience an overwhelming yearning to have Mr. Horton back. If only he were still alive and living in his bachelor pad across town, he would have surely been able to convince Tristan about the truth of who he really is. And then maybe Tristan and I would still be together.

Mr. Horton is not around to help my and Tristan's situation, though, and I realize all too well that if anything is going to happen between us, it is going to happen all on its own. But if I allow myself to dwell on this reality, I get exhausted over the idea, and with my recent good health being tenuous at best, I decide it is best to put my mind in neutral and do my best to let go of these thoughts. If I am to convince all that are inclined to worry about me that I am getting better after my recent hospitalization, I need to focus on letting my mind and body heal completely. Because the minute I permit myself to perseverate on the negativity of the situation, I feel my physical condition slipping backwards.

Zepher is on the list of those who seem to want to worry about me. Well, maybe not worry exactly, but at least be of some type of help so that I can continue healing. Determining there must be *something* I need, he stops by on several occasions to see of what aid he can be. I think that in some ways he feels directly responsible for my near-death encounter, telling me more than once how he should have just gone down to find Nate on his own instead of letting me go with him. And oddly enough, there are days when he seems willing to talk about what all went on that day when he helped me search for Nate, including the guilt he feels over not going in my stead. And yet there are days when he seems perplexed by my questions, and he does his best to change the topic.

Today is one of those days.

"Remember, Bethany . . . we agreed," Zepher says as he lightly tweaks my nose. "No talking about that disturbing day. It is not good for you. And right now I'm here to help you have fun." For a moment he pauses as his smile fades. "And that day wasn't fun."

"All right. Agreed."

An hour earlier Zepher had stopped over to take Nate for a swim. Afterward Nate had gone down for a nap, and Zepher had begun gathering some scrap metal to take to the recycle yard. Pausing to let me know he will be finishing the project up on another day, he'd found me in the side yard pulling weeds from a flower garden. Just when I think we've finished our conversation and he is leaving the premises, I feel an ice-cold trickle of water seeping down the back of my neck. Yelping, I jump to my feet.

And find Zepher, who I thought had already gone, standing right in front of me with an empty glass in his hands. Laughter leaves his throat, echoing over the sound of the distant waves. His blue eyes are dancing, and his dimples are indented to the max. Narrowing my eyes, on impulse I reach out to smack his arm.

"Nice . . . Zepher!"

He laughs some more while I wipe my hand over the back of my neck. "Sorry, I . . . I couldn't resist . . . you looked . . . I thought you might be hot."

"Maybe, but not cup-of-ice-water-down-the-back-of-my-neck, hot."

"I don't know; that is debatable."

I roll my eyes. "You know . . . there are such things as paybacks. And I hear they are hell."

Zepher winks. "You have me scared . . . I'll be waiting."

Now I am blushing, and I feel like an idiot. Turning my back to him, I concentrate on my flowers. "Don't hold your breath for anything too fun. Trust me, when I return the favor, I'll make sure you won't like it," I say in dismissal.

Zepher's laughter reaches my ears, but instead of waning into the distance as I expect, it gets closer, landing right next to my ear. Kneeling beside me, he eyes the garden. "You missed one." He points to a large cluster of weeds. In response I nudge his arm. I get what he is doing: trying his best—as he put it moments before—to help me have fun. I decide to appease him. *Okay, I can have fun. See, I am perfectly okay, Zepher. I can have fun. Watch me.*

"Smart alec," I lightly tease.

"Okay, so you missed *more* than one . . . like two or three. Or maybe more like one hundred. Do you want my help?"

"Oh, I don't know, I think I can handle it."

"All right, but don't say I didn't offer, and don't come complaining to me tomorrow when you're all sore from leaning over the dirt for several hours." Out of my peripheral vision I can feel Zepher's eyes on me, but his tone is playful, so it doesn't make me feel uncomfortable.

A soft giggle escapes from my throat. "Got it." I run my thumb and forefinger across my lips as I turn to face him. "My lips are zipped . . . you won't hear one word of complaint from"—I stop and a small gasp of air leaves my mouth—"me." The last word of my sentence comes out in a faded whisper. Zepher's gaze doesn't leave mine even for a second, and now I am frozen in place. *Don't do this, Zepher,* I try to warn him with my eyes. But even as I am thinking this, he continues to watch my face. I can tell he is leaning toward me ever so slowly. I swallow hard.

The soft tone of his voice causes me to strain my ear even at this distance. "You sure . . . that you can handle it . . . handle everything? Because I—" My heart pounds in my chest as his face is now just a few inches from mine. *Oh, Zepher, please don't . . . we shouldn't.* But somehow in spite of the warning signals that are flashing through my mind, I am paralyzed in place, unable to move. I'm not sure if it's the strong gust of wind that whips between us right then or just a sudden moment of clarity, but at the last second I turn away.

Laughing nervously, I wipe my dirty hands on my pant legs and jump to my feet. Zepher's blue eyes shoot up at me from where he is still sitting on the ground, looking a little stunned. I exhale a large breath. "Zepher . . . it's not a good idea . . . you should probably . . . ah—" I motion toward the water.

He shakes his head as if to unclutter it. "Yeah, sure . . . I'll just—" He clears his throat and jumps to his feet as well. Offering a two-second pause, he shakes his head once again. "Yeah . . . I'll just go."

I look right at him, albeit somewhat uncomfortably. *Still friends, right?* I ask him with my eyes. Then afterward, nodding, I offer a small smile as he turns to leave.

It's the phrase, *still friends, right?* that keeps echoing through my mind into the evening after Zepher is gone, and then well into the nighttime hours when everyone else is asleep. I hope so. Because I really like Zepher as a friend—like him and Seth both. But especially Zepher. He has been a really great friend during all of this—ever since Tristan disappeared in the West Coast accident. But due to other past incidences, I'd been suspecting that he was carrying around some type of nonplatonic feelings for me, edging him into another category besides friend. And now after today, I am completely sure. I let out a long sigh. Why did this have to happen? I don't want to lose Zepher as a friend. Is he mad at me now that I rejected his advances today? Now I bury my head in my hands as I lean against the kitchen countertop. "Uggg!" Unable to sleep, after checking on Nate in his crib I'd slipped into the kitchen for a drink of water.

Still friends. right?

Again the silent plea I'd spoken in my mind as Zepher left earlier in the day shoots through my mind as I swallow down the liquid in my glass. But this time the words are interrupted by the sound of a voice groaning in the other room. I freeze in place. *What was that?* My heart begins thudding loudly in my chest, causing me to strain that much harder, listening intently over the sound of the thump-thump, thump-thump. For a long minute everything is quiet but my deafening pulse. Then all at once, I hear the mumbled groan once again. This time I can tell it is coming from my brothers' room. Startling into motion, I tiptoe from the kitchen into the living room, pausing outside their door to listen. By the randomness and restlessness of the words that are being spoken, I can tell someone is talking in their sleep. I furrow my brow. *Is this something they do often?* Had I just not paid attention before? It's seldom that I'm up in the middle of the night roaming about the house, so it is definitely possible that I would have missed it had they done it on prior occasions. Pressing my ear against their door, I concentrate harder, trying to decipher what I am hearing. Twice I catch what sounds like the name Freddy being mentioned, or rather moaned. *Freddy?* Narrowing my eyes, I shake my head. The name holds no meaning to me, but for some unknown reason it causes goose bumps to form on my skin.

I make a mental note to ask Mom about the sleep talking. It is quite possible that this is just a habit I never knew my brothers had. But it would have been nice to know. Carefully I push their door open to make sure all is okay inside. Peeking through the dimly lit interior of their room, I watch for several minutes as both Josh and Jake toss restlessly in their beds. Eventually they appear to become more relaxed, and the movement subsides. After no more words are spoken, I edge myself quietly back out of their room, not wanting to wake them from what now seems like a relatively peaceful slumber.

The following morning I am a little groggy from lack of sleep as I make my way down to check on *Blue.* My mind had been intermittently stirred overnight up by the *still friends, right?* phrase echoing through my brain and then afterward with questioning thoughts about my brothers' sleep talking. It had stormed somewhere close to the midnight hour, and I couldn't remember whether *Blue* was covered or whether I'll need to now bail water. So tired or not, I head down to the beachfront to make sure all is okay.

After finding the boat swaying gently in the waves, completely covered, I sigh in relief and turn to make my way back to the cabin. I am almost off the dock when I notice Seth heading my way. At first glance I question whether it is Zepher, and my heart rate accelerates. But by the time he is a few yards away, I realize with relief that it is Seth, and I let out a soft expulsion of air as I am taken back to the day before. If Seth notices my momentary distress, he doesn't let on. In fact, if anything he seems almost humored at the sight of me, and for a moment I imagine that I detect a smirk crossing over his features. Which isn't that unusual for Seth, so I let it go and listen as he tells me that he'd just run into Tristan. And Tristan wanted him to ask me if it was okay for him, Tristan, to stop by and visit Nate later that day even though it wasn't originally planned. *So many recent changes in the schedule.* I press my lips together contemplatively, almost obstinately. I could be difficult and refuse.

But of course I'd never turn Tristan away. And besides I can't help but think back to Tristan's last visit and the way that Nate's middle name caused a spark in his memory. Suddenly a small thrill shoots through my veins. *What if he's remembered more?* What if that is the reason for moving up this next visit? What if he wants to be around me to see if something will trigger his memory further?

What if he already *has* remembered more, and now he can't wait any longer to come tell me?

For a moment a feeling of uncontrolled elation surges through my body.

It's hard to tame the butterflies that are fluttering around in my stomach as I wait for Tristan to show up at the cabin. Nate hears the sound of his arrival before I do and rushes his little toddler legs to the door. Rounding the corner from the living room, I head down the hall and find Nate whacking the screen as he peers out at his dad. My heart beats hard in my chest at the sight of Tristan's lean, muscular frame standing on my porch. He has on low-slung jeans and a light blue tee shirt that hugs his chest. My eyes reach for his as I turn the knob and push open the door. But he is looking at Nate, a smile lighting up his face. For a moment my heart sinks. Then I remind myself that this is what he is here for—to see his son—and just because he is excited to see him doesn't mean anything negative where we are concerned.

"Hey, guy," Tristan says as he lifts Nate into his arms, throwing him into the air before straddling him safely against his chest. Nate lets out a surprised whoosh of air and then starts laughing. Tristan carries on the repartee by talking playfully to Nate, periodically tickling him in the tummy while I stand by watching with a tentative smile on my face. Nate babbles an enthused conversation in return. After many moments of Tristan paying exclusive attention to Nate without a single glance in my direction, my smile begins to fade. I am just thinking about taking a step backward in order to silently disappear into the house, leaving father and son to have alone time, when Tristan finally looks my way.

But there is no real eye contact.

"Thanks for letting me come by to see him today. I had something come up and today just works out better."

As I fold my arms across my chest, an unexplainable disheartening feeling settles in my stomach. "No problem," I say. But by now Tristan is facing Nate once again. My hand reaches for the door knob. "Well, I'll just go grab his things for you."

Tristan nods in acknowledgement to my statement as he continues to hold eye contact with Nate, laughing as Nate reaches out to grab his nose. My steps are unhurried and heavy as I make my way to the bedroom where Nate's bag is waiting. Throwing it over my shoulder, I head back to the porch where father and son are both thoroughly enjoying each other's company. Even though I've stepped through the screen and am standing right in front of them, neither seems to notice. Suddenly my stomach feels queasy. Clearing my throat, I shove the bag in Tristan's direction. "Here you go."

Finally Tristan looks my way, appearing somewhat surprised by my curt behavior. "Okay . . . thanks," he says as he takes the satchel from my hands. For a brief instant our fingers brush against one another during the transfer. An electric thrill shoots along the nerve endings of my skin, and I almost jump in response. Tristan notices my reaction and casts a speculative glance in my direction. What it is I see reflected in his green eyes I'm not sure. But for one plummeting moment I think it is guilt. Now the queasiness in my stomach turns to full-fledged churning.

Fighting away the urge to puke, I look into Nate's sparkling green eyes while blowing him a kiss. "I'll see ya later, baby. I love you."

Nate sends me a heartwarming smile. For a long moment his eyes transition from green to blue as he watches my face. "Ma ma ma," he babbles while sending me a look that says *It will be okay, Mommy. Don't be sad. I love you and that's all that matters.* His empathetic expression is too much. Suddenly I get an uncontrolled impulse to cry. Tears sting the back of my throat as I begin the retreat back to the cabin.

Tristan's voice stops me in my tracks. "Hey . . . can you . . . ah . . . do you want to come down to the water for a bit while Nate swims?"

Swallowing hard, I take a moment to compose myself before turning back around. Finally I shrug my shoulders. "Yeah . . . all right."

Our jaunt down to the shoreline is made mostly in silence, and I am left to question why he bothered to ask me to join them in the first place. Oblivious to the tension in the air, Nate continues to speak gibberish along with a mix of newly discovered words as we walk along the path. In the nearby distance, the ocean playfully rolls and splashes in response. When we reach the beach, Nate wastes no time wading in. "Wait for me, Nate," Tristan calls to him. "Don't go in too far yet."

Nate glances over his shoulder, apparently listening, and I am momentarily impressed by Tristan's sway of authority. For a period of time Tristan stares out at the waves as if he is searching for something. Narrowing my eyes, I follow his gaze. A few seconds later a smiling, dark form shoots out of the depths, heading toward the shallow water where Nate is standing. *Drake!* Obviously familiar with the aquatic creature, Nate squeals in response. Drake skims speedily through the surface until he reaches Nate's eager smile. Immediately the two begin interacting. Apparently satisfied with what he sees, Tristan allows his steady gaze to shift away from the swimmers. It takes me a moment to realize what is going on. Tristan has just called upon Drake to stay and play with Nate, keeping him safe and well occupied in the shallow water. I suck in a breath. *Amazing!*

Shaking my head, I turn away from Nate and Drake and keep my eyes focused on the sand. Beside me I can feel the strong presence of Tristan's form. But I can't tell if he is looking at me or not. My heart thuds loudly in my chest. Obviously there is something he wants to say to me without Nate here to interrupt. But what?

Silence surrounds us.

Holding my breath, I stand frozen in place, too scared to glance to my right or left. Beside me I can hear Tristan's feet shifting in the sand. The sound of his knuckles cracking causes a spike in my heart rate. Finally he lets out a long expulsion of air. "I wish I could remember you, Bethany."

The air exits my lungs.

Tristan sighs again, heavily. "I'm really confused. I'm not . . . I'm just not sure what to do," he says, then pauses. Out of my peripheral vision I see him kicking at the sand with his feet, apparently trying to choose his words carefully. "But I just can't remember you."

More silence.

I don't know what he wants from me. Does he want me to look at him? *Because I just don't think I can.* Fighting to breathe, I will my runaway pulse to quiet down. I don't want to lose control. *I feel like I'm going to lose control!*

"I mean, I want to be part of Nate's life if that is still okay but"— *Still okay? Still okay but what? I don't get it*—"I can't remember you . . . us."

Finally I dare to look over at him. My arms are shaking as I hug them to my chest. Running fingers through his tousled hair, Tristan glances back uneasily at me. The troubled expression in his eyes causes my heart to ache. I can tell there is more he wants to say but is having a hard time spitting it out. I clench my jaw in preparation. For a long moment he turns back to stare at the water, seemingly watching Nate and Drake who are lost in play. My eyes drift there too. The sight of their spirited, carefree interaction should comfort me. But it doesn't.

He clears his throat before continuing. "All I can . . . all I can remember is . . . Rye." *What?* A knife is stabbing me in the chest. Narrowing my eyes, I gasp for air and turn to face the sound of Tristan's voice to see if what I am hearing is for real and not just some figment of my imagination. Tristan catches my gaze and holds it for an uncomfortable moment to let me know he is serious. His green eyes are flooded with guilt as they stare into mine. "I'm not sure . . . but I think—" For a second he pauses to look away. Then he looks back. "I think I might have some type of feelings for her . . . for Rye."

Now the blade of the knife has hit its mark, sinking deep into the main arteries of my heart.

For a moment I sit in stunned silence as I wait for the bleeding to begin. Then startling into motion, I reach for my mouth to stop the gagging motion that is threatening to kick in. I feel like I'm going to puke. A worried expression covers Tristan's face as he glances over at me. "O . . . k . . . k . . . okay," I finally manage to spit out. Nodding my head, I gesture to the trail behind me. "I'm gonna just . . . I got to—." Fighting back the tears that are attempting to spill at any moment, without saying another word, without waiting for Tristan to say another word, I begin making my way down the path that leads back to the cabin at a rapid pace. I can feel Tristan's eyes on me as I make my retreat, but this doesn't change a thing. Not one freakin' thing that is said or done is going to change a thing between us ever again.

By the time I reach my bedroom, my vision is a liquid blur. Pulling open the sliding doors of my closet, I fall to my knees in a state of devastation. With sobs pouring from my throat, I reach for the handle of the searchlight that sits on the floorboards shining a blinding light up into my eyes. The overpowering glare of it causes a flash of disorientation to shoot through my brain. I shake my head to focus my gaze. Hands trembling, it takes me a few moments to locate the power switch. Without a moment's hesitation, my fumbling finger curls over the knob.

Then less than a second later, I snap it to off.

Chapter Fourteen

Immediately the crying stops.

Seriously? You had me follow you down to the beach for this?

It's this thought alone that penetrates my mind. Over and over I say the phrase in my head. My brain is numb to any other reality. There *is* no other reality! Just this one thought. Putting it on repeat, I play it over and over in my mind until finally falling into an exhausted sleep. Curled up into a ball on my closet floor, I lay beside the darkened searchlight until sometime into late evening when I awaken to the sounds of Isabel talking to Nate in the next room.

In the middle of the night after I'd tucked Nate in and woken from a fitful slumber back in my own bed, the deluge of tears starts up again. Not wanting to wake Nate, I pad into the living room on shaky legs and plop onto the couch. For the next couple of hours I pour my heart out to a throw pillow and a box of Kleenex. Finally the tears taper to an occasional, hiccupping sob. *Well, this is it—it's finally ended!* Game over.

And Rye has won!

Dabbing my swollen eyes and adding one more piece of tissue to the wadded-up pile on the floor, I finally take the time to contemplate the future. And one thing I know for sure. I never want to see Rye again. Or Tristan. Hopefully they will take their budding romance off land and settle into their new life together deep, deep down in the sea. Just the thought of Rye's gloating face as she runs around town on Tristan's arm makes me want to be sick all over again. No—if I have my way I'll never see her or Tristan again. I will just have to figure out a way for him to continue his visits with Nate without having direct contact with me.

That way comes in the form of Lucy.

"Of course, I'll do that for you." Lucy flashes me an understanding smile. She is sitting next to me on the couch with a fuzzy blanket stretched over both of our laps as I flip on the remote. We are getting ready to watch the movie *How to lose a Guy in Ten Days.* I'd called her earlier in the day to tell her I could really use a friend right then, and she'd made arrangements to come over later that evening after work to lend a sympathetic ear. Now after hearing the abridged version of my and Tristan's dissolving marriage, when posed with the question of whether she could help by bringing Nate to Tristan for their father-son visits so that I wouldn't have to see him for a while, she is happy to oblige.

I am instantly relieved. It will be one less thing I will have to worry about for a while: having to lay eyes on Tristan's beautiful physique, reminding me of what I no longer have, but Rye has instead, causing the knife in my chest to twist and plunge that much deeper.

As the opening previews begin to light up my TV screen, Lucy snuggles deeper into our blanket and looks over at me. "You know . . . every bad thing that could possibly happen in a relationship you've had happen to you. Two years ago I thought for sure that you and Tristan were meant to be together after all. But now—" she pauses to take a handful of popcorn out of the bowl that is resting precariously between both of our thighs, "after all of this has happened, I hate to say it, Bethany, but I am seriously having my doubts."

A thoughtful frown forms on my lips, but I can't disagree. Deep down I know that she is right. How much grief can one relationship withstand?

"I mean, think of all you've already gone through in the past . . . and then the accident and now Tristan's amnesia. How many people do you hear this sort of thing happening to? Next to none probably. It is so unbelievable! I can't believe that it's happening to you."

Unexpectedly the sound of laughter escapes from my lips, and Lucy looks momentarily startled. With mouth slightly agape she looks questioningly into my eyes. The surprised expression on her face only causes me to laugh harder. It isn't long before she is laughing too. Hard, gut-splitting laughter is coming from both of our throats. Soon tears are rolling down my cheeks, this time caused by hysterics instead of sadness. The release feels so good.

The popcorn that is balanced between us begins to topple, and Lucy reaches to steady it. She is still snickering. "I mean right? Am I right? This whole thing is just so insane!"

Attempting to tame the chortling sounds that are coming from my lips, I reach for the Kleenex box and begin wiping the tears that are streaking my face. "No . . . you are . . . completely"—I shake my head to stifle the giggling bursts that are still continuing to come—"right! This is ridiculous. Enough is enough, right?"

Our laughter continues on well into the movie as the heroine, Andi, works overtime trying to drive her counterpart, Ben, crazy in her attempt to *lose him*. But the bet Ben has made to *land her* is causing him to endure her annoying and foofoo antics even though it's the last thing he wants to do. And although I've watched the movie several times before—most of them being with Lucy—this time is just as funny as the first. Maybe even funnier. I have just about convinced myself that this is the perfect medication for a broken heart when at the end of the movie romance wins out. Andi and Ben are able to work through their deceptions and end up discovering that they have actually fallen in love with each other in spite of everything.

Uggh!

As the ending credits roll, I sit with my knees tucked under my chin staring absentmindedly at the list of names that are disappearing into the top of the screen. Lucy is still picking at pop-corn, but my appetite is now all but nonexistent. Setting the bowl aside, she reaches a hand toward me, resting it lightly on my knee. All is quiet around us but the reverberation of the ending theme song playing softly in surround sound. Finally my eyes leave the TV as I slowly turn to look at her. Once she has my gaze locked, she crinkles her nose. "Maybe a scary movie next time?"

I nod my head. "Yeah . . . maybe."

Lucy's lips curl into a pout. "Aw . . . shoot, Bethany, it's gotta get better. It's going to. It's just going to!"

She is right, it *has* to get better. And I am right too. *Enough is enough!* But in reality will it ever really be enough? Because even though I can attempt to erase Tristan from my mind, I won't ever be able to get rid of him for good. I will always have Nate as a reminder. Sweet baby Nate who I love more than anything. Sweet baby Nate who looks identical to his dad. Sweet baby Nate who will continue to have interactions with his dad for a lifetime, causing Tristan to be in my life for good one way or the other. The thought is deeply depressing.

That night Lucy sleeps over at the cabin, showing her moral sup-port just like we did for each other in high school. Slipping out to her car just before sunrise to get ready for work, she leaves me with a blown kiss as I snuggle deeper into my covers, not yet ready to get up and face the day. *Remember, it's going to get better,* she tells me with her eyes before disappearing through my door. But Nate has other ideas than mine as he begins stirring beside me. What starts as a babbling conversation soon escalates into cries of protest for being held hostage in his crib.

"All right, baby, I'm coming," I moan before rolling out of bed. After a diaper change, with Nate straddled on my hip I pad out of the bedroom heading toward the kitchen. On our way past my brothers' room I notice that their door is ajar, so I decide to peek inside before closing it. I know that they will appreciate the peace and quiet if I latch it shut in order to continue their newfound habit of sleeping in. A quick glance in the dimly lit space reveals a large pile of laundry next to their bunks, and it occurs to me that I must be falling behind in that area. *Odd that they didn't mention anything.* On second glance, though, I realize that what I am seeing is not clothing at all, but a rumpled pile of blankets. I push the door open a few more inches and realize that it is not just blankets that I am seeing, but a sleeping form covered in just a single blanket. *Jake.*

Now my gaze shifts to take in the bottom bunk, and I notice another sleeping form draped over the edge, as if it wants to be as close as it can to the one on the floor. The light brown, sunstreaked hair lying on the pillow lets me know it is Josh. One roll and he will be on the floor. Or rather on top of his twin. *Odd.* Had Jake plummeted off of the top bunk during the night, and if so, why hadn't I heard the crash? Or had he chosen to sleep on the floor? Glancing back at Josh's dangling limbs that are hovering centimeters away from Jake's, it occurs to me that it looks as if they are trying their best to huddle together—as if for comfort like they would when they were young boys growing up. Or as if something had them scared. *But what?* Unexpectedly a chill creeps up my spine, and I shake it away just as Nate begins to wiggle in my arms. Backing out of the entrance to their room, I softly close the door behind me before he decides to verbalize his thoughts and wakes his uncles prematurely in the process.

It's noon before my brothers stumble into the kitchen for breakfast. But that is not at all unusual. By now this is their daily norm. I am walking past where they are standing, cupboard doors ajar while they peer inside searching for something to eat, when I see Jake shove Josh out of his way. On first glance I assume this is an everyday playful gesture like the ones I'd witnessed growing up. But when Jake turns so that I can see the angered look in his eyes,

I realize that I am wrong. Josh wastes no time retaliating by punching his brother in the arm.

Jake rubs his arm and shoves at Josh once again. "Son of a bitch. I said get out of my way."

Josh's blue-gray eyes flash irritation as he takes a step to his right, now blocking his brother's way completely. "No! You get the hell out of *my* way!" *Yikes!* I am just about to step into the room to offer an intervention when Jake abruptly turns to put Josh in a headlock, his normally handsome features scrunched up with rage.

"Hey . . . hey . . . what is going on?"

At my questioning words the boys reluctantly separate, but their countenances still resonate some semblance of hostility. Periodically they shoot each other dirty looks as they stand side by side, facing me with their backs to the cupboards. Observing their unsettled expressions, I have to wonder at the transformation from wanting to sleep so closely together during the night to this now openly shared opposition.

Winding my ponytail so that it rests over my shoulder, I look pointedly into their faces. "Rough night?"

At this Jake's eyes go wide, and Josh looks at the floor. Jake is the first to speak. "Not really." His tone is flippant. "Just hungry and dumb ass won't get out of my way so I can get some food." Josh clenches his jaw and curls his hand into a fist. Hastily I clear my throat.

"How about some eggs and bacon?" For a brief moment a semblance of relief flashes across both of their faces. Picking up a container filled with banana nut muffins, I hand it over to them while raising my eyebrows at the same time. "Here, snack on these while I cook. I'll have it ready soon, and maybe your angry stomachs will settle down a bit."

"Thanks," both boys mutter sheepishly. Looking a little guilty, they settle into chairs around the table and begin munching on the food I've given them while I busy myself at the stove. Thankfully no more outbursts occur over the next hour, but I do notice that their overall dispositions are more subdued than normal.

And this doesn't change throughout the day, even when I announce that their blond girl friends, Anna and Elle, are at the door. With some reluctance they leave their lounging on the couch and go to greet the girls at the side entryway. As they walk past me down the hallway, I can't help but notice the unkempt condition of their hair. What once was borderline sexy on them has now grown into an unappealing, shaggy mess. But though I've mentioned the idea of haircuts on a couple of occasions, neither seems in a hurry to get it done. Surprisingly, it's as if they don't really care. And if the smiles that are lighting up the girls' faces as they talk to Jake and Josh on the porch are any indication, they don't seem to mind my brothers' slovenly new looks either. Shaking my head, I attempt to decide whether the attraction is in their handsome faces that are still showing through the scruffy mess.

The boys let me know that they will be taking the girls out on the boat to meet some friends in town, so I spend the day alone at the cabin playing with Nate. Due to an orthodontist appointment, Isabella won't be coming over until later in the day. It's early afternoon after naptime when I decide to appease Nate's need to be by the ocean and take him down to the beach for some closely supervised water time. After loading up a bucket of sand toys, I have just finished walking down the path that leads to the beach with Nate on my hip when I hear sounds coming from the direction of the dock. Taking a step over a patch of dune grass, I freeze in place as I spy Jake intertwined with the shorter blond, Anna, while they proceed to make out with each other next to the shoreline. Slightly embarrassed, I look away as I consider heading back to the cabin undetected. But then remembering that this *is* my beach after all, I stay my ground, refusing to be chased away. Besides, I promised

Nate, and by now I know that he understands full well the meaning of "do you want to go for a swim." So no, I'll be the one staying. There will definitely be screams of protest if I try to retreat now.

As I prepare to clear my throat in a way of announcing my arrival, Nate notices the couple mixing it up in the sand as well and beats me to the punch. "Ja ja ja," he begins calling loudly while pointing and wiggling to get out of my arms. Immediately Anna breaks free from Jake's embrace and turns to face us with a stunned look on her face. Moments later, Jake arranges himself into a sitting position and looks our way too. Expecting to see his cheeks highlighted in red from embarrassment at getting caught by his sister in the act of making out, I am surprised to find an air of boredom emanating from his eyes instead. I press my lips together and send a little wave.

"Greetings, guys. I am going to let Nate swim for a while. So if you don't mind—"

Brushing the sand from his legs, Jake rearranges his shirt. "Yeah, no problem." Rising to a standing position, he offers me an aloof grin. Anna stands as well but does not make eye contact. For a brief moment I scan the beach looking for Josh, but he and Elle seem nowhere to be found.

It isn't until almost evening that Josh and Jake both finally show back up at the cabin unaccompanied by the girls. Nate, satiated from his afternoon swim, is sitting on my lap while I read him a book. And Isabella is preparing to leave for the day. Both boys appear distant as they skulk into the house and head to their bedroom, barely offering Nate, Isabella, or me a nod. "Hey, hold up, guys. How did it go? How was your day?" *Or should I rephrase? I know how your day went, Jake, but what about yours, Josh?*

The twins freeze in place and pivot to face where I am sitting. Josh offers the reply with a trace of tedium in his voice. "Not too bad. It was okay." Out of the corner of my eye I detect Isabella shooting a look in Josh's direction, seeming to study his face. Josh avoids her gaze, almost guiltily. A type of sadness radiates from Isabella's chocolate eyes as her stare drifts back to the floor. For a brief moment I have to wonder what Josh, himself, had been up to this afternoon. Had he been somewhere on the premises with Elle, engaged in a similar activity to that of Jake and Anna? Had Isabella run into them on her way in to work? Suddenly my heart aches for the girl who continues to be so starstruck by my brother even though the love she is feeling is unrequited. Thinking back to Isabella's earlier arrival to the cabin, I try to recall the expression on her face at the time. Was there anything to alert me that she had seen more than she wanted to see on her way through the yard? Nothing significant stands out in my mind. It's hard to say whether she could have ran into Josh and Elle or whether her sadness is from the current rejection she is feeling from Josh due to his lack of eye contact or acknowledgement toward her in any way at this very minute.

After Isabella is gone for the day, I decide to ask the boys about their feelings toward the pair of blonds that seem to be making repeated appearances at the cabin.

Jake shrugs his shoulders in response. "Aaanh."

I can't hide the surprise in my voice. "Aaanh?"

Josh turns his head unhurriedly in my direction. "Yeah, mostly aaanh. I mean they're okay. But mostly boring I guess." *Really? Because the two bubbly blonds that I saw at the cabin earlier today seem like they'd be anything but boring.*

I furrow my brow. "How so?"

Once again Jake shrugs his shoulders, and Josh turns back to fidgeting with the mobile device in his hands. "I don't know how to explain it . . . they just are. Boring," Jake says.

"Well, I have to say that surprises me to hear that coming from you, Jake, especially after the way you and Anna were all over each other on the beach today. I'd say you didn't look too bored then."

If I expected a reaction from Jake, I don't get one. "Yeah, I guess." His voice holds no inflection as he begins digging in his pocket for his own phone to let me know that as far as he is concerned, the conversation is over. For just a moment Josh stops what he is doing and looks up, but the expression on his face is unreadable, offering me no answers to my questioning.

I am still contemplating the boys' blasé attitudes toward the girls—and their attitude about life in general really—over a cup of coffee the following morning when a pounding noise resonates through the open window in the kitchen, grabbing my attention. After peering through the screen and not finding the source of the sound, I grab a hoodie and my ceramic mug and head outside to see what it is all about. After a quick scan through the yard I discover one of the twins, Zepher or Seth, up on the roof of the shed, nailing away. Upon my approach the twin turns, and I realize it is Zepher. *Oh crap!* Right away I think back to the close call that we had the other day. *The thwarted kiss.* My cheeks heat up with the memory.

"Oh, hey, Bethany," Zepher smiles. "I hope I didn't wake you. I never did finish the patch work on the roof of your shed, so I thought I would try to get it—" For a moment his voice fades as he studies my face from his elevated position. "Are *you* okay?"

At this my pulse picks up in tempo, and I immediately chastise myself for not being able to keep my thoughts and reactions under control. Now my face is bright red, I'm sure. Why is it so easy for him? Did he already forget about the whole we-almost-kissed-the-other-day scenario? Was it not really that big of a deal after all? Maybe we're letting bygones be bygones and we are *still friends, right.* Well, that is good news! Relief washes over me like a tidal wave. Letting out a slow expulsion of air, I allow my shoulders to relax and will the coloring in my cheeks to recede. "Yeah . . . I'm fine. I just wasn't expecting anyone, I guess."

Zepher studies my face for a few seconds longer. "I *did* wake you then!"

"No . . . no, it's okay . . . really, I was up. But once again, thanks for the roof."

Zepher shakes his head to make light of my gratitude. "No problem. It's no big deal."

"Well, it is a big deal to me. So thanks for all you do around here."

Zepher motions to the roof. "All right . . . well, I better try to get this done before it gets too hot so—"

I begin backing away. "Okay . . . yeah. If you need anything, just let me know."

Later in the day, after Zepher has completed the roof project and is inside using the bathroom, I feel his silent approach while I sit at the kitchen table folding some of Nate's freshly laundered clothes. For a moment he stops and watches me work.

"Do you want to talk about it?" *What?*

I freeze in place and meet the concerned look in Zepher's blue eyes. The tiny shirt that I'm holding in my hands begins to slip through my fingers, and I catch it at the last second. *The kiss!* It did mean something after all! *Aw crap!* I clear my throat. "Ta . . . talk . . . about it?"

"The light."

I furrow my brow in confusion. "The light?"

"You know . . . the light," Zepher answers as if that should explain everything. Though the idea that he is not referring to the kiss after all offers me some semblance of relief, the empathetic look on his face has me feeling a little unsettled, but for different reasons. "Your closet door was opened as I walked past your room on my way to the bathroom, and I happened to notice that the light that you like to keep on all the time is no longer on."

I suck in a breath. *How does he know?* Biting my lip, I shoot him an inquisitive look. *I mean* does *he know?* I think back to the time that I emphatically stopped him from turning it off, but that wouldn't exactly explain the reason I was keeping it on. He couldn't possibly know the meaning behind the on and off button, could he? But the compassion I feel emanating from his gaze as he stares down at me is telling me he knows *something*. Now I just need to find out what. I sigh. "So what all do you know about the light?"

"I know that you've been keeping it on nonstop since Tristan went away. I also know that it must be some sort of symbol for your faith in his return." He pauses. "His return to you."

My eyes widen minutely. I guess I hadn't been all that successful at keeping the representation of the light a secret even if it was in the confines of my own bedroom closet. I hadn't been all that diligent at keeping the sliding doors shut. Maybe it hadn't been all that difficult for anyone who knew me well to figure out the gesture after all. Focusing my vision on the shirt in my hands, I begin nervously playing with the delicate collar.

"And," Zepher hesitates, his voice becoming soft as he continues, "I know that you've shut it off now, and I'm also pretty sure I know the reason why."

By the time I look up there are tears streaming down my cheeks. Using my fists, I begin self-consciously wiping them away. Zepher looks shocked. I don't think he expected this type of reaction. He takes a step toward me and then takes a step backward, seemingly at a loss of what to do now. And this surprises me. This definitely does not seem like the Zepher who a couple of days before was so eager to move in for a kiss. If anything, this situation seems like the perfect opportunity for him to put the moves on me in the guise of comforting the brokenhearted, wronged wife. Instead he seems at a loss of what to do next. Suddenly I feel the need to speak in order to make him feel more at ease.

"You are right." I chuckle lightly to cover the awkwardness of the situation, knowing that if I don't, the floodgates are going to open at any second, and then what—Zepher will really feel uncomfortable. I shake my head. "I don't know how you figured all of this out exactly. But you *are* right about the whole thing."

Zepher takes the few steps that he needs to close the gap between us. Now he is standing at my side. Reaching a hesitant hand in my direction, he wraps it around my shoulder and begins rubbing my arm. "I'm sorry," he whispers. "For your sake, I wish I wasn't right."

Nodding my head, I try desperately to fight back the tears. Finally I glance up at Zepher. "You know about Rye then?"

Solemnly he nods one time. "Yeah." His voice is a muted sigh. I swallow down the giant lump that is forming in my throat. *Oh my word, he knows! Everyone must know!* The whole sea community. I was probably the *last* to know. Zepher squeezes my shoulder. "Hey . . . what do you say we go for a walk? Maybe some fresh air will do you good. It can't hurt."

He's right, it can't hurt. After making arrangements with Isabella, I am out the door in twenty minutes taking a walk along the shoreline with Zepher at my side. Swinging my flip-flops in my hands, I allow the gritty feel of the sand to soothe my temperament, along with Zepher's sympathetic, listening ear. For more than an hour he nods his head, paying close attention to the all the sad thoughts and feelings that seem to pour effortlessly from my throat as we saunter along the winding, nautical trail that leads into town. Occasionally he offers his rather unbiased, albeit sympathetic opinion on the matter. But mostly he just listens as I talk. And it feels so comforting to have his strong, steady presence at my side.

When we reach town, he tells me with a reluctant expression on his face that he needs to go, and asks if I'll be all right walking back on my own. Never once does he attempt to give me any prolonged looks or in any way take advantage of the vulnerability of the situation by moving in for a kiss. Not even one hug. I am amazed and rather impressed by his ability to do a one eighty and respectfully back off after our previous intimate episode.

After he leaves my side and heads around a bend in the shoreline to the remote area where I know he will make his discreet entry into the sea, I take a deep breath and begin to think about heading back myself. Eyeing the waves of the ocean at my right, I roll my shoulders and notice that the weight of them has lessened considerably after pouring my heart out to Zepher's listening ear. Now although still not close to 100 percent, I feel that much more ready to face my daily life and all that the world has to offer as I think about making the return trip to the cabin. Giving one last glance toward the sea, I finally commence into motion. I am rounding Larkin Road onto Bluff Avenue, just about to pass by the pedestrian trail that leads to East Beach, when suddenly all the newfound fortitude gets sucked out of me. For a moment it takes all I can do to breathe, because stepping into my path, blocking my way, is Tristan. Just as frustratingly beautiful as usual.

And he looks pissed.

Chapter Fifteen

Stifling an audible gasp, I allow a mask of indifference to cover my face. I can't let Tristan know how easily just a simple run-in with him on a downtown sidewalk can throw my whole equilibrium out of whack. The last time we were together he made sure to let me know that he doesn't think of me in *that way*, but *is* having feelings for his childhood flame, Rye, instead. And along with having no romantic thoughts for me, he is not having *any* thoughts of me. He can't even remember me at all! *Some type of impact I made on him during all of our time together!* Suddenly it's all I can do not to spit on the ground at his feet. Instead I set my jaw and mentally plan the easiest route of escape around his firmly planted body. *By the way, why is he looking at me that way—staring all kinds of daggers in my direction?* Doesn't he remember that he is the one that gave *me* the slip?

Unable to figure it out, I send a brief salutatory nod in his direction and begin edging my way off the cement so that I pass by his well-built form without making any physical contact. *Especially since he doesn't seem to be moving an inch.*

"Bethany." Tristan says my name in return greeting to my nod. His deep voice causes me to practically jump a mile, but I cover it up by pretending like I just stumbled over a loose rock.

"Tristan," I mutter back, while doing my best to hurry on down the path that will take me out of town—as far as I can go away from him.

"Bethany, wait." *What?*

For an instant I get a strong urge to ignore the directive and just keep right on walking. Instead, I pause in place. As I plant my feet on the sidewalk, I feel his green eyes boring into my back. I don't want to turn around. I don't want to see him or talk to him at all. But after taking a deep breath, I finally begin rotating toward him anyway as if in slow motion.

And there he is, standing only feet away from me as I knew he would be, but the way he looks, *so hot*, in his white shorts and the pale green button-down shirt that is hugging his chest causes my heart rate to increase triple time. I can tell his sunstreaked hair has been freshly cut, but it is still just long enough to look windblown and sexy. *Still long enough to run my fingers through during a kiss.* Pressing my lips together, I fight to keep the runaway thoughts of indecency from showing on my face. I hate him for making me feel this way even after he's declared his feelings for Rye. As my eyes discreetly move to scan his perfectly sculpted cheekbones and soft lips, for a moment an ache in my chest emerges, becoming almost more than I can bear. Swallowing hard, I inwardly long to look away—just long enough to give my eyes a little reprieve. Instead I set my jaw and stare hard into his eyes.

The green eyes that are looking formidably back at me.

"So tell me, is it true?" *So much for niceties.* Seriously? The last time he sees me he unloads a bucket of rocks on my chest—he has feelings for Rye instead of me—and now this is how he starts up a conversation the next time we have an encounter? Has he not given any thought to how I might have been feeling since he delivered that type of life-changing, heartwrenching news?

The hostility written into his question catches me off guard. *Is what true?* I lick my lips. "I'm sorry, what?" I am surprised by how much enmity my own voice holds. My mind begins spinning a million miles a minute as I contemplate what could have sparked his ire? I hadn't tried to stop his visits with Nate after his latest announcement, so it couldn't be that. And I hadn't attempted any more deep-sea dives since the latest hospitalization, so it couldn't be that. But even if I did, *so what*, he has made it more than clear that he doesn't care about me. So by all rights he shouldn't care about how deep I dive. I blink as another thought occurs to me. Had he seen me talking with Zepher just now? Because if he is mad about that—that is just crap! He can be with someone else. But I can't? The blood in my veins begins to heat—quickly reaching a near boil.

For a moment Tristan's narrowed gaze sweeps over my face. "Are you good at tricking people?" *Again, what?* The mixture of sarcasm and disdain in Tristan's voice causes goose bumps to form on my skin. *So unlike him.* What has gotten into him? What happened to the Tristan that I used to know? The Tristan that I once loved so much?

"I'm not sure what you are talking about, but—"

Tristan runs a hand through his freshly cut hair as he interrupts. "You know, I'm just trying to put everything together . . . so I can put my life back together. And I've been hearing things about you . . . about you and me . . . and the reason why we got married in the first place."

My heart begins pounding in my chest. This is so unexpected. What do you mean *why we got married in the first place?* In a flash I return to the night of our wedding—the first night of our honeymoon on the island. And the way his gaze never left mine even for a moment while he showed me how much he loved me. All night long. All the things he said and did to me, making me feel like I was the most cherished person in the world. I press a trembling hand to my lips. *I thought . . . I mean, we got married because we . . . you and I . . . we loved each other and didn't want to be apart.* Suddenly my mouth feels dry and I have to swallow twice before I can speak. When I do my voice sounds cracked and uncertain. "I still don't know what you are talking about. I don't know what *things* you are talking about. We loved each—"

Tristan begins shaking his head, causing the words in my throat to disintegrate into the ocean breeze that is winding its way up from East Beach. "Is that what you call love? Using pregnancy to trick someone into marrying you?"

The air leaves my lungs.

What?

After a long moment I take in a breath and shake my head in confusion. Instantly my mind begins swirling in mayhem. "What"—I clear my throat—"are you talking about?"

"Is this part of your mastery at tricking . . . the ability to play dumb? Are you going to deny playing the pregnancy card so that I would marry you?"

The accusations that Tristan is throwing at me are so unexpected and unbelievable I am at a complete loss for words. Sentence fragments in my brain begin tripping over one another as I fight to organize my thoughts. Over the tree line and the tops of the summertime cottages I can see the steadiness of the ocean waves as they repeatedly advance toward the shore. Drawing strength from their equipoise, I finally look into his accusing eyes. "I don't know what you've learned about the time line of things in your past, but if you carefully study the dates of the major events of your life, you will find that the date of our marriage and the date of Nate's birthday are well past nine months apart."

"I *have* looked at those dates. But I'm not talking about Nate. I'm talking about . . . did you fake a pregnancy to get me to marry you and then fake a miscarriage after the ceremony was over to cover it up?"

Now I am angry!

My cheeks heat up in rage as realization floods through my veins. *Rye!*

"Oh my word . . . Rye told you this, didn't she?" I pause to steady my voice. "And you believe her! You flipping believe her!" *You complete jerk!* "Well, I guess it's my word against hers"—I place my hands defiantly on my hips as fire flashes in my eyes—"and I also guess you'll just have to choose who you are going to believe."

Not giving Tristan a chance to respond, on shaky legs I turn to leave, trying desperately to hang on to my anger so that the tears that are clawing at the back of my eyes will hold off a little longer. At least until I have rounded the corner that will take me off of Bluff Avenue, far away from Larkin Square, far away from the reach of Tristan's glare so that he can't see my shoulders shaking from the sobs that are about to come.

"Wait."

Tristan's voice reaching my ears causes me to stop in my tracks, but I don't want to turn around. I don't want to see all the hurt that is emanating from my eyes, for him to see all the tears that are trying to come.

"You still didn't answer my question."

Finally, reluctantly, I turn to face him. "And I'm not *going* to. Like I said . . . you are going to have to figure that one out yourself." The words as they leave my lips are low and steady—dripping with ice crystals. This surprises me. Because I didn't know I had it in me—especially now.

Obviously Tristan is surprised by my tone because now he is staring at me, perplexed, as I prepare to leave once again. With deceptive calm I turn away from where he is standing at the entrance to East Beach, all the while doing my best to hide the emotional upheaval that is taking full custody of my body.

Is that what you call love?

I am walking along a Connecticut shoreline with Nate by my side the following day, and the anger that had been present during the confrontation with Tristan has resurfaced to replace my most recent bout of tears. I had been crying on and off throughout the night, and all I have left inside of me is incensed exhaustion. I keep hearing the venom in Tristan's voice as he says the hurtful phrase over and over again in my head. *Is that what you call love?* And I really do have to question—*is that* what I call love? Because it sure doesn't seem like it anymore. The way Tristan talked to me earlier by the path to East Beach doesn't seem like anyone I could ever love. Those days of intimacy and love that we shared together are waning into the distance, becoming more and more blurred by reality.

Sometimes to the point where I have to wonder if they actually happened at all.

Except that I still have Nate to prove that they did. *But oh, that's right, I might have just taken advantage of Tristan and tricked him into my bed in order to come up with Nate too. Maybe it wasn't love at all!* Biting my lip, I clench my jaw and feel my fingers on the arm opposite of Nate tighten into a fist. *What a creep!* Out of the corner of my eye I sense Nate's blue eyes looking up at me in question.

What's wrong, Mommy? Are you okay?

Squeezing his tiny hand as it rests in mine, I send him a reassuring smile. There has been no mistake made or deception here. Nate was meant to be. And he is perfect. *Screw Tristan and his ideas! Or rather the ideas that Rye is feeding him!* Although, thankfully, he never really did say anything negative about the creation of Nate. But then again I did leave the conversation prematurely; who knows, maybe I never gave him a chance to get to the subject of Nate. Once again my free hand unwittingly forms into a fist. *I dare him to go there!*

Rolling my shoulders, I work hard to relax and let go of the angst in my mind that is eating at me. Right now I have other things to worry about—the news that had reached me of another oceanic disturbance occurring late yesterday afternoon, around the same time that Tristan had been confronting me. *By the way, shouldn't Tristan really be spending his free time worrying about the state of his ocean instead of worrying about assaulting me with false accusations?* Inhaling deeply, I let out a long, slow breath as I will the muscles in my neck and back to loosen. I am digressing. Glancing down at Nate's small frame as he toddles along beside me, I try to focus on the task at hand. As soon as I had heard about the series of miniature tidal waves that had stirred up the water off the coast by Mystic Connecticut, I knew I had to go check out the damage. The story went that after popping up unexpectedly miles offshore, the waves had thrust themselves onto land causing all sorts of havoc in the process. Now I've arrived onsite and am about to investigate the report personally.

After parking the black jeep on the outskirts of town, I take Nate in my arms and begin making my way toward the quantified scene. Once the water enters our sight, Nate immediately wiggles to get down. Now I hold a secure grip on his little fingers as we edge by the crowd that has gathered to investigate the rumored descriptions. In an attempt to avoid the mob, I snake down an unused footpath. While rounding the corner by a large steel building used for boat storage, I suddenly become scared of what I'm going to find when our view clears. Creating my own trail, I step around a section of dune grass on the side of the oversized structure, and finally the full panorama hits my vision.

On initial glance, I instinctively pull Nate close to my side and gasp for breath.

Everything is black!

What I'd expected I'm not sure, but the deluge of black that fills the shoreline is completely alarming. It's as if death has descended to swallow up the beauty of the once-shimmering blue water and the powdery sand that lined the coast. And now all that is left is a barren wasteland—a barren wasteland filled with ebony-colored mud and miscellaneous debris. Immediately Nate buries his face in my legs and begins to whimper. Picking him up, I pull him to my chest and begin slowly walking through the scattered rubble.

Soothing the back of Nate's head where his cheeks rest against my breasts—away from the view of the wreckage—I take in the pieces of strewn lumber and garbage. Piles and piles of garbage. Where did it all come from?

I am looking down at the dirt that is covering my feet and sandals, realizing that I've worn the wrong kind of footwear for the excursion—*but how could I have known*—when I notice a compilation of wood only feet from where I am standing. On closer inspection beneath the covering of murky refuse, I can tell that it had once been some type of intentional construction. For a moment I stare at the conglomeration, trying to decipher what it is that I am seeing. Then it dawns on me. *A ship.* It is a piece of an old ship. I lift my eyes to scan the rest of my surroundings and begin to notice other similar pieces, not easily detected upon first glance due to the mask of dirt and debris that is covering them. Soon I visualize what I can now tell is a rudder and a crow's nest from a wooden ship popping up from the wreckage. My vision shifts again, this time to the blackened ocean. Studying the pattern of the waves, I watch as the water splatters a murky substance onto the shore. Ensconced in the opacity, a long, pointed bowsprit floats aimlessly back and forth in the liquid. Back and forth. Back and forth. Lifeless and black.

Old ships, garbage, and miles of filth. Where did it all come from?

Turning away from all the waste and wreckage, I swaddle Nate's trembling body a little more tightly into my arms. Suddenly overwhelmed with the defiled coastline, I feel a desperate need to leave, for Nate's sake and for mine. Turning my back on the dismal scene, I begin weaving my way through the hordes of onlookers until finally making my way back to the jeep. As I am driving back to Watch Hill, I glance in my rearview mirror at Nate's car seat, and it occurs to me that there is one more stop I need to make before heading back to the cabin.

An untouched shoreline.

I need to show Nate that his ocean is still there. That it is still alive and vibrant and beautiful. That it is not a forsaken place filled with death and monsters that are trying to get you from underneath the bed. As I make a last minute decision to pull over at Tristan's beach, I secretly hope that he is not there. But I need a place that I know for sure humans don't go, a place that is completely untouched by anything but the sea and all that lives in it. The minute Nate sees the sparkling waves, he lets out a squeal of glee and rushes for the water. And I know I've just made the right decision.

"Don't go in too far," I breathlessly call to him while his toddler legs begin splashing through the shallow water. I am following close behind. For a moment Nate stops. When he turns to look at me, I notice his eyes are green and bright—possibly the greenest they have ever been. Obvious relief shines through their vibrant color, causing them to practically dance. And at that moment, I know what I need to do.

Even though I don't want to.

When I think of going near that forsaken shoreline again, a chill shoots down my spine. Even the thought of laying eyes on it from a distance is unwelcoming. But to actually spend any amount of time immersed in the depth of the rubble is not something I'd relish doing anytime soon. Probably never. No, I never want to see anything that annihilated and depressing ever again.

And yet that is exactly what I'm going to do. I'm going to volunteer to help clean it up.

I couldn't live with myself, knowing that I'd allowed the ocean and the shoreline to remain in that ravaged state. I have to at least try to repair the damage and restore the nautical landscape to its original existence—the word "try" being key. Because after viewing the condition of the wreckage, I'm not sure that it is even remotely possible. But I *have* to make an attempt. There was a time I would have done it for all mankind—to save the beauty of the earth. And then after I met Tristan, something had stirred inside of me, and I would have done anything to protect the ocean for him, and in so doing protect it for his people as well. But now—well, now it's a whole new playing field. Everything has changed.

I glance to the water and watch as Nate dives below the surface and reemerges with a spirited grin on his lips. Looking up into my face for approval, he catches my eye and attempts another playful plunge. My heart squeezes inside my chest with so much love I want to burst. Yes, now everything has definitely changed. Because now I will do anything to help protect the future of this little guy who is so lightheartedly splashing in the water in front of me.

Thick mud pours down my throat, filling my lungs—pervading every crevice of my body until it begins seeping out through my eyes and ears, through every pore in my skin. *I can't breathe!* I had gone for a swim in the ocean, but now the water has changed—completely transformed into the mud that has taken its place. Faster and faster the mud is becoming more dense, now changing into mortar. I am becoming a brick. Solid and unmovable. *I can't breathe!*

Shooting up from my supine position in bed, I fight to swallow down air while my heart palpitates hard in my chest. *It was just a dream!*

But an awful one. The sight of the ravaged ocean earlier in the day must have affected me more than I thought. Glancing over at Nate's sleeping form next to my bed, I quietly throw back my duvet and begin tiptoeing to the kitchen for a drink of water. My throat is parched. *From all of the mud?* I shudder. What a dreadful dream! *Nightmare is more like it.* My whole body is now out of sorts as a result: pulse hammering, limbs shaky, breathing depleted, esophagus dry, nerve endings on edge. Taking a calming breath, I push open my bedroom door, hoping that it won't squeak and wake Nate. But a second too late the creak in the hinges elicits a sleepy moan from inside the room. *Oh crap!* With hand on the knob, I freeze in place. Maybe if I don't make any more noise, he will drift back off.

It only takes a few moments of concentration for me to realize that the moaning sound I just heard was not coming from inside my room at all—but from down the hall. An uneasy chill shoots down my spine. *Are Josh and Jake talking in their sleep again?* Padding the rest of the way toward their room, I pause outside their door. The mumbling and groaning sounds I hear coming from inside seem restless and disturbed, not like a coherent conversation at all. Clearly one of the two of them *is* talking in their sleep. Maybe even both. Not able to stand another minute, I push open the door. As the light from the hallway casts a faint glow on their bunks, the anguished sound of the word *Freddy* echoes into the shadows of the room. The tortured way it is uttered causes my skin to prickle. *There is that name again!* Am I hearing it right? Who is Freddy? And what nightmarish significance does his name hold? Staring at my brothers' restless shapes, I wait for more words to emerge. But after one or two additional unintelligible moans nothing more is said.

"So, who is Freddy?" I ask at breakfast the following morning. I can no longer pretend that all is okay where my brothers are concerned. And as far as I can tell, the name Freddy seems to be right in the center of it all.

Josh swallows hard, and Jake almost chokes on his Frosted Flakes. But neither one looks at me. From where I am standing at the kitchen sink, I take in the faint line of a shadow that hangs below both of their downcast eyes. Their hair hangs into their face, continuing to grow more and more unkempt on a daily basis. Even their clothing seems in complete disarray: unmatched, wrinkled, and ripped. *Well, ripped means nothing where teenagers are concerned really.* But right then and there while taking in their appearances, I determine to send them both for a haircut later in the day no matter what. At this thought I run a self-conscious hand through my own hair as I draw it into a bun at the nape of my neck. For a brief moment I consider my own appearance after last night's disconcerting dream. Once more I relive the terrifying feeling of breathing down a lungful of mud, and a shudder rips through my body. It's not just the boys, it is me too—it's all three of us. We all look haunted and tired. It's like the whole house is unsettled and disturbed. *Well, with the exception of Nate.* I glance over to where he is seated in his highchair. He seems happy enough as he repeatedly shoves Cheerios into his mouth, apparently oblivious to the strain in the room.

Expecting an answer, I continue staring at my brothers. Finally Jake clears his throat. "Freddy?" he says. "I'm not sure what you mean."

"Really? You too, Josh. Does that name not ring a bell for you either?"

For a moment a look of worry seems to flash through Josh's eyes, but seconds later it is gone and his youthful, normally handsome features just look exhausted instead. He shakes his head. "Nope. Not sure what you are talking about." He takes another bite of cereal, still not looking in my direction.

"What I am talking about is you guys talking in your sleep. I've heard you more than once. And I keep hearing the name Freddy being mentioned. I am just wondering who that is and what is going on with you guys. Is this something you do often . . . talk in your sleep?"

Jake looks pointedly at Josh. "Maybe it's that guy Eddy we met from Connecticut. Remember that big wipeout he had on his surf board that day? That was pretty crazy . . . maybe that has us talking in our sleep."

For a moment Josh looks confused while Jake continues to stare over at him. Then finally he shakes his head as if to clear it, his eyes filling with clarity. "Yeah . . . Eddy . . . yeah, we were probably talking about Eddy. We talk in our sleep a lot . . . so I wouldn't worry about it too much." Finally his eyes connect with mine, and he offers me an apologetic grin. "I hope it isn't keeping you or Nate awake though."

Furrowing my brow, I watch their faces a while longer, but nothing more on the topic is offered from either of them. "No," I shake my head slowly. "No, it's not."

I am still contemplating the ominous cloud that seems to be hanging over the cabin, causing all of our nightmarish dreams and increasingly strange behavior from the boys, when Zepher and Seth show up to take Nate out for a swim. I am so happy to see them, sure that Nate could use some carefree time away from all of the hovering gloom. After the earlier interrogation at breakfast, I'm not positive that I am buying into Jake's and Josh's flippant answers over the whole sleep talking thing. But what may actually be going on with them I'm just not sure. They are teenagers after all. Who knows what all social hardships they may be having to endure? Inside I have to question, although they have each other for support, do they know they can come to me if it ever gets too bad? I make my mind up to convey this to them the next opportunity I get.

"You can go too." Seth's blue eyes sparkle playfully as they sweep over my frame. We are standing on the side porch, and I have just kissed Nate good-bye before Zepher scoops him up into his arms as they prepare to head toward the beach.

"I'm not sure, but I think I might slow you down just a little." Offering my sarcastic reply, I shoot one more look in Nate's direction. The solemn expression in Zepher's eyes as he watches my face catches me off guard. For a split second I suck in a breath, remembering. *Remembering the close kiss encounter.* Out of the corner of my eye I can see Seth looking on, his eyes darting between the two of us. Biting my lip, I contemplate the expression in Zepher's gaze. I thought after our recent platonic shoreline walk all was okay between us. Bygones were bygones.

"You could take *Blue* out, and one of us could take turns keeping you company on the boat while the other stays under the water with Nate." Concern is evident in Zepher's voice as he makes the proposal. Self-consciously I reach a hand up to smooth my hair as realization dawns on me. Maybe this has nothing to do with the almost-kiss. Maybe what I had seen in my brothers over breakfast, he is seeing in me now. How dark are the circles under *my* eyes? Maybe his concern is legitimate. Maybe I look awful!

Chuckling lightly, I try to make light of the situation. *I'll be okay, Zepher,* I tell him with my pointed glance. *Really!* "No . . . I have a lot to do around here. You all go on. Nate looks so excited . . . he can hardly wait. And that makes me happy."

Zepher studies my face for a second or two longer. "Okay . . . if you are sure—"

"Yep . . . I'm sure," I adamantly interject. As I say the words, for a moment a look of worry flashes through Zepher's eyes. But it isn't that look of worry that keeps flickering through my mind as I turn to reenter the cabin. It's the way Seth's dimples keep indenting as he works hard not to smile while standing across the yard.

Like he wants to break into gut-splitting laughter at any moment.

Chapter Sixteen

I wonder if my brothers are sneaking out at night.

I have been trying to give them the benefit of the doubt, talking myself into believing their answer about Eddy, that he is just a guy that had worked his way into their nightmares by worrying them with a surfing accident. I keep telling myself that their unkempt appearance isn't really that big of a deal. Maybe they are just going for the grunge look. I mean, teenagers do that all the time. But the more I observe their somnolent presence around the cabin during the daytime hours, the more worried I become. *Something is going on with them!* So I have to wonder, even though they appear to close their door and go to bed on most nights—are they really sneaking out of their window at some point instead? If this is true, it would definitely explain their perpetual lethargy and the dark circles under their eyes. I think back to a summer not all that many years ago when a certain girl I knew used to do that very same thing. *Sneak out the window with her boyfriend Tristan.* Without warning, my cheeks heat up.

Yes, the sneaking out of the window at night thing is a definite possibility.

And really the thought of Josh and Jake sneaking out on a rare occasion isn't all that unsettling. It's the way they are acting so dead to the world that has me convinced that whatever they are up to needs to stop. And although I'd like to ask them point-blank about it, somehow I get the feeling they wouldn't tell me the truth if I did. This disconcerting thought gives me a chill. Why do I get the feeling that whatever it is that they are up to is bad enough that they wouldn't want to share it with anyone? Especially me. It's this notion that causes me to create a plan to wait up at night and see what I can find out.

It's two o'clock in the morning when I first hear the music.

I had been sticking close to the exterior of Josh and Jake's bedroom door since they had made the announcement that they were *exhausted* and were going to *crash*. That was ten o'clock last night. I think back to the first part of the summer, remembering how for my brothers ten o'clock was the beginning of the night, the time when they were just getting energized for the next bonfire on the beach in front of the cabin or the next party in town. And now they are acting like two retirees obsessively worried about getting to bed on time. The only difference being they are not popping out of the covers in the morning like a retiree, all chipper, ready to face the day. As this consideration burns through my mind, I narrow my eyes, concentrating harder to overhear any noises that might be sifting through their door. Once again I am reminded of my conviction that there is more to the story. Because the whole thing is just not adding up.

And tonight will be the night that I find out why.

Although I had heard a brief interval of hushed tones as they first prepared for bed, there had been no more sounds or conversation to indicate they were doing anything other than going to sleep. But besides occasionally checking on Nate, out of sheer determination to solve the problem, I had stuck close to the exterior wall of their bedroom listening to the silence anyway.

The first reverberation from the beat of the song causes me to jump from where I am seated on the floor, knees bent, just feet from their bedroom door. Fine-tuning my hearing and focusing on the noise, for an interval I wonder if I just imaged the sound of music. But the longer I listen, the more I am sure that I was correct in my original assumption. A song is playing. *Now is the time.* They must just be getting up, turning on their stereo speakers—getting ready to go out for the night. *I knew it!* And now I will finally be able to confront them about all their nocturnal carryings on. Stealing over to their door, I press my ear to the wooden structure, eavesdropping—waiting for just the right time to confront them. For a fleeting second I consider going outside the cabin to wait by their window, thinking that this might be the most effective way to catch them. They must be sneaking out this way. But moments later I sink to my haunches instead. *No, better that I just wait in here, right here by their door.* Besides somehow the thought of going outside suddenly seems rather exhausting at two o'clock in the morning. *Yes, way too tiring.*

Soon I am settled onto my bottom, knees pulled to my chest as I rest my head against the wall straining to hear something—anything. Trying to decipher what song it is that they are playing. Trying to untangle any sounds that they might be making as they prepare to go out for the night. Because I don't want to miss a thing. Tonight is the night that I will finally catch them in action. But the more I strain to listen, the sleepier I become. *Crap!* Apparently I am no longer a middle-of-the-night type of person, because I can barely stay awake. Shaking my head, I pull my eyes open to clear the drowsiness. But the harder I try, the more I seem to be losing the battle. The last thing I remember is the sound of the music facing slowly away.

The following morning I wake with a start. Every part of my body aches. With a quick jerk, I move my head to take in my surroundings. *Seriously?* I had fallen asleep curled into a heap on the wooden floor of the hallway outside the boys' room. *Figures!* How could I have let this happen? Rising to a standing position, I stretch and curse over my throbbing limbs before turning the knob on their door. Not sure of what I'm exactly expecting to find, I peek inside to find both of their nestled forms, sound asleep, dead to the world.

And this proves nothing except that they are both lying less than a foot apart from each other on the floor instead of on their respective bunks. This in itself seems odd. *See, I knew it! Something strange is going on!* And I would have caught them if I had only been able to stay awake. But now as it stands I'm not sure they will ever be forthcoming of any pertinent information that will lead me to the answers I want to know. For a moment I pause in the doorway, staring at my brothers' sleeping forms. And as I do, it occurs to me just how youthful and innocent they look with their eyes closed, oblivious to the world around them. Unexpectedly my heart squeezes in my chest. For a while longer I continue to watch their resting shapes before getting called away by the sound of Nate's insistent chattering from the next room.

In the days that follow, I begin observing Jake's and Josh's faces carefully, looking for some sign of drug usage. Maybe this is what is causing the change. Although I hate to admit it, at this point I have to consider that this might be a strong possibility. It would definitely explain their peculiar, rather sluggish behavior. And although I can't rule out the sneaking-out-at-night theory because I wasn't able to stay up long enough to prove it either way, I have to face the idea that a chemical substance might be what is playing a powerful role in the boys' life.

But after trying my best to unobtrusively scrutinize my brothers' appearance, I come to the conclusion that maybe it's not drugs after all that is causing their change in behavior. While sneaking discreet glimpses at their faces while they are engrossed in their video games or staring at the cereal box over breakfast, I have discovered that their eyes—while showing signs of tiredness, a distant stare, and lined with dark circles—are not glossy, red, or dilated: signs I generally attribute to being high. But although slightly relieved about this deduction, it leaves me with more unanswered questions about the altercation in their overall persona.

And this doesn't allow me to rest easy about the whole situation. If anything, it is a greater cause for concern, because now I am in a complete quandary over what is going on. This I do know—for sure it is *something*. Even their interactions with each other have become increasingly strange. Many times when I peek in their bedroom in the morning, I find them huddled together, sleeping side by side on the floor or with one on the bottom bunk and the other close by on the floor as if they are too frightened to be alone. They don't even seem to want to be one bunk apart. And yet during the day, though they still hang in relatively close proximity, it seems as if they are completely irritated with one another. I often catch them shoving the other out of anger or making annoyed wisecracks that are laced with underlying elements of rage. And the times they are having some type of ordinary conversation, I notice they can't even look each other in the eye. It's this last oddity that gives me a sick feeling in the pit of my stomach. *Why would this be?*

On the occasions when I approach them about the changes I've noticed, they make light of the situation, inferring that I'm being a hovering, big sister and I just need to *chill.* Or else they act closed off and won't give me more than one-word answers followed by an imminent exit from the room. But if I think that their behavior toward me is curt, it demonstrates far less insolence toward me than to each other. If I didn't know better, it is as if they hate each other. *Do I know better?* Surely that can't be true. Soon I decide enough is enough—it's time to call my mom. It's time for my brothers to get away from Watch Hill and go back home.

"Hi, Bethany." Mom's voice sounds cheery as she answers the phone. More upbeat than usual. "How are things going?"

"All right." *Well, not really, but give me a few sentences before I get into all of that.*

"Oh great . . . how are the boys?" she pauses for a second, but continues before I can answer. "They don't call or text often enough. I suppose that means they are having a lot of fun. But fun or not, they still need to keep in contact with their mom . . . will you tell them that?"

"Ah . . . sure . . . but—"

"Thank you, honey. I'm sure you will. It is so nice of you to let them stay this summer. I can't tell you how excited they were to go visit you. I'm sure when they look back on it, this will go down in their memories as one of the best summers ever." *Ugh, no! No, it won't. There is something I need to tell you.* "So thank you, Bethany," she continues, buoyant and happy.

"Mom—"

"Oh, and I should tell you. I am so excited." *Yeah, I can tell.* "Your dad and I have decided to take advantage of our free time. We have decided to take an anniversary trip. Thankfully he was able to get the time off of work, and so we are just going to do it. We're finally going to do it."

I suck in a breath as my mom comes up for a moment of air. "Aw, that's . . . that's great, Mom. You deserve it." Immediately I flash back to that summer when they almost didn't make it, the summer when they were very close to getting a divorce. They made it through that and had been working hard to stay together ever since. But I know first hand just how hard *it is* to make things work. And now they are finally getting the opportunity to take a trip together, a much-deserved, probably much-needed trip. How can I ruin that for them? *But the boys.* I swallow hard. "When . . . when will you leave?"

Mom sighs happily into the phone. "At the end of the week. I wanted to talk to you first of course, but we've tentatively booked an all-inclusive in Jamaica starting this Sunday. But hey, listen to me rambling on and on. You were trying to say something to me, and I think I must have interrupted several times already. What were you getting ready to say, honey?"

"Oh . . . oh nothing. I . . . I was probably just going to ask how things were going back at home. But I can see they are going well." *And I just wanted to talk to you about Josh and Jake. I hope they will be okay, Mom, because there is something going on with them. Something strange and I'm worried. But I can't ruin your much deserved getaway with Dad, so have fun and we will figure everything out with the boys when you get back.*

Hopefully! I cross my fingers.

"Yes . . . things couldn't be better, but I better get going. I have some errands to run and some shopping to do. This is so crazy last minute. I hope I can get everything all tied up before we go."

"I'm sure you will. Have fun. You'll pull it all together. Everything will work out fine." The sound of enthusiasm conveyed in my voice is astonishing. I didn't know I had it in me. Pressing the off button on my mobile device, I sigh heavily. Because I'm not sure who I am trying to convince more, her or me.

One morning shortly after the phone conversation with my mom when I am watching my brothers' sprawled out forms on the couch while I stand in the entryway to the living room, my eyes are drawn to the television. The first unusual thing I notice about the picture on the screen in the agedness of the film. It looks to be created in the 1970s or 1980s. *Strange that Josh and Jake would be interested in something this dated.* Especially with all the high-tech recordings that are out these days. Even the music playing in the movie sounds tinny and outdated. Maybe they are just using the television as white noise—something monotonous to fill up the gloomy space. Out of curiosity, I saunter to the far corner of the room and unobtrusively glance back at the twins' faces where they sit huddled side by side, both wearing old sweat pants and ripped tee shirts; at least their new haircuts that I had insisted on look relatively presentable. But their eyes are so glued to the screen that they don't even notice that I am there. *Okay, so they are interested.*

My vision shifts back to the screen with increased inquisitiveness.

Immediately my attention is drawn to the ocean on the set: miles and miles of turquoise water filled with frothy whitecaps, lined with sandy beaches. Instantly I'm hooked too. *My favorite setting for a movie.* Soon characters are added to the set. It's a short time later when I am watching a dark-haired girl stepping out of the surf as if from out of nowhere, that my heart stops briefly and then resumes beating double time in my chest. *What is this? What are they watching?* Why do I have the unsettled feeling that this is not any old girl out for an afternoon swim? Now my eyes, too, are glued to the TV. Am I making too much of her sudden manifestation in the water due to my relationship with Tristan and my awareness of sea people? For how many minutes I continue to watch I'm not sure, but I can't seem to turn away.

But it's not until the main character, Magnus, a young man in his early twenties, speaks to a wrinkled old lady, a local in town, and finds out that the dark-haired girl who he's encountered swimming in the ocean does indeed reside in the depths of the water after having sold her soul to the devil two centuries before, that a chill climbs up my spine. Once again my eyes shoot back to my brothers. But if they detect my anxious scrutiny, they don't let on. If anything, their attention is more focused on the screen than ever. With eyes narrowed and jaws slack they stare straight ahead, seemingly taking in every detail of the events that are being played out in the film. Suddenly I can't take it anymore. Apprehension circulates throughout my voice.

"What are you watching?"

Startled, Jake and Josh look over at me, and it takes a second or two for them to answer. Clearly they hadn't realized I was in the room with them. Finally Jake clears his throat. "It's just a movie."

I furrow my brow. *I get that.* "What movie?"

"*The Bermuda Depths.*"

"Did you find it on TV? Where did you get it?" *Why can't I stop my heart from beating so fast? Why can't I conceal the urgency in my voice?*

"We checked it out of the library," Jake answers.

"Really? . . . Why? . . . I mean did someone tell you to or . . . how did you hear about it?"

Immediately Jake gets a closed-off expression on his face. *I've just pushed too far.* Josh continues to look on uncomfortably but says nothing. I stare back, waiting for some type of answer. Finally Jake seems to snap out of his momentary escape and lets out an edgy chuckle. "Geez, Bethany, why the sudden panic? You look all freaked out or something. You don't believe in this stuff, do you?"

What? What stuff—sea people and all that? I swallow hard before letting out an awkward chortle myself. Jake sits waiting for my answer with a hint of a smirk on his face, while Josh's gray-blue eyes continue to get rounder, almost appearing frightened in a strange sort of way. "No," I choke. "No . . . of course not."

It's not until the closing credits of *The Bermuda Depths* are rolling that I get a sudden inclination to extract the boys out of their lounging positions on the couch and on to more productive things. Suddenly I've had enough—seen enough. They may have to stay in Watch Hill for another week or two, but they don't have to stay idle—allowing time for their young minds to get into trouble. I can find plenty of projects around the premises to keep them well occupied. Determined to follow through on my newest idea, I proceed to tell them I have a list of things that need to be done starting with cleaning the boats down at the dock.

Begrudgingly the boys peel themselves out of their sedentary spots on the comfy cushions and begin rounding up buckets and rags to wash the boats while Isabella, who has just arrived to watch Nate, does her best to stay out of their way. But I can't help but notice the way her chocolate eyes keep straying to Josh's form every time he comes within seeing distance. Or the way her cheeks heat up in a blush each time her vision encounters the youthful muscles of his bare chest even for a few seconds. And just once I detect Josh return the favor when he thinks Isabella isn't looking. I catch the way his gray-blue eyes drink in her newly formed curves as she reaches down to pick Nate up into her arms. Or the way his gaze narrows thoughtfully as she swings her long, wavy brown hair over her shoulder.

Recent memories of their stolen glances at each other are floating through my mind an hour later when I am preparing lunch. Packing up a basket full of sandwiches, grapes, and chocolate milk, I go to find Isabella where she is playing with Nate in the living room.

"Isabella, would you mind bringing this lunch I've prepared for Jake and Josh down to the beach?"

Momentarily stunned by my question, Isabella goes still. The dimples in her cheeks indent as she contemplates an answer. For a second the brightly colored building block that she is holding in her hand almost drops, and she reflexively steadies it in her grasp. Nate detects the movement and reaches his tiny hand toward the cube. She easily acquiesces to his curiosity and allows him to take it from her fingers. "Okay . . . sure . . . I—"

Not leaving room for uncertainty or potential argument—though I really doubted Isabella would present much of an argument—I quickly interrupt the unsteadiness in her voice. "Here you go." Reaching toward her, I hand over the container filled with food. "And I have nothing pressing. I have plenty of time to watch Nate while you are gone . . . so take your time."

"Oh," she gulps. "Okay." For the second time that day I watch Isabella blush bright red, this time as she agrees to the arrangement I've just presented. And I can't help but smile as she makes her way slowly out the screen door and onto the path that will take her down to the beach, down to where the boys are working on the boats. Down to where Josh will be more than happy to take the lunch from her unsteady hands.

I've just stepped out of the shower the following morning and am contemplating what other jobs I can conjure up for the boys to do today when I hear my phone vibrating on the counter. Towel-drying my hair, I use a free hand to pick it up. It's a text from Lucy.

(Unlock) Where have you been? Been texting you all morning. Tristan is coming over . . . like now. Hope you get this soon . . .

What? Quickly I peruse my screen and discover all of the missed texts from earlier. *Crap!* I am just about to set my phone back down when I hear a *knock knock* coming from the side exterior door. For a second or two I freeze in place while my heart pounds hard in my chest. *Oh crap, it's him—already! It's Tristan.* Taking a quick glance in the mirror, I hurriedly pull on a pair of jean cutoffs and a baby blue tee shirt and head for the door, all the while attempting to comb through the wet strands of my hair with my fingers. By the time I've unfastened the locks, my initial shock at the idea of Tristan unexpectedly arriving on the premises is replaced with my former ire from the last time I'd encountered him by East Beach. *What does he want anyway?* I thought our current arrangement of using Lucy as a mediator to schedule visits with Nate was working just fine. *Maybe he is here to throw more false accusations my way.*

By the time I open the door, my jaw is set obstinately and my blue eyes are like steel. It takes all I can do not to shout "What do you want?" when I first see him. Instead, I don't say anything, and there is a momentary pause between us as he stares at me with perplexed eyes, seemingly at a temporary loss for words. Finally he shakes his head as if to clear it.

"Uh . . . hi . . . I ah . . . just wanted to—" Pausing for a moment, he begins to crack his knuckles. *Why is he suddenly so tongue-tied and doing that knuckle thing again?* As I contemplate this, a large drop of water rolls down my face, leftover from my recent shower, and I wipe it away with the back of my hand. Tristan's eyes follow the movement. I notice then that in my haste to get to the door, I'd never really dried myself off properly, and there is still liquid plastered to the skin on my arms and legs as well. *Nice!* This only serves to make me more irritated. *I should have just made him wait until I was completely dried off instead of running to the door like a swooning schoolgirl.* My fingers curl into a fist at my side, and I press my lips together as I wait for him to continue. His eyes sweep from my face down to where my tee shirt is plastered wet against my stomach and then back up again. "Yeah . . . I just wanted to stop by and see—"

"And see Nate?" I interrupt. "I thought we had an arrangement. And I thought it was working well."

"No, it's not Nate," Tristan hastily interjects. "I mean . . . sure, I'll see Nate too, if he's . . . if I can, but—" *But what, you're really here to prosecute me for tricking you into a fake marriage so you can be free to love Rye all you want? Well, go ahead and be with her. You don't have to clear the air with me.*

I sigh impatiently.

Tristan shoves his hands in his pockets, looks down at the floorboards on the deck, and then back up at me. And he looks so young and innocent and so incredibly good-looking in that moment, for a split second my heart catches hard in my chest. And immediately I hate myself. His voice, soft and steady, breaks through the spell, causing me to fleetingly shake it off. "But I just need to talk to you. Do you have a minute?"

All right, here it goes. I glance at the hallway behind me and then resignedly back in Tristan's direction. "Yeah . . . okay. I have a few minutes." *Make it quick.* "Nate is napping right now."

For some unexplainable reason, Tristan looks slightly relieved, and I figure it's due to the fact that I am not hiding my crossness over him being here, so he can't be confident of whether or not I'll agree to a conversation with him. He is probably smart enough to realize that my irritability is due in large part to our last encounter and how much I didn't appreciate his allegations. I also hope that by my stern presentation I am helping to lay the groundwork, letting him know that I am not interested in more of the same. No more accusations. So if that is what he is here for, he can just be on his way and exit the way he came.

"Do you want . . . can you come out?"

I nod my head and step out onto the porch.

Tristan leans against the porch railing. "I get the sense that you are busy, so I'll get right to it." *Okay?* My eyes stare into his formidably as I wait for the blow. For a split second Tristan appears to hesitate. Then he looks right at me. "Can you tell me all you remember about my cousin Keuran's death?"

I suck in a breath. *I should have known!* I should have known she would go there. *Rye!* I should have known that she would convince Tristan that Keuran's death was my doing—my fault. And in many ways it was. But Tristan had never made me feel that way. He had assured me that Keuran's innate evil was his own undoing, causing his death. But now standing here on my side porch being faced with the task of having to recap the whole scenario to Tristan, nothing seems all that black and white anymore. Maybe Tristan's memories about Keuran are of a blood relative that he grew up with, who was for all practical purposes his brother—*not an enemy*. The closest thing he would ever have to a brother. And now I have to tell him just how I went about destroying that for him. Suddenly all my ire from earlier is gone. And all that is left is a quiet sadness—a resignedness. *Okay, just shoot me now. I did it!* Inhaling deeply, I heave a long, slow breath. "What do you want me to say? Whatever you've heard . . . just go with it. Let that be your truth. I don't see what else I can say to add to the story that will be of any help."

Narrowing his eyes, Tristan runs his hand through his hair. "Still

... if you don't mind I'd like to hear it from you ... I'd like to hear what you have to say."

Biting my lip, I pull my arms across my chest in a hug. Suddenly I'm cold. "I don't see why you need a reaffirmation from me—it's not going to change anything—" *It's not going to make you believe or not believe me. It won't change your opinion of me or your feelings toward me.* "But here it is ... I didn't believe you that Keuran had ah ... issues ... so I continued to hang out with him the summer of 2016, stirring up all sorts of trouble ... finally provoking his anger enough to have him display a show of force towards me. You arrived on the scene to save me. There was an altercation between the two of you, and Keuran ended up getting killed in the process. It was all my fault." Pausing, I begin to soothe the unwanted goose bumps that are forming on my arms. "Is that story close to the one you've been told?"

Silence.

Please, don't do the silent thing. Freaking say something! On second thought, no, don't say anything. I don't need this. I'm out of here. Pivoting on my feet, I prepare to leave. Suddenly, Tristan's head shoots in my direction. And I can't help it; in spite of my determination to escape the scene, my gaze is drawn in by the puzzlement and contemplation I see reflected in his green eyes. Like everything is *not* cut and dried to him after all. Like he is trying hard to figure something out. I freeze in place.

"Keuran wasn't a good person, was he?" Tristan's voice is deep and pensive. It's more of a reflection than a statement or question. What does he want me to say? Does he want me to say anything at all?

I shake my head faintly, my eyes now glued to Tristan's.

"And," he pauses, as if realization is just dawning on him, "he didn't like me all that much, did he? In fact ... in fact, he hated me."

What do I say to that? I am not going to be the one to tell him. "I ah ... well—"

Suddenly Tristan straightens into a standing position, seemingly in a rush to leave. "Never mind. Okay, well thanks. Thanks ... that's what I needed to know." He begins backing away until finally completing a one eighty. "I'll, ah ... I'll guess I'll see you," he hastily calls over his shoulder as he prepares to exit my porch.

My forehead furrows in confusion as I stand, stunned, watching his retreating form. *Glad I can help?*

Chapter Seventeen

"So tell me, what was that all about?" Lucy's chocolate eyes are inquisitive as she glances over at me while we walk along the beach of Napatree Point. After having dinner with work friends at the Olympia Tearoom I had run into Lucy on the sidewalk outside of the restaurant. From there she suggested going for a quick jaunt out to the point, giving us a chance to catch up with each other. "Why did Tristan suddenly need to come over so bad? I thought you guys kind of had this unspoken rule about using me as the go-between for visits with Nate. Did he decide to come over and get Nate himself this time?"

Attempting to tuck a strand of my blond hair behind my ear, I contemplate Tristan's visit. *What was that all about?* Clearly he was on a mission to find out more about the death of his cousin Keuran. But what I had originally thought was going to be a finger-pointing session turned out to be quite the opposite. In the end it didn't seem like he was accusing me of anything at all. *Go figure.* I shake my head, and immediately my unruly wisp of hair pulls free into the wind once more. "You know, I'm not sure exactly, but I think he is trying his best to put the pieces of his life back together." *Excluding me, of course.* "And his cousin Keuran was a big part of that. He must have felt the sudden need to know more about his death."

Lucy picks up a handful of sand and lets the grains slowly slip between her fingers. Having reached the point, we've stopped walking and are standing, watching the foaming surf as it spills repetitively onto shore. Finally she looks over at me, and for a split second a token of sadness passes over her countenance. Right away I interpret the look as empathy. "So how did it go . . . did you tell him what happened?"

I nod, trying to recall all that Lucy actually knows about the circumstances surrounding the death of Keuran. Not much really, except that he had had a tragic accident. "Yeah . . . I told him. But I'm not sure if it helped or not. I don't know, in some way I think it might have jarred his memory a little, the way he acted like all of a sudden he was remembering something." I shake my head. "But I'm not positive really . . . I guess I'm just not that sure about anything when it comes to Tristan anymore."

"I know what you mean." *What?*

My head shoots in Lucy's direction. The sadness that I had detected moments before now seems tenfold. Now she is kicking her foot repetitively at the sand. "How is that?" I question.

Lucy sighs and I can't help but notice the radiance of her natural beauty in spite of her apparent glumness. *What is going on with her?* This new melancholy mood is so unlike her usual upbeat personality. "It's Ethan," she murmurs.

"Yeah?" My voice is soft, encouraging her to go on.

"Yeah . . . he's . . . I don't know, acting funny lately. Strange, I guess."

"Really . . . how so?"

Lucy shakes her head. "I don't know . . . it's probably not that big of a deal. It's most likely nothing. Nothing I need to bother you with at least."

My eyes go wide, and I deftly proceed to nudge her in the arm with my elbow. "Are you kidding me? How many times have I burdened you with all of my problems? Big deal or not . . . you better tell me."

At this Lucy sends me tentative smile. "All right . . . he's just acting kind of distant lately. Closed off. And when he goes out with his friends he is staying out later and later." Pausing, she lets out a long, slow breath and begins playing with a topaz ring on her finger. "One night a few days ago he didn't even come home at all."

Yikes! I hesitate. My voice comes out concerned and soft. "Have you . . . talked to him about it?"

"I've tried, but like I said he's being closed off so I'm not getting much in return. And then after he didn't come home the other night we haven't"—Lucy's lip begins to quiver ever-so-slightly—"spoken since."

"Aw, baby." I pull her into my arms. *I knew it! Ethan Vaughn is a player! He's got to be—someone that looks and acts like him.* In spite of Lucy's attempt at bravado, her tears begin to emerge, wetting the skin that is peeking out from my tank top as she cries into my shoulder. "I'm sorry . . . Give it time. Maybe it will all turn out okay. And if not . . . he doesn't deserve you." *That creep!* "You are a beautiful girl . . . inside and out . . . you only deserve the best. And he is blind if he can't see that." *Why do these words sound so familiar?*

Lucy continues to cry softly as I stroke the back of her head with my fingers. How strange it is to be on the other end of things, soothing my best friend instead of being soothed. My heart aches for her because I know what she is feeling all too well. Either way it is no fun—hurting inside for yourself or hurting for someone else. But regardless, I will be there for her no matter what. She's been there repeatedly for me all of these years.

Pulling back from me, Lucy begins wiping her cheeks with her fists. "Sorry," she says, her lips forming into a sheepish grin in spite of the liquid that is still shimmering in her brown eyes.

"Hey," I say, while reaching up to wipe away one tear that she missed. "Don't be sorry. You needed to cry. You'll get through this. We'll get you through this together." *We'll get through all of this together.*

We always do.

I am dropping off a completed work project at the Center for Marine Studies of Rhode Island the following morning when I come upon a group of my co-workers all huddled around a cubicle. *What's up?* Right away I wonder if the cluster is a work-related gossip party or something bigger. Curiosity getting the best of me, I head over to the assembly, exchange a few hellos, and ask what is going on.

"You haven't heard?" a dark- haired guy named Joe asks. "There was a huge explosion of water in the ocean last night . . . like a tidal wave . . . huge."

At his words, all the nerve endings in my body instantly stand on end. "No, I hadn't heard . . . where at?"

"Just off the coast by the Rhode Island/ Connecticut state line. Right now they are saying some boats are missing. Search teams are out, but they haven't detected any sign of them yet. It's been all over the morning news."

"*Really . . .* what type of boats?"

"From what I've heard a couple of private yachts, some fishing boats, and a dinner cruise."

An uneasy feeling settles into the pit of my stomach. "Wow, that's—"

"It's scary is what it is," a girl named Mandy who has now taken over my cubicle since I've elected to work mostly from home after the birth of Nate says. "They are saying it was completely unpredicted. So if that is the case, how can anyone feel safe going out on the ocean? Something like this might arise at any time, and if you are out there in the water when it happens, you are screwed. As it is, it did some damage on land too."

Visions of a black shoreline fill my mind—the shoreline I'd been helping to scour in my spare time. *What a mess.* Even with city and volunteer cleanup crews working diligently on a daily basis, the damage was so extensive it might take months or years to restore the nautical landscape. Now from the sound of it, there will be even more to do. *What is going on? When is it going to stop?* It is only getting worse. Now boats are missing—people are missing—swallowed up in the tidal wave explosion. *Yes, something is definitely going on.* And it doesn't seem to be related to weather patterns. It seems to be directly related to the sea itself. And although I don't understand how that is possible, and because I know that there is a whole world of fellow-humans who wouldn't understand how that would be possible either, I realize I need to talk to someone about the situation who might very possibly get what is going on. An expert in the field. An expert who is the last someone I want to approach and discuss the matter with. But a someone I need to contact none the less.

Tristan.

I close my eyes and inhale deeply. I don't want to chase Tristan down so I can confer with him about the increasing oceanic disasters. But what choice do I have? He is my best solution for getting some answers—for getting to the bottom of the problem. *If there even is a bottom to the problem.* Yes, Zepher and Seth are an option, but neither are the experts that Tristan is on the matter. But if I do end up tracking him down, how he will react when he sees me? Will he treat me coldly or with contempt? Is he still carrying around the thought that I'd tricked him into marriage? The last time he'd come over, he was still obviously searching for answers about how his relationship with me had affected his life. And I'm sure many of the scenarios of our time together may be coming out looking tainted, less than picture perfect. Especially when portrayed from Rye's dishonest perspective.

Rye!

A new thought occurs to me—when I do find Tristan, what if he is not alone? What if he is with Rye? Suddenly my stomach feels queasy. What will I do then—if I see them together? Will I just turn around and walk away? *Run away?* Is getting to the bottom of the sea disturbances really worth all the potential trouble I might encounter along the way? Swallowing down the feeling of unease that is screwing with my thoughts, I fill my mind with resolve, jump in my car, and head toward the place where I know I will have the greatest chance of finding him.

I have parked my jeep and am winding down the path that leads to his secluded beach when one more consideration flashes through my head. Will discussing the recent sea problems stress his recovering brain? I had been instructed to let him heal in his own time. Will focusing on this dilemma be too much for him? I don't want to put an added strain on his mind. But surely he's faced the topic on some level already. He *is* back to work after all. Sifting through the uncertainty of my thoughts, I make a final decision and round the bend that will lead to a clear view of his private inlet. *Here goes.*

When I first see Tristan, part of me is relieved that he is there, alone. *I really do need to talk to him about what is going on with the ocean.* And yet a part of me wants to turn around and retreat the way I came. *What was I thinking?* We don't even share that type of familiar relationship anymore—the kind where I can easily approach him about a heartfelt topic and expect him to confer or empathize with me about it. But now here he is less than a basketball's throw away, and any second I will certainly draw his attention, and he will turn to see me and what then? Suddenly I can't breathe. Just the idea of speaking to him has me completely tongue-tied and flustered.

While these anxious thoughts are pummeling through my mind, I imagine that I hear the sound of a musical chord being strummed on a guitar. For a two-second interval my heart pauses in my chest, and I freeze in place watching where Tristan sits bent over an instrument, plucking on the strings. *It's his guitar!* Strumming two more chords, he pauses, then begins to play what sounds like a little ditty. Now my heart pounds hard. *Oh my word—that tune.* My jaw goes slightly slack. *It sounds like our song.* Instantly my mind becomes a chaotic mess, and my breathing comes in loud hisses. Scared my deafening exhalations might give my presence away, I lift a hand to my face in an attempt to cover my mouth. But he doesn't look my way. Instead he stops playing only briefly, then attempts a few more chords. And they sound so familiar—so close to the real thing that I find myself holding my breath, wishing. Willing it to happen. *Doing everything in my power to make the song take off on its own accord.* He stops, then starts one more time, nearing precision—right on the verge of breaking into a recognizable rhythm. I keep shaky fingers pressed to my lips, silently encouraging. *Keep going, Tristan. Keep playing.*

Eventually he relaxes the guitar marginally in his arms and closes his eyes like he trying hard to remember something. *Trying to remember the chords and melody to the song—our song.* The thoughtful look mirrored in his expression along with his finely chiseled cheekbones suddenly makes me feel weak all over. In a blink of an eye I want him all over again. So completely, it hurts. And although the logical part of my brain is sending warning alerts to my heart, renewed hope begins to surge through all of my veins. *Please remember, Tristan.*

Signaled of my presence by some unknown influence, Tristan snaps out of his reverie and turns in my direction. When he sees me, a startled expression crosses over his face. For a long second our eyes lock, and then we both look away self-consciously. So much has happened in the past month since his return, none including this type of unsettling connection between us. Now all of a sudden seemingly out of the clear blue, here is this awkward moment, and it seems we both don't know what to do. I clear my throat.

Lifting my hand uncertainly, I point toward his lap. "Your . . . ah . . . it sounds good."

Tristan's green eyes shift to his guitar, looking slightly relieved that I have been the one to break the uncomfortable moment of silence. "Oh ... yeah ... thanks." He shrugs his shoulders. "I've been picking it back up ... playing with it a little bit lately. Nothing fancy ... just—"

His voice fades into the sound of the surf and when it becomes apparent that nothing more is going to emerge from him, I begin nodding my head in an effort to take up where he left off. "It's good though ... yeah, it's ... it's good."

At that he looks over at me with an almost timid, schoolboy-ish smile. Unexpectedly a swarm of butterflies begins to flutter in my stomach. Lacing my fingers together, I bite my lip. *Oh my word, what is going on here?* For an instant a flicker of surprise or something else registers in Tristan's eyes, then he sucks in a barely detectable breath and turns to face the ocean.

I follow his lead and turn in the same direction. In spite of all the disconcerted energy that is flowing through me, I am immediately pulled in by all the sparkling blue water and the stateliness of the waves. Digging my feet into the sand, I watch while a sailboat rocks gently in the outlying surf as it veers toward the horizon. Beyond the boat I detect a familiar black head bobbing up and down, waiting patiently, biding its time. *Drake.* I can't help but smile. High above a seagull soars and swoops, looking for his next place to land. Allowing his wings to glide, he keeps an eye out for a jutting rock or a floating piece of driftwood—any piece of solid material that seems like a transitory safe haven in the midst of this giant, stirred-up body of water. *The ocean!*

Oh yeah, the ocean.

Suddenly the original purpose for going to Tristan's beach comes bursting into my brain. Bending over to pick up a partially hidden seashell from the pale granules at my feet, I turn away from the water, looking Tristan's way instead. His gaze is still focused out to sea. Under partially lowered eyelashes, I view his profile. The carved angle of lightly tanned cheekbones peeking out from underneath his tousled, blond hair causes me to momentarily digress. Once again I almost forget about what I came here to ask him. Swallowing hard, I shake my head to clear it. "Hey," I pause, and he looks over at me, causing my heart rate to accelerate marginally. I ignore it and keep talking. "So have you heard about all of the recent tidal waves and disturbances in the ocean?"

He is just beginning to nod in answer to my question when I hastily interrupt. "Wait a minute . . . what am I saying? Of course you have. The ocean is your life . . . it's not like what happens in it is a secret or anything. We are probably just beginning to discover the coming and goings of the ocean here on land when it's already old news to you and your people."

Tristan sets his guitar next to him on a piece of driftwood. Hopping up, he runs fingers through his hair. "Yeah, pretty much."

"So you've visited the aftermath then . . . seen all the damage?"

This time Tristan's nod is solemn and thoughtful. "I've seen it." For a moment our eyes connect, and the disconcerting depth of the destruction is conveyed between us. An involuntary shudder escapes me, and I look at the ground. At the crème-colored sand that is lightly sprinkling over my toes—gracefully blanketing the shoreline, extending out for miles onto the ocean floor. Without warning the pale granules transition to a murky hue in my mind, and I shudder.

"What you saw . . . was it all black?"

Tristan lets out a long, slow breath. "Yeah."

"It's pretty bad, isn't it?" Shaking my head, I close my eyes in reflection, calling to mind every inch of the seaside ruins. When I open my lids again, Tristan is watching me with a puzzled expression on his face. My heart rate accelerates. He looks away and shoves his hands in the front pocket of his jeans. The repetitive sound of the waves swallows the transitory burst of silence that is hanging in the air. For a moment I begin to wonder if he is going to confirm my questioning statement at all. When he finally speaks, his deep voice causes me to practically jump.

"Yeah . . . it's bad," he confirms, then pauses. "I don't really think all of this stuff going on—the wave surges, the blackened water, and the sunken pieces of ships and other paraphernalia emerging—is just random. I think this is something big. But I'm not sure what." Walking over to the water's edge, he wades a foot into the surf, and I briefly wonder if he's decided our conversation is over—he has said all he is going to say on the matter and is now heading out to the waves, getting ready to make his exit. This thought makes me sad. I remember back to all of the times in the past when he had confided in me about the state of the ocean, about the pollution and damage inflicted on it at the hand of the human population. And then I recall how we had shared our love for the preservation of its beauty, making it a healthy place for everyone—for those that reside in the sea and on land. Now those days are gone, and by the way he is easily dismissing our conversation, he apparently doesn't want to include me in any future plans.

Awkwardly shuffling my feet in place, I contemplate whether this is my cue to leave. My face heats up with uncertainty, suddenly feeling stupid for having come here in the first place. I should have known. Tristan and I don't have that type of familiar relationship anymore. What made me think I could just come here and discuss this with him and arrive at a solution? I should have known he wouldn't be interested in discussing it with me. But *really*? Is he really just going to walk away without even a good-bye? I inhale a sharp breath as disappointment begins to mix with irritation.

Tristan stops walking, the water now up past his knees, and I hold my breath. *Now what? Should I leave or stay?* Turning toward me, he reaches down into the surrounding liquid and scoops up a handful of grit and tiny pebbles. Appearing to study the contents in his upturned palm, he lets it all slip slowly though his fingers. *Maybe he is not leaving after all.* "At first I thought it might be due to offshore testing"—the sound of Tristan's voice delving into the particulars of the case sends an unexpected flurry of relief through my chest—"but now I think there is more to it. Something else is going on. All the disturbances are affecting my people, throwing off their equilibrium, causing unexplained dizziness and nausea . . . things like that."

"I can see why. The times I've witnessed the momentary fluctuation in the pattern of the waves, everything, all the fish, everything, seems topsy-turvy. That's enough to throw off anyone's equilibrium. And—" I pause. "I've been thinking . . . lately, as I've been helping to clean up the shoreline down on the Rhode Island /Connecticut state line, a thought has occurred to me. Maybe it's not the land that needs to be focused on so much . . . maybe it's the ocean. I think that—"

At this, Tristan casts me a surprised glance, interrupting my train of thought.

I stop talking as I study his expression. He seems to be looking at me funny with a whole new light reflecting in his green eyes. My breath catches in my throat. "What?"

"I don't know . . . it's just that *you get it.* I mean you are exactly right. Many don't get that it's not the cleanup of the shoreline that needs to be focused on. It's the ocean. Cleaning up land is like treating the symptoms instead of the disease. The focus needs to be on cleaning up the ocean, and then homeostasis can be restored and the disruptions and all the ugliness will stop." Goose bumps form on my skin. Although I wasn't trying to impress Tristan with my insight into the situation, inside I am secretly pleased that I have. "And I have a strange feeling," Tristan continues cautiously as he watches my face for a reaction, like he is unsure how I am going to receive what he is about to say, "that it's the ocean itself that we are dealing with here. It's almost as if the sea is trying to purge itself from the threatening levels of pollution that have accumulated over a period of many years, the pollution that continues to only get worse."

The sea personified. The thought sends an unanticipated chill spiraling up my spine. Nodding my head in agreement, I attempt to show that I do get it, that I believe what he is saying. We are completely on the same page. Instantly a measure of relief passes over Tristan's features.

He blinks. "I have a hunch if the polluting doesn't stop, the effects of these disturbances are only going to get worse and worse."

"What can we do to make it stop? There has got to be something—"

Again Tristan glances over at me in bewilderment. Like I completely dumbfound him. "Do you want to *help*? I mean—" His tone is incredulous. *Why is he is looking at me like that?* Suddenly I feel tongue-tied and uncertain.

"Yes." My one-word answer comes out choked and soft, and at first I don't think that he hears me.

But when he says, "Well let's make a plan then," I know that he does.

Chapter Eighteen

Soon after digging into the meat of the matter, the unease that is hovering between Tristan and me fades into the salty sea air, and we are able to focus and formulate a plan—a desperate, large-scale plan to halt pollution on the East Coast. Tristan will talk to his work, NEC Systems Group, about aiding and backing him in spreading the word to all Atlantic harbor cities. All pollution must stop—effective immediately. Even the type of pollution that companies are pretending doesn't exist, like the attitude—*this little bit of dumping won't hurt anything, and it meets code, so it's okay*. It has to end—pronto.

After running back to my car to grab my laptop, I begin to formulate ideas to add to the plan while Tristan looks on. As I pull up the Ocean Conservatory's website, the title International Coastal Cleanup catches my eye. Scrolling through page after page of information, I begin reading about the worldwide effort to establish a day for volunteer cleanup of our oceans and shorelines. Although the cleanup is set to take place later in the fall, I have the idea that we can copy their example and implement something similar on a smaller scale—concentrating on the Atlantic, moving up the date to suit our urgent need.

Eyes quickly skimming link after link on the site, my attention is drawn to the Trash Free Seas Act, which is set in place to increase the national focus on marine debris. A flash of light goes off in my mind. I will contact the senate for exigent help. Massive amounts of cleanup effort need to begin straightaway.

Or we all may be in danger.

Later that evening while allowing Nate to crawl across my lap, I sit with my back resting against the couch on the living room floor and begin perusing the screen on my mobile computer once again. The minute Tristan and I parted ways on his beach earlier in the day, desperate to get our plan into action, my research had begun as I hunted for contacts and phone numbers. Now after a short break to eat dinner, I am back at it again. With the worsening sea disturbances increasing at an alarming rate, how much time will we have before the devastation is irreversible? And even if we do implement a massive effort to reverse the problem, will it be enough? Will the ocean put a halt to all the destruction and the furor it is now sending our way? Or is it too late? All of these years we've spent giving very little thought to destroying its crystal-clear waters, and now, finally, it is fighting back. If we raise our white flag high in the air, will it have any effect on the ocean's maritime depths?

Not if our actions don't match our desperate pleas.

"Mom ma ma ma," Nate says as his chubby little fingers reach for my face. His inquisitive blue eyes seem to be searching mine as he pulls on my hair to steady himself. *What is it, Mommy? What is making you look so worried?* Pulling to an upright position, he now stands balancing himself on my legs, blocking the view of my PC.

Setting my computer off to the side, I lean forward to kiss his nose. "It's the ocean, baby. Your ocean. For years we've been making it all dirty, and now it is finally really mad. It's time to reverse our mistakes. Say we are sorry and take action. It is time to make the ocean happy again." Brushing a lock of Nate's blond hair off of his forehead, I smile into his gaze in an attempt to soften the harshness of the message. A one-year-old boy shouldn't have to worry about things like this. "And that is what Mommy is working on. Mommy is going to try to do her best to help make it all okay again . . . Daddy too."

Nate crinkles his nose, making me laugh. *Such a silly face! Why is he doing that?* Then it occurs to me: I'd had been crinkling *my* nose as I was telling him the tale of the ocean's troubles. He is mimicking me. And he looks ridiculously cute in all his efforts. A warm feeling settles in my chest.

"Baby Nate, you are too much," I chuckle.

"Wa wa wa," he says in return. Dubiously I shake my head as I study the expression on his face. It's almost like he gets it—what I'm talking about—the water, *his* water. But I know that he can't really understand. It isn't possible.

"Someday, baby. Someday I will tell you all the ins and outs of everything in greater detail. When you are older—much older. And then you will understand. Hopefully by then it will all be history, and the world will be a better place. And you will just waggle your head in disbelief about how we treated the ocean so cavalierly for all of these years."

I have just finished talking when Nate stops all babylike antics and stares deeply into my eyes. The baby-soft pads of his fingertips slide down the sides of my cheeks, eventually adding just the slightest pressure as if to focus my head in his direction. And then right in front of my watchful gaze his blue eyes transition to green. Vivid emerald green, the color of the sea on the brightest sunny day. Goose bumps cover the skin on my bare arms. I don't look away. I can't look away.

I understand, Mom, he tells me through his exposed manifestation.

I swallow hard. *Okay, okay baby, I get it. You do understand.* Breaking our gaze, I pull Nate's head to my chest and proceed to cradle him in my arms while running my fingers through the silky strands of his hair. *Though I don't know how or why, I get that you do understand.* Resting my chin on the crown of his flaxen-colored mane, I breathe in his toddler scent, so powdery-fresh and innocent.

"Well, you understand then. You understand that Mommy has lots to do, lots to do to help make everything all right again."

Nate lets out a quiet sigh and snuggles deeper into the comfort of my embrace.

The sun beats down heavily on my shoulders as I stand behind my jeep out in the parking lot of McQuades Market Place. Arranging and rearranging. I am trying to fit the last of my grocery bags into the rear compartment. But I've apparently bought too much, and each time I try to close the hatch it doesn't fasten. *Blast it!* I arrange and rearrange some more. Isabella is back at the cabin watching Nate while I do my best to squeeze a few errands in between all of the recent business of helping to initiate the coastal cleanup. I am about to slam the rear gate one more time when a grocery bag topples from its volatile position and sends a series of grapefruits and oranges rolling on the pavement's downhill incline away from the car. "Aw, piss!" *I don't have time for this.*

Right then a deep chuckle grabs my attention. "Need some help?" My heart rate increases marginally. *Tristan.* Turning to meet his form, I find him scooping up wandering fruit, a glint of humor in his eyes. He straightens with a deftly acquired armful and lifts an oversized orange into the air. "Troubles?"

I roll my eyes and sigh. "I guess I should have listened to my mom . . . *hurry doesn't help.*"

Tristan walks over to where I am standing, one hand resting on a precariously positioned bundle of purchases in an effort to keep them from plummeting to the ground as well. Reaching behind me, he places the produce in a safe place. I try not to notice that the strong muscles of his arms are only inches from mine, or that he is standing so disconcertingly close, parts of our bodies are almost touching. *Just one move to the left and*—I blink. He doesn't feel that way about me anymore. I shouldn't feel that way either. "Busy these days . . . the ocean cleanup?"

"Yeah."

Tristan motions for me to let go of a lopsided bag while he takes possession of it, allowing me to straighten and level the other two that I had been trying to juggle. His hand brushes over mine in the process. Fire shoots across my skin, and I work hard to fight back a blush. For a second Tristan does a double take in my direction, standing so close by. But then just that quickly he looks away again and steps back from the jeep. "There . . . I think everything might stay this time. Try closing it." As I swing the hatch shut, this time successfully, Tristan resumes talking behind me. "So I've been wanting to run into you . . . wanted to find out how our plan is coming along."

I turn around to face him. "I think it's going well . . . the coastal cleanup is a full scale operation. It seems like the sense of urgency is catching on—" I stop talking as Tristan runs his fingers through his hair. For a quick moment the normally tan skin on his cheeks turns pale. He shakes his head and the color returns. I furrow my brow. "Are you okay?"

He laughs lightly, almost nervously, and glances up at the sun. I look up too. *It is hot out but*—He clears his throat. "I guess I've been busy too. Maybe *too* busy . . . I haven't paid attention to the time." For an instant he regards me uneasily like he isn't sure if he should share anything more. But then finally he continues. "I ah . . . think I might have been out of the—" He motions to the ocean behind him.

"Out of the water too long, you mean?"

As soon as the words leave my mouth, Tristan shoots me a questioning look laced with a measure of relief. Relief that I understand about the whole he-needs-to-be-in-the-ocean-every-so-often thing. *I was living a married life with you, you dumb shit. Of course I know about that.* Inwardly I sigh. He really *doesn't* remember. He nods his head. "Yeah . . . I think so." Jerking his thumb behind him, he continues. "Hey . . . I really want to talk to you some more about all that we have going on with our plan so far, but I just . . . I just need a minute. Would you, ah . . . mind . . . would you wait for me while I take a swim?" He stops and sighs, pointing over his shoulder toward the ocean once again. "I really need to take a swim right now."

Unobtrusively I peruse my watch. I really am in a hurry. I still have so much to do today: put groceries away, meet with two more city commissioners, have dinner with Nate, and help with the beach cleanup to the north. Lifting lowered lashes, my eyes land back on Tristan. And he is standing there looking so sexy and uncomfortable from having too much air and sun. And yet hopeful at the same time. *Hopeful?* My pulse begins to thud. When had I ever been able to say no to him? "Okay . . . yeah, I'll wait."

Tristan has me follow him down a shoreline trail until he reaches a secluded area. Sending me one last glance over his shoulder, he wades into the water and dives below the surface. Then I am left alone to pace the beach while he swims somewhere below the waves. Minutes feel like hours. How long will he be gone? Hugging arms to my chest, I continue to wander through the growing tide, stopping and starting, shivering in spite of the hot sun. Why am I so nervous anyway? This is a business meeting, nothing else. I am the one who went after Tristan to get some help, to confer and lay out an agenda for getting to the bottom of the matter. To give it one big, hearty try. I owe it to Nate. We both owe it to Nate. And now this is just a follow-up visit, you might say.

Still my reaction to Tristan's wet body as he reemerges from the water feels like anything but a professional encounter. Running fingers through dripping wet hair, he finally reaches my side. And I just can't deal with the sight of him—swallowing hard, I look away.

"Hey . . . you okay?" His voice is soft coming at me while I inhale a long, slow breath. *Oh my gosh, he just doesn't get it!*

Shaking my head to clear it, I look back up. "Yeah . . . I'm fine." His green eyes staring at me with a combination of confusion and concern are almost my undoing. I blink. "So anyway . . . how are things going on your end? Has your work been helpful?"

"Very. We've been able to reach many harbor town corporations. The urgency has been conveyed and they are responding. I think all of the news coverage of the tidal-like waves has helped. How about you . . . did you get ahold of the ocean conservatory?"

"I did . . . they are of course happy to be on board—" I stop talking, my words becoming choked sounds in my throat. Just beyond where we are standing, a small, dark-haired figure is commencing our way, the glint in her gray eyes looking less than pleased. *Rye!*

Sensing a new presence close by, Tristan turns in the same direction I am looking. But it is not Tristan that Rye addresses first like I expect. "Bethany," she draws out my name with sugary sweetness. *Complete fakeness.* I want to puke. "It's been so long . . . what have you been up to? What are you up to now?"

For a second I consider not even answering. I could just send Tristan a curt nod, tell him I need to get going, and then leave the way I came. In my mind it seems like the logical thing to do. But the way Tristan is looking at me, so expectantly, like he is waiting for my answer, causes me to cough, clearing the sentence fragments that are strangling in my esophagus and reply. "I was just discussing the ocean disturbances with Tristan."

For a three-second count Rye's irises become very dull, and a chill creeps up my spine. *Something is seriously not right inside her head.* But then the moment passes and a flash of anger emanates from the pewter depths of her eyes before she breaks into laughter. "Tristan—?" The word rolls off of her tongue as if she is playing around with the sound of it. Afterward another peal of laughter escapes from her lips as she looks up into Tristan's face. "Oh my word, Tris, I haven't heard you called Tristan in *so* long." Taking a step toward him, she reaches for his arm. Intertwining her own slender one with his, she leans into his sturdy, well-built frame.

"You always did hate it when people called you that. For your sake, I thought the long version of your name had been all but obliterated by now." Her mocking gaze falls on me as she shrugs. "Guess not."

My whole body heats up, all the way from my toes to the undisclosed evidence that is now being displayed on my bright red cheeks. Anger and embarrassment begin circulating through my body at lightning-quick speed. Embarrassment because I feel so stupid. Carefully I avoid making eye contact with Tristan as he stands directly across from me. *I never knew.* All of these years I'd been calling him *Tristan* and he never said anything. He never told me he didn't like it. And so I just kept right on calling him that, each time probably sounding like fingernails on a chalkboard to his ears.

And anger at Rye for once again making me feel like an idiot. *Time to leave!* I begin playing with my ponytail, focusing my sight out to sea, skimming over the tops of Tristan's and Rye's heads. I can't bring myself to lower my gaze a few inches and make eye contact with either of them as they stand so closely together looking like the couple of the year. Or rather couple from hell. Finally I find my voice. "Well . . . I think we've covered all we need to for now. Sounds like everything is in place and happening like it should. So I'll go now. I have a lot of things to still do today."

Very quickly I turn away, vigilant not to connect my vision with Tristan's. With complete purposefulness I focus my ears on the drone of the waves in order to tune out the sound of his voice, or rather the absence of his voice—clueing me as to whether he cared enough to bother with a good-bye. But in spite of my assiduousness, I can't help but notice a flicker of concern springing from Tristan's expression as he passes through my peripheral view in the midst of my escape route. And I can't help but wonder if it is the sound of my name I hear being called over the crash of the surf as I hastily make my getaway from the shoreline. Ignoring these illusory notions, I continue on my way, wiping fists at my eyes in an attempt to clear my irritatingly now blurred vision, all the while hoping that my groceries have not begun to overheat in the car.

Let it go. This is the phrase that keeps echoing through my mind the following day. Over and over again I try to erase the particulars of the conversation I'd had with Rye on the beach less than twenty-four hours before: how stupid I feel for calling Tristan *Tristan* all of these years, not realizing that he hates it; or the way I'd begun to be secretly drawn in to his good looks and charms again, thinking that because he was giving me certain glances and friendly retorts he had some type of renewed interest in me. Only to get the reminding jolt a short time later that he is still with his childhood sweetheart, Rye, and has no intention of going back to the wife who he can't remember. We are only two associates working on the ocean cleanup project together. Nothing more.

Let it go. Forcing my mind to hold onto that thought, I walk away from the kitchen and into the entryway hall, watching while Josh and Jake gather up their fishing gear as they prepare to go down to the water. "How long are you boys going to be gone?"

Jake picks up a canteen of water and looks over at me. "I don't know . . . why?"

I try not to stare at the shadows that are hovering below his eyes—is the darkness fading or growing more prominent as the weeks of the summer press on? *At least they are going fishing.* I can find reassurance in that. Going fishing is a healthy, productive thing that normal fifteen-year-old boys would do. Not only that, recently they have been going with me on a daily basis to help with the shoreline cleanup at the Connecticut state line, albeit for a short duration by the time I actually drag their butts out of bed.

"If you get back early enough, I might have you go with me to do some more shoreline damage patrol."

At my words Jake's expression becomes guarded and he glances away. "Okay . . . yeah, sure, whatever."

I peer over at Josh sitting on the welcome bench, lacing up his tennis shoes. He hasn't looked at me once since I've walked into the hallway, but the minute I mention the word cleanup he flinches ever so slightly, and his fingers freeze mid-loop. Finally he resumes tying, a lock of his sandy blond hair covering his eyes so that I can't see into them. While I am intently looking for signs of angst on his downturned face, suddenly a thought occurs to me—something I have been meaning to mention to him. Something that I have been growing increasingly sure of as the weeks of the summer go on. Something that might distract, at least him, from the stronghold of whatever is dragging him and his brother down this summer.

"Hey, Josh." At my acknowledgement Josh's eyes look up from his shoes, briefly skimming my face, then back to his laces. "When you guys go down to the boats to go fishing, you will probably run into Isabella and Nate on the beach. Isabella has Nate down there swimming. Just check in on them for a minute before you leave, okay?" As I talk, I continue to watch Josh's countenance. But if I expected a reaction, I get none. He keeps twisting and threading without pausing. Inhaling a deep breath, I make a quick decision and proceed ahead anyway. "You know, Josh, I'm pretty sure Isabella has a crush on you."

Now both Jake and Josh look over at me with surprised expressions on their faces. Quickly, shock turns into apprehension. Jake glances uneasily at Josh as if to check on his reaction. Ignoring his brother's glare, Josh startles into motion. Having completed both of his shoes, he stands up and brushes his hand against his faded jeans. "I doubt that," he says.

"I don't doubt that. I am quite sure I am right. It's true . . . I can tell. Besides, in case you haven't noticed, she is a pretty girl and—"

"And she is also thirteen," Josh interrupts.

"Almost fourteen," I say. "And besides you are only fifteen, it's not that big of a gap really."

Josh presses his lips tightly together, and I detect the little muscle in his jaw twitching. From all appearances he is really bothered by what I've just revealed to him. Jake is seemingly ignoring the conversation, busying himself by gathering up the bucket and other paraphernalia that they will need to take with them on their fishing excursion. Disregarding Josh's distraught countenance, I focus my gaze his way. *So?* I ask him with my eyes.

At first I think he isn't going to answer, and I might have to actually pose the question aloud to obtain a reply. But then he sighs and looks at me through lowered lashes. "Thirteen, fourteen . . . it doesn't really matter. Isabella doesn't want to mess around with someone like me." *What?*

Unease and confusion begin to spread throughout my veins. *What is he talking about?*

Freezing in place, I cock my head in question. For a moment Jake stiffens too, staring hard at the floor. The aluminum pail that he is holding begins to swing back and forth, ostensibly of its own accord. And then before I can gather my wits enough to ask for clarification, Josh turns to Jake and says "ready," and they both head out the door without another word, letting the screen door slam behind them.

On two later occasions I try to dig back into the conversation and elicit a response from Josh about what he could possibly mean by the statement that Isabella doesn't want to mess around with a boy like him. But both times he blows me off, once making light of the account, and once getting visibly irritated, telling me that it meant nothing; let it go. *Let it go*—there was that phrase again, the one that I was trying so desperately to make my new anthem, the phrase that was sometimes so difficult to follow. I don't bother him about it after that. Instead I decide to concentrate on doing my best to keep both brothers engaged in the cleanup projects, assigning them to this site and that site. Hopefully it will help to keep them busy and deterred from whatever trouble is following them.

I stay busy too, of course, busier that I have ever been: lobbying state representatives, meeting with coastal city mayors, and contacting a variety of save-the-ocean interest groups—not to mention spending my free moments at the shoreline wreckage sites. In the midst of all the transactions, there is a part of me that speculates if I'll ever run into Tristan somewhere along the water so that we can update each other on how things are progressing. Although the cleanup seems to be effectively spreading, the ocean is still continuing to have outbursts, and I have to wonder whether we are even on the right track with what we are doing. How much will need to be done in order to satisfy its demand for restitution? Is there any placating that will be enough for the vast bodies of water that make up the majority of our planet, or is it really just too late?

These are the types of things I would like to bounce off Tristan, but since seeing him last with Rye when we had our initial planning discussion, he has yet to make an appearance. Although I keep trying to separate my feelings for him from our professional relationship, at times both get tangled into one. I can't help but wonder: is he staying away, not checking in for updates because he just can't stand being with me? Surely he would not pick acting on his lack of feelings for me ahead of saving his life source—the water. What then? After two weeks of not making contact with him, I decide to ask Lucy. She is still bringing Nate to Tristan for scheduled visits. Had he mentioned anything in particular that would clue me as to what is going on? How are things going on his end?

It doesn't take much probing on Lucy's part during Nate's next visit with his dad before she comes up with something. Yes, Tristan is still busy with the cleanup. NEC Systems Group has really jumped on board. The initiative is spreading quickly. But something else has procured his attention, keeping him preoccupied as well— Rye. Somehow something has happened to her. "He said something about her being dehydrated because of lack of water or something.

And now she is sick." Lucy pauses to shake her head in confusion as she relays the story to me. "I don't know, it sounds kind of strange to me. He almost made it sound like Rye had been held captive. As if she had been in the dessert or something, away from any water source . . . like there was no water available for her to drink. Weird. Almost like it was against her will or something. And because of the lack of water, it is taking a while for her to recover. So of course he is having to spend a lot of his free time by her side helping her out with that. You know, the whole recovery thing."

Of course he is!

I narrow my eyes. What is Rye up to now? How could she have possibly been held hostage, not able to get to the water? The water that Lucy thinks she needed to drink. The water that I know she really needed to breathe. What game is she playing? Well, of this I am certain—whatever it is that happened, whatever kept her from getting to the sea in time, she did it to herself, most likely as an attention-getting gimmick to elicit Tristan's time and sympathy. Probably after she realized that he and I would be spending time together working on the ocean project. I begin clenching my jaw as the realization of it dawns on me. Whatever her plan, apparently it is working. Because Tristan isn't coming around.

Chapter Nineteen

A spray of water hits my face. And I don't care. It feels so good—cleansing and therapeutic.

I have been working exceptionally hard recently, juggling work at the Center for Marine Studies of Rhode Island, being a mom to Nate, and as of late, spending all sorts of overtime on the ocean cleanup project. Now I am out for a run, trying to clear my mind of everything except the feel of the wind on my skin and the way the sand and surf are skimming the soles of my feet. It is a blustery day, and the waves are roaring beside me in response to the turbulent airstream. Occasionally a surge of liquid comes in contact with a boulder next to where I am running through the unsettled tide, and the result is a slosh of fluid against my hair, eyes, tee shirt and shorts. Every hit feels like a baptism. I really needed this shoreline jaunt today.

Above me a dark gray sky hangs low and heavy, filled with spitting rain, emitting just enough drizzle to keep my arms and cheeks continually damp between the larger gushes of water. It is a natural air conditioning, enabling me to run faster. The harder I sprint, the more I heat up. In turn the tiny beads of precipitation emanating from the clouds keep cooling me back down, allowing my body to maintain a comfortable temperature. Today's pace is the quickest I've kept in a long time. My feet are hitting the ground in a repetitive motion, matching the tiny wafts of air that are coming from my lips. Rounding a bend in the nautical landscape, I detect Watch Hill Light towering in the distance. For a quick second I glance at the watch on my wrist. *Geez, I have made good time today.* The recognizable outline of the business district is less than a mile away. Lengthening my stride, I put added force into the use of my muscles, flexing and extending with each step. Slap, thud, slap, thud, my feet hit the sand. Hiss, puff, hiss, puff, short breaths come and go from my throat. Now the downtown boardwalks are only an estimated half mile away at the most.

Using every ounce of energy that I possess, I kick my speed up one more notch—putting my tempo into high gear. Way above high gear. With lightning-quick speed I finish my trek into town in an all-out sprint. Coming to a stop, I begin pacing next to the boat slips until my breathing eventually slows to an even, relaxed cadence. The dreary day has kept many of the tourists at bay. The sidewalks in front of the shops are virtually empty. I am taking a long swig from my hydration bottle, wiping the sweat that is pooling at the back of my neck, observing the lack of pedestrians, when I catch the glimpse of copper highlights heading in my direction.

Ethan Vaughn.

Just beyond him I visualize the familiar sign that reads Hill Cove Marina. He must be coming from work. It has been a long time. I try to think back to the last time I'd seen or talked to him. That one time with Lucy at the Music on the Green. *Lucy.* Immediately my mind spirals back to all she had confided in me about the relationship trouble she and Ethan were having. Had things improved since then? Had they gotten worse? Surely not or she would have told me. There were times when I wanted to ask her, but I didn't want to bug or pry. If there was any more information to divulge, certainly she would've shared it with me. I take another sip of water and watch as Ethan's form edges closer. Involuntarily one or two butterflies begin to flutter in my stomach. On the inside I am shaking my head. *Yikes! Poor Lucy. How does she deal with it? Anyone that good-looking is bound to be breaking hearts all over the place.* Is Lucy now going to be included on that list? *Hopefully not.* Steadying myself from the wobbliness leftover from the run, I wait as he continues my way. It appears as if he is lost in thought, because as of yet it seems he has not recognized me.

I know for certain the moment our vision connects. A flicker of light filters through his perpetually upturned eyes as they widen marginally and link with mine. Grin forming on my lips, I anticipate the gesture of greeting that is sure to follow—only it never does. Instead he astutely focuses his gaze away from me, appearing to look around for someone or something across the street, like he never saw me at all. *What?* I pause my own hand midwave and lower it back to my side. *What was that all about?* If I didn't know better, I'd say Ethan Vaughn just avoided me. *Big time.* I blink and allow my eyes to follow his trail where he is now walking on the opposite side of the road. *Away from me.* Know better—bull crap. I am absolutely certain! Ethan Mr.-Sexy-Voice Vaughn has just successfully evaded my company. Immediately my heart begins to sink in my chest, because this does not fare well for my best friend Lucy.

The following morning I climb out of bed and reach my arms high into the air for a stretch. I am in desperate need of a cup of coffee. I have so many things to do today, and now I've overslept. It has been one of those rare times when Nate was content to sit in his crib and babble while entertaining himself with his favorite stuffed toys, allowing me to continue snoozing. Focusing my thoughts on Lucy and Ethan's troubles, I hadn't settled into a restful sleep until well past midnight. Hence the need for sleeping in. Picking Nate up out of his crib, I plant a good-morning kiss on his cheek. Once again my thoughts shift to Lucy. I should really get ahold of her so she can tell me all that is going on, lend a listening ear. But I have so much going on with the ocean project, it will have to wait until later. As I recall the way Ethan didn't want to face me when I saw him in town after my run, I experience a stab of empathy for all

Lucy is going though. Yes, I will definitely call her, if not now, soon.

"Mom ma ma ma," Nate says as he wiggles in my arms, embracing the new day with typical toddler energy.

I tweak his nose. "Hey, baby Nate. I love you," I say. Hugging him a little tighter in my arms, I pad into the kitchen to see about preparing breakfast. Isabella will be over soon, and I want to be ready to go when she arrives. After the sound of the coffee percolating begins to fill the air, I set a handful of berries on Nate's highchair tray for him to munch on while I fix hot cereal for both of us. After it is prepared, I sit back to eat. Between bites, I help Nate, so that his portion does more than get plastered on his tray and face. I am just scraping the last spoonful from the bottom of my bowl when I hear a knock at the door. Contemplatively, I go still. *Friends of the boys?* Hopefully not. I don't want to disappoint anyone, but I know I won't be able to pull Jake and Josh out of bed at this midmorning hour. But I know it can't be Isabella though; she never knocks. *Who then?* I take a large swig of water and head toward the entryway.

Unfastening the interior locks, I peer through the screen that is currently the only thing separating me and the person that I can now see is Tristan. My heart begins to beat double time. This is so unexpected. Since our arrangement began with Lucy taking Nate to him for visits, he has rarely showed up at the cabin—especially unannounced. And I have just checked my phone. There were no texts to alert me of his pending visit. Now he is standing here on my porch looking so hot, and I am suddenly tongue-tied. Recalling our last time together when Rye revealed how much he hated being called *Tristan,* suddenly I am embarrassed all over again. Unwittingly my cheeks heat up.

"Hey," Tristan says. His hands are shoved in the front pocket of his jeans, and he is looking at me with an uncertain expression on his face. Involuntarily my eyes sweep over his well-built frame. He looks so good it hurts.

"Hey," I breathe, immediately wanting to shoot myself for sounding like a smitten schoolgirl. *What is wrong with me?* Besides, he has made it clear that he and Rye are a pair. This visit isn't about me.

Tristan points to the threshold of the house and then cracks his knuckles one time. "Can I come in . . . or can you, ah, come out?"

I shake my head ever so slightly to clear the daze. "Um . . . yeah." I turn the screen handle and pull it open. "Yeah . . . come on in."

Tristan steps inside and I take two steps back, almost tripping over a pair of mud boots that are stationed in the hallway. Now there is no wire mesh to separate us, and suddenly I am mindful of my just-woken-up appearance. Self-consciously I run a hand through the tangled strands that are falling around my face. Tristan's eyes follow the movement, and for a second a look flashes across his countenance that makes my pulse come alive. But then he averts his gaze, and I feel stupid for always making too much of every little thing when it comes to him. Pulling my hair into a ponytail at the side of my neck, I clear my throat and make my best attempt at conducting myself in a professional demeanor.

"So what brings you by today?" My voice comes out sounding surprisingly businesslike.

Tristan's head snaps back up as if he hadn't expected my tone. For two seconds he says nothing. Then he blinks and an expression flashes over his face like he is just now remembering the reason for his visit. "I came to tell you about this area I discovered out in the ocean. It's the strangest thing I've ever seen . . . a giant pot of water bubbling out of nowhere like a volcano. Yesterday I went there and just sat and watched it for a while." He pauses for a moment and bites his lip like he is contemplating an idea. "I not sure, but I think it may our nucleus."

I furrow my brow, completely tuned to his story. "Our nucleus? How so? What do you mean?"

"Well, from all appearances it seemed to be pulling things into itself like a magnet—a strong, super-powered magnet."

"What? What types of things?"

"Debris, dark liquid . . . like, I don't know, oil and other types of fluid waste. Bottles, all sorts of trash, you name it . . . anything you could possibly think of. Pollution basically."

"Wow . . . it sounds—"

"Crazy . . . unbelievable?"

I begin to nod my head and stop as Tristan stares hard into my face. *I live in the water . . . that's crazy too, isn't it.*

Suddenly my throat feels dry. I swallow hard. "It's just that . . . some things are hard for me to wrap my mind around."

Tristan's expression softens. "No . . . yeah . . . I get it. It was hard for me to believe at first too. And I'm *from* the water." At that we both let out a light chuckle, and any unease between us seems to dissipate minutely. The idea that he is willing to share this type of huge information with me makes me feel warm inside. "So anyway, after studying it for a while, I think I've figured out that it seems to be sucking pollution to itself in direct lines. There appear to be several direct streams of refuse heading toward the center of it, direct lines of feed."

"Really? So it isn't just randomly sucking it from everywhere?"

"No, that to me is the oddest part. The tributaries are definitely coming from every direction encircling the core. But they seem to be direct feeds coming from somewhere." For a moment Tristan appears pensive. Lifting his hand, he rakes it through his hair. "I think . . . I'm not completely positive, but I think it might be pulling debris from heavily polluted areas. If I can figure out where these areas are and concentrate on ending the pollution there, I think I may be able to stop it. I hope so at least."

"Stop what?"

Tristan looks right at me. "Stop the whole thing from blowing like a volcano."

I suck in a breath and lift a hand to my mouth. Tristan continues.

"I think this might be the source of all the ocean disturbances we've been experiencing. It is like the ocean is fighting back, sucking up all the pollution and spewing it out, causing all the havoc we've been witnessing lately—what we've been working so hard to clean up. But if I'm right, and I think I *am* right, when it finally has had enough, when it finally blows, it is going to be catastrophic. I just hope it can be figured it out in time."

Goose bumps cover my skin. "Wow . . . this is incredible. I hope so too. What are you going to do? How can I help?"

For a quick instant Tristan's eyes sweep over my frame, and I hug my arms to my chest in response. Suddenly appearing nervous, he begins shifting back and forth on his feet, seemingly unsure of how to continue. *What is it? What is going on?* That quickly the tone of our conversation has changed, and I'm not sure why. Finally he begins to speak again. "Actually . . . that's why I came over. I wanted to see if you could . . . if you wanted to—"

"Da da da." Nate's emphatic voice reaches us from around the corner to the kitchen. He has just figured out his dad is in the house. Immediately Tristan stops talking and cocks his head, listening. He starts laughing. I start laughing too.

"Someone knows you are here."

Tristan sends me a questioning look. He clearly wants to go see his son, and of course I would never stop him. Motioning for him to follow me, I lead him into the kitchen. Nate squeals the moment he sees Tristan. "Da dad da." His green eyes are smiling, his tone high-pitched and happy.

"Hey, little buddy," Tristan says in return. I hand Tristan a wet cloth, and he wipes Nate's messy fingers and face before lifting him into his arms. For a moment a stab of melancholy rips through my body as it occurs to me that this is how it could be—me and Tristan and Nate living under one roof, doing life together on a daily basis. Fighting back that sentimental notion, I send a smile toward the two of them. Tristan tosses Nate into the air and catches him, repeating the action several times. Watching the gesture, I cringe, hoping Nate's freshly eaten breakfast won't come back up, landing all over Tristan's chest. I start to say something to that effect and then bite my tongue and cross my fingers instead. Somehow I just can't bring myself to ruin the moment.

Thankfully Nate's stomach contents manage to stay down. For several minutes Tristan continues to focus his attention on Nate, playing and interacting with him, while I stand by watching, not able to stop the grin that keeps forming on my lips. Finally Tristan turns in my direction, seeming to study me over Nate's blond curls. Unexpectedly a blush creeps onto my cheeks, and I start to look away. But then Tristan clears his throat and begins talking, holding my attention. "So . . . I never got to finish what I was going to ask you. I came here to see if you wanted to go out on the ocean and check out that site with me. That site I was just telling you about . . . see what you think of it."

I consider the many things I have to do today. None of them include taking a boat ride with Tristan. But really, we would be going to inspect the main source of the problem, so technically that should trump the things that are already on my list. Besides, when have I ever been able to tell Tristan no? Through sexy green eyes Tristan waits expectantly for my answer. *Crap, he is so gorgeous!* Excitement at the thought of spending time alone with him wells up inside of me. I force my voice to sound nonchalant. "Um . . . yeah, sure. I think that could work out . . . yeah, I'll go."

After Isabella arrives at the cabin, Tristan and I walk down to the beach and board *Blue.* A short time later we are trolling though the waves, heading toward the open waters of the sea. The wooden bow of the boat parts neatly through the sloshing liquid that is ensconcing our vessel. Behind us Drake is diving in and out of the wake. The sky is blue and endless, causing the ocean to sparkle and shimmer with a vibrant color of blue. I glance over at Tristan's profile, and an electric thrill shoots down all of my nerve endings. It has been so long since I've been in this type of intimate situation with him. Sitting less than a yard away from him, I can't help but wonder what type of thoughts he is having. Are his thoughts traveling along any of the same lines as mine? Does he remotely feel what I'm feeling—the energy and the heat from us being alone together? Am I only imagining it? Is it only one-sided?

The boat picks up tempo, causing the increased wind to whip through our hair. Discreetly, I take one more glimpse of Tristan's lightly tanned cheekbones just as he runs a hand through his tousled locks in an attempt to keep some unruly strands out of his eyes. He catches me looking. *Busted!* For a long second our vision collides. In an instant my mind spirals back to a self-assured, sexy Tristan smiling over at me from the driver's seat, making my insides feel like Jell-O. But then I blink and am taken back to the present, with Tristan watching my face uncertainly and yet with what appears to be a type of curiosity as well. Confident or confused, it doesn't matter—either way the effect of it causes me to blush bright red as I turn away.

After that the engine roars as he accelerates to full throttle. Relieved for the distraction, I lose myself in the speed. We are going at such a brisk pace the water is now passing by us in a blur, obscuring my mind at the same time, leaving no room for thoughts—good or bad. Reaching down to the leather material under my thighs, I grip the sides of my seat, holding on for dear life. *Good idea, Tristan, the faster the better. Let's just forget it all. There is no past or future. Right now there is only us and the speed of this boat.* He appears to read my mind. Reaching for the control lever, he revs it up one more notch. Now there is no higher point on the power handle. Our watercraft has reached its utmost momentum, and it feels exhilaratingly crazy. And so good.

Instantly the world around us becomes a blue haze. Blue water, blue sky, our boat, *Blue,* all becoming a mixture of blue. Are we in the water? Are we in the sky? I'm not sure, but it doesn't matter. Because for miles around us there is only Tristan and I traveling through an indistinct phase of time, shrouded by an unspoiled sphere that is the color blue.

On and on we go until abruptly the boat slows. The change is jolting. Catching my breath, I finger a mass of tangled hair out of my eyes. The new silence due to the boat motor's lack of acceleration is deafening. My inner ears are still buzzing from the wind that was pelting my face only moments before. Turning my head slowly, I allow my vision to sweep over our new surroundings. Nothing but water and more water. Tristan's deep voice nudges me back to reality. "You hear that?"

Briefly I glance toward Tristan, then cock my head. *Nothing.* My head is still humming from our fast ride. I strain my ear to concentrate some more. *Still nothing.* I shake my head. "No."

"Huh . . . well, let me get a little closer. Let me know when you hear something."

I am sitting on the edge of my seat looking and listening, still not exactly sure what it is that I'm about to encounter. The boat continues to edge forward at a gradual rate. Finally my head begins to clear from the drone of the leftover blasting air. The roaring noise that replaces it is hard to differentiate at first. But the more we glide through the rippling current toward the sound, the more I become sure of what I am hearing. Finally I nod my head. "Yep, I hear it now. I hear *something* . . . like a roar?"

"That's it . . . that is what we're heading for."

I keep my eyes glued to the water. "Will I see it soon?"

"Pretty soon. I'll pick up the speed in a minute, and we'll be there shortly."

There is something about the tone of Tristan's voice that causes me to jerk my head in his direction. He is staring straight ahead, seemingly lost in thought, his arms draped over the steering wheel. I furrow my brow. *What is it?* Tristan lets out an uneasy chortle and kind of half glances over at me. Then he faces forward again and sighs. Now everything is quiet, except the sound of the roar in the distance that is steadily increasing in decibel.

"What? What is it?" I finally ask.

Tristan sighs again. "I don't know . . . I've been thinking, I just wish things were—" He stops, again peering over at me, albeit briefly. My heart begins pounding in my chest.

I swallow hard. "You wish things were what?"

Tristan runs his fingers through his hair, and his expression becomes pensive. "I just wish things were easier . . . more clear cut."

"Like?" The word sounds cracked and uncertain as it leaves my lips.

Tristan's mouth forms into a thin line, and the little muscle in his cheek begins to twitch almost undetectably. I press my hands into balls at my sides. It's so hard not to reach out and trace my finger along the edge of his jawline. But that is not my right. He is not my territory anymore. "I don't know," he finally says.

Again a stretch of silence.

In the quiet my mind begins spiraling with an influx of overwhelming thoughts. What do I say to him? What could I say to make him open up and talk? I know that I only have seconds to react to his statement, to encourage him to clarify. What should I say? In some ways I know it might sound like a complete change of topic to him. But to me it may very well be related, so without giving myself a chance to change my mind, I blurt. "How is your guitar playing coming along?" What I really want to ask is *How is the song coming along? Do you remember our song yet? If you could just remember, it might make everything easier.*

At my question, Tristan turns toward me, a slightly surprised expression on his face. *Oh no, wrong question!* "My guitar?" he finally asks, then pauses to shrug his shoulders. "Actually I haven't been able to find my guitar lately. I . . . I must have misplaced it somehow. It is missing. Why do you ask?"

Missing? A bad feeling settles into the space below my ribs. The guitar seemed like our one link. Our one connection to the past. And now it's gone? Suddenly it's all I can do to keep myself from shaking, to stave away the feeling of desperation that is trying to swallow me up. *Oh no! What is going on with me?* I thought I'd gotten beyond this. "I don't know . . . I just wondered—"

"Well, anyway"—Tristan's voice, clear and self-assured, snaps me out of my newfound funk—"I think I'm just referring to the whole thing with the ocean and stuff. I just wish we knew for sure exactly what to do to make everything okay again. You know, like I wish we could be 100 percent sure that what we have planned is going to work." Looking over at me, he flashes me a smile. And for some reason the abrupt cheeriness in his tone feels anything but reassuring. "I wish that whole thing was clear cut . . . so we just knew for sure."

My heart sinks in my chest. "Oh . . . yeah . . . yeah, I know what you mean."

Again Tristan smiles. "Well, all right . . . let's go find this thing so I can show you what I've been talking about." Pushing the lever on the control panel into an upward position, Tristan coaxes the boat into a faster speed once again, this time a steady trot.

I don't know what catches my attention first, the sound of the thunderous roar rising up to meet my ears, or the magnitude of the churning, volcanolike trench we are approaching. All at once the breath leaves my lungs, and my jaw drops. I look over at Tristan, and his face is now focused and serious. "See what I mean? It's nothing to play with," he shouts over the reverberation of the churning waves.

I nod my head, eyes wide, knowing that it would be too difficult to speak over the level of the noise. Rising to a kneeling position, Tristan leans toward me and points toward the chaotic bubbling on the waves while talking loudly into my ear. "See that over there? See how that appears to be a dark line?"

Squinting my eyes, for many moments I study where he is pointing. I am just about to shake my head no to let him know that I can't find what he is referring to, when I finally detect the outline of a streak that seems to differentiate itself from the rest of the churned-up water that is leading up to the center of the agitating hub. *Yes,* I nod. *Yes, I see it.*

Tristan appears relieved. "Watch," he shouts. "Watch how each thread is getting sucked into the middle . . . into the nucleus of it all. Like large snakes traveling through the water. Can you see the movement?" It is similar to the underground snakelike movement in the movie *Tremors,* I want to say to him, but I don't think he'll be able to hear my voice over all the din. So I decide to tell him about that later. Tristan leans in closer, but he still has to shout. "Well, anyway . . . I'm trying to see where all the feeds are coming from. That will be my focus."

Okay, I nod back to let him know that I get it, that I think he is right on track.

The ride back to the cabin is quick but not high-speed-blur-fast like on the way there. After we pull up to the dock and tie the boat, we spend some time lingering on the beach, discussing what we've just seen out in the water—all that Tristan has already studied and analyzed, and my impressions and opinions of the whole matter. On the whole I feel like Tristan is correct in his thinking. If he concentrates on the sites that are heavily supplying the pollution, then maybe the brewing epicenter will calm. Maybe. Hopefully. It is definitely worth a shot. Possibly our *only* shot.

Tristan continues to talk on and on, his green eyes wild and fervent, as he shares his strategy for saving the ocean and all that will be affected by the threat of the imminent eruption. I can tell he seems pleased, almost relieved, to have someone to confide all the details to. And of course I am an interested listener. After all I've been doing on my end, I'm zealous too. It's nice to finally have the right someone to connect with, someone to be partnering with as all we are doing begins to fit together like pieces to a puzzle. But although I'm happy to be the one Tristan has found to relate with on this fervid topic, at some point while we are in the midst of our conversation, for a brief moment I have to wonder if there is no one else who shares his enthusiasm on the same level. Not his family? Or other sea people? Not even his girlfriend, Rye? But although in some ways this seems unbelievable, on the inside I am secretly glad that from all appearances the certain someone happens to be me.

Finally our discussion dwindles, and we say our good-byes. I am getting ready to begin walking on the path that winds up to the cabin when I hear the sound of Tristan's voice calling to me.

"Bethany."

I stop. *Maybe there is something else he wants to tell me—something he forgot to mention about the plan.* Pivoting my feet through the sand, I turn back around. "Yeah?"

My heart skips a beat as I meet his gaze. The green eyes that were smiling only moments before as we were discussing our strategy have now changed, glinting with something else I can't put my finger on. That something else is what sends tiny shivers traveling down the nerve endings on my skin. "I just wanted to tell you . . . that I don't mind you calling me *Tristan.*" Pausing, he bites his lip like there is something more that he wants to say. *What could it be?* I wait in silence, my heart beating wildly in my chest. Finally a soft sigh escapes his lips and he adds, "I, ah . . . I just wanted to let you know."

Nodding twice I press my lips together, afraid that if I speak my voice might come out sounding funny. "Oh . . . okay," I eventually murmur. For a second longer we hold eye contact. And then I turn back around and continue heading toward the cabin.

Chapter Twenty

How are you doing, girl? I haven't talked to you in a while. *(send)*

This is the second text I've sent Lucy today. It is early evening, and I still haven't heard back from the first one. That is not like her. If she is having problems—and after running into Ethan down by the docks and having him purposely avoid talking to me I can safely assume that she still is—then she needs someone to shoulder her difficulties. Not being used to how Lucy responds to trouble— trouble had not found her too much over the years—I am uncertain if she prefers the talking-over-dark-chocolate-with-a-friend route or the shut-herself-away-in-the-closet-and-cry-alone route. Either way I've been trying to get ahold of her to confirm which she has decided to choose. I can't just leave her hanging, all alone, not knowing if she is in desperate need of consoling.

After three unanswered texts, I decide to change my plan of attack and go find Ethan instead. Pulling my hair into a messy bun, I dress in an oversized sweatshirt and leggings and drive down to Hill Cove Marina to see if I can locate him. I know in the past he tended to put in late hours at the boat works. But once I arrive, instead of running into Ethan, I find David Chambers, my old boss, just closing up the front office instead. He tells me that Ethan is not there, but there might be a good chance I can find him hanging out down at Waves, a local sports bar. He has been spending a lot of time there lately. Telling him thanks, I jump in my black jeep and head to the other side of town.

Eyeing the neon sign that reads Waves, I hesitate briefly before walking through the door. On the exterior, nothing has changed much since the last time I was there. Since having Nate, there hasn't been much time for frequenting pubs, so it has been quite a while. And now with the whole ocean project going on, there is even less time for hanging out. But this is different—this is for Lucy. It needs to be done.

When I step into the entryway, it takes a moment for my vision to adjust to the darkness. Perusing the dim interior, I keep my eyes peeled for any sign of Ethan amidst the array of decorative surfboards and other beachy paraphernalia adorning the walls. Televisions flashing panoramic color are mounted everywhere, displaying golf, baseball, and a variety of beer commercials. My gaze fine-tunes to the screens that are displaying the Red Sox and then to the seats in the direct line of their view. But still I don't see Ethan. A few times I detect a head or two swiveling in my direction, ogling me, hoping for some fun—a single girl out alone. But I ignore them and keep looking, weaving in and out of chairs and tables. I am just about to give up, deciding that Ethan is not here after all, when I spy copper highlights staring up at a soccer game from a far corner booth. *I guess I'd been looking for the wrong sport.*

"Ethan," I say upon reaching his table. If he is surprised to see me, I can't tell. In a leisurely motion his vision leaves the TV screen and sweeps over my form instead.

"What's up, Bethany?" By the slur of his words I can tell he is well on his way to getting drunk. He winks and even though I don't want them to, goose bumps form on my skin. "So . . . come looking for your old boy Ethan, did you? Am I finally good enough now that Tristan's given you the slip?"

Swallowing hard, I try to disregard the insensitivity of his statement, knowing that he has probably had a few too many. But somehow my temper gets the best of me, and I hold up the middle finger on my left hand in reply. Instantly I regret it. *Oh crap, that's not going to elicit the conversation I want to have from him.*

But instead of retaliating, unexpectedly he laughs. Hard. "Sit down," he finally says.

Heaving a sigh, I slide into the seat across from him. Taking in the large assortment of long-necked bottles that are covering the table, I gesture toward them. "Are these all yours?"

Again he laughs. "At this point, yes, but I can order one for you, and we can start sharing the collection if you like." In spite of the tipsy edge to his voice, the gravely sound reaches out to me, drawing me in. His perpetually crinkled eyes are holding my stare, asking me a question. *And the answer is—*

"Stop it, Ethan," I finally declare. He jerks back, looking unexpectedly wounded. And I can't tell if he is being genuine or if he is just mocking me, inebriated as he is. For a brief moment I wonder if I'll really be able to get anywhere with this conversation considering his current state. He definitely does not seem in the mood for a heart-to-heart. And if he calls my bluff, I am going to soon fold. After all, this is Ethan Vaughn—completely unnerving and sexy. I am definitely not good at dealing with his type. Will I be able to carry out my serious stance and get to the bottom of the matter about Lucy, or will I become all tongue-tied and wilt? I clear my throat just as our waitress stops at the table. "I'll have a lemon water and he'll have a coffee . . . black," I say. Astonished by my own forthrightness, I wait for Ethan to respond and humiliate me to the point of crawling under the table. But he lets the order go and says nothing. There is a two-second pause after the waitress leaves.

Finally he looks at me pointedly. "Not much of a drinker?"

"It really depends on the occasion. Right now I want to talk to you . . . I think you know about what." Pressing his lips together, he looks away. Inhaling slowly, I push on, pretending like I am not completely intimidated by his unsettling persona. "So, I want to know . . . what is going on with you and Lucy?"

Our beverages arrive, and he surprises me by taking a long swig of his coffee, trading it in for his current flavor of beer. I press the glass of water to my lips and take a sip as I wait for him to answer. "It's over," he finally announces. *What?* My heart takes a deep dive in my chest. *Oh no, poor Lucy. It can't be!*

I take a large breath and hold on to the seat cushion beside me to stop myself from getting up and going to find my best friend and wrap my arms around her. "What? When did this happen? I mean does Lucy—"

"Know? Does Lucy know?" Ethan interrupts. "Probably. It would be kind of hard to miss it. But no . . . we haven't made it official if that is what you mean."

For a split second I close my eyes as I experience Lucy's pain. When I open them again Ethan is watching me, a wounded expression in his own eyes. For some reason this surprises me. *Maybe this isn't just a use-and-dump job on his part.* Maybe there is more to it. Gathering my resolve, I decide to press on and find out. "Is there . . . is there someone else?" I have to know. Lucy deserves to know. With a guy like Ethan that has got to be it—the reason behind the breakup. But if that is the case, by the look in his eyes he obviously feels guilty.

Silence.

My heart falls even further. His lack of dialogue is telling me all I need to know. *Well, you creep,* I tell him with my eyes. *Say something, you idiot! Just be a man and admit it!* The silence continues. And suddenly I've had enough. Setting my drink back down, I push away from the table and begin to slide out of my seat. For a quick second I narrow my gaze at Ethan, my voice filled with hostility. "Just do me a favor. Don't drag this out. Man up and end it so she can move on. She deserves to know what is going on."

The injured look in Ethan's eyes as he watches my departure is slightly confusing, but I continue my exit from the booth anyway.

Standing up, I turn to leave. "Wait." His voice causes me to stop midmotion. "Sit back down." *What?* I glare back and he rephrases. "I mean *please* . . . sit back down." I do as he asks. But instead of talking, for a long moment he stares at me uncertainly, and I wonder if he's changed his mind again and doesn't have the guts to spill the goods on himself after all. I glance at my watch. "Lucy is better off without me," he finally says.

Looking up, I narrow my eyes in question. *Please don't tell me that it's because you are a cheater and she doesn't deserve your continual infidelity.* "Why is that?"

"This town is too small for her. I've watched her with her work, and she is loaded with talent. Any marketing firm would be happy to have her. Any big city. And here she is stuck at the edge of the world with me, manager of a boat marina. If I'm getting bored, I know she has to be too. I'm just holding her back—she deserves more."

Out of all the possibilities that Ethan could present to me about the reasons for his and Lucy's breakup, this is not one of them. I shake my head to clear the shock from the forefront of my mind. "Have you talked to her about this?"

"No . . . no, I know that if I do, she'll just tell me she is happy here with me . . . that she doesn't want more. But I know that would be a lie. So I am doing her a career favor and cutting her loose. If she is not emotionally attached to me, she'll be free to go. Someday I'll read about all the lofty things she is doing for some big company somewhere. And I'll still be tying boats up to the docks here in town."

For a while longer I sit with Ethan while he drinks cup after cup of coffee, laying out all the reasons why Lucy would be better off without him. And although at times I offer some heartfelt advice about why he might be mistaken in his thinking, mostly I just listen. After leaving Waves, I shoot a text to Lucy again.

WE REALLY NEED TO TALK! TEXT ME! SOON! *(send)*

There is a huge end-of-the-summer party at the Fredericks, and they are advertising it as family friendly—kids are invited. This piece of news is a welcome sound to my ears. Even though I am exceedingly busy with the ocean cleanup, I will be happy to take a much-needed break to attend. Besides, kids can come too. What a great way to induct Jake and Josh back into the land of the living. Make them remember how much fun they used to have hanging out with the summer gang: attending parties, talking by oversized bonfires until late evening hours, playing football or volleyball in the sand. As of now these are activities that they've all but given up on. Even their innermost circle of friends have finally stopped dropping by for visits. Now all their days consist of are intermittent periods of me dragging their butts out of the house to help with the shoreline trash-elimination ventures and hours and hours of sleep.

In my mind Mom and Dad can't come back from their anniversary trip soon enough.

Late evening is fast approaching when I finally get a chance to tell Josh and Jake about the party. They are walking up from the beach trail together, faces downcast, footsteps sluggish, when I shout, "Hey, guys," and wave them over. Nate is tucked into bed, fast asleep, and I am using my few minutes of free time to do some much-needed gardening. His crib monitor is hanging from the waistband of my cutoff jean shorts, allowing me to hear his soft, rhythmic breathing while I work.

At the sound of my beckoning, two pairs of blue-gray eyes look in my direction. For a moment I detect hesitation on both of their parts, then they begin to advance toward me, albeit apathetically. Ignoring the lack of emotion in their step, I force enthusiasm into my voice. *I'm excited about the party; they should be too.* "Hey, Jake. Hey, Josh. Thanks for all help you've been giving to the ocean cleanup lately. You've been working hard." *Well, not that hard, really, but nevertheless*—At my words of acclamation, they both visibly stiffen. "Anyway, I just heard about a large party the Fredericks are having this Saturday, and I found out you are invited too. It is going to be huge. And their estate is amazing . . . It goes on forever: fountains, patios, pools . . . you will love it."

When I start talking, describing the party, Jake's and Josh's eyes widen slightly, and they both take a step backward. Apprehension mixed with escape. Overlooking this not-so-subtle reaction, I keep talking, working hard to keep my tone upbeat. "Last time I was there, they even constructed a dance floor in the middle of their lawn. I wonder if they—"

"No," Josh practically shouts his answer as he interrupts. I go still. *What?* He runs a hand nervously through his hair while forcing an even tone into his voice. "I mean, no, I don't think that is going to work out . . . but . . . but thanks."

Shocked by my brother's adamant refusal, I compel myself to remain calm. Suddenly I feel very young. Pinching the side of my leg to get a grip, I to try to stay focused and not freak out. I am the older sister in this situation. I have to remain levelheaded. But something is going on here—something really strange, and I don't know if I can handle it. Inhaling a large breath, I turn with a hopeful expression to look at Jake. But his demeanor is only an echo of Josh's—possibly even worse. Appearing almost panicked, he jumps in with his own reply. "No . . . ah . . . no, I don't think we can. I mean we have to . . . we have to go to—" He quits talking and turns toward Josh, his eyes reaching out in silent desperation. Begging, pleading for help.

I don't give Josh a chance to come to his brother's rescue. "You have to go where?" I demand. "What plans do you already have that obviously seem so important?" For an interval, neither brother says a word, so I raise my voice a decibel and continue. "Someone better start talking . . . because it is obvious you have plans, and since you are currently staying at my house and because you are both fifteen years old and I am your acting guardian, I have the right to know . . . so someone better—"

"Whoa . . . whoa . . . whoa, chill," Josh eventually says, his tone reproachful, yet laced with a thread of anxiety. "You always make such a big deal of things. It's no big thing that we don't want to go to the party. I'll bet you never really checked out those parties in detail. In case you want to know, most of the kids that go to those are drinking underage. Maybe we just don't want to partake in that stuff; did you ever think of that?"

I furrow my brow skeptically. *This is new news.* In the earlier part of the summer when the twins were having all of their beach blowouts, I never once detected leftover liquor bottles thrown in the dune grass or any crazy, loud behavior on the part of their visiting friends which would indicate underage drinking. "Really . . . this is the first mention of this. If this is a problem, how come you never told me before?" *And since when had my brothers become so sanctimonious?*

"Well, you never really asked," Josh answers. Then after glancing discreetly at Jake, who is now staring intently at the ground, he continues. "And no, we don't have any special plans. It's just that we've been busy helping you with your cleanup thing lately, and Saturday there are more projects going on; we'll probably be tired out and ready to go to bed at a decent time that night is all."

Squeezing my eyelids tightly together and then slowly reopening them, I release a long, tired sigh. "Okay." My voice comes out sounding breathless and exhausted. They've won. I could force them to go to the party, but what would be the point? The thing is, even though I'm not really buying the story about the drinking, I have to believe that they really don't have any particular plans Saturday night. Lately, I haven't seen them leaving the vicinity to hang out with any friends at all. But this thought only leaves me in a quandary. I just don't know what is going on with them.

The minute I say the word *okay*, releasing them from the hot seat, some semblance of relief passes over both of their features, causing me to feel that much worse. There was a time, when the twins had first arrived for the summer, that there would be no stopping them from attending a blowout party like the Fredericks'. So what has changed? As I watch their countenances while they stand restlessly waiting for their informal dismissal from my presence, an ominous feeling shoots through my veins. At the same time a shadowy light from the dusky sky falls across their faces creating a ghostly ambience around their youthful frames. As if for the first time, I look through unveiled vision to see the reality of their appearances: unusually pale skin, hollowed cheekbones, and dull, sunken eyes.

I gasp for air.

In a flash, time rewinds. Clear as day I can picture Jake's and Josh's enthusiastic smiles as they are first arriving in Watch Hill less than two months ago: bright eyes; overconfident, teenage-boy demeanors; and virile good looks. For just a moment I can hear the sound of their eager voices as they take their first glance around the cabin, vibrant and alive.

I always did love this place. This place is total awesomeness. I can feel the good times coming on already.

And suddenly it becomes very evident just how much they have changed over the course of one summer. *Oh God, what have I allowed to happen?* My brothers! What have they become? And what is wrong with me that I would permit it to take place under my roof? My mind turns to panic, and for a minute it becomes difficult to reason things out in my mind. *Think. Think. Think.* How about Mom and Dad? I take a calming breath. Yes, I just need to do it—I just need to get ahold of Mom and Dad. It's what I should have done in the first place.

I close my eyes.

No! No, Mom and Dad are on their anniversary trip—and they really need the vacation time alone after all that they've been through. *Think.* I exhale slowly through pursed lips and reconsider. Mom and Dad will be home soon. And when they arrive, I will get the boys back to them. As quick as I can.

Before they are completely destroyed!

The Fredericks' party is as big and festive as I remembered from the last time I attended their social event. No expense is spared on the part of the hosts: live music, hors d'oeuvres, gourmet delicacies, freely flowing drinks, canopy-covered lounging areas, sand volleyball, enormous bonfires. And endless numbers of people partaking in it all. Although still concerned over Jake and Josh's refusal to come with me, I had prodded myself along and taken pains to make my appearance fashionable. After donning a beige sundress, I slipped into coordinating tan, wedged sandals. Letting my hair hang in long waves down my back, I placed a tiny barrette to the left of my temple to draw back my bangs. Then after taking a final glance in the hallway mirror, I made the trek across town to the happening affair.

Once there, it doesn't take long before I am sucked into the festive atmosphere, enjoying the upbeat music and the energy of the crowd. Grabbing tidbits from circulating trays of food, I spend time mingling among the mass of people that are gathered, meeting up with many familiar faces and running into those I haven't rubbed shoulders with in a long time. But old acquaintances or everyday cohorts, it doesn't matter, the conversations all eventually seem to settle on the same topic: how unusual it is that we are suddenly experiencing such random surges from the ocean, what we are currently doing to clean up in the reoccurring aftermath, and if after all that we've done and are doing—will it be enough to stop the destructive problem? In the end, none of us really know—me included. But we have to keep trying. What they don't know, however, is about the discovery Tristan had made out in the ocean—the direct feeds of pollution to the bubbling water-volcano. The average person would never buy into the idea that the ocean is capable of being a functioning power of its own. So that little detail I keep hidden in my brain as I carry out each conversation, all the while hoping that Tristan's efforts to focus on the heavily concentrated pollution locales is going to pay off in time. In time to stop the ocean from blowing sky high.

Soon a group of work companions call me out to the dance floor, and for a while I leave all the discussion about the latest nautical problems behind as I begin moving to souped-up music that is exploding beneath an overlay of flashing lights. It's while I am lost in the beat of the song that I allow myself to wonder for the briefest moment whether Tristan happens to be at the party. If I look around hard enough, will I spot him somewhere in the crowd? And if I do happen to see him, will he be alone?

The hypothetical answer to the last part of the question causes a stab of melancholy to shoot through my stomach, so I decide to trade in the dance floor for a few minutes of solitude. Breaking away from my friends, I leave the lights and the music and the energy of the crowd behind and begin heading down a secluded path that leads to the ocean. By the time I reach the edge of the shoreline, I discover I am not the only one who has decided to escape the party. Almost immediately I have a near collision with an older man out for a walk, bottle in hand. After acknowledging each other with surprised laughter and offering sincere apologies for getting in each other's way, we both continue on in opposite directions. Feeling slightly vulnerable as I continue on down the coastline, I perform a discreet glance over my shoulder to make sure he is still walking away from me. And he is. While breathing a tiny sigh of relief, I keep walking, only to advance upon muffled sounds coming from behind a sand dune on my right. *What the—?* I turn in the direction of the noise only to discover a couple engaged in a make-out session. Unobtrusively, I edge around them in a far circle while wading a few inches into the water in the process. *Crap. Now I am wet.*

For a brief moment I consider going back. Twilight has just arrived, and it is getting harder to see much of anything anyway. But in spite of my second thoughts, I talk myself into going just a little farther. Rounding a large bend in the landscape, I experience a little nudge of joy at finally finding a protected alcove—at long last, a great place to be alone. Spying a rock to sit on, I am about to make myself comfortable when I detect movement near the far side of the nook. As an obscured figure shifts in the emerging shadows of dusk, I practically jump a mile discovering that once again I am not alone. Rising to my feet with the intent of heading back the way I came, I do a double take in the direction of the stranger at the exact same moment as I hear a voice calling out to me.

"Bethany?"

I go still in my tracks. "Tristan?"

We both laugh nervously at the same time. This is clearly an unexpected visit for both of us. Padding through the sand, I go to the place where he is seated on a piece of driftwood. "Well, this is a surprise," he says as I come near. "What brings you out here?"

"I was at party at the Fredericks. I had enough of *loud* and went for a walk to be alone for a while."

"And you thought you *were* alone until you figured out that you had company—" Pointing to himself, he looks playfully into my face. Some of his features are shrouded by the emerging night sky, but I can see enough of his unnerving good looks that my stomach comes alive with butterflies. "Me."

Fighting the flustery feeling, I transfer nervously back and forth on my feet. "No . . . it's okay. You're okay. I wasn't going stay away from the party long. I just—" My vision moves to where his legs are sprawled out in the sand, and for the first time I notice his guitar where it is resting on his lap. Suddenly I lose my train of thought. "Hey, you found your guitar." I can't hide the sound of surprise in my voice.

Tristan looks down at the stringed instrument that is balanced on his thighs and then back up. "Oh yeah, I did find it . . . *finally.* Rye had borrowed it, and I just didn't know." As he mentions the name Rye, he gets an uneasy look on his face as if he doesn't feel comfortable talking about her.

You mean stole it, more like. I offer the semblance of a nod and shrug my shoulders at the same time. "Well, anyway, I'm glad you got it back." Once again I am reminded that I shouldn't be hanging out alone with Tristan on the beach. He is obviously still spending time with Rye, who he has feelings for, and I don't need to deal with getting my hopes up and growing more attached to him, just to turn around and get hurt again. It would be different if we had the ocean business to tend to. But since we don't, I point behind me. "Well, I think I'll just be going. It is getting dark and—"

Tristan interrupts me by playing two random chords on his guitar that I don't recognize. Then he stops. I can barely see his face in the now almost completely faded daylight. "You sure . . . you just got here." *What?* My heart slams hard against my chest.

*Not sure at all actually, but then there is the Rye thing, so—*I begin fidgeting with the hem of my dress. "Yeah . . . yeah, I better." Lifting my hand in the gesture of a wave that I'm not sure he can actually see in the dimly lit sky, I turn to leave.

While I begin striding though the sand on my exit route, behind me Tristan plays one more chord on the guitar and then says something under his breath that sounds like an unintelligible curse word. Afterward his voice becomes soft and wistful. "I just wish—"

I stop walking. Even though I am leaving, I get the feeling he is talking to me. *Does he want to tell me something?* After a two-second count I slowly turn around. "Wish what?"

Tristan sighs heavily. We are several feet apart, so I creep forward slowly, heading in his direction. When I feel close enough, I stop. "I don't know . . . it's this guitar. It is frustrating me. There are a couple of songs, one in particular—" It is officially dark now, and the light of the moon is shining through the tree line, landing on Tristan's form. Now I can see all of him, every gorgeous inch of his head and his body. For some reason this makes me want to cry. He runs his fingers through his hair in apparent vexation. I hold my breath, scared that if I let it out or make just the wrong move he'll quit talking—quit confiding all that he is feeling about whatever it is that he is about to tell me. He clears his throat. "It is plaguing my mind . . . sometimes keeping me awake at night. It's right there . . . on the very edge of my memory. But I can't seem to remember it." For a moment he pauses and I bite my lip, wondering if there will be more. "But," he finally continues, "I really wish that I could." *Oh my word!* Suddenly it is hard to breathe.

I close my eyes. When I open them again the moon is shining a spotlight on both of us. As I look right at Tristan my voice becomes a whisper. "Yeah . . . I wish that you could too."

Tristan's eyes, now so green in the reflected glow of the night sky, lock onto mine as he contemplates my words. For a moment we stand frozen, watching one another, neither saying a word. Then finally, Tristan breaks the stare by offering a slow nod and eventually looking away.

Chapter Twenty-One

I don't have much time to dwell on Tristan's struggle with the guitar or how close he is to possibly remembering our song. Or why it is that when I am with him lately something feels different. Like at times he is looking at me funny, studying me as if he is trying to figure something out. Or how now that he is acting this way, with a flicker of possible interest in his eyes, I am suddenly ten times more jealous of the relationship he and Rye share—that when he leaves me after our brief interludes together, he is most likely going to her. And is probably doing things with her that make me want to vomit onto the ground, leaving a trail of emptiness from the bottom of my stomach all the way to my heart.

All the way to my very broken heart.

But I don't have much time to dwell on these matters at all because very soon after our encounter on the beach in front of the Fredericks, the pollution extrication plan is stepped up one hundred-fold. Time is now of the essence. The ocean's need is growing greater, and disturbances are escalating. I am thrown into a tailspin of meetings with the government at federal, state, and local levels. Not to mention the plethora of committees and organized groups put together for the sole purpose of the cleanup who I make an effort to contact on a daily basis just to make sure all of our conjoined efforts are being maximized. Any of my leftover free time is spent at the beach, cleaning. And I know that Tristan is expending the same amount of energy focusing on the cities that he has identified as direct feeds to the bubbling corpus of water that is getting ready to blow—soon.

Bag thrown over my shoulder and keys in hand, I am on my way out the door to check on a group in Stonington, Connecticut, another cleanup in action, when Zepher surprises me by walking up to the cabin by way of the beach path. For a split second my heart flip-flops in my chest as I recall some of the intimate encounters we've had over the summer. After the most recent letdown—the thwarted kiss—he had seemed to ease back into a platonic relationship with little problem. But each time I meet up with him, I have to wonder what he is currently thinking. Is he still okay with us being friends and nothing more? At times I think he is perfectly fine, and yet there are others when he is still flirty, and his eyes hold more than friendship in them. During these moments I realize that we may be digressing. Watching as he makes his way across the yard toward me, I have to wonder which Zepher today will bring. He is still fifteen feet away from where I am standing on the edge of my wooden porch step when I know for sure.

"Hey, where are you going? You are not leaving, are you? I just got here," his playful voice calls out to me as I jiggle my car keys nervously in my hand. His blue eyes, lit up and provocative, instantly put me on alert. Today will most definitely not be a *just friends* day.

I smile uneasily. "Hey, Zepher. Yeah . . . my time has been pretty well tied up lately. I was just heading out."

Zepher's lips form into an exaggerated pout, causing his dimples to indent as he keeps heading toward me. I can't help it, I laugh in response. *He really is cute.* In another time and place I might have been easily attracted to him. Something may have actually happened between us—an actual relationship. But the way it stands now, I can't get past Tristan. And really, we *are* still married, even if Tristan can't seem to remember that. "Damn," he says teasingly as he closes the distance between us. "I keep missing you. You are a hard one to keep up with lately."

Inwardly I wince. "Really? I take it you've stopped by recently then and I have been gone?"

Zepher is now right in front of me, and his eyes lock onto mine for an uncomfortable second. "You might say I stopped by once or twice." He winks. "Or maybe more." *Oh crap!*

Swallowing hard, I point to my jeep. "Well, I'm sorry that I'm going to miss you again today, but I really have to go."

"All right, I'll let you go." He feigns indignance. "I can tell when I'm being blown off."

"No . . . it's not like that. I just have to keep working on the ocean project . . . you know, with how bad everything is getting and all. It's kind of scar—"

Zepher's blue eyes immediately grow serious. "No . . . no, I get it. You *have* to go. You are doing a lot for the ocean. And we've been doing all we can too. All of us. Underwater . . . behind the scenes you might say."

"I've heard. And that is great. But of course you would. You would want to protect the ocean. It is your home. But it's sad that it has come to this, because it's not your fault."

"Yeah . . . I guess you could say it's been difficult to watch the pollution escalate over the years. And now it's—" *Scary,* I know. *We don't know what is going to happen.* He shakes his head. "Anyway, let me walk you to your car."

I nod and we begin walking together closely, side by side. *Too close.* His arm keeps brushing up against mine every few steps. On the inside I am bristling with each contact. *Zepher, please, I like you, but I thought we were past this. Why can't we just be friends?* I increase my gait in order to get to my vehicle more quickly. Reaching my jeep, I click the remote and pull open the door. Before sliding in to the driver's seat I turn to offer Zepher a polite good-bye. And he is right there in front of me. So close. I suck in a breath. His eyes are watchful and quiet, but for a moment his lips twitch, and I think he is going to break into a grin. This strikes me as rather odd. *Is he getting all serious preparing to put the moves on me, or does he just think it is funny to watch me squirm?* To avoid his gaze, I focus on the beauty mark above his lip.

He takes a step toward me and I lean into the doorjam. My heart begins tripping out of control seemingly of its own accord. *Double crap!* He clears his throat, and his voice grows soft. "Do you . . . do you think that maybe after . . . after all of this is over we could—" My eyes widen. *No, Zepher, don't say it. Please don't*—"that you and I could go, I don't know, do something. Just hang out or whatever. I know you said before that we should just—"

Just be friends! I thought we agreed to just be friends, and you were okay with that! I begin trembling all over. I don't ever want to have this conversation, and now it looks as if it is going to be forced out of me here and now. And I am so scared. So scared to hurt Zepher's feelings, so scared to lose a friend. I close my eyes.

While my lashes are still resting against my cheeks, I hear a rustling noise coming from the corner of my yard and then, "Hey . . . what is going on?" A familiar male voice calls in our direction. My lids flash back open. Zepher takes a step backward, away from me. And we both turn toward the approaching figure. *Seth?* From my distance Seth appears to have a perplexed, almost irritated, look on his face. Ignoring me, with narrowed eyes he focuses his gaze on his brother. "I said, what is going on, Seth?"

Seth? I shake my head, thinking I've just heard wrong. Zepher takes another step backward, creating a clear distance between us. For just a moment a flash of worry crosses over his features before it is replaced with a wide grin. Seth keeps advancing toward us. When he is only a few feet away, I observe the challenging look in his countenance and gasp for air, suddenly completely confused. *His face! His mouth! The beauty mark above his mouth?* Over and over my eyes dart back and forth between the brothers. *What is going on?* Who is who? Suddenly, I have no idea.

Because both have beauty marks above their lips.

The brother who I assumed was Zepher detects my disconcerted expression and bursts into laughter. But the other brother who I now have to believe is the real Zepher doesn't look at all amused. "What?" he questions through narrowed eyes. "What do you have painted on your face, Seth? What are you trying to prove?"

"Just having a little fun."

A little fun? I am completely speechless, and still feeling puzzled. Suddenly I experience an imperative need for clarification. Shaking my head, I try to gather my muddled thoughts. "So . . . what? What is going on? Who is exactly who here?" I sputter incredulously.

"Wipe off your face and show her, Seth," comes the command from the newly arriving brother. Acquiescing, the twin who I had thought only moments before was Zepher proceeds to wipe his hand across his upper lip, smearing what I had assumed was a beauty mark, causing it to disappear. I gasp. *Oh. My. What?* Suddenly I am angry and relieved at the same time. And yet my mind is still whirling in confusion as I try to recall all the times I'd had intimate, flirty encounters with who I always uncomfortably assumed was Zepher. My good friend Zepher. Was it ever Zepher at all? Or had it always been Seth? *Oh my word, I feel so stupid!*

Who I now know is really Seth appears to be practically bent in two, holding his stomach in laughter, obviously feeling proud of the elaborate prank he has been able to carry out. And the real Zepher looks pissed. My cheeks heat up as I realize that ultimately I am pissed too. Suddenly I feel desperate to know how far this has gone. How extensive was his scheme? Was it today only? I turn toward Seth. "How long has this been going on?" My voice is demanding, edged in anger, and Seth sobers slightly.

"Long enough. Let's just say long enough to say that either I'm a genius, or else you are completely gullible and don't know Zepher as well as you think you do."

At this statement I am completely horrified. Sheepishly I glance over at the real Zepher to see how he is now reacting. But although he is avoiding eye contact with me, I can't tell if his incense is really directed toward Seth. I can only hope so. I heave a sigh and look back at Seth where I focus my gaze on the leftover dark stain on the top of his lip. *That jerk!* A multitude of feelings are coursing through my brain, causing me to feel overwhelmed: anger, betrayal, embarrassment, hurt, and complete puzzlement. *How could I have been so dumb?* "I'm glad you think this is so funny!" I tell Seth.

At the obvious sound of ire in my words, Zepher now levels his gaze on his brother. He appears furious. But in spite of the multitude of daggers being sent Seth's way, Seth continues to beam. "Oh, lighten up, both of you. It was all in fun." Pinching his forefinger and thumb together he continues. "And maybe a teeny bit of an experiment, but geez, no one was hurt by it, so relax. And besides," he says as he stares his brother Zepher directly in the eye, "I was only doing you a favor, bro."

At this Zepher's face turns bright red and he looks away. And my confusion only continues to deepen.

After Seth and Zepher leave, in a dazed-state I contemplate all that I have just discovered about the one-sided switch-up with the brothers. Taking a quick trip down memory lane, I try to recall all of the encounters I'd had with Zepher since Tristan's disappearance. *There were so many.* Piecing all of the actions together with who I know to be the true Zepher, I try to decide which engagements were actually him and which could have been Seth. Surprisingly enough, it is not that hard to separate and assign episodes to the correct brother. This only adds to the anger and relief and stupidity I've been experiencing since the whole revelation of the hoax. At the time I had trusted so much in the discovery of the beauty mark to differentiate between the two that I never once jumped to the conclusion that it could have been the other twin playing a prank on me. And what of Seth's last statement to Zepher about *only doing him a favor*? What exactly did that mean?

I shake my head in slight trepidation. *Hopefully nothing.* Not having much time to dwell on the situation, I begin sliding into my car once again so that I can start toward Connecticut when I realize something is absent from my back pocket. I'd left my phone in the house. Turning tail, I begin a quick jaunt back to the cabin to retrieve it but stop short when I detect hurried movement coming from the beach path. Briefly I wonder if it is one of the twins coming back. But then the figure emerges from the surrounding foliage, and with a heart-hammering jolt, I realize that it is Tristan. Tristan is coming toward me, soaking wet, rushed, and breathless. *What is going on?* My first thoughts go to Nate, but I know that he is inside the cabin safe and sound with Isabella.

"Hey . . . Bethany. I am so glad I found you."

"Hey . . . what's up?" My voice matches the urgency in his.

"The roar is getting louder . . . have you heard it? Can you hear it now?"

I shake my head in confusion, straining my ear to listen for something that I can't hear at all. *What is he talking about?* "No . . . no, I don't hear anything. What do you mean?"

"The roar from the volcanic section of the ocean," he replies as if I should already know what he is referring to. "It is getting louder. I can hear it so I wondered if you could too." Once again I shake my head while Tristan keeps hurriedly talking. "I want to go out there . . . and check it out. I need to check it out and see what is happening with it. I've done all I can do for now with the pollution feeds. I need to find out if the ocean is going to respond and back off. Or—" He stops and runs a hand through the dripping strands of his hair, leaving little leftover droplets of water on his cheeks. "Or whether it is going to blow." For a moment he closes his eyes. When he reopens them, his expression is laced with worry. In response my pulse starts tripping on high alert. "And if so, we need to start warning people . . . everyone. I don't know how far spread the ramifications of this is going to be. But it might be devastating."

I suck in a breath. This is getting real. *Too real.* The end of life the way we know it may be just days or hours or minutes away. How bad will it be? Will anyone lose their life over it? Or in all actuality, will anyone on the Eastern Seaboard even survive at all? Panic rushes through my veins, and my vision locks with Tristan's as he seemingly reads my thoughts. Silently I plead with my eyes for him to tell me that I am wrong—asking him to say something that will refute all that I am imagining. But he never does. Instead he clears his throat. "Come with me . . . will you come with me and check the scene out again? Offer a second opinion. Help me make the decision about the next move . . . there might not be much time. We'd have to leave now."

I don't have to think twice. "Of course . . . let me just get the keys for *Blue*." While I run into the cabin to grab my phone and now the boat keys as well, I can hear the sound of Tristan closing the ajar door on my black jeep. Minutes later we pull away from the dock in front of my house and head toward the open waters of the ocean at breakneck speed.

The sun shines down in a deceptive manner as we skim along the surface of the waves, giving the impression that it is a perfect day. But I know all too well that what we are about to come upon in the far reaches of the sea is going to be anything but pleasant. I close my eyes and allow the warm rays to saturate my face, trying hard not to imagine the worst. But it is difficult to pretend when I have a foreboding feeling in the pit of my stomach. *This is going to be bad.* Since the minute I'd encountered Tristan today, his whole persona seemed to hold a type of urgency. Would the catastrophic explosion occur soon? Possibly even while we are out on the ocean? Will this be the end? Will I ever see Nate again? Suddenly I feel desperate to go back. I need to hold my baby boy just one more time. Taking a deep breath, I try to push away that thought. *No, I need to help Tristan.* What if there is something we can do to help stop this? *What if.* Then I can feel the sweetness of Nate in my arms for many more years to come. Sensing Tristan's gaze on my face, I open my lids again and look in his direction. For a moment our eyes lock, and all the anguish and turmoil I am feeling is shared between us. *He isn't sure either.* He doesn't know what the outcome is going to be any more than I do. Swallowing hard, I turn my head toward the rising wake of the boat.

We are going so fast and the engine is so loud that it takes a few minutes for me to figure if the roar that I am hearing is just Tristan stepping up the accelerator. Or something more. Another thirty seconds later I determine with bone-chilling realization that it is indeed something more. *Something way more!* Ten times louder than what I'd heard when I'd been out here with Tristan on the previous visit. No wonder he had been able to hear it from miles away. Now I speculate why I hadn't. Maybe I just hadn't been tuned in. Again I turn toward Tristan, and this time he nods his head slowly. His face is serious. I don't have to say a word. He knows that I am now hearing the thundering drone, and that I am realizing its intensity. All the potential implications. He doesn't attempt to offer any comforting looks. *This is going to be ravaging, and we are going to have to be brave—together.* With wide eyes, I offer a slight nod and swallow deep.

Oh, God, help me—am I ready for this?

The moment *Blue* starts to bounce up and down on the increasingly choppy water, I know that we are approaching the volcanic site. But one glance at the stirred-up waves gathering around me tells me that the circumference has grown. Our watercraft is already starting to struggle in the unsettled ripples, and yet the epicenter is not even in sight. At this viewpoint we are not even able to get a glimpse of the core. I shake my head. Who are Tristan and I that we thought we could help? We are just two kids. And this is big. *Too big!* This is the ocean we are dealing with., the massive force that takes up over 70 percent of the earth. *Let's face it, it's over.* It is time to go back. This is too much. Let's go now, lay down with Nate, and wait to die. From the deafening sound of things, it won't be too long until that happens.

I am just about to express my newest conviction to Tristan when he suddenly swerves the boat to the far left and begins darting in and out of the turbulent rapids, finding zigzagging streams of passable waterways in which to guide the boat through. *Holy shit, this is crazy!* Gripping the leather cushion under my legs for dear life, I attempt to keep myself in a stable, upright position. But one curve of the wheel is too strong, and I go flying across the seat toward Tristan, landing against his strong, muscled arm and thigh. *Oh my word!* The wind whips against my face, blowing strands of hair into my eyes. I can hardly see. Attempting to maneuver out of my precarious position, I try to scoot back over. But gravity is holding me in place. In spite of the desperateness of our situation in the chaotic sea, unbelievably I am somehow embarrassed that I've ended up this way—pressed against Tristan's side. Surely he won't think that I've manipulated my way over here in pretense of not being able to hang on. "Sorry," I manage to yell into his ear. But he keeps twisting and guiding the boat through the water, seemingly not affected by the way my body is pressing into his. Twice I try to pull away, but I can hardly move an inch.

Finally, amidst the finagling of *Blue*, he leans his head toward me. Inwardly I cringe. This is so awkward, but what can I do? *What is he going to say?* Again I attempt to wrench myself away, this time using all of my strength. But in midmotion he lets go of the steering column and reaches out to grab my arm. "Don't," he shouts. Stopping my struggle, I focus my ear in the direction of his voice. "Don't try to get back. Just hang on. Forget it. Hang on to my waist . . . this is going to get rough."

Immediately I am relieved. He doesn't think I am trying to pull something. Of course he doesn't. This is life and death. For a brief moment I feel silly for even allowing myself to think that way at all, but then the boat jerks and I am forced to do as he says—put my arms around his waist and hang on for dear life. As my body presses up against his, for a two-second interlude I deceive myself into thinking that I am safe. Completely and utterly safe—protected from all that life has and is about to dole out—tucked snugly into Tristan's strong physique. Then I blink and peek out from his arm to face the turbulence of the water. Instantly reality comes crashing in. My fleeting feeling of security was only an illusion.

The roar is getting louder, and the churning motion of the waves is getting stronger.

For a while longer *Blue* continues to snake and surge through the enraged breakers that are closing in on us. Several times I think the boat is going to flip and I close my eyes, tightening my squeeze around Tristan's rock-hard abdomen. When it seems there are no more passable waterways, he finally draws back on the accelerator, and we stop going in a forward motion. Gravity's strength lessens. Unwinding my arms from Tristan's middle, I scoot away. At least a few inches. That's all I dare to move. The volcanic activity is great. I am certain that we are now staring into the face of the nucleus. Daring to lift my arms, I cover my ears. Up close the reverberation of the churned-up water is disturbingly loud, to the point of pain. Tristan offers me a cursory glance and then rises to his knees, shifting his gaze to the area surrounding the boat. Peering over the glass windshield, his head begins darting this way and that as he appears intent on finding something. *What is he looking for?*

All around us the waves continue to gyrate. Our watercraft, no longer being in a forward motion, is being tossed and turned uncontrollably, like a toy ship in a spa tub. A swell of water heaves toward us and smacks me in the face, soaking my entire body. For a split second I think this might be our end. But after shaking my head, my sight clears, and I realize that we are still afloat, albeit somewhat haphazardly. Tristan runs a hand quickly though his drenched hair and continues his search. I lean toward him. "What are you looking for?"

"The heeds." A thundering boom swallows his voice.

Oh God, it's getting worse. I grip the sides of my seat. "The what?" I call out, crinkling my nose in confusion. Tristan shifts his position and cocks his head.

"I said the feeds." *Oh, the feeds.* I nod my head. *But why? What is going on with them?* Another wave reaches up and saturates us. For a second I can't breathe. In the midst of the soaking I feel Tristan's hand gripping my arm. Once again the water clears. For a second I sputter and cough while Tristan watches me. "You okay?" he shouts. *No. I don't know. I guess.* Spitting out the taste of the salty liquid, I nod. He continues. "I don't see the feeds. The dark streams of water that we saw before. They aren't here anymore." I can barely comprehend what he is saying.

"What does that mean?" I yell back but I'm not sure if he can understand my question. At this point I can't even hear my own voice. Tristan studies my face, trying to interpret my lips.

"Hopefully that there is not enough pollution to feed the core. It should—" A large explosion of water interrupts his answer. In front of us a giant geyser skyrockets into the air. All around it a sea of unsettled fluid bubbles and churns, growing into an unrelenting force. Our boat rocks and tips and finally stabilizes for the time being. Tristan increases his voice to a higher decibel and tries again. The unrelenting roar does its best to drown out his words, but I watch his lips with great precision so that I can catch what he is saying. "I hoped that if we had done enough cleanup on shore, the feeds would stop and it might be enough to prevent a catastrophic explosion. And now, since the feeds no longer seem to be playing a part in this thing, since they seem to have stopped, I thought that maybe our efforts were going to pay off." Tristan sends a brief glance toward the oceanic volcano and then shakes his head as he leans back in. His face looks grave and sad. "But I don't know. Maybe we were wrong all along . . . or maybe we are just too late."

A sickening feeling settles in the pit of my stomach as my eyes leave Tristan's face to take in the conditions of the worsening sea. And all at once, I know that what Tristan has just said is true. Apparently it *is* too late. Our plan has not worked. And now it will be too late to make it back and warn everyone on land. Even if we were able to pull our boat out of this unbridled mess, there wouldn't be time to evacuate the Eastern Seaboard. *This is it.* Finally the end. Suddenly, out of nowhere, my heart aches to be with Nate, to see his rosy cheeks and watch his eyes turn from blue to green one more time. Just one more time. When the water comes sweeping over the land with a vengeance, will he be scared? Will Isabella be there to comfort him? Will it happen quickly so that he won't have to suffer?

Once again a large, shooting eruption of water reaches up toward the sky, spraying a large circumference on its way back down, including us. Our boat pitches forward and turns sideways, coming very close to capsizing. At the last minute it rights itself, but by now there is at least a foot or more of water covering the floorboards. It won't be long. I close my eyes and lift them heavenward. *I am ready.* Sensing Tristan's stare, I open my lids again. His face holds a tender expression as he watches me succumb to the inevitability of our predicament. I can tell he feels bad: feels disappointed that our plan didn't work, and feels responsible for dragging me out here only to die. In slow motion he opens his arms.

I hesitate. I am no longer his. It wouldn't feel right. Biting my lip, I blink away the water that is dripping into my eyes, leftover from the last soaking wave. But on the other hand, it couldn't be more right. I make a decision. Abandoning my spot on the seat, I slowly enter his embrace. Cradling me with his strong biceps, he pulls me to his chest and holds me securely in place while we wait.

While we wait to die.

Even Tristan's ability to swim underwater won't be enough for this powerful cogency. It will soon devour us all. An earsplitting detonation shakes the air, but I can't bring myself to look. Shuddering, I bury my head into Tristan's neck. Crushing me against his body, Tristan rubs his hands up and down my back repeatedly in a comforting motion. The irony of what it finally took to put me back in Tristan's arms does not escape me even during this life-ending event. With tears now streaming down my cheeks for several different reasons, I hold my breath and brace myself for what will most certainly be the final explosion.

Only it doesn't come.

Instead, a series of several blasts fill the air until all at once it hits me that the roaring noise is no longer painfully loud. It is actually tolerable. I can actually hear things besides a deafening drone, like the creak and whine of the boat rocking, or the sound of water bubbling and mixing all around us.

But no longer exploding.

The water is no longer exploding!

Lifting my head from Tristan's chest, I dare to look at our surroundings. I suddenly want to shout for joy and break into a sobbing fit all at the same time. I am momentarily stunned. Clearly the threat is dissipating. I can't believe our good fortune. Below me, I sense the shifting movement of Tristan turning to look too. I can almost physically experience the relief as it resonates through his body. *It worked! Our plan and all of our efforts have worked!* The ocean has conceded. It is settling down. It is no longer threatening to explode. We are safe. We are all safe. I pull back from him, tears still streaming down my cheeks.

And he is right there looking back at me, an expression of victory illuminating his face—his perfectly beautiful face. *We did it! We did it together! Just let yourself imagine the far-reaching effects of all of our efforts!* I smile back, letting him know that I am echoing his thoughts. For a few moments the light from his green eyes collides with mine, and it feels like we are on top of the world. Our unspoken victory is like fireworks on the fourth of July. Inside I am singing and dancing and whooping at the top of my lungs, and I can tell he is too. But then, that quickly, something changes and his smile fades. Now the victory dance has taken on a different tone, and a new rhythm arises between us. Something deep and inherent. A desperate need. My heart begins to beat hard against my chest wall. Suddenly the few inches that stand between us seems to be thick with a magnetic pull. I let out a slow expulsion of air, and Tristan inhales it down afterward. It is like we are one breath. I breathe out, he breathes in. One time, then another, and then again. I can feel my body leaning forward. I can sense him leaning too.

And then the boat lurches, and I jerk backward. The moment is gone. Now when I look back at Tristan, my cheeks feel hot and red. I glance awkwardly away. He too seems suddenly self-conscious and tongue-tied, opening his mouth to speak and then shutting it again. Turning away, he moves to position himself behind the steering column, and I scoot way over to the other side of the crème-colored leather interior seat where I had been when we originally started the trip. Tristan heaves a sigh. "Wow," he finally says. "That was some freakin' craziness. Too close." *What was too close, our near death experience, or our near kiss?* But I know what he is referring to. The ocean, of course. That *was* close. But thankfully it is over now, hopefully never to occur again. Hopefully people will now take the pollution thing seriously and make long-term plans to protect the ocean environment for good.

Chapter Twenty-Two

I am jumpy for days after my and Tristan's near-death experience on the open waters of the ocean. My nights are filled with nightmares about loud, explosive, whitecapped waves that reach up so high they block the light of the sun. I know that when they peak and roll back downward they will surely wash away everything on the Eastern Seaboard. Complete devastation is only moments away. At times I wake up gasping for air, just sure that I am swallowing down large gulps of water as the surf plunges over my head. Next to me Nate, who I've woken by my restlessness, watches me through the rungs of his crib with a concerned look on his face. But aside from me and my nightmares, the entire town of Watch Hill and all the surrounding areas that had been affected by the disturbances are now relieved and happy. The big threat is gone. Of course they don't understand the entirety of the situation. They don't know about the actual volcanic area that had existed in the ocean and about the direct feeding lines that needed to be severed. All they know is that pollution was upsetting the natural marine balance which was in turn causing the unsettled waterway. And now due to everyone's hard work, everything seems to be better.

I'm happy too. Immensely relieved. But I know too much. I understand the complexity of everything. I know how close we all were to complete devastation. And of course, I witnessed everything firsthand with Tristan, so it takes a little more for me to land back on my feet. To wipe away that image of the stirred-up, angry ocean from my mind. To do normal, day-to-day things once again without all my limbs shaking over the most trivial occurrences.

So when Lucy texts me to tell me she wants us to meet for lunch, I welcome the plan wholeheartedly. *Spending time with Lucy*—that is about as normal as it gets for me. After my heart-to-heart conversation with Ethan at Waves, I had relayed all he had told me to Lucy. After that, the ball was in her court. I know that she hadn't wasted any time going to him. But so far I hadn't heard the final outcome.

"Hi Bethany," she calls to me with a wide smile on her face the minute I step through the door of St. Clair Annex. Inwardly I relax. *She is smiling, that is good.* I wave and walk over to where she is sitting at a parlor table in the center of the room.

Pulling out a chair, I take a seat across from her. "Hey." I take note of the slender, liquid-filled flute on her placemat. "Did you already order?"

She shakes her head and takes a sip out of her glass. "It's just lemon water. No, I was waiting for you."

"Well, let's get some food. I am dying to know how it went with you and Ethan, and once we start talking I know I won't want to interrupt to place an order." At that, Lucy chuckles and we go up to the counter. Minutes later we return with steaming bowls of clam chowder and thick slices of artesian bread. And for me a tall glass of sweetened tea. I take a spoonful of soup and blow in it. My breath mixes with the vapor. It still looks too hot, so I set it back down and eye Lucy. "Well?"

Lucy begins stirring her soup, glancing up at me with a combination of happy and sad at the same time. Little warning signals begin to flicker in my mind. *How can these conflicting emotions be present on her face all at once?* Steeling my heart, I prepare for the many ways I might have to console her if the outcome is not what she'd wanted. *But what of the smiley face?* I really am confused. Finally she sets her spoon down, looks me in the eye, and beams. "Well . . . we worked it out!"

A comforting feeling washes over me. "Oh, Lucy . . . that is awesome. I am so glad."

Her doelike eyes are brimming with exhilaration. "I know . . . we really had to talk. And we had to agree to talk in the future instead of running from our problems. Now we are on the same page. Looking back, I can't believe this even came between us. It is silly. Bottom line, we decided we want to be together no matter what. No matter where."

I sputter on the drink of tea that I'd just sucked between my lips. "Where?" *What do you mean, no matter where?*

Now the happiness that was filling her countenance dissipates slightly, and a type of melancholy moves in to take its place. She bites her lip, and I notice she is having a hard time looking me in the eye. "Yeah," she sighs. "The thing is, we talked about it and he was exactly right, I am getting restless here. But so is he. As it turns out, we are both feeling the same things. We are both feeling stagnant in our careers. So—"

So? I hold my breath.

"—we've been looking into some things. Ethan has signed up for classes at University of Chicago to get his masters in business and—"

"Wait, what? Chicago?" I interrupt. "I am confused."

Now Lucy looks really sad, and I have a big premonition I know what is coming—what she is about to say next. Immediately a lump forms in the back of my throat as I wait for her to explain. "So . . . yeah, Chicago. And I'm going too." For a moment she pauses as she waits for the words to sink in. My face becomes a mask, hiding the shock that I am now feeling. I know I need to listen to what she has to say without ruining her pursuit for happiness, so I wait for her to finish. "I have two interviews set up there for marketing positions. One with Sears Holdings and one with Motorola."

Fighting back the tears that are hovering just behind my eyes, I force the most genuine smile I can muster. "Wow . . . Lucy, that is . . . wow. That is big time. I am so . . . so happy for you. For both of you." *And so completely devastated at the thought of you leaving this town. Of you leaving me at all.*

At my words, her face lights up again. I can tell she is so relieved that I have given her my blessing. But the night after Lucy relays her news to me, she is added to my dreams. Now when the midnight waves catapult high into the air, she is swept away with them, balancing on their crest, terrified, waiting to plunge back to earth. And I am terrified too—where will she land when she falls? Will I be in the right spot to catch her? Up and down the shorelines I run with my eyes glued to the sky. All through town, in and among the quaint cottages and tourist shops, I scuttle looking for just the right angle, just the right station to position myself in order to cushion her descent. But it never seems like the perfect place. It always feels like I'm going to miss her plunge.

I am deep inside my latest dream, observing a giant gush of water being hurled into the air, when I hear my name being yelled from somewhere in the distance. The summoning is urgent and desperate, and for many moments I am sure that it is Lucy. Lucy is calling to me, and this time I can't see her anywhere. "Lucy, Lucy, hold on, I'll find you," I moan into my down-filled duvet. Thrashing against the mattress, I begin my search down a lonely shoreline only to feel two strong hands gripping my arms, shaking me.

I wake with a start.

And come head on with the frantic expression on my brother Josh's face. *What?* It takes me a few moments to focus and realize that I am not still in a dream. Was I calling out in my sleep, disturbing the whole household? The look in Josh's eyes tells me no—this is not about me. Immediately my nerve endings jump into high alert. The sound of panic in Josh's voice sends a series of chills down my spine. He is frenziedly trying to tell me something, but his words are all running into one. All I can make out is "She has him, she has him," over and over again. I shake my head to clear it and fix my gaze on Nate's crib. He is all curled up, sleeping soundly. Instantly a measure of relief fills my entire being. *Thank goodness!* I turn back toward Josh's desperate form. Breaking free from his grip, I sit up in bed and in turn curl my fingers around *his* arms.

"Josh . . . Josh. You have to slow down. I can't understand you. You need to tell me what is going on, but you have to slow down!"

Josh's eyes are wild. "It's too late . . . drown . . . she's got him."

All I hear is *drown*. Gripping his shoulders, I shake him hard. "*Josh . . . slow . . . down!*" My tone becomes severe—a military police-man. "Tell me what has happened!"

"He . . . she . . . water." Josh's voice, switching from panic mode, is now on the edge of tears. I am losing him. He is shutting down. Alarm pulses through my veins. Forcing gentleness into my words, I look him directly in the eye.

"Josh . . . try your best. I need to know what has happened so that I can help you. I am going to help you, but I need for you to explain."

For many moments his lip quivers while I continue holding his gaze. I refuse to look away. Even in the darkness of the room I can detect tears streaming down his cheeks. It feels like a punch in the gut to see him like this. My once on-top-of-the-world, strapping, young brother reduced to this pathetic mess. For a brief second I wonder what time it is anyway. Out of my peripheral vision I see the bright red numbers on my alarm clock: four thirty in the morning. Finally Josh takes a deep breath. Afterward his shoulders begin to shake, and I wonder if he is going to completely break down. Instead, he severs my hold, wipes at his face, and averts his gaze as he begins to speak. "We've been hanging out with an older girl."

I swallow hard. Am I going to be ready for this? Nodding my head, I encourage him to go on. But his eyes are still focused on my bedcovers, so I'm not sure if he even notices.

"We knew it was wrong . . . that she was dangerous. But we

couldn't seem to stay away." Josh stops talking, and I wait patiently with my heart pounding in my chest. As hard as this is for me to hear, I know it is that much harder for him to say. Now his eyes are completely downcast. Through the window pane the pale moonlight filters in, revealing the embarrassment that he is trying to hide. "She made us do things . . . to her . . . both of us . . . all of us, that we knew we shouldn't. Dark things. We tried . . . we tried to stop. We wanted to quit . . . to quit going to her. But we couldn't. I stopped wanting to do anything else. Jake too. All our summer friends that we'd been hanging out with suddenly seemed boring. All of the girls from town couldn't compare to the dangerous high we got from being with her. All we wanted was her and all the things she had us do. Many times she'd have us do things that involved asphyxiation both above and below the water. It would take us to the edge of death. But we always survived . . . then we'd want to try it again to see if we would survive again."

It feels like my lungs are collapsing into my stomach. All this had been happening to my little brothers while I refused to get too involved in their lives, making only feeble attempts at confronting them about their peculiar behavior. I am sick. Ashamed, now it is my turn to avert my gaze. How can I face my sibling knowing that I've let him down—that I've done very little to stop all that he and Jake had been going through all summer? At this Josh's blue-gray eyes shoot upward to confront my mortified expression. Suddenly his voice is emphatic, as if he wants to convince me. "We did try to stop though. We made pacts with each other . . . to quit. And for days we would. And then . . . and then the sleepwalking began. We'd remember going to sleep in our own beds and then we would wake up and be with her instead. And we couldn't even remember how we got there. In the morning, somehow we'd wake up in our room again. We knew we were screwed. There was no stopping it. What was happening, we couldn't stop it." Once again his voice takes on a panicked tone. "And now—" His eyes shift toward me in desperation, and his breaths begin coming in rapid succession, interrupting his train of thought. He appears to be on the verge of hyperventilating.

"And now what, Josh?" I keep my tone soothing even though on the inside I am a complete mess. "Talk to me, Josh. Tell me what has happened." This is the punch line I've been waiting for, what he initially came to the bedroom to tell me. He can't bail now. I needed him to clarify his erratic statements by taking me back to the beginning. But right now, I need for him to finish. I need to know exactly what is going on at the moment so I can do my best to help.

Josh's face becomes absorbed terror. "And now she has taken Jake into the water. And they haven't come back . . . she is going to drown him."

The veins under my skin turn to ice. My voice becomes a choked whisper. "Who? . . . Who has Jake, Josh?"

"Rye."

Oh God, no! Suddenly the room begins to spin out of control, and the mattress that I am clinging to feels as though it is tipping sideways. My grip on reality is quickly diminishing into thin air. I am sinking fast. Too fast. I can't think straight. I can't focus at all.

"Bethany? Bethany?" Josh begins calling my name throwing me a tiny thread of lucidity. Grasping on tightly to that small tendering, I begin pulling myself back to the present. I have to get control. Taking deep breaths in though my nose, I release dead air through pursed lips. Locating Josh's silhouette on the bed, I use his face as a focusing point. With an escalating voice he meets my gaze and keeps talking. "Her name is Rye . . . She has Jake, Bethany. What can we do? We've got to try to help him. How can we help him? How can we help Jake?"

I blink. "Where were you when she took him? Do you know how to get there by boat?"

"Yes."

Josh's answer stirs me into motion. After reaching Lucy by phone, she comes over to the cabin to stay with Nate while I gather my things to take down to the boat. Outside it is still dark. Clouds are now covering the moon, and precipitation has begun coming down in a steady mist. By the time I reach the dock, my rain slicker is already coated in moisture. As I undo the ropes that hold *Blue* in place, my mind keeps sinking back into a chaotic mess. Over and over I jerk my head to bring myself back to the here and now, to focus on the problem at hand. Lifting my face upward, I silently call into the murky sky. *Why, Rye? Is it not enough that you've already tried to steal my son? You've taken my husband. And now my brothers too? When is it ever going to be enough?* Situating myself in the driver's seat, I lower my eyes. Grasping the steering column, I begin edging the boat out to the open sea. My thoughts are still on Rye. Does her resentment and hatred for me over marrying Tristan go this deep? Immediately my body begins to tremble, partially due to the cool, damp air that is now whipping at my face, and partially due to my unnerving predicament. Rye already has Tristan; shouldn't that be adequate repayment? In my mind she has already won. Why isn't it enough for her? Why won't she stop?

Josh knows the nautical landscape well, even in the dark. But of course he does; he'd been going there with Jake night after night while I slept soundly in the comfort of my own bed. Directing us northward, he helps me to guide the boat around bend after bend in the coastline, skirting around small, unoccupied islands until finally reaching a jetting, rocky terrain in the middle of nowhere. After pulling *Blue* as close as we can to the beach, we wade the rest of the way in, calling Josh's name with each step. The water is warmer than the air, causing an early morning fog to rise off of the surf. It is difficult to navigate around protruding boulders and pieces of driftwood hiding beneath the vapors that are now covering our feet.

Finally we reach the shore. "This is where we last were before she took him," Josh finally tells me through choppy breaths.

We decide to split up in order to cover more ground. Using a flashlight I search through rocks and bushes, hoping to locate Jake's form resting somewhere, probably shaken, but hopefully safe. The whole time I am rifling through the undomesticated shrubbery and rock-strewn terrain, one thought keeps rushing through my brain: Will we even locate Jake on land? If Rye really took him, then Josh is probably right—she probably has him somewhere out in the water. Will she really drown him though? Will she really go that far? After what feels like a long search, finally, empty-handed, I turn back to find Josh.

When I run into him, he too is alone. His whole persona radiates desperation. Once again I detect tears dripping from his eyes, running onto his cheeks. A now-steady precipitation falls against his face, helping to wipe them away. "I haven't told you everything," he blurts upon seeing me. I go still in preparation for whatever it is he is about to share. He continues. "Rye had a friend named Freddy." *Freddy!* Goose bumps cover my skin as I recognize the name I'd heard my brothers call out in their sleep on more than one occasion. *I guess Freddy wasn't really Eddy after all.* "We were all in the boat. At first we were just goofing off. But then Freddy started making jibes, comments . . . comments about me and Jake. There . . . there was a fight. We were all fighting. And then—"

"And then what, Josh?"

Josh runs shaky fingers though the wet strands of his hair. He is staring out to sea with a glazed look in his eyes. "And then I pushed him. I didn't mean to push him that hard. But I did. I was so mad about what he was saying. About what he was saying about me and Jake. When I pushed him he fell in . . . he fell in the water and drowned that night."

I swallow hard trying to digest everything he is telling me, and a smattering of rain slides down my throat. Wiping the back of my hand against my lips, I swallow again while sorting through all the ramifications of what Josh has just presented. It is almost too much. But I have to remain calm. Josh is falling apart in front of me, and he needs me to keep it together. Suddenly he makes an unintelligible noise that resembles a sob, and his distraught voice breaks through my musings.

"I killed Freddy, Bethany. I killed Freddy. I am a murderer. We kept waiting for the police to come, for something to be on the news . . . but it never was. But it's going to be. Someday he'll be discovered missing, and the trail will point back to me." Josh stops talking and looks right at me. His eyes are wild and desperate. "All the problems with the ocean . . . all the big waves and the destruction and shit on land, it is all my fault. The police never came after me, so this was my punishment instead—my punishment for causing someone to drown." *What? No, he can't think that!*

"Whoa, stop, Josh." I practically yell. "The ocean thing was not your fault. It was due to all of the pollution. And look . . . after cleaning it up, it has stopped now. So it can't be your fault."

"It *is* my fault! And now Rye has taken Jake to drown him, and that is my fault too. It is my payback. It is my payback for killing Freddy." Josh buries his face in his hands to hide the weeping sounds that are now pouring from his throat. I momentarily close my eyes to squeeze away the grimacing sound that wants to escape from my own. For a few seconds anxiety threatens to overcome me, and I consider going to join Josh in his overwhelming grief, allowing the floodgate of tears to open. Together we could just sit here on the shoreline and cry until there is nothing more left inside either of us. For hours or days—as long as it takes.

But what then?

Taking a deep breath, I begin walking slowly in Josh's direction. Reaching him, I place a gentle hand on his arm. My voice is placid, as if I am talking to a small child. And really Josh is a small child, a small child in a grownup's body who has had everything about his innocence stolen from him over the course of a few months' time. "It's not your fault, Josh. All of this is not your fault. It was an accident. Just an accid—"

I stop talking. The splashing sound of neatly parting water captures my attention. I look to the ocean. And my heart jump starts in my chest.

Jake is sluggishly wading through the surf, heading in our direction. Joy fills my chest. The sound of Josh crying stops and he too turns to see what I am seeing. *Jake! Jake, living and breathing and walking our way!* Josh abandons his spot on the shoreline and goes to meet him out in the water. I am only seconds behind. "Jake . . . Jake," Josh calls as he runs, all the while wiping fists at his eyes.

But Jake doesn't answer. Nodding his head, his whole body begins shivering uncontrollably. Immediately Josh and I converge on him to wrap him in a hug. Situating ourselves on either side of him, we sling one of his arms over each of our shoulders and help him onto the boat. Taking a dry blanket from a cubby, I place it around his shoulders and prepare *Blue* for departure.

"What happened out there, man?" Josh questions his brother as the boat trolls softly through shallow water. We are still fairly close to shore. "I thought . . . I mean you were out there so long. I was sure she was going to drown you." Still Jake doesn't answer, and I keep sending worried glances his way while Josh continues to inquire. "Were you under the water, man? How could you have stayed under the water so long?"

Though continuing to shake, Jake remains quiet. Josh looks worried. Inside, I am alarmed.

"Why aren't you talking, man? I knew it . . . Rye is a witch," Josh declares emphatically. Inwardly I gasp. "I saw you go under. You were underwater that whole time, weren't you Jake? Just *tell* me!"

Jake's eyes seem to take on a new light, and eventually he offers a barely perceptible nod. Josh notices though and it is just enough. Just enough for his eyes to register some semblance of satisfaction as if relieved that he is finally getting somewhere. I cough. *No! I can't let them think that it's true!*

"She is a sea witch. She has got to be." Josh nudges Jake in the arm. "Tell Bethany, Jake. Tell her how we've suspected that she is a witch. Tell her about how she used to hypnotize us. She'd sing to us and we'd fall asleep. And then we'd wake up and be doing—" Josh stops talking and looks away. For a split second I detect a flicker of pain interrupting the dull expression on Jake's face. It makes me want to vomit.

It makes me want to find Rye and kill her.

Instead I clear my throat. *This line of thinking has to stop.* "Rye is not a witch . . . I mean she can't *really* be a sea witch." Both brothers are now looking in my direction, Jake's teeth chattering, and I realize that what I say now is going to matter. I have a trusting, captivated audience, desperately searching for answers for their hellish summer. And what I come up with now as a possible explanation is going to make a serious impact. *I'd better make this good.* Licking my lips, I taste the rainwater that is still coming down in a light, steady stream. "Don't get me wrong. She *is* a bad person. It sounds like she is a *really* bad person. Downright evil. And who knows, I can't say for sure that she isn't dabbling in witchcraft, maybe you are right. But there are explanations for the things you've been through. I think she must have been giving you drugs—"

"But we don't do drugs," Josh interrupts.

"Of course not . . . not on purpose," I quickly clarify. I don't need to add to their already well-established guilt. "But she may have been slipping them to you somehow unbeknownst to you. She sounds crafty enough to do something like that. That would explain many of the things that were happening. You couldn't help them.

You weren't aware of what she was doing to you. And maybe Jake wasn't really in the water as long as you think. He was probably drugged so he couldn't know the *actual* length of time. It makes sense." *More sense than the alternative.*

Jake lowers his eyes to the floorboard of the boat, and I get the feeling that deep down he isn't buying into my explanation. But maybe he will make a conscious choice to believe it anyway. Maybe what I've just offered as a rationalization will influence his thinking in such a way that someday he will look back on it as the truth. *I can only hope.*

Josh meets my gaze. *But what about Freddy? Accident or not, I still killed Freddy,* he asks me through troubled eyes. Holding his hurting stare, I send him the most empathetic expression I can conjure. *I'm sorry, Josh, for that I have no answer,* I convey back to him as I hang my head and slowly turn away.

Chapter Twenty-Three

I am not surprised by my parent's reaction when they arrive at Watch Hill to pick up my brothers. They are completely disturbed. Upon first glance Mom brings a hand to her mouth and gasps aloud. I can tell that tears are stinging the back of her eyes. Dad swallows hard and stares fiercely in their direction, his hair appearing to grow more gray by the moment. In return, with shoulders slumped and shadows etched beneath their eyes, Josh and Jake stand beside their baggage anxiously watching my parents, looking more than ready to depart for home. It's as if they can't get out of town soon enough. And I can't blame them—they have been through much. Too much. Will they ever be the same again?

The minute my parents had gotten back from their anniversary trip, I had made the dreaded phone call that filled them in on the twins' condition. *Sorry to tell them Jake and Josh had gotten mixed up with the wrong group of kids, that on one unfortunate occasion they had witnessed the near-drowning of one of their friends. It affected them so badly they may need counseling to sort through everything. And FYI, should they ever come up with peculiar or fanciful ideas about what happened, the girl that they were involved with, who was the ringleader, may have been slipping them chemical substances to alter their perception of reality.*

Upon hearing the story, my mom was completely incensed. *Why hadn't I told them about this sooner? They should have been there for the boys. They would have skipped the trip had they known any of this.* Cradling the phone against my ear, I had closed my eyes tightly and sighed inwardly as I listened to my mom's inquisition. Maybe she was right. Maybe I should have just interrupted their anniversary getaway and called them sooner. What would happen to my brothers now? Even with counseling, would they ever recover from all the hurtful things they had experienced this summer conducted by the hand of Rye?

After speaking with me, my mom had hung up the phone to get ahold of my dad and then called me back again less than ten minutes later. *They were coming to get the boys—now—pronto. They would have come to get them a long time ago had they only known!* A sour feeling filled my stomach as I listened to my mom's voice lecturing on the other end of the line. I knew right then that my parents had officially had enough of Watch Hill. She didn't even have to speak the words aloud—I knew what they must be thinking. *First our daughter was shattered by that stupid place in the course of one summer. And although having experienced a fleeting bout of happiness, is going through the whole thing over again only in a slightly different form—by the uncanny form of amnesia that has all but destroyed her short-lived marriage. And now our boys? Our precious baby boys!*

And of course my parents were right in their thinking. What *is* wrong with this place? What is wrong with me that I keep coming back to it? That I keep dragging the people I love here to get hurt right along with me? *Except Lucy.* From all appearances it looked like Lucy was going to end up being okay. But then again, she was leaving town. Was that why? Was that why she would end up being okay? Was that her way of unknowingly escaping the hurt handed out in this place? Was it the town then? Was it the people from the water we encountered who were involved in the town? Or was it the water itself? One thing I did know for sure: the sea had changed me forever. And now, one way or the other, the sea had changed my brothers too.

As my brothers are preparing to load their things into the back of my parents' car, I detect Isabella standing in the far corner of the yard. Her brown eyes look sad. She busies herself picking up Nate's toys that are strewn about the garden as if she is not paying any attention to the twins' departure. But every now and then I catch the wistful glances she is sending Josh's way. She is still crushing on him, in spite of the apparent unrequited love. My heart goes out to her. Will Josh break her heart further by leaving without even a glance? For a moment I consider going to him—telling him to do the right thing, to at least offer some semblance of a good-bye.

But surprisingly I don't have to.

My thoughts are still contemplating the matter when I notice that Josh has stopped walking midstride on his way back to the cabin from stowing his last bag in the back of the car. His eyes are on Isabella's form, watching. For a moment indecision is written on his features. Then abandoning his original path, he switches route. Hands shoved in the front pockets of his jeans, he begins heading slowly in her direction. Finally he reaches the spot where she is standing, pretending to focus on yet another of Nate's toys to pick up from the ground. She lifts her eyes. Briefly they hold each other's gaze, both looking very nervous. *Josh shy around girls? This is a first for my brother.* He clears his throat. "So ah . . . I guess we're leaving."

Isabella nods her head, her long brown hair hanging in waves around her shoulders. She looks stunning. Surely her beauty must have some type of effect on my brother. How could it not?

Josh motions behind him, pointing to the car where my parents and his brother are waiting. "Well . . . I should . . . it was nice to meet you—" He turns to leave and then as if thinking better of it, stops and faces Isabella again. Once more he clears his throat and this time his voice sounds strangely cracked and uncertain. "So . . . ah, maybe when I'm . . . feeling better . . . I'll try to get ahold of you . . . text you or something?"

"Okay." Isabella's one word is spoken in a barely audible whisper. But I can't help but notice the little flicker of light that flashes through her brown eyes as my brother Josh walks back to the car.

After my parents leave with the boys, Isabella goes inside to wait for Nate to wake up from his nap, and I decide to take a walk down by the seashore to clear my mind. To pray for my brothers' swift return to normalcy. To try to forgive myself for letting this happen to them. To contemplate why a drowned body had never turned up on one of the Rhode Island beaches. Surely Rye must know the answer to that. *Rye.* Just the thought of her name causes my hands to form into fists at my side. She has succeeded at singlehandedly destroying my life. And now my brothers' lives too. What will happen to them if they are indicted for murder? Will they be able to prove it was an accident? Will Rye tell a lie and testify against them? Should I go to Tristan in hopes that he might be able to elicit truthful answers from her? Because if I go to her on my own the way I'm feeling toward her now, I'm afraid the scene won't be pretty.

Heaving a sigh, I wade a few feet into the ocean. Vexed and frustrated, I kick at the encircling water, creating a large splashing sound. Beneath my feet wet sand sinks around my toes. It feels soothing and much needed. Moving forward, I continue to tread through the surf. Then I stop. Close by I hear another splash echoing my own. Frozen in place, my feet are completely swallowed up in pliable granules of silt and sand. Glancing over my shoulder, I search for the source of the sound. But no one is around. *Possibly just a fish then.* I keep going. Immediately my mind goes back to my brothers' situation and I keep sorting through the possibilities of what ifs. The should haves, could haves, and what nows. But minutes after descending into the particulars of Josh and Jake's predicament, I am catapulted back into the present with an eerie chill.

Because something doesn't feel right.

Once more I glance to the right, to the left, behind me, taking in the complete circumference of my surroundings. But there is nothing and no one around, and no more remarkable sounds since the last splash. Still, I can't shake the unnerving feeling I am experiencing. My vision shifts to the outlying ocean, but nothing unusual stands out. *Maybe it had just been too long of a night—too long of a day.* I am probably still shaken and on edge from all the worry over Jake's disappearance and the fresh discovery of everything that had been happening with my brothers. All at once it hits me how exhausted I really am. Coming to the conclusion that my mind is starting to play tricks on me, I decide to go back.

Beginning my retreat back to the cabin, I have only started to pivot in the water when I feel a body converge on my back, and something sweet-smelling covers my face. For one split second panic surges through my entire body. And then all becomes dark.

My head feels like a lead balloon. I attempt to open my eyes, but everything is blurry. Trying to pull myself out of an oblivion, for a minute I remain with lashes frozen against my cheeks. I feel like I am in a time warp. *Where am I? What has happened?*

I remember going for a walk on the beach.

I try opening my eyes again. Everything is still fuzzy. And I feel completely drained. Shaking my head which feels like it is filled with twenty-pound weights, I attempt to concentrate. For several seconds my vision goes in and out of focus as I take in my surroundings.

Rocks, rocks, and more rocks. And lots of water.

I am no longer on the beach in front of the cabin. *The beach in front of the cabin.* I was there to think and clear my mind of all that had happened with the boys. The boys left to go back home to Philadelphia today. *Today? What day is it now? Is it still the same day?* Furrowing my brow, I continue taking in the landscape with repetitive sweeps. A shoreline filled with pebbles instead of sand. Medium-sized stones. Large boulders and towering, rocky cliffs.

Panic!

I remember feeling sudden panic and the smell of something sweet all at the same time. Before that, noises—a splash in the water. *But no one was there.* Suddenly terror comes swooping down over me as realization pummels through my brain.

Someone was *there!*

"Enjoying your accommodations?" A familiar voice calls me out of my pondering. Choking, I gasp for air.

Rye!

I am preparing to turn to the sound of her greeting when she speaks again. "Well, don't get used to it, you little bitch; you are about to move."

Anxiety tingles through my body. I should have known! I should have known that after all she'd been up to this summer, now that my brothers were gone she'd come after me next. She's done toying with peripheral veins, now it's time to go straight for the jugular. My jugular. After all, when it all comes right down to it, her biggest problem is me after all. Recalling all she's done to my brothers, a surge of anger shoots down my nerve endings. Shifting my weight, I attempt to rise to a standing position, and I find that my arms are tied up. Suddenly a new alarm wells up from my chest. *What is Rye up to this time?*

"It's about time you woke up. I didn't think that stuff was sup-posed to last that long. But at least it got you here without me having to fight you. I'd hate for you to wreck my plan." Rye is now standing in front of where I am seated on the pebbly ground. With unkempt hair and a crazed look in her gray eyes, she stares me down. But in spite of the demented, villainous demeanor, I am reminded of her small stature. *How was she able to get me here all by herself?* Wherever here is.

When I go to speak, my mouth feels like glue. I attempt to clear my throat. "Wh . . . where am I?"

Rye's eyes flash anger. "Shut up, you damn whore, I never asked you to talk. If you say too much, I'll gag you."

I turn my head away. I'm really too tired to talk anyway. Whatever she had given me is making me feel very lethargic. And clearly she has not brought me here to communicate. What exactly she is planning on doing with me, I am not sure. But something inside of me is choosing to cling to the idea that maybe it is just her little way of teaching me a lesson. Let me sit, bound, while I listen to her reasoning why she has triumphed over me and has obtained Tristan as the ultimate prize. *Well, go ahead, but first chance I get I am going to make it clear that she will pay for the abduction and abuse of my brothers.*

Soon Rye begins talking again, interrupting my thoughts. This time her tone is light—too light. High-pitched and almost childlike. A disconcerting chill fires down my spine. "But since you asked, I'll tell you . . . it's my very own island. How do you like it? I discovered it myself and since no one else has ever seemed to claim it, I've adopted it as my own. It has its own charm, don't you think? No sand . . . all rocks and cliffs. It wasn't too difficult getting you here. You float pretty easy." She doesn't wait for me to answer and offer my opinion of her desolate parcel of land. Nor do I intend to. Now switching gears, her proclamations take on new tenor yet again, this time emanating complete bitterness. "Quite a far cry from the little island Tris likes to call his own, don't you think? The one you tricked him into marrying you on and then stole from him what was supposed to be mine on our wedding night." Cocking her head, she maneuvers in front of me, making sure that she has my attention. Each word she speaks is stilted and spewed with venom as she looks me directly in the eye. "I'll . . . *never* . . . forgive you . . . for that." Without wanting to, I flinch at the maliciousness of her tone.

Taking a deep, huffing breath, she moves away. The resentment that she's been harboring deep inside moves with her. "I've had a hard time forgiving Tris. But I guess he can't be blamed really. He just needed to escape from your sorcery in order to remember what he really wants in life, remember who it is that he really loves." *Sorcery?* Inwardly I am shaking my head, but I am too tired to argue. I'm not going to argue. *Not yet.* "But I guess your spells finally reached their limits, didn't they? When Tris went away and had his accident, he was finally able to break free from you. I can't forgive what you did though. You were such a demon; you kept him tied to your bed for too long. Far too long. I'm glad I was finally able to escape from where they were holding me hostage all that time while you were convincing him to sleep with you. I'm glad that I finally persuaded my people to my line of thinking . . . that there is nothing wrong with me. That I'm okay to walk around in public. That I no longer need therapy. I have no need to be constantly supervised. It's nice to know that my people now know that *you* are the one with emotional problems, not me. They've watched you cry your little heart out over Tris . . . tsk, tsk, tsk . . . so unstable." Rye takes a break from her ranting. Running her fingers through her hair, she attempts a smile. An unsettling, bone-chilling grin.

I keep looking away, pretending that I'm not affected.

Today I'll sit back quietly and endure her creepy, offbeat reasoning, and then another day, very soon, I'll come back to get her with reinforcements on my arm. If not Tristan, then Zepher and Seth, Britton and Charlize—anyone I can convince about the truth of what she's really been up to this summer. I will make sure that she pays for what she has done to my brothers, make sure that this time she is locked up for good.

While I'm mentally formulating the plan that will get her permanently reinstitutionalized, the sound of laughter jars me into the present—the shrill, feverish pulsation of hilarity coming from Rye's lips. For a moment I almost believe that she is seeing into my thoughts, that she can read my mind, that she thinks my strategy for retribution is pathetic and ridiculous, that it will never work.

Refusing to be intimidated, I set my jaw. Then finally she lets out one last chortle and settles her gaze back on me. "I am so good . . . so good! My plan not only went well, it went better than I thought—exceptionally well." Avoiding the warped, triumphant expression on her face, I pick a rock on the ground to stare at, focusing my eyes on its pyramidlike shape. *What is she talking about?* "I worked it all out. Tris would have an accident on the Pacific, and that would be it. All finished, end of problem. If I couldn't have him, then neither would you."

What? My vision leaves the little rock. She has broken my resolve. I can no longer remain subdued. I gasp loudly. *This I hadn't expected.*

Rye rolls her eyes at my reaction. "Oh, quit being so self-righteous. In all actuality it was you who caused his accident, not me. If you hadn't tried to steal him from me, the accident wouldn't have had to happen. But as it stands, it ended up working out even better than I thought. He didn't have to die after all. I couldn't have planned it better if I tried. I couldn't have predicted that he would end up living through it, having amnesia instead. It turned out perfect. Now the truth is finally aired for all to see. In the end he couldn't even remember you. The truth is, deep down all he ever really wanted was me."

Somehow the lethargy that I'd been experiencing since waking is now swiftly receding. And the anger that I've been trying to hold inside is suddenly unleashed as I begin twisting my arms back and forth in an attempt to loosen the bindings on my wrists. "If you are so sure that you have him, why spend all the effort on this? Why bring me here today?"

With lightning-quick speed, Rye turns to confront my squirming form. This time there is no hilarity to light up her countenance. Narrowing her dull, gray eyes, she looks directly into my face. Her voice is like ice. "Because I think it is time . . . I think it is time to end this whole thing. Tris needs to choose once and for all."

"Choose what? According to you, the choice has already been made!"

"Shut up. I told you not to talk." Pulling a cloth out of her back pocket, with shaky hands she pours liquid onto the material. Much of it falls to the ground, but a little manages to land where intended. Charging in my direction, her small frame looms over my bound form while she holds the damp fabric over my nose and mouth. As the sweet smell reaches my senses, once again everything goes dark.

"We'll just have to carry her then," I hear a voice say. My head feels heavy, and I am so tired. I open my eyes and everything tilts sideways. Immediately I close them again. Why does that voice sound so familiar? *Rye!* My lids shoot back open. My vision is blurry, but I can make out rocks. Many rocks. Rocks of all sizes. And a narrow but deep gorge. *What is going on?* Rye's island. I am on Rye's rocky island. *What is she going to do to me?* Obviously she keeps drugging me with something. What are her plans? Sensing someone close by, I angle my head to the left.

And someone is right there! Right by my face. I am being carried—or dragged, really. But it is not Rye. I try to scream but all that comes out is a weak sound. "She is waking up," a male voice says next to my ear—a male voice I don't recognize.

"Good, I want her to be awake for this. I want her to see for herself who Tris chooses once and for all," Rye answers.

Tristan. Where is Tristan? And why does Rye keep talking about him choosing? How will he choose? I'm pretty sure he has already made his choice, and it is her. It's Rye. He had already left me for her earlier this summer. Although I seriously doubt he realizes that she tried to have him killed. That she is the real reason he has amnesia.

"I'm tired. I need a break," the male voice says.

"Oh, all right. Just set her down," Rye snaps back. "But we have to do this soon." *Do what soon?* The male voice who was carrying me plunks me down on the ground, and a pile of gravel scrapes against my face. For a brief moment I am able to get a view of his brown, stringy hair as he steps away. I try to lift my head, but it feels like it is filled with bricks. Stones and grit are imbedded into my cheek while I lay sprawled on my side. My mouth feels like the Sahara Desert.

"Do you think we are going to be able to get her out there without it collapsing on the way?" the male voice asks. *Collapsing?* My nerve endings begin to come alive. *What is he referring to?* Out of the corner of my eye I can see Rye. She looks upset.

"I am going to get her out there, and you are going to help. You promised me you would help with this, so you better quit whining, Freddy." *Freddy?*

My eyes pop wide open, and suddenly everything comes into focus. A surge of adrenaline shoots through my body, and I am suddenly able to prop myself up on an elbow. "Freddy?" I try to say, but it comes out sounding more like "Setting." My voice is loud enough to draw Rye and Freddy's attention, however, and their heads both spin in my direction.

"Don't let her get up." Rye's tone is edged with irritation. Freddy comes to stand next to me. I lift my face to take in his medium-built frame and his beady, gold eyes as he stands hovering so close by. I wiggle in place and discover my hands are still tied up. With a rush of strength, I manage to bring myself to a sitting position, and Freddy takes a step closer.

I cough to clear the thick, pasty feeling from my throat. "I thought—" I sputter. My tongue feels so thick, it is hard to speak. I try again. "I thought Freddy was dead."

"What? What are you talking about?" Rye narrows her eyes.

"Drown . . . he drown," I manage to say. Freddy's watchful gaze turns toward Rye. *Apparently he does not answer for himself.*

For an instant Rye looks confused, and then she begins to laugh. "Oh that is right, he drown." She looks at Freddy. "You drown, remember, Freddy?" Now Freddy is laughing too. I'd like to laugh too, but I am not quite getting the joke. On the contrary, I am becoming more and more irritated by the moment as I wait for clarification, as I recall the devastation on my brothers' faces as they live with the guilt of another person's death. "The thing is . . . it is kind of hard to drown when you already live in the sea." *What?*

"But my brothers—"

Rye laughs some more and Freddy grins, looking almost relieved that Rye is apparently in such a good mood. "That was so funny. Your brothers were so freaked out when they thought they killed Freddy. At first I was going to let Freddy come back around them again so that they would know he survived, but then I decided it was a whole lot more fun to watch them squirm. And it was even more fun to hold it over their heads." Looking directly at me, she sends me a spiteful smile laced with inherent evil. "Your brothers are pretty accommodating when you need them to be."

Anger shoots through my veins. Balling my hands into fists, I attempt to break free from the ropes that are tying my wrists. But my movements only serve to rub the skin on the inside of my arms raw. Finally I give up. Taking a deep breath, I try to calm myself back down with the consoling thought that first chance I get, I will reassure my brothers that the person they thought they had killed had survived after all. *I, of course, would leave out the part that because he is from the ocean it was impossible for him to drown anyway.*

"Come on, Freddy—let's get moving," Rye suddenly barks as her labile mood switches gears once again. "It is getting late, and you still need to go get Tris." Once more I contemplate the pending plans she keeps referring to. *What is she going to do with Tristan?* As if reading my mind, Rye points to the narrow gorge I'd noticed earlier. Her gaze focuses on me. "We are going to be crossing that bridge up there, and if you don't cooperate, you will fall off and die. So you better not make the wrong move . . . you better do it just right. Because you will *not* ruin my plans."

My vision moves to get a better look at what she is referring to. At first I don't see any bridge, but then I detect a thin slice of something hanging precariously across the canyon up ahead. My heart rate skyrockets. The spindly contraption that I see swinging back and forth does not look like it will hold much of anything, let alone the weight of more than one human body. Surely she will not trust me enough to send me across by myself; besides, my hands are still tied. That means at least two of us will have to cross together. A shot of fear quakes through my insides, threatening to induce panic. *She still hasn't told me the complete plan. Where is all of this heading?*

"Now listen close, you little bitch. You are going to do exactly what I tell you to. We are going to cross that bridge until we come to the platform I built. Then you are going to crawl up on it and wait. I'll be balanced on the other half."

I furrow my brow in confusion in an attempt to ignore the terror that is trying to take over my thoughts. *She is completely nuts. What are we going to be doing up there?* It won't matter—with her it doesn't have to make sense. She is bat shit crazy, and she is going to get us both killed. "We can't go up there. That isn't safe," I finally blurt.

"Do you think I give a crap about safe, you stupid wench? This isn't about safe. This is about Tris making a choice once and for all. I am so sick of the way he goes off all moody much of the time . . . always thinking about something . . . always playing his damn guitar like he is trying to figure something out. Doesn't he know I realize that he isn't spending all that free time daydreaming about me? He already *has* me. He doesn't need to *think* about having me. I'm tired of him having another choice so close by. He needs to make up his mind once and for all so that he and I can get on with our lives together. Today he will finally know for sure that it is me he wants. After today there will be no question in his mind. And then he will spend the rest of his life making it up to me. Making it up to me for having to suffer for such a long time. While I was being held hostage deep down in the ocean, he was up on land spending his time screwing you. No one knows what that feels like. No one will *ever* know."

My brain begins whirling a million miles per minute. I still don't understand her ultimate plan. But I do know that she is demented and sick. Whatever she has concocted won't have to follow a rational thought pattern. But it may very well be deadly for us all. I blink to focus and try to force the anxiety from my voice. "But you *do* have Tristan, Rye. There is no need for all of this. He is already yours. He realizes he made an earlier mistake with me, but it is only you that he wants. That he'll ever want. Go to him and let's end all of this. You don't need to do this."

Rye's head snaps in my direction. Her expression is almost savage. "Oh no . . . you won't talk me out of this. This is going to happen . . . today. Tris will choose today. Tris. His name is Tris, so quit calling him Tristan. It sounds so juvenile. You are going to do as I say and crawl up on that platform. Then Freddy will help me to get on the opposite side. It is built to be like a teetertotter. It has to be balanced just so, with one person on each side, or it loses its stability and tips off of the bridge. It isn't very strong, so Freddy will have to make it quick going to get Tris. By the time Tris gets back to us, the platform should be about to break. He will only have time to save one of us. When he pulls one of us to safety, the other will fall to their death at the bottom of the gorge."

Inhaling deeply, I press my eyes tightly together to stop myself from shaking. To stop myself from coming completely undone. Now there *is* no more guessing.

Now I know the plan!

Chapter Twenty-Four

"Don't make me do this," Freddy pleads. By now his face looks worried. Brown, stringy threads of hair fall over his brow, and he pushes them away to reveal desperate eyes. "I don't want to tie you up, Rye. I don't want to go get Tris. What if he doesn't pick you? What if he decides to save her instead and it's you that falls into the pit and dies?"

"Shut up, Freddy. Just get over here and do it. You promised. Stop sounding so negative. He *will* pick me. Why wouldn't he? What is the matter . . . do you think that he won't?"

Freddy flinches. "No . . . no, I don't think that, it's just that—"

"It is just that you need to get over here and tie me up. *Now!*"

I turn my head away from the two of them and feign exhaustion. But on the inside my mind is very alert—whirling with all the possibilities of escape. So far I'd come up with none. The minute Rye had forced me onto the narrow, swinging bridge I'd pretty much accepted that my life was over. It looked poorly constructed and old, rickety with several boards missing. Surely it would not hold up under the weight of our crossing forms. With each step we took I could feel the structure creak and sway beneath our feet. I kept telling myself to look straight ahead. Not to look to my right or left. Not to let my vision stray to the cracks and large gaps in the spindly wooden planks or pay attention to the deep culvert that was waiting below. Not to be affected by all the jagged rocks that stood ready to tear my body apart on the way down.

But somehow I couldn't help myself. I couldn't bring myself to stop investigating the view that would soon be the vehicle to my death. An overpowering feeling of dizziness had swept through my brain. Gripped with anxiety, my body began to imitate the fall. My hands were tied up. I had nothing to hold on to; I could no longer keep my balance. Seemingly helpless to stop the motion, I closed my eyes and gave in to the sensation. Immediately I began to tip.

Rye's hands quickly reached out to steady me. "Oh no, you don't!" she shouted into the back of my head. "You will not ruin this plan." For the rest of the walk across the bridge she held on to my shirt with a tight fist. I didn't think the situation could get worse, but it did. As it turned out the platform that she had been talking about was not a platform at all, but two thin, rotting boards, piecemealed together. Teetering on the center of the bridge, the tips of the makeshift apparatus were barely resting atop the rocky precipice on either side of the narrow ravine. There was virtually no support. Any second it would snap and plummet to the ground in pieces. Instantly my eyes widened. *She wants me to do what on this?* Paralyzed with fear, I was unable to move. My hesitation was immediately detected. With a firm grip on the waistband of my shorts, Rye gave me a shove. "Crawl over to the edge of those boards," she breathlessly commanded. The combination of words mixing with the uneven puffs of air coming up from her throat gave it away. At that point I knew she was scared too. Once more I tried to appeal to her reasoning, but with no success. "Just shut it I said, and get over there," were the last words she told me before I began inching across. While Freddy held weight on the other end, Rye proceeded to secure my arms and legs to the boards. As an afterthought she also placed a gag in my mouth. Afterward she'd shimmied over to her side in order for Freddy to do the same—tie her in place.

Only Freddy doesn't want to.

But after several feeble attempts at arguing with Rye, he finally acquiesces by fastening her to the other end of her own contraption.

Speculating, I wonder why she needs to be tied up anyway. How exactly is this part of the plan? While Freddy is working to secure her, several times the wavering planks almost tip toward their side. Their combined weight was obviously not thought out. Petrified by each abrupt tilt, I hold my breath and wait for the outcome. Inside I am shaking my head. The irony of all three of us having to die for this ludicrous scheme all of a sudden seems that much more horrific. Finally, after pausing to intermittently rebalance the slats, Freddy finishes the job to Rye's satisfaction. Afterward he carefully shimmies off the platform in order to go after Tristan. Albeit unhappily.

The minute he is out of my sight, I begin eyeing the cliff that is just to my right. If only I could edge myself over. *I'm so close.* But the second I attempt to maneuver my position in the slightest, the wobbly stand I am sitting on threatens to give way. I bow my head in defeat. Out of the corner of my eye I can see Rye on the other side of the bridge with a dull gleam of satisfaction in her eyes. *She really is sick! Completely twisted!* Why would she want to risk her own life for something like this? If she really wants me out of her and Tristan's life, why not just take me out into the deep water and call it an unfortunate accident? In her mind she must be relatively certain of today's outcome, or surely she would not have put herself at this type of risk. She must be confident about Tristan's choice. A chill shoots down my spine at the thought of Tristan standing here choosing who to save. The Tristan I know from the past or even the present would not *want* to choose. Although he has made it clear that he has feelings for Rye, he is not the type of person that would wish death on anyone. But in spite of that sense of altruism, like it or not, he is going to be forced into a decision. *Rye or me.* If he hesitates at all, soon the boards will crack, and we will both die. He will have to make a quick decision or watch us both fall.

And in the end, Rye will have played her cards exactly right, because if it is her that he truly loves—and I am sure that it is—ultimately, when backed into a corner with only seconds to fool with, he will end up saving her. The way this teetering device is constructed, he will have no other choice. And he will never know the truth of what actually happened today. He will never know that it was really Rye that caused his accident out on the West Coast. Or that she had originally set out to plan his death. The mishap accompanied by the amnesia was only a bonus. In the future will he ever get his memory back at all and remember that he once loved me? Or will he live out the rest of his years in Rye's company, never knowing all of the deception that surrounds their relationship?

Suddenly a wave of nausea washes over my body as it occurs to me how close I am to the end. There are so many things left unsaid and undone in my life. The thought of never being able to share love with Tristan hurts so bad I can practically feel my heart breaking into pieces: first the valves, then the arteries, then the chambers. I suck in a breath in an effort to stop the progression of the painful annihilation. *I didn't know!* I didn't realize until now just how much hope I still had buried deep down inside, how much I had hoped that Tristan would someday remember and come back to me—that we could still live out our lives together in love.

My stomach continues to churn, and I bite onto the cloth that serves as a gag. My thoughts shift to my brothers. If I die, Jake and Josh will never find out the truth of how they never actually killed someone. They will carry that burden with them to their grave. As it stands, their young lives are all but destroyed by something that never actually happened.

And then there is Nate!

My beautiful baby boy, Nate, that I will never get to see again after today. Bile rises into my throat as I try in desperation to picture the last little smile he gave me when I tucked him into his crib for a nap earlier in the day. Was Isabella alarmed that I hadn't come back to the cabin from my walk on the beach? Maybe she just assumed that I decided to go for a long run or do some errands in town. This whole thing will probably go down before anyone has the chance to realize anything is amiss. Will Tristan willingly step into his role as full-time dad after I am gone? Will Nate miss his mommy as much as I imagine missing him? Will he grow up even remembering who I was in his life? Or will he end up forgetting me too? Just as Tristan has. After today, will life move forward as if I never spent any time in Watch Hill at all? Mr. Horton died. Lucy and Ethan are moving. Will it seem like as far as this little ocean town goes, I didn't even exist?

Suddenly it takes all of my effort not to puke into my muzzle, knowing that if I do, I'll be forced to swallow it back down, most likely ingesting it into my lungs. Will that be my ultimate end? Will I end up drowning on my own vomit sitting up here on this shabby little post constructed at the hands of Rye? Will she then take over my life?

"Tris, Tris . . . help . . . oh Tris, help." Rye's voice screaming in desperation across the gorge jolts me out of my end-of-life reflections. Immediately my eyes begin sweeping over the landscape of the rocky terrain. Is Tristan here? Had he already arrived? "Help . . . help, Bethany did this. She tied me up. She is trying to kill me. She is sick . . . help me Tris, I'm going to fall. I'm going to die."

Somewhere in the back of my mind it occurs to me how ludicrous this situation is, how well thought out Rye's plan is. She is forcing Tristan to choose, all right. Now I know the reason for her tied-up limbs. She is making him believe that I am the one who is attacking *her*! I am the one who has concocted this whole warped scheme. She is playing the damsel in distress. Will he buy it? In the recent past he has believed all the other lies she has convinced him of. Will this be the final one? My eyes keep sweeping over the bridge and the entrance to the bridge—over every visible rock that makes up Rye's island as I look for Tristan.

Finally I find him. With shoulders back and legs parted, he stands at the far end of the canyon by the entrance to the bridge. For some reason the familiarity of his tousled, blond hair and line of his sculpted cheekbones causes an ache to well up in my chest.

For a moment I watch his reaction as he takes in the whole situation. With narrowed brow, his eyes peruse the dangling walkway, the deep, rocky gulch, and finally, the poorly constructed platform in the center of it all that Rye and I are currently tied up and balanced on—one of the two of us waiting to plummet to our death. Although from my distance I can't see the fine details of his facial features, I imagine that for one instant his eyes widen faintly, and with a slight shake of his head he mouths the words *"What the hell?"*

My heart begins to pound in my chest, and sweat pours off of my skin as the wooden planks squeak and crack below me. *This is it! The end is coming soon. My end!* Within minutes Tristan is going to choose who it is that he wants to save, and the other person is going to plummet to their death. Involuntarily my eyes shift to take in the deep gully directly below where I am seated. The chasm is so deep I can barely see the bottom. Instantly I become dizzy with fear. For one second I imagine how the first impact is going to feel as my head makes contact with one of the many jagged rocks on the way down. Taking a deep breath, I try to put my mind in neutral to block out the pain of what is soon to come. If only I can make myself go into shock, I won't even know what is happening.

"Help . . . help, Tris!" Rye calls out again. Her voice sounds despairing and completely believable. Tristan's gaze shifts toward her cries. *Oh God, no! He is buying into her pleas.* Without making a conscious choice to act, I begin shouting into my muzzle. But all that comes out is a weak, stifled sound most likely undetected from where Tristan is standing. Now Tristan's eyes move across the bridge and land on me. *Did he hear me after all?*

"Mmmm . . . mmm," I yell some more. But I can barely hear my own voice, so how can he?

"Damn," he appears to say before looking away to focus on the swaying bridge. Now his eyes look wild and focused. The urgency of the matter is evident on his features. *He gets it.* Time is of the essence. This whole makeshift platform thing is going to split at any moment, and Rye and I are both going down if he doesn't hurry. I can tell he doesn't want that to happen. He looks driven and desperate. There is definitely *someone* he wants to save, but I don't know who.

The hanging bridge begins to sway beneath the transfer of Tristan's body as he crosses, careful to avoid missing boards and rickety sections that are sure not to hold up below his weight. My breaths are now coming in quick pants. My mind is a jumbled mess. Across the gully Rye is still calling out over and over again, guiding Tristan to her tied-up form with her frantic pleas. Although the words that are leaving her lips consist of mostly *"Help me, Tris,"* her message is blatantly clear. *Save me . . . I am scared and desperate . . . I am the victim of this deranged plan . . . I need you . . . come get me soon! I don't want to die!* She is manipulating the situation, doing everything in her power to make sure she has his attention. I am only a silent afterthought.

Finally he reaches the center where our boards are poised and teetering. Steadying himself on the groaning planks, he surprises me by turning in my direction. For a second he looks me directly in the eye and I get an unexpected surge of hope. *"Something something,* Bethany," I think I hear him say, but I can't be certain because right then a strong gust of wind rushes through the canyon, and the bridge that Tristan is standing on begins to swing back and forth unsteadily. The volatile pieces of timber that are holding me and Rye up immediately become unbalanced. Instantly I begin to tip. My heart lurches in my chest. Panic devours me. Death is now seconds closer than I originally anticipated. Our platform is microseconds from going down.

The look in Tristan's green eyes is frenzied as he dives to steady the pieces of wood that are tilting, getting ready to send Rye and me to our deaths. For a few seconds I think it's not going to work—no matter what Tristan does. The imbalance is too great. Gravity has been set into motion. I am going to fall along with the weakening boards. Back and forth the makeshift bench under me slides and I with it. My hands are still tied. There is nothing for me to hang on to. I can taste the air that is rising from bottom of the cavern as it calls me into its swirl of death. Soon enough I will be swallowing a whole lot more of it on my way down.

But Tristan keeps hanging on, trying to subdue the center of our platform. And finally it works—for the time being. The planks under my bottom are no longer slipping. I am not going to die, at least for the next few seconds. I can't believe how much those few seconds mean to me. Suddenly I want to cry out in relief. But I can't, of course, with the rag in my mouth still blocking the sounds coming up from my throat. Tristan's gaze shoots back and forth between Rye and me to make sure that both are safe. Momentarily satisfied, he rises to his feet. But the minute he stands, the thin panels that are housing me begin to creek and groan. Suddenly a loud splintering sound fills the air and a large crack forms down the middle. The material is wearing thin. It is no longer going to be able to hold my weight. Now I realize just how short those few cherished seconds are actually going to be.

Tristan hears the noise, and his head snaps in my direction. His vision takes in the boards that are in the process of splitting beneath me. My heart pounds in my chest. *This is it!* It's do or die. He has to make his decision. There is no more time. Will he try to save me? Or will he let me die? There is something about the way his gaze connects with mine that tells me that there is still something between us, that he has some type of feelings for me after all. But then the thought occurs to me—could what I am seeing reflected in his green eyes just be guilt? Guilt over what he is about to do next.

The answer to that question is revealed seconds later as he turns away from me and begins edging out onto the opposite planks. My heart plunges. He has made his decision. He is going to save Rye. And now clear as a bell I finally understand what he had been trying to say to me a few minutes earlier. *Forgive me, Bethany.* Now I get it—I completely understand. What he meant was *forgive me, Bethany, I don't want to let you die. But since I have no choice, I have to—I am going to save Rye instead of you.* I don't know what hurts more: the idea that Tristan has just turned his back on me for good, or the idea that my time is up and I am not ready to go.

"Hurry, hurry, Tris. Oh thank God, Tris," I keep hearing Rye scream from the other side of the makeshift platform. My boards continue to creak and split, widening the gap down the middle. *My time is coming soon.* Making my peace, I look to the sky and focus on a white, fluffy cloud. Funny, how in some ways it reminds me of the material from one of Nate's baby blankets. Allowing my mind to rest in the comfort of that thought, serenity settles over me.

"Good-bye, Nate," I whisper.

"Noooo . . . Tris . . . nooo." It is the bloodcurling sound of desperation in Rye's voice that causes me to turn my head, abandoning the tranquil place that I'd just created. Once again my heart jump-starts in my chest. *What is Tristan doing now?*

Stopping at the halfway mark on his route toward Rye, he is now placing rocks onto the planks. *Where did he get them? What is he attempting to do with them? What is his plan?* I have little time to consider the absurdity of the scenario before the slats under my legs make a complete split. Now I am just hanging on by a thread, practically suspended in midair. Frantically I attempt to find the cloud I had been eyeing seconds before. *If only I can find that cloud. I'm ready to go now, I just need to find the cloud.*

But I never do find the cloud. Before I have time to realize what is going on, Tristan is reaching out to grab me. With lightning-quick speed he pulls me safely against his chest while the boards that were holding me up finally give way and fall in a pile of splinters to the bottom of the gorge. At the same second Rye's end of the teetertotter pulls in a downward direction without my weight on the other end to keep it balanced and erect. The sound of her screams fills the air, growing more distant as she plummets toward the rocky bottom of the canyon. And just like that she is gone. Her plan had backfired. Obviously unexpected by her, she is the one of the two of us who has become the recipient of death. *Suddenly it is too much!* I bury my head against Tristan's tee shirt.

"Noooo . . . Rye—" I hear a voice call from the side of the cliff. *Freddy!* Where had he been this whole time? I lift my face from Tristan's chest in time to see his brown, stringy hair wavering on the edge of the rocky precipice as he looks down, searching for Rye's fallen body. Rye, who obviously meant the world to him. Rye, who Freddy's love and devotion meant absolutely nothing to in return. Before Tristan or I have time to call out to him, he flings himself over the threshold and begins to plummet like a dead bird dropping from the sky. I close my eyes to wipe away the ghastly vision of his suicide from my mind. But the sight of Rye and him falling one right after the other are there plain as day, assaulting my brain. Shaking from head to toe, I begin to cry.

"Shshsh," Tristan whispers into my hair as he begins to carefully guide me step by step off of the hanging bridge. The minute we reach the safety of land he collapses to the ground while I am tucked beneath his arms. With my head buried against his chest, he squeezes my trembling body to his ribs. Then rubbing his hands over my arms and back, he hangs on like he can't get enough of me, like he never wants to let go. Now he is crying too. We are both crying together. We can't stop crying. Or shaking. "I remember the song," he keeps telling me over and over through the sound of our tears. "I finally remembered our song."

Epilogue

The sun is shining brightly, turning the water into sparkling topaz jewels as it splashes against *Blue*'s swaying outline. Tristan and I are sitting side by side on the end of our dock, watching while Nate goes for a swim. As is his habit since the return of his memory, Tristan has an arm draped protectively over my shoulder. Spiritedly diving below the liquid layers of the ocean, Nate resurfaces from the waves only to dive under once again. This is something we only allow him to do in a private setting such as the property of our own home. The average person would go into a near panic if they witnessed the way we permit a young toddler such freedom to play and experiment in the water. But we know that this is the best thing we can do for him. It is his favorite way to spend free time. And we would never deny him that. It is a gift—his ability to breathe in and out of the water for an unlimited amount of time. He is the future, the liaison between land and sea.

For a moment Nate stops swimming to shoot his mom and dad a contented grin while the water laps up around his small body. In an instant his eyes transition from blue to green and then back to blue again. He seems so happy now that Tristan and I are back together as a family. Of course I am happy too. Tristan had explained to me that the minute he remembered our song his memory had come sweeping back to him like a giant tidal wave. He was suddenly desperate to come find me, to tell me how sorry he was that I had to suffer like I did while he floundered, trying to figure things out.

At that same moment Freddy was on his way to find him. And then the whole catastrophe with Rye on the bridge went down.

Tristan just hoped it wasn't too late, that I could still find it in my heart to love him like before. And of course I do. He already knew he loved me though. Even *before* he got his memory back. Every minute he spent with me, the more time we shared together—he knew. His messed-up intellect prevented him from understanding what exactly he had shared with Rye in prior years. But he *knew* he was falling in love with me now. Then it started to dawn on him: the feelings he had for Rye weren't romantic in nature. It was a type of brotherly affection initiated from early childhood. But he wasn't attracted to her at all.

Now as we sit watching Nate, I feel Tristan's eyes on me transiently before he focuses back on the gentle movement of the surf. His fingers are still resting on my arm. "You know," he hesitates like he isn't sure whether he should utter his thoughts aloud, "it has been occurring to me . . . even the ocean . . . seemed a little out of sorts while we were apart." *A little?*

I glance over at him in astonishment. "You were thinking that same thing too?" At my words he turns back to face me, and for a few moments our eyes connect. There are no words to describe the depth of this revelation between us.

"Da dad dad . . . Ma ma." Nate's voice interrupts our ruminations.

"Hey, Nate," Tristan calls back. Then moving away from me, he reaches under a pile of towels that are resting on the dock. Pulling out a bulky object, he lifts it into the air, pointing it toward Nate. A clicking sound reaches my ears, and then a light illuminates the water in spite of the brightness of the day. *The searchlight!*

My jaw drops open in surprise. "Hey, where did you get that?"

"I found it in the back of the closet. For some reason Nate likes it when I turn it on." Tristan takes the beam off of Nate and points it toward me. His green eyes are playful and completely sexy at the same time. Immediately my heart rate accelerates, a frequently occurring phenomenon that I am getting reacquainted with since the return of Tristan back at my side. Somehow I can't help it, he just does that to me. Now I am on stage. "Ladies and gentlemen, people of the land and sea . . . introducing my beautiful wife, Bethany

Alexander, who I have a complete crush on . . . who I am completely in love with."

My mouth forms into a smile. Biting my lip in contemplation, I have to wonder which is shining brighter: the searchlight in Tristan's hand, or the light from my own blue eyes while I watch his perfect features as he leans in for a kiss.

The end

Acknowledgements

I want to thank God for all the blessings
he's poured out on my life.
Every day I stand in awe.

Also, I want to thank all of those
who have joined with me in the process of writing
and publishing this book series.
It has been an amazing ride.
My husband, Steve, for his continual love and strength.
My parents for urging me to follow a dream.
My family and friends for their ongoing support.
Once again the AMU/EMCU girls have
surrounded me with encouragement
as they readily embrace
each new book.
Your enthusiasm is like sunshine in Michigan.
Thank you to my rough draft readers: my mom,
Nancy Root, my daughter, Haley Flach,
Chris McDonough, Alyssa Woodin, and Kayla Martin.
I appreciate your opinions and ideas.
And to all that continue to let me know
how much you are enjoying the series and
keep spreading the story
by sharing the books with friends,
it really means a lot.

~Thank you~

CPSIA information can be obtained at www.ICGtesting.com
Printed in the USA
BVOW06s1022261015

423984BV00006B/11/P